Fish of Souls

Gary Williams

Copyright © 2002 by Gary Williams

All rights reserved. No part of this book shall be reproduced or transmitted in any form or by any means, electronic, mechanical, magnetic, photographic including photocopying, recording or by any information storage and retrieval system, without prior written permission of the publisher. No patent liability is assumed with respect to the use of the information contained herein. Although every precaution has been taken in the preparation of this book, the publisher and author assume no responsibility for errors or omissions. Neither is any liability assumed for damages resulting from the use of the information contained herein.

This is a work of fiction. Names, characters, places, and incidents either are the product of the author's imagination or are used fictitiously. Any resemblance to actual events or locales or persons, living or dead, is entirely coincidental.

ISBN 0-7414-1144-X

Published by:

PUBLISHING.COM

519 West Lancaster Avenue
Haverford, PA 19041-1413
Info@buybooksontheweb.com
www.buybooksontheweb.com
Toll-free (877) BUY BOOK
Local Phone (610) 520-2500
Fax (610) 519-0261

Printed in the United States of America

Printed on Recycled Paper

Published July, 2002

This book is dedicated to my sons, Josh and Jeff. Their imagination far outshines any stories I could concoct.

Acknowledgements

The author would like to acknowledge a multitude of people for their contributions beginning with editor, Jerald E. (Jerry) Hanks, whose encouragement proved to be the ultimate motivation. Also, thanks to Les Williams, Wayne C. Kryspin, Teri Hanson, Martin Letourneau, Maryanne Pease and Sharon Moran for their assistance. In addition, a special thanks to Christine Mangum whose photography graces the cover.

And with deepest gratitude to my family, who listened to me peck on the keyboard into the wee hours of the morning.

Create your vision
Look in your soul
Make your decision
You're in control

--You Choose
"Big Al & the Kaholics"

CHAPTER-ONE

The year was 1571. A man slowly trudged through the soft sand destined for the sea. His dark skin perspired as the early morning sun crested on the horizon. His long black hair caressed his broad shoulders with each stride.

Civilization would eventually tender its hold on this section of coastline but not for years to come. For now, he was alone. Alone as any human had ever been since the beginning of time. And for him, time would become an eternal nightmare.

Ahead, the waves playfully gathered and foam settled on the shore with each reach of the tide. Seagulls pivoted on the beach, back and forth, squawking their early morning discontent for the intruder. The air was still and lifeless and the man wore no expression. Each step seemed to burden his heart further as he approached the shoreline.

As his toes touched the water, he stopped and looked up to the sky. He closed his eyes and lifted his arms upward in praise. The bright rays warmed his body but all he could picture were the bleak visions of things to come. In his sheltered darkness he was oblivious to the crashing waves and the frantic cries of the birds.

He opened his eyes, lowered his arms, and continued into the surf. With each step through the broken seashells, the chilly water captured more flesh and bone. When he could no longer feel the sandy bottom without submersing his head, he began to swim.

The swells beyond the breakers fought to keep him near shore but his determination drove him out. He swam as hard and as fast as his body would allow. Any indecision had to be squelched. Second thoughts briefly entered through a small crack in his resistance but he quickly slammed the door.

This was finite.

This was how he wanted it.

Once past the point of turning back, the mark where he instinctively knew further progress would seal his fate, he understood his purpose was absolute. With inner strength, he drove the last of his fear across the ocean far away.

Not long after, fatigue consumed his body yet left him content. Images formed a mosaic story of the last four years of his life. As he willfully gave up, he dissolved below the surface, looking up just long enough to see a beautiful blue rippling sky dancing overhead. Then he closed his eyes firmly and exhaled. Water invaded his lungs with a coarse burn. A bright blue light arched across his conscience.

For him, the life that God had originally planned, as it should have been, was over.

Minutes later, the disturbed surface of a small inland pond relaxed. The ripples dissipated. Feathers floated lightly on the surface spinning in a clockwise motion. More feathers brushed onto the shore.

Beneath the calm, the creature sat motionless, gazing upward.

CHAPTER-TWO

Hundreds of years later, the waves crashed down around Curt with a force that made it difficult to keep his grip on the one thing keeping him afloat. He bobbed furiously gasping for air. The burning in his throat was wretched and the sky above seemed to fade from black to a burnt orange with each new mouthful of saltwater. The water drained from his forehead streaking into his eyes, blurring his already impaired vision.

He looked around and saw others struggling feverishly in the massive swells. Some were treading the violent elements better than others. Curt noticed one man who was under more than above, fighting valiantly to remain topside but obviously doomed from the ordeal. On the fourth submersion, the man did not reappear as Curt involuntarily held his own breath. The man had been consumed by the churning water.

Curt could see other men being thrown mercilessly to and fro like toy army men in the bathtub of a child throwing a temper tantrum. The gusting wind and the pelting rain stung his face making it difficult to keep his eyes open. He desperately clung to the piece of wood as the waves ferociously attempted to end his life.

Squinting upward, the sky suddenly glowed a brilliant white as the fingers of light stretched down on the horizon to his right. The jutting extensions were followed by a billowing thunderous roar, causing the air to shake violently. Positioning back to the left, he could barely make out a shoreline through the dimness. The trees created a dark wall hovering in the distance. But it was shore. Even as he rode the waves, that much he was sure.

As his body fought to stay above water, he continued to be lifted and dropped in the relentless waves. Without really understanding why, he decided to release his lifeline and swim for land. Something inside convinced him to do this with little exploration of his options. Riding the waves to shore would have taken an eternity and remaining at the mercy of the elements – the wind, the rain and the lightning, was a grim alternative.

Strangely, amidst the wet crushing blows and driving rain, he felt amazingly strong and capable. But the moment he let go of the wood, uncertainty captivated his thoughts.

My God, what did I just do. I could have continued to float. Now I've let my security go!

The fear partially paralyzed him as he began to tread water in a deluge of insanity. The momentary lapse of purpose nearly killed him as the next swell catapulted the wood back toward him. He submerged to avoid contact and the briny water uncomfortably entered his nostrils. His lungs ached from the sudden inhale as the board passed overhead. If the plank had struck, it would have gashed his head, rendering him unconscious or even killing him.

Surfacing he refocused, searching for the shoreline but the dark shadow of the trees was gone. The only image before him was an endless roving terrain lit briefly by the heavenly activity and then victimized by the darkness of the stormy night.

Did I just imagine the shore? No, it was there. Think! Think! Don't lose it now. I've got to remain rational.

He slowly closed his eyes. His body and mind fought to stay calm. Spinning 180 degrees he quickly adjusted and rediscovered the shoreline. Taking a few composure-gathering breaths, Curt swam as diligently as he could, lowering his head and kicking his arms and legs with vigor. The tumultuous water beckoned him on as it crested and fell with driving thrusts. Often the waves drove him under and he was forced to claw his way back to the surface. Moving closer to the treeline, he stopped to rest, flapping his arms just enough to remain afloat. It was then he noticed the men around him in the water heading inland, swimming in unison as if in some odd Olympic competition.

A wave slammed his head forcing him back to more pressing matters. Again he looked through the gray toward the beach to mark his position. Not wanting to be left behind by the other men advancing inward, he lowered his head and began paddling. The skies continued to flicker and the sound of thunder rolled on in a seemingly endless cascade sending ripples through the night air.

Proceeding at a steady clip, he was amazed at his own perseverance. Not only was he keeping his head, but his stamina was limitless. Physically he believed he could continue swimming for hours. Was it the adrenaline pulsing through his veins? Was the terror of the elements pushing him along at an advanced rate? One was probably influencing the other. Whatever it was gave him hope.

As Curt churned his arms and legs just beneath the surface, he experienced contentment. The fear was gone and he continued almost effortlessly. The waves had little effect on his course and he occasionally caught one for a free ride inward.

He paused again to check his distance and was surprised to find he could stand upright. He planted his bare feet on the sandy bottom and glanced around. He could see the dark silhouette of men straggling onto the beach and lying in exhausted piles not far ahead. Some were motionless while others paced like cats circling a spot prior to lying down.

He turned to look out to sea and was blindsided by a wall of water. The surge pummeled Curt squarely in the chest, sending him backward, but somehow he managed to catch his balance. Not waiting for another assault from the ocean he continued inward. The shore appeared less than 20 yards away.

Then fatigue found a home, as if his body had finished fooling his mind and now was ready to admit the awful truth. His muscles ached and he labored for air as he sluggishly stumbled forward. Each step was a monumental effort. He looked down wondering if he was stuck in the mud.

The lightning continued but the thunder had subsided and neither the waves, wind nor rain had created an inkling of sound since he'd come within walking distance of the shore.

Suddenly, the silence was harshly interrupted. But it was not the typical sounds of a beach. Not seagulls or pelicans or tourists chatting. It was a radical noise that was cold and shrill. Sounds of terror that alternated between low-pitched howling and shrieking yelps. Curt looked up and saw that other men had invaded the beach. They moved quickly and were prodding the exhausted survivors to their feet and, for those who did not respond, they administered the ultimate penalty. Curt froze, watching the terror with disbelief. What he saw was a carnival of human decadence. The survivors were being slashed and chopped with long dark objects that occasionally caught the dancing gleam of distant lightning. Limbs and heads from men who had just fought a life and death battle with Poseidon only to wash up on the beach from Hell were being strewn about the sand while their bloody cries for mercy were coldly denied. The exhausted men who did not get up were the first to suffer. But even those who obeyed were hacked apart. The brutality made Curt wince as the horror of the cries echoed down the shore. He watched several more men suffer the brutality, the last, a man hacked about the skull and shoulders until his screams went silent.

Without options, Curt turned and swam out to sea, his body shaking with fear. The sky had turned a dark shade of orange and the lightning had ceased. The water was calm and smooth and he glided along the surface, stroking as fast as he could as his heart raced. As he moved further out he briefly turned to look back at the soldiers on the beach to see if anyone was following. To his relief, no one was in pursuit. Now his plan would be to continue farther out then, once beyond their view, he would turn and go parallel to the beach until it was safe to come ashore. With luck, the butcherous pack of men would not worry about a lone survivor.

The progress this time was slow and strenuous as he battled fatigue. Little by little he distanced himself from the bloody screams but they continued to echo in his mind.

Why had those men been slain? What had they done to deserve such violence? What had *he* done to deserve to die?

As he swam his thoughts jumped and swirled. Obviously, he had been on a boat or ship, maybe even a plane, with the rest of these poor souls. But what happened? Had they crashed? Shipwrecked? The void in his memory was agonizing and he could feel the shivers stemming from his stomach and the nausea revolve through his intestines as he swam. He was fleeing barbarians and he had no idea who they were or why. Or how he even came to be in the water.

With each stroke the exhaustion of his limbs became reality. He did not know how much longer he could go on. He stopped again to look back at the activity and was relieved to see nothing but the black shoreline with the dark towering fence of trees hovering over it. He could no longer see the men and still none had given chase.

But the minor elation was short-lived. As Curt remained stationary, treading water, he felt a sharp, cutting grasp sink into his left ankle and he was ripped under the surface and pulled toward the ocean floor. As he went under, he instinctively closed his eyes to guard against the burning salt water. Panic gripped his soul and he tried to reach down with his hands to knock away whatever held him. But the speed at which he was descending made it impossible, the water forcing his arms to trail above his head.

The sharp clutch on his ankle turned into a warm, biting sensation of pain. It was as if his skin was being pierced by hundreds of tiny razor sharp knives. But the pain was secondary to his fear of drowning and he plummeted wondering how long he could hold his breath as the pressure pushed against his lungs and salt water filled his nostrils.

Then, another voice entered his conscience. It was his friend Scott, the voice of reason. "Kick him!" Without hesitation Curt coiled his right foot back and kicked in the proximity of where he thought he would make contact. But his foot swung past the spot. The swipe had been a clean miss. He backtracked his leg again coming up empty.

Still falling at a phenomenal speed, Curt briefly wondered how much farther down he could go. Even a quarter mile from the shore the depth was probably no greater than 30 or 35 feet. Surely he had passed that by now. His lungs felt ready to burst.

For the first time he gazed downward in the direction of his tortured ankle. The rushing water tore at his pupils but he forced his eyes to remain open. Through the pain, a cloudy image began to materialize at the end of his leg.

In the dim light, another pair of eyes met his. They appeared out of the darkness completely void of a body, at least none that he could see. Glowing white and glistening as if completely filled with water, the creature's pupils appeared to serenade back in forth in their sockets, lifeless yet surreal as they spun in oblong circles. The sight was so hideous Curt simply closed his eyes and kicked violently again and again but incredibly missed with each swing. The certainty of defeat was growing. This thing with the demonic eyes, and serrated teeth wanted him dead and it was about to get its way.

With a horrifying finality, Curt gave up.

In an instant, he arched his back to look up. His lungs grew exponentially until they exploded and Curt let out a scream that sent air bursting toward the surface.

When he woke up, Curt was soaked in sweat. He was so disoriented that he could tell his vision was blurred even in the darkness. What added to his bewilderment was how wet he actually was. His underwear, his pillow, his sheets, everything. It took a minute of controlled breathing to help stabilize his thoughts and convince himself he was indeed in his bed and no longer submerged in water. When he calmed, he reached to the side and flipped the table lamp on. He wiped the sweat away from his eyes allowing time for his pulse to slow. Curt reached over to his nightstand for a glass of water. As he was about to drink he hesitated. He wasn't sure if it was fresh or from the previous night. "What the hell," he said out loud before guzzling half the stale fluid as the horrific images of the dreams still ambled in his mind. He lowered the glass and looked at the clock. Squinting at red letters, he read 3:18.

Curt returned the glass to the nightstand and settled back into bed. He wasn't ready to drift into sleep. He was afraid of slipping back into the dream. That sordid, terrifying dream. The one that had just scared the crap and perspiration out of him. He was sure if he closed his eyes now he'd be just in time for *I Still Know How You Swam Last Summer*. He was equally sure he would object to the ending.

Lying there on the moist sheets he wondered what had provoked such a nightmare. Even now he almost believed he could smell salt in the air. Of course, in the morning he would reason that notion away as suggestive persuasion.

But what fragment or subliminal information stored in the recesses of his mind had created such a harsh scenario? Such a wicked beast, whatever it was. A creature that he never got a good look at other than the eyes. *Those eyes*. Where in the hell did he come up with *those eyes*? Maybe it was the pizza he had consumed after 9 p.m. It was loaded with the usual suspects; pepperoni, sausage, beef, onions (that was probably the culprit, onions always gave him gas the next day), and an assortment of other toppings. Maybe the gastric fluids had an adverse reaction to the Italian delicacy and decided to make Curt's subconscious pay the price. But whatever the cause, *those eyes* were ghastly. He couldn't recall seeing anything so scary even in the movies. Spielberg would kill for those ocular effects.

Deciding it was safe to go back to sleep Curt looked up at the ceiling fan, which turned barely fast enough to create any wind flow. He decided it best to change the mental subject and began concentrating on work items. The billing collection project he was going to personally own starting in the morning and the editing that still needed to be done on the E. O. Brunner website.

After a few minutes his body relaxed and he fell back to sleep with the light still on. For the remainder of the night his rest was peaceful and without dreams. At least none he would remember in the morning.

CHAPTER-THREE

It was Friday, September 18, 1999. The air outside desperately hung on to the summer heat as it usually did this time of year. In Florida, there really is no spring or fall. It's more of a long summer briefly separated by eight weeks of winter. In the Sunshine State, Floridians consider it winter anytime the temperature goes below 50 and stays there for more than an hour.

Jacksonville, located so far north in Florida that it is sometimes referred to as South Georgia, is no exception. Jack Frost usually doesn't arrive until late December or even January and could more aptly be termed just *Jack*. Until then, the warm weather clings to the area with a vengeance. The thermometer the last few days exemplified this. Since Monday the temperature had been stifling and the recent intermittent rain showers as a result of Hurricane Cindy, which had passed 432 miles to east, had only made the damp air more humid.

Hurricane season officially ran from July through November with September as the most active month for these massive storms to sweep along the eastern Florida coast. At one point Cindy's eye was aimed just south of Jacksonville, directly at Daytona Beach, but veered off 48 hours before making landfall. Due to her unusually large size, 125 miles wide, the outer clouds had dumped torrential rains on northeast Florida for the last week backing up sewers and overflowing small ponds and lakes.

On this particular morning Scott Seymour had left his house at 7:30 a.m. and was traveling to work east down the winding back roads. Mandarin, a quiet area of Jacksonville known for its huge oaks and historic homes nestled along the St. Johns River, offered a shady, rustic drive.

When searching for a new home last February, Scott had instantly fallen in love with the two-story home nestled in a quiet cul-de-sac the moment he saw it. For him, a strong appeal was the backyard pond stocked with bass, bream and carp and the adjacent setting to a horse ranch with stallions and mares gallivanting in the field. The view from the back porch was uniquely country in spite of the fact it was still very much in the suburbs of Jacksonville. His wife Kay didn't have the instant affection her husband did but she came around quickly after seeing the vast living space compared to the small ranch home they'd been in the first 16 years of their marriage. Their three children: Cody 5, Katie 12 and Lindsey 15 were all enamored with having upstairs rooms that looked over the serene backyard setting.

This particular morning at the Seymour abode had been a hectic one for a Friday. At 5:30 a.m. Scott was rudely pulled from sleep by a rattling piece of paper dangling over his eyes. A few feet away was Kay staring down at him, arm extended. It was a note from Cody's kindergarten teacher regarding an incident at school. Apparently, after a recent viewing of the movie *Blade* (in which Wesley Snipes plays a vampire exterminator) with his parents, Cody took it upon himself to tell a girl in his class that he, too, was a blood-sucking demon of the night. Scott and Kay both assumed Cody had slept through the majority of the movie. They had watched the rental from Blockbuster last Saturday night and Cody had cuddled up between his parents on the couch and faded off to sleep not long after the opening credits. Somehow he caught more than they had thought. Now Scott was paying the price.

As Kay began reading the note out loud, Scott attempted to shake the cobwebs out of his head. He was stuck in that mind-numbing phase, a gray area between sleep and consciousness. Scott truly wished she had found the note the night before but fate was not on his side this particular morning. As Kay read, her excitement gained momentum. Unfortunately, Scott's thought process was still at a virtual standstill.

After finishing the teacher's dissertation, she hesitated and Scott quickly drifted back to sleep. He was startled back awake as Kay posed the question, obviously for the second or third time, in a resounding voice, "What are we going to do?!" Without giving it much thought and just wanting her to go away until the cerebral part of his brain became operational, Scott made the mistake of replying, "Guess we won't let him watch *Blade 2.*"

It was 7:00 a.m. before she began speaking to him again. After a cup of coffee and examining the teacher's note firsthand, the alleged incident hit Scott as a little suspicious. Not that he denied his son might attempt to scare a little girl. He only had to regress to his own childhood to remember pulling little Suzy's pigtails or when his best friend Johnny put a bug down Sally's shirt. It's just what little boys do. What Cody had done was just a slight variation on the physical torture Scott and his cronies had used. In a way, Scott was proud of Cody's use of mental harassing, not usually found at the kindergarten age. Wouldn't Darwin have found this interesting? Even practical jokes evolve over time. But what Scott found particularly intriguing was the note that the teacher said came from the little girl's mother. The teacher's letter read:

> "Tina's mother sent a note to me that Cody had a conversation with Tina and told her he was going to be a blood sucking vampire when he grew up. He also told Tina that he was guided by the Devil and would soon transcend his primortal existence and regress into a being that only came out after dusk had fallen in order to propagate the order of his domain and subrogate the species of the dominions. Cody also said the apocalypse was upon us and destiny had been defined by the established machine that had preceded the chaotic and cataclysmic downfall of our dogmatic existence. Tina's mom said Tina was very upset by all this."

Hell, so am I, Scott thought. With a vocabulary like that, Cody should be writing best selling novels and bringing in some cold hard cash to the family. Scott was also pretty impressed that Tina understood all this because he sure didn't.

Since Cody's IQ is a tad short of 625 (about 615 point shy to be exact), Scott felt assured that there had been some miscommunication between Tina, her apparent Bible-thumping Mother, and the teacher. But since his son had recently had a haircut, and a crew cut at that, to be on the safe side, Scott decided to check Cody's scalp at the breakfast table. Seeing no "6's" Scott walked him in front of the mirror to check for a reflection, simply as a precaution. Kay found little amusement in all of this.

Content that his son was indeed human, Scott had a brief conversation with him about movies and "what's real and what's fiction" and then sent him upstairs to brush his fangs . . . um . . . teeth. Afterward, Scott showed him the lost art of how to successfully place a lizard down a girl's shirt using a fountain pen for practice and encouraged his son to try this in place of his vampire dialogue tactic.

"It's much more immediate and kindergartenish," Scott told his youngest son. This time Kay was unable to suppress a smile. She was pleased to see that her little boy was now on the right track.

With the crisis resolved and after a quick shower, Scott jumped in the Blazer (or the *Blader* as he referred to it this morning) and focused his thoughts on work. His calendar was relatively full this morning with meetings and other appointments, but the afternoon, at least after 2:30 p.m. was clear.

This gave him hope of possibly leaving early and getting some chores accomplished around the yard in order to free up some Saturday time for more pressing matters such as the 3:30 p.m. kickoff between Scott's alma mater, Florida State, and Georgia Tech. Scott had graduated from FSU with a B.A. in Business Marketing in 1985 and relished any opportunity to watch the Seminoles play.

Scott drove to work east on Baymeadows past the Gate Station at the intersection of Old Kings Road. His thoughts became preoccupied with the trip he and two of his managers were scheduled to make to New Jersey in two weeks to conduct a post mortem of his client's system implementation. The project had begun in February and, as expected, had been a tremendous strain on his team. With a crunched timeline, stress had been high throughout the implementation. The technical support staff working with his operations group had been busting their collective asses to remain on track, but it was almost an insurmountable task and took a Herculean effort during the last two months to come in on time.

Unfortunately this had the residual effect of creating enormous frustration for everyone involved. For all intents and purposes, the visit to ATB Telecommunications was the conclusion of the project. The application had been plugging away for over two weeks now with minimal problems. And the discrepancies that were uncovered had been isolated to some off-time project runs that wouldn't affect the daily production process. In all, a very high profile, successful implementation. His job now was to complete a summary document based on the post mortem in New Jersey and then develop a Business Continuity Plan in the event of a disaster.

But the project had also taken a personal toll on Scott as Kay had watched him transform from a happy-go-lucky prankster who was always in a good mood to a man composed of nerves, tension and limited humor. It was just in the last few days he began to feel like himself again. Kay found his wit over Cody's little incident more welcome than he could have imagined, contrary to the looks she gave him.

As usual the stop light in front of his building was red as he rolled to a standstill. Waiting his turn for it to cycle, he slowly tapped his fingers on the top of the steering wheel as lyrics from a Dan Fogelberg song flowed through his head. Scott stared at the light waiting for some color other than red when he happened to focus his vision beyond.

The blue sky was cluttered with an array of clouds. He had no idea what kind of clouds they were. He never could tell the difference. He remembered a science teacher once referring to a particular formation as "cumulous nimbus." To Scott, that had a nice ring to it. Anytime his children commented on cloud designs, he would confidently tell them they were "cumulous nimbus" and they would "oooh" and "aaah" as if he had actually taught them something special. Dads do stuff like that just to impress their kids. But today Scott had no one asking him about the clouds he spotted nor did he say out loud the words "cumulous nimbus" to keep in practice.

His attention was drawn to something unusual that caught his eye and he strained to watch.

One cloud appeared to be resisting the rest of its surrounding brethren and formed and reformed into images at an exceptionally fast rate. Not inkblot images that kinda-sorta looked like a particular object. No, these pictures were clear and defined. Scott wiped his eyes as if his mind had somehow abandoned its consciousness.

The lone cloud just to the left of the red light moved with an extra zip as if the winds up high had singled it out. Bending and stretching its soft cotton-like features for a moment, Scott swore it resembled a sword. It immediately mutated into a circular shape that waved with a groundswell. As he watched with his mouth open, not really sure if he trusted what he saw, the white puffs rapidly formed into a skeleton. It took a second longer for this image to develop but Scott could make out a more distinct pattern of the backbone, ribs and a tail.

The image was like nothing he had ever seen. Living or dead. Current or prehistoric. The creature was elongated with a curved spine and oversized head, with large protruding teeth in a very formidable manner. The tail was split with the longer portion on top and a second, smaller piece underneath. Or maybe it wasn't a tail at all, maybe it was some other sort of appendage. Maybe the second appendage was . . .

Scott banged his head on the rear view mirror at the sudden honking of the horns behind. Gathering himself, he saw the traffic signal had turned green and stepped on the gas making the right turn into the parking lot as his tires squealed on the pavement. He slid into the first available spot, jumped out of the car and was almost hit by Pamela Steed steering her Pontiac into the adjacent space. If not for her quick reflexes and new $68 brake pads, he might have had a very bad Friday. As it was, she nearly took off his door that hung wide open as he stared upward, searching for the magical cloud again.

But it had vanished. Scott was amazed to see there were no clouds in the sky at all. None on the horizon, none up above. It was as if the clouds had disintegrated.

Pamela stepped out of her car and yelled, "You okay?"

He responded with a pleasant, "Good morning. Yeah, I'm fine. Just admiring the beautiful day," he said not wanting to admit he'd probably experienced some psychosis brought on by the recent stress.

She gave him a bewildered look and then began strolling toward the sidewalk. He watched until she reached the covered walkway before turning again to look at the sky. But the puffy white cloud was gone. Instead, he saw a large dark bank of clouds building on the west, signifying that Jacksonville would probably see more rain soon.

Where the hell did those come from? Scott asked himself. Shaking his head as if to remove the last chunk of irrational thought, he headed toward the covered walkway that led to the entrance. As hard as he tried to repress the visions, his mind continued to replay the metamorphic images.

He approached the main door, listening to the internal bantering in his mind between the rational and irrational explanations of what he'd witnessed. Scott was a very methodical man, who usually leaned on the theory that events occur for simple reasons and because of simple circumstances. It's just that in this case, he was having a hard time coming to any satisfactory resolution over what he had witnessed. What he thought he had witnessed.

As Scott entered the building he was no longer tempted to look up at the sky and go cloud hunting. He arrived at the elevator and pressed the call button. He reached his office on the fourth floor and turned his concentration to work. That's what he was paid to do, not worry about unnatural cloud structures.

He didn't give the wavy images another thought until walking outside at 5:20 p.m. So much for leaving work early and cutting into the Saturday chore list. What had started out as an empty afternoon calendar had quickly filled and become an exceptionally busy Friday. As for the morning cloud, Scott was now sure he had just imagined seeing a sword and the bones of some odd animal. Stress can do strange things. Kay was right. He was probably due for some rest and relaxation.

Scott crossed the parking lot and for a moment forgot where he'd parked. He had been so flustered this morning, he had disregarded his normal habit of parking toward the back rows.

Moments later he spotted the *Blader*. He approached the SUV and as he opened the driver's side door his cell phone began to chirp.

"Hello."

"What-up man," Scott heard a voice say that he instantly recognized.

"Just leaving work. I had all intentions of getting out of here about three hours ago," Scott said. "So much for getting a jump on the honey-dos. I'm not missing that game tomorrow so I guess I'll be doing chores when I can this weekend."

"You never leave early. You're a workaholic. Just admit it. Admitting your addiction is half the cure you know," Curt said.

"I'm just a responsible guy. What can I say," Scott replied.

"Hey, we still on for taking the kids skating tomorrow?" Curt asked.

"Yeah. One o'clock right?"

"Sounds good. I'll meet you there," Curt said.

"Hey, what's up tonight?" Scott asked.

"I'm doing the single-guy thing. Probably Schotzy's."

"I know this advice will limit your choices but don't pick up any strange women," Scott said with a laugh.

"Are there any other kind?" Curt replied with a chuckle.

"I guess not. Okay, I'll see you tomorrow."

"Bye," Scott responded as he heard Curt hang up. Scott had known his friend since high school and they had remained close ever since. As with most good friends, they had been through the good times and the bad. Scott had fond memories of the apartment he and Curt had shared in their early twenties and had many humorous pictures and stories stored in his mind from those days. Generally, they had stayed in touch through the years but there had been intervals, like early in both their marriages, when the two hardly spoke, not by design but as a result of their hectic lives.

Now Scott, 37, and Curt, 36, had reestablished the connection and frequently found time and circumstances to get together. It was also convenient that they each had children and that Cody and Julie were only a year apart, at 5 and 6, respectively. This allowed them opportunities to convene in the daddy role at the movies, birthday parties, picnics and in the case of Saturday, the skating rink.

Scott drove home reflecting on the turmoil his friend had experienced during the last year and a half. Curt and his wife had finalized their divorce three months ago after 11 years of marriage. It had been a tremendous strain on Curt. His friend was the victim of a wife who fell out of love but refused to be honest about the situation. Instead of confronting Curt with the truth, she had taken the slimy path of initiating an affair with an old high school love. Curt suspected something since the sex had been literally nonexistent for two years.

Instead of trying to solve their relationship, or at least get to the truth, Curt focused his time and energy on the one female who really appreciated him, his daughter Julie. He now realized he was wrong for ignoring the situation but it was a natural defense. It wasn't until after the divorce that he realized the affair had been going on for some time. The ugliness of the circumstances still infuriated Scott and he kept wondering what he would say to Sheila the first time he ran into her in public. He had a strong opinion he wished to express.

Although six-year-old Julie seemed to be handling the divorce with amazing resilience, Curt had not. He desperately missed the time with his daughter. Over the last year, he had spent almost all his free time with her doing father and daughter things. Now he was able to see her at scattered intervals during the week and to keep her from Friday till Sunday twice a month. But he sorely missed the normal routines of family life.

It had taken awhile but he was slowly adapting. Scott had recently noticed the turnaround in Curt's outlook. Curt had even resumed some hobbies he had abandoned, or seldom allowed time for, such as archeology and fishing. Curt even slowed down the time spent at work as a part owner of Ticomet Inc, an internet design company. It had been a painful lesson and Scott was glad to see his friend enter the dating scene again, if you could call going to a bar and meeting women dating. The image of Curt getting shot down in Schotzy's after attempting some lame pickup line on a drunk brunette made Scott smile as he turned left onto Timmon Road.

After picking up Cody from the Little Kings & Queen's daycare center, Scott proceeded home, hearing all of the daily goings-on of kindergarten. They pulled into the driveway a little after 6:10 p.m. Kay had gotten home 15 minutes earlier and was already busy making dinner.

CHAPTER-FOUR

Long before the Inca civilization would leave its profound mark on history or the Egyptians would construct the Great Pyramid of Giza, an old man stood peering over the wooden rail of a massive ship, looking at the water slowly receding below. The journey with his family had been harsh and not without sacrifice. It was as he had expected. As he had been told it would be.

But they had made it safely and the cargo was intact. He had done what he was asked. Now maybe he could relax, as an elderly man should, and just enjoy the remainder of his existence with his wife.

Behind him on the deck, in a barrel half-full, the water churned. A creature whipped just below the surface. It stared upward waiting for sustenance to enter its domain, swirling in a frenzied pattern as it had since the journey began 12 weeks ago. Now, with the mission's conclusion, the old man turned and looked at the container, wondering what he would do with the beast that had fulfilled its purpose.

Would it be taken away? Surely the intent was not to allow it to exist with mankind.

But how? When? Soon his extended family would debark the mighty vessel and remove the living cargo. The creature in the water had no further use. He had been assured of that. But what was to become of it?

The old man moved closer to the barrel then stopped several feet away, fearful of what moved inside. He waited for instructions as the water slapped against the wooden sides, sending shivers through his body.

Patiently he waited. There was no response. Communication had been oddly severed.

Since the very beginning, the creature had unnerved him and his family. They avoided the barrel as much as possible on the long trip, going near only when necessity dictated.

They understood its intent and had used it frequently. Now, as the ship quietly sat perched more on land than sea, the old man had grave concerns about how to dispose of the creature, a beast whose power was unlike anything on earth he had ever witnessed.

He edged closer to get a better look inside. The beast was rapidly gliding beneath the surface hugging the curved walls creating a downward vortex. It's eyes peered upward and transfixed on the old man's stare, keeping contact even as it circled.

Its presence alone chilled the man's soul. But when he had to actually look at the creature, as he did now, the sight was hideous. How could such a thing be used in such a glorious manner? He never would get an answer to this question.

Later that afternoon, with his family's input, and accepting he would receive no official guidance, the old man and his sons worked the barrel to a covered opening in the deck, careful to keep their hands on the outside. The hold below was empty. Earlier the cargo had been removed and set upon the land.

As the creature frothed the surface, waiting for any opportunity to feast, the men, squatting down, pushed low on the barrel and slid it next to the opening. After lifting the door, in unison, they slowly tipped the container. When the weight finally shifted past midpoint, the barrel fell over sending water and the beast into the empty hold, 35 feet below.

A piercing screech resonated from the bowels of the ship. The old man's eldest son quickly threw back the hatch door to seal the opening. The man and his sons rose to their feet and backed away holding their ears.

The horrifying sound continued for several minutes. The women on board watched from a short distance away and sobbed uncontrollably.

Several hours later the old man and his family had completely stripped the ship of anything useful and were prepared to abandon their temporary home for a more permanent solution. But curiosity over what had become of the creature secured in the hold became the topic of conversation.

Prior to final departure and unknown to his father, the eldest brother made a trip to the main deck. With considerable trepidation he opened the hatch, not knowing what to expect. Cautiously moving to the edge he gasped at the site below.

Most of the hold was caked in darkness. Sunlight sought out one small square area on the flooring below. And in the middle of the illumination an animal's brilliant white skeleton lay dormant.

The *creature's* skeleton. In a mere several hours it had gone from a living, breathing thing to a perfectly clean carcass.

The son closed the hatch and stood on the deck, momentarily confused about what he would do next. A strange desire overcame him and his initial resistance was overruled. He was not alone. Someone or *something* was very close. Close enough to make his skin tingle. In the sun's warmth his vision blurred and the daylight suddenly went insipid. He fell to his knees and nearly fainted. Colors scattered and the deck wavered. His body became tight and rigid. It was as if his soul had been invaded by another presence and there was not enough room to accommodate the two entities.

Panting he could see the beast's skeleton through the deck. The image was as clear as when the hatch had been open. Now, somehow, its presence was clearly distinguishable through the solid flooring! Again, colors spun in front of his eyes and he fell to the deck.

When he woke, his clothes were bathed in perspiration from the sun's warmth. Sleep had obviously been brief. Now his head ached and his stomach tossed in sickening turns as he recalled the dream of the creature in the hold. He closed his eyes and his stomach calmed and the anguish passed. Opening them he slowly gained his vision and the world around him oriented to normal. He stood up and looked down at the wooden deck.

He knew what he had to do next. He just didn't understand why.

CHAPTER-FIVE

The small pond in the Seymour backyard was no more than 60 feet across and about 45 feet wide. It was relatively barren on all sides except to the east where it was bordered by bushes and trees from the uncleared property to the left.

Scott had been an avid fisherman since he was five. He'd spent many hours of his youth landing croakers, trout, sheepshead, and blue fish out of his father's 16-foot, 40-horsepower run-about. Most of the time they'd fish the St. Johns River near its mouth leading into the Atlantic. The picturesque view of the jetties reaching toward the ocean, the assortment of aircraft carriers, cruisers, and destroyers docked at nearby Mayport Naval Station and the early morning sun cresting on the horizon had left indelible memories in Scott's mind. To him, fishing was as natural as walking or riding a bike. It was just something he had loved as far back as he could remember. As an adult, the sport represented a method for acquiring some semblance of solitude. Whether he caught a dozen fish or never got a bite, it was his own personal way of recharging his psyche and preparing to face the next round of challenges life threw at him. It had the same cleansing effect that jogging has on runners. It clears the mental palette, erases the anxieties and calms whatever stress hovers in the air.

In Scott's early thirties he had hit those years of relentless hours of work and, along with Kay, of raising two young children and a baby while keeping all life's other distractions at bay. There was a multiyear period in which Scott never held a fishing rod in his hand. It took that long for him to realize he wasn't the same relaxed man he'd been most of his adult life. Between working 10 hours a day and the mountain of activities that had to be tended to each evening at the homestead, he felt like he was dipping into a subtle depression. Eventually he understood the missing element was the occasional escape to the great outdoors to refresh and he had resumed the activity whenever time allowed.

That evening, 30 minutes before dinner, Scott, Cody and Katie went out to the backyard to catch some bream. On the average, during the spring and summer, they fished the pond about three times a week. It was a no-lose situation. The Seymours constantly kept the area baited to draw the fish in. The bream were conditioned to come to the edge of the bank nearest the house. Scott referred to the finned creatures as the "Stepford Fish." He could bait a small hook with a ball of bread, toss it in and almost immediately watch the red and white bobber disappear.

Sometimes the kids hooked the fish. Sometimes they missed. But there was always the next cast. Each time a bream was landed, Scott quickly removed the hook and placed the fish back in the pond. Having a pond in the backyard was something he had only dreamed about as a kid. He was glad to see his children take advantage of the opportunity.

As Dad patiently rolled the first ball of bread, Cody became more and more impatient.

"Hurry Daddy! Hurry Daddy! Before they run away."

"They're not going anywhere, honey. These fish are related to Pavlov's doggie."

"Huh," Cody said with a confused look.

"Nothing honey. Okay, you're ready to fish. Toss it out there."

Cody wheeled the rod back over his head as if he intended to toss the bread 80 yards out, but instead brought it forwarded with an equally slow move, landing the bait, hook and bobber only four feet from shore.

"Watch, I'm gonna catch a lunker," he said.

"I'm sure you will," Scott replied as he watched Katie bait her hook and toss the line in the water about 18 inches to the left of Cody's.

"Daddy!" Cody screamed. "Katie is trying to hit my bobber with hers. Tell her to stop."

"You're okay, Cody. There's plenty of fish in here for both of you."

At that exact instant, Cody's bobber jerked down twice barely escaping the surface. The third time it was gone and the excited little five-year-old began winding the reel as though he was "The Old Man and the Sea."

"I got him! I got him!" he shouted as Katie took two steps to the left to move her line a little farther away so not to get tangled with Cody. Dad had taught them well. Fishing etiquette, Scott called it.

Cody wound furiously. In a moment he lifted the five-inch bream into the air for Scott to retrieve and release. Simultaneously, Katie hooked into a slightly smaller version. She brought it up about the same time Scott was grabbing for Cody's hook to bait. Scott's daughter, who did not mind the "baiting" part of the sport, did have serious issues with clutching a slimy fish, propping its mouth open and extracting the hook. This resulted in Scott continuously alternating between baiting Cody's hook and removing the bream for his kids as fast and furious as they could catch them. On a good day, each kid would catch 10 to 12 fish before they got tired. Scott really didn't mind though. He loved the idea they had come to embrace one of his passions so intently.

Fifteen minutes later, Cody and Katie informed Dad they were going inside to get carrots and feed the horses over the wire fence at the back of the property. This was about their average fishing duration, give or take five minutes.

Scott, on the other hand, could be at the pond for hours. For him, it was pure relaxation. Upon notification from his kids that they were done, Scott walked back to the porch and replaced the two smaller rods with an Abu Garcia rigged for bass. He returned to the bank and, after adjusting the seven-inch red shad plastic worm, made a cast into the middle of the small body of water. He paused momentarily allowing the 1/16-oz weighted lure to sink to the bottom amongst the rubble of fallen tree limbs from the surrounding pines. He worked the worm slowly as it crawled over the branches and other assorted structures along the bottom. Scott concentrated on sensing movement in the line. Bass fishing is a very patient sport and can also be very unproductive for long periods of time.

As he stood on the shore slowly retrieving the lure, Scott's mind wandered back to the cloud he saw that morning. Or probably had *imagined* that morning. It seemed so long ago now. Watching the smooth surface of the water and admiring the quiet of the late afternoon, he wasn't sure if it had been real or just a daydream. He mentally slid back into the seat behind the wheel of the Blazer and could see the images of the sword and the creature's skeleton. Had it really taken such defined shapes? How was it possible the cloud had transformed itself at such speed and, why, apparently, had no one else seen it?

Thinking back, it was like something out of a cartoon. But as much as he wanted to convince himself it had all been an illusion, maybe even some sort of weird flashback to a Stephen King story, there was something in his psyche that wouldn't let go.

As Scott mentally debated the issue, he did what any proud man would do. Instead of accepting defeat, he decided to think of something else. He turned his concentration back on the worm that he had recast slightly to the left of the pond's center.

As the bait settled to the bottom he immediately felt a sharp tug. Before he had time to set the hook properly, the fish ran, ripping line and taking drag. The rod tip bowed sharply. Scott was so surprised he nearly lost his grip.

"What in the . . .?" Scott said catching his tongue with the children around. The fish was not behaving like a bass and Scott immediately considered it to be a catfish or even one of the large carp that occupied the pond. Whatever it was never broke the surface as a bass typically would, instead, staying toward the bottom of the pond, which reached eight feet in the middle, and running toward the far end. Scott adjusted the drag with his right hand to try and slow the fish. But the increased tension had no effect. The resistance seemed to anger the fish and it gained speed as the drag screeched.

There is nothing in this small body of water that should behave like that. Nothing this strong.

Scott considered the alternatives. Maybe an alligator had migrated to the pond and was about to strip the line completely off his reel. Florida was famous for alligators and it was quite common for one to move from pond to pond during the warm months. Again he adjusted the drag, this time to full force and, in an instant, the line snapped cleanly. The sudden release surprised Scott. He had been using his weight as leverage by leaning back stretching the fiberglass pole into a near perfect loop. With the loss of tension, he fell onto the ground, landing square on his backside. Cody and Katie had turned to watch their dad struggle with the fish and broke into laughter upon his fall. Scott sat on the ground for a minute as the stinging pain from the landing slowly subsided. He didn't want to let on to his kids that it had hurt dear old dad. Besides, he knew it hadn't done any permanent damage. Fortunately, he had landed on a flat spot of grass.

He slowly rose and brushed himself off while staring into the pond, looking for any surface disruption. Normally a fish that keeps a hook frantically tries to dislodge it by crashing about. But the water was as calm and silent as it had been before the strike. The whole encounter had been very bizarre.

For several minutes Scott watched the small body of water, wondering what exactly he had fought. His curiosity had not only piqued, it had ballooned. He hated losing a fish, no matter what the circumstance. That quote about "It's better to have loved and lost than never have loved at all" did not apply to fishing. He'd much rather not get a strike than to hook a fish only to lose it in the ensuing battle.

But was it a fish? Unless a freshwater tarpon had evolved in his pond, the thing had just been too strong. An alligator was a more rationale explanation but not one he was happy with. Even a small alligator would have probably broken the surface during the fight. Besides, alligators need air to breathe so why hadn't it come to the top? What if it was a snapping turtle? This was possible. Turtles had been known to take lures occasionally, especially snapping turtles. Scott and Kay had noticed six or eight residing in the pond during the early summer. Kay had taken to feeding them small crunchy pieces of cat food, which she tossed on the surface. The buoyant food was devoured by the turtles within minutes.

But that was some seven weeks ago. Scott assumed the turtles had moved on, although to where, he had no idea. The thing that bothered him about the turtle solution was the strength of whatever he hooked. It had been tremendous. He didn't think a turtle would be strong enough to put up that kind of a fight. But maybe it had been a large one. Yeah, like one the size of a Volkswagon he thought with a concerned grin creeping to his lips. The biggest turtle they had seen during the summer was maybe 14 inches around. Could one that size reel off drag and then snap the line without ever slowing? It didn't sound plausible. He was pretty sure the Teenage Mutant Ninja Turtles were just a cartoon, not creatures living in his pond.

Without exploring other possibilities he decided it was time to go inside. He instructed the kids to do the same. If it was an alligator, he wasn't taking any chances. A gator with a stainless steel barb in its jaw might be more than a little annoyed. He thought back to stories of gators killing small animals and even children strolling on the banks of waterways in Florida, lying in wait until the unsuspecting victim would approach and then lashing out with those deadly jaws packed with razor sharp teeth. Anyway, it had been more than 35 minutes since he and the kids had come out. Surely it was time for dinner.

A little past 8:30 p.m. and after tackling a medium pizza that had been delivered to his apartment, Curt drove to Schotzy's. It was Friday and he was in a much better mood than he had been on recent Fridays. Even though it was not his weekend to have Julie, Sheila had consented to let him take her Saturday for a while. He was beginning to get used to the fact that he was single and there was life after marriage. He had recently made a few female acquaintances at this particular pub and felt very comfortable with the locals who frequented the place.

It had been a strange transition though. The dating scene had never really been his strong suit. But the demographics of the female patrons of Schotzy's were ideal. Most were of the 30-and-over crowd and many had also been married at one time or another. Misery loves company.

As it turned out, the evening was uneventful for Curt and the bar was relatively quiet for a weekend night. As the evening had progressed Curt felt the effects of the day catching up to him and on more than one occasion he found himself suppressing a yawn. He had risen early that morning and had gone full speed at work all day long. It was not going to be a late night.

Friday night at the Seymour resident was marked by a "bisghetti" feast accompanied by garlic bread and Coca-Cola. When all was said and done (and eaten), Cody wore more on his face than he could ever possibly get in his 38-pound body. After gobbling his fill, the lips and the surrounding skin of the five-year-old glowed a bright orange tint. Upon finishing, Kay ordered him to the upstairs bathroom to cure. The other kids had done their fair share of damage as well. Lindsey, who ate at the speed of light, had been done before Scott even finished pouring the drinks and had excused herself from the table. Katie, who was developing the teenage mentality, had yet to cross over the bridge. Yeah, she could huff down a plate of food within minutes but she was still young enough to enjoy sitting around the dinner table with Mom, Dad and little brother for some of the conversation and humorous stories or comments from Scott.

In many ways, Scott was sad Lindsey had outgrown the nightly camaraderie, but he didn't blame her. He had done the same thing to his parents about the time he turned 14. Now he had a much better appreciation of the mixed emotions they must have gone through. But at least he still had two, soon to be one, that appreciated the time they shared. And Scott tried to make the best of it.

When Cody returned from the bathroom, Scott was helping Kay clear the table. Cody still donned a huge orange moon around his mouth.

"Scott, do you mind giving him a bath?" Kay asked. Scott was the family bather. This was a much easier job than it had been a few years ago when he had multiple kids to tend to. Now it was down to one.

"C'mon Sketti face. Let's dunk you in the water," Scott said to Cody.

"Daddy do I have to?" Cody said with a grimace.

"You heard your mother. You need to be clean so that you won't offend anyone with your stinky body or the dirt behind your ears when you dream tonight," he said with a straight face watching for Kay's reaction out of the corner of his eye. As he stared into Cody's puzzled expression he saw his wife momentarily give him "the look," again suppressing a smile, as she went about the business of wiping down the table. With that, father and son made their way up the stairs to the hall bathroom where the re-beautification of Cody would commence.

Now as Cody easily entered the warm water, Scott settled down on the toilet seat beside the tub.

Cody never bathed alone. Drifting aimlessly around him were a series of plastic Pokemon characters. In addition, Cody also had five army men, which remained in a plastic cup on the side of the tub for such occasions. After allowing for play time, which included a life and death battle pitting Char and Peek against the army dudes, Scott went about the task of putting the soap to the body and sanitizing the young Seymour. When he was through, he lifted Cody out of the tub and pulled the plug. His son giggled at the small cyclone of water funneling downward above the drain and carrying three of his floating army men circling to their plastic death.

"Look daddy," he said with a childish cackle. "Those Maroons can't swim." "Maroons" was Cody's term for the Semper Fi crowd. The few and the proud. As the Maroons continued to struggle (with no success) against their destined fate, Scott placed Cody on the bath mat and immediately covered him with a towel and began drying before the shivers set in. Starting at his short wet hair and quickly wiping off his back and then chest, stomach and finally his legs. With the rub down finished, he prepared Cody's underwear for the skin-is-still-slightly-damp-one-leg-at-a-time entry method whereby Scott stretched the first leg hole so wide it formed an oversized opening that a Lebanese Yak could have gone through. Once accomplished, step two was to repeat step one. Once the underwear was on, the big tee shirt followed. It went on much easier as Cody gladly welcomed the warmth of the covering.

Now dressed for bed, Scott continued toweling his little guy's hair. As he did, Cody held onto his dad's shoulders and leaned forward to kiss him softly on the nose. Scott looked into his son's eyes and returned the favor by gently holding the back of his head and rubbing his cheek against the boy's forehead, careful not to give him razor burn. At that moment Scott thought how deeply he loved his son. All his children. His wife. For that matter, most everything in his life. Scott really lived a charmed existence for the most part. He felt very fortunate to have what he had and was proud of all that he had accomplished so far in life. And at that moment, the undeniable truth was his family was his strength.

After putting Cody down, Scott grabbed a beer and joined his wife in the den. Several hours later, at the conclusion of a "B" horror flick, Kay retired to bed. Scott stayed up to catch *Sports Center* and strolled to bed at 11:22 p.m.

As soon as he hit the pillow he was asleep. But it was a light sleep. His brain shot fragments of thoughts that misfired and landed in a disrupted pattern. He awoke after half an hour and could not relax. Something gnawed at him. The feeling lingered just out of reach, neither close enough to grasp nor far enough to release.

He turned on his side to the right and then rotated back to his left as he listened to the rotors of the ceiling fan gently humming above. Whatever had cemented itself deep in his conscience, rose only enough to shine minor glints of light to signal its existence. Otherwise, it remained buried. Not ready to give up its position. It's quiet, peaceful position.

Scott sensed *it* (whatever the *it* was) had a yearning to be discovered. Whatever had sunk in had taken roots and would not be removed easily. Something he'd picked up from the day. Was it the clouds? He'd pretty much written that off to stress and eye strain.

What troubled him now was more than that. It was something tangible. A *need*. A *need* for discovery that he somehow knew was best left unrevealed. Yet he *could* not. As the sleepless minutes drifted by, the nagging pervaded as he struggled to unearth what lay below. What was so disturbing, so very disturbing, was the uneasiness that crept in. He began to wonder if someone close had passed away. He'd heard stories of such premonitions affecting the living. He lay in bed somewhat expecting the phone to ring with bad news.

The minutes passed and the feeling remained embedded. At quarter till one, he got up and popped three Motrin. After several attempts to divert his thoughts elsewhere he finally faded off to sleep around 1:20 a.m.

At 11:15 p.m. Curt paid his tab, gave up his bar seat and headed home. He stopped by Krystals for five cheeseburgers and a coke and ate them on the drive back to his apartment. After a quick scan of the cable channels, he lay down shortly before midnight. The moment his head hit the pillow he was wide-awake. He could not relax. Thoughts of the previous night's dream flickered in his head and every minute noise in the apartment seemed magnified. It was several hours before he drifted off but dozed only sporadically throughout the night.

CHAPTER-SIX

Without his father or family's knowledge, the old man's son retrieved the small skeleton from the hold. He hid it neatly within the confines of his sheepskin smock and left the huge ship. When he arrived at the gangplank, the others were busily securing supplies on the pack animals. The father had decided the family would stay together and travel toward the valley.

Several weeks later, after the father was comfortable that all was taken care of, his sons and daughters, with their spouses, set off on their own. All this time the eldest son had taken great care to keep the skeleton hidden, even from his wife and children. When allowed to proceed on their own, the son ordered his family to uproot their meager camp. He led them on a northwestern course that several months later took them to what someday would be known as the Black Sea.

Once there, they set up camp. Beginning that first night along the shore, long after his wife and children fell asleep, he went about fashioning a wooden container made from the trunk of a thick birch tree. With the crude instruments available, he meticulously carved an 18-inch opening in the three-foot section. It took several weeks, working secretively at night, to achieve the desired results. All the while, his family, without question, went about finding food, preparing the meals and thatching together a meager abode from the local vegetation. They understood their place in the world implicitly. And it was not to question husband or father but simply to do as was instructed.

Sixteen days after first laying eyes on the great body of water, the man retrieved the small carcass he had buried in the dry sand the night of their arrival. Under the cloak of darkness he placed the skeleton in the carved wood encasing and used leaves and tree sap to seal the opening. He carefully placed the entire assembly on a large inland boulder far away from the family's camp. He patiently waited nearly a month for the sap to harden into an airtight seal entombing the skeleton inside.

One evening, nearly seven weeks after his task had begun, the man rose in the middle of the night while his family slept. He walked inland through the blackness and, guided by forces he was unable to comprehend, found the wooden coffin with the small skeleton neatly tucked away inside. He made his way back to the shore several hundred yards west from his quiet family and walked into the gentle surf. When the water was easily breaking over his knees, he placed the section of tree with its cargo softly on the surface and let go. It gradually receded beyond the breakers and into the darkness that prevailed. He would never see the skeleton again.

At that moment the man became aware he was standing in water and had absolutely no idea where he was or what he was doing. He instinctively walked back to his family and lay down.

When he woke in the morning he remembered nothing about the skeleton or wooden casing that would afford the carcass its dry journey.

CHAPTER-SEVEN

Curt rose at 7:30 a.m. to the blaring of "Hotel California" on his clock radio. After a cup of coffee he shaved and showered and was out the door by 10 minutes after eight. Sheila would give him flack for showing up early but he didn't care. He was getting his daughter for most of the day and he was in a great mood. Besides, it would take him 30 minutes to get into Arlington and that would put him at Sheila's at 8:40, only twenty minutes ahead of schedule. She would have to live with it. He'd called and spoken to Julie at 8 and she was rarin' to go.

He arrived as expected, twenty minutes early. Sheila didn't seem to mind as she had errands to run. Julie met Curt at the door with a huge bear hug around his neck. Curt stood upright still clutching Julie as her legs dangled happily in the air.

"Daddy's here! Daddy's here!" she shouted in a shrill but happy voice.

"Hey Cupcake. Have you been a good girl?"

"Uh huh," she said still holding on with a jaws-of-life grip on his neck. "What we doin' Daddy? What we doin?" she asked looking into her father's eyes with childish inquisition.

"Well, I have a big day planned, Cupcake. You'll just have to see. Stick with me and I promise you some fun."

By this time Sheila had made her way to the door and they exchanged pleasantries. For Curt the bitterness of the divorce made it very difficult to have any respect toward the woman. But she was his little girl's mother and for that reason, he worked very hard at playing nice.

After confirming the time Sheila expected to be back and when he would bring Julie home, father and daughter were off, ready to tackle a Saturday of fun, relaxation and togetherness. They backed his blue Mustang out of the driveway at 10 minutes till nine and began their adventures.

To Curt, the morning passed within a moment. After leaving Sheila's, they went to Shoney's for the all-you-can-eat buffet bar. Forty-five minutes later they waddled out and drove to the Avenues Mall where Curt dropped an easy $20 playing video games and the like with Cupcake. Afterward, they traversed the stores and finally landed at the Oasis for a couple of hotdogs before heading back into Mandarin. Destination: *Skate Place*. It was 12:50 p.m. when they arrived and Scott and Cody had not shown up yet. Julie was elated when she found out whom they were meeting.

"Cody gonna skate with me?" she said with honest concern that he might come to the rink and ignore her.

"Of course he is. They're just not here yet. Uncle Scott always runs late when he's supposed to meet Daddy somewhere. I think he does it to test Daddy's patience," Curt replied as they sat in the car awaiting the Seymours arrival.

"They'll be here soon," Julie said grabbing her father's hand to comfort the distraught man.

"I know, Cupcake. I know," he said smiling into her big brown eyes and wondering if it was humanly possible to squeeze out any more love for her than he already felt. He wasn't sure but he'd keep trying.

In time the Blazer rolled up and Scott and Cody hopped out. "Been waiting long?" Scott asked.

"Don't get me started," Curt responded with a smirk and then smiled at his friend. "Is Cody ready to skate?"

"Does the Pope poop in the woods?" Scott whispered leaning into Curt's ear.

"I have no idea. I don't keep track of the Pontif's fecal events. But I'll take that as affirmation."

The foursome crossed the parking lot and entered the building.

The air coming from the beach was crisp and clean as the man opened his back door and stepped onto the patio. He carried the box containing the bound pages he'd been reading for the last day and a half. He picked up a plastic chair and moved it to the front left corner of the deck. It was the one spot the sun had yet to uncover. The large palm trees lining the back fence saw to that. He sat down in a slow precise manner and then scooted in place until he felt comfortable. Damn old age. Twenty years ago he would have plopped down on a piece of wrought iron and would have been fine. Now he had to wiggle and squirm to accommodate his over-seventy-body in a position that would be comfortable if he was to remain sitting for more than 15 seconds.

The man held the closed box in his lap as he admired the day. Another beautiful September morning in Florida. Sure he lived in the middle of hurricane central having experienced one recent scare and knowing that another storm was building hundreds of miles to the east, but it sure was worth it. The setting could be as serene as a postcard and when the winds died and the ocean surf was flat, the quietness would filter a man's soul, cleansing him of any wrongdoings in whatever past lives he may have existed.

As he watched one lone cloud streak the sky he realized how tired he was and contemplated closing his eyes. But there was no time for that. He had work to do. He was actually being paid for something that came perfectly natural to him. What a great country this is even if they have no clue how to make good champagne.

He lifted the box lid and placed it on the deck to his right. Removing the bound papers and tossing the rest of the box on the ground, he winced as his intestines locked up. It felt like someone had a firm grip on his stomach and then slowly, agonizingly slowly, released its hold like air being pinched out of a balloon. The pain was so intense he nearly blacked out.

"Ooooh," he said in a long drawn out breathless voice. The ache had caught him completely off guard. With each new intake of air, the intensity faded. He repositioned his hindquarters in the seat to make sure the pain had completely subsided. The movement was meant to replicate the discomfort if it was still present. This time he was prepared to receive it.

"Go ahead dammit. Let's get this over with!" he said in defiance. Since turning 70, his body had given him more than a few shocks for unknown reasons. He wanted to make sure there were no more surprises with the next deep inhale. It was better to meet the pain head on when he knew it was coming.

"C'mon," he said, "I can take it!"

As he sat in the chair anticipating the next swell of frayed nerve endings, his ears detected a sound coming from the beach. But the Central Control Unit didn't get the message. The CCU had taken a coffee break and had left no one to tend the store. Several minutes later, when his mind caught up with his senses, he would question what he had heard. What he *thought* he had heard. A powerful yet weak, hideous, desperate noise. It must have been some odd combination of the gulls and wind. A trick to the old mind.

The man sat with his spine taut, continuing to grit his teeth and bracing for the volts. But the pain did not return. Breathing easier, he opened the pages to the place holder, a marker advertising the First Baptist Church of Ponte Vedra he'd gotten in the mail with an invitation to attend their service. He read for a moment and then delicately turned the page. He reached over to the side table and grabbed a pencil and pad. He scribbled some cryptic notes and returned to reading.

Soon his shady spot, which had been so well protected from the sun's UV rays, was under full attack. He gathered up the contents of the box and placed them away. He rose and went inside. With the heat continuing to build outside, the air-conditioned environment would make his work much more tolerable. Curt Lockes man would be over this evening and he had to be done by then.

That afternoon at the skating rink, after the kids went their merry way, Scott and Curt settled into a booth with four small cokes purchased from the snack stand. Their table represented the pit stop for the Indy 500 Racers. The kids swung by every few laps to indulge in the liquid refreshment and catch their breath while Scott and Curt watched the sights and talked about guy stuff.

"So what grand plans do you have for this evening? You want to come over and have dinner?" Scott asked.

"Thanks for the invite but I've got an appointment with a man."

"An appointment? For what?" Scott asked with a look of concern.

"It's not a doctor's appointment. I'll tell ya tomorrow. It may be nothing. The again, we'll just have to see. I'll give you the details when I know more. Oh, by the way, I've wormed my way into participating in the Indian burial dig off A1A, across from the old ferry ramp. You want to come along? We're going to start next Saturday and continue for 12 to 14 days."

"Gee, Curt, I'd love to but I have this little time occupier called a job. I don't own my own business and therefore can't take two weeks off on the *sperm* of the moment."

"Man. You should get a new job," Curt replied with a chuckle.

The rest of the afternoon at the Skate Place was filled with the two friends sharing stories, jokes, opinions and observations about everything under the sun. Every so often the Andretti twins would pull in for a refill and then be back on the track to blaze the rink. It was an enjoyable afternoon and before long the clock over the floor marked the three o'clock hour and they departed their separate ways.

Scott pulled into his driveway at 3:20. As soon as he killed the engine, Cody hit the seatbelt release button and flipped the handle on the door. "Can I go play in the backyard?"

"Yeah, just stay away from the pond," Scott replied.

He watched his son run around the left corner of the house and strolled to the mailbox to check for incoming. There was the usual clutter. The Sears bill, some mixed advertisements, one from Dr. Claude Leopar introducing his practice to the Mandarin area, a flyer for Pizza Hut and one from Centrinex Mortgage Company wanting to give him a home equity loan for up to $35,000 to pay off all his outstanding debt. With the exception of the Sears bill, which was really Kay's since it was in her name, the rest found their way to the circular file near the refrigerator in the kitchen.

"Where's Cody?" Kay asked coming from around the corner, carrying a basket of laundry.

"I left him at the roller place. He picked up some 24-year-old babe and I didn't want to embarrass him by telling him it was time to go home. Hope you don't mind."

"Not at all. She doesn't smoke does she?"

"Only hash. But she doesn't inhale," Scott replied.

"Oh, well, that's fine," she said with a grin.

The remainder of the afternoon Scott spent watching the Seminoles mash helmets against the Yellow Jackets. The game was a nail-biter that came down to a last second field goal by FSU's kicker, Jiloski, with 1:22 left to play. It was one of those games Scott thoroughly enjoyed even though his nerves were frazzled by the end.

Curt took Julie home at four o'clock. They actually arrived before Sheila, who had gone to her sister's. As they sat in the car in front of the house, Curt kept the radio on and, against Julie's wishes, scanned the stations in search of more intelligent music. There is just so much bubble gum music that an adult over the age of 18 can endure in one afternoon and he felt it was time to move on to more mature art. Although the pop music of the Back Street Boys, 98 Degrees and NSYNC was fun and kept a smile on Julie's lips, he was relieved to catch the beginning of Creed's *My Own Prison* on Rock 105.

"Where's mommy?" Julie asked about half way through the song as Curt realized he had the radio up a little too loud and quickly adjusted the volume.

"She'll be home in a few minutes. Did you have fun today, honey?" he asked as he smiled into his daughter's eyes.

"Of course," she responded in a matter-of-fact voice. "Can you stay when Mommy gets home? You can play in my room with me," she said, hoping for a positive answer.

"I'm sorry honey," he said as he felt his heart sink. "Daddy has to go to a meeting. But remember next weekend, you get to stay with me for two whole days," he said, holding up his right hand and displaying his pointer and middle finger to make sure she understood the significance of the numbers.

There was a look of despair in Julie's eyes as she gazed down at the floorboard almost crying instantly. Curt could tell she was fighting back the tears as valiantly as any six-year-old ever has. As if joined by forces of the universe he felt her disappointment and would have done anything at that moment to make her happy. Shaking off the bitterness, he thought quickly.

"Hey, Cupcake, you wanna play hide-and-go-seek until your mother gets home?"

She looked up at him slowly and at first he thought she was still upset about her father not *wanting* to play with her in her room. Her expression was flat. No smiles no grimaces. Just those beautiful brown eyes peering into his soul. "What'd you say?" she asked to check to make sure she'd heard him right.

"C'mon, let's play until mom gets home," Curt said with enthusiasm. Julie was out the door and standing on the lawn before dad had released his seatbelt. After 20 minutes of hiding around the corner of the house, in the bushes (where Curt momentarily stood in a bed of fire ants) and in the alcove by the front door it was apparent that he would never outsmart his little girl in this game. She was a natural. Inspector Julie. More capable of tracking down fugitives than Tommy Lee Jones.

Just after 4:30 p.m. Sheila pulled her Ford Taurus into the single car driveway. After another brief exchange of niceties and a big hug and kiss from Julie, Curt was in his Mustang heading toward his next stop. He had a five o'clock appointment that he would now surely be late for. Oh well, it didn't really matter. The old man had nothing better to do. It wasn't like if he got there late he'd be off on a hot date or heading to the beach to go skinny-dipping in the late afternoon sun. The man was a hermit from what Curt could tell. He didn't really impress him as a people person, content more with just riding out the rest of his existence sitting in the backyard as the wind cut through the palms or watching the Classic Movie Channel till he fell asleep in his Lazy Boy at nine o'clock at night. But the man had a skill few did. As Curt turned off Southside and onto the cloverleaf that would lead to J. Turner Butler Boulevard, he thought of a remark someone had once made regarding living in America. The comment was made in response to a slur from a redneck in a bar several years ago that Curt happened to overhear and it had always stuck with him because it was such a great comeback. *Foreigners can do something most Americans can't. Speak two languages.* That talent was the reason Curt had employed the old man and the reason he was anxious to meet with him this evening.

As he sped along the road that would lead him to the coast, Curt began thinking about the dream he'd had the night before and those eyes from the thing that had relentlessly carried him to the depths. Those floating, horrific eyes that gazed up at him, that nearly drove his sanity on a one-way trip just north of his wits. The memory caused him to shiver and he reached down to crank up the volume of the radio. He'd never experienced a dream that had been so mind rattling. Nor one in which his recollection had been so concise, so vivid.

Never.

As the Mustang cruised along in the right lane he had a disturbing premonition. Nothing concrete. Nothing he could hold or grapple with. Just an unsettling feeling something wasn't right and that there would be despair before things would get better. In a lot of ways it resembled the feeling Curt got anytime he was leaving on a business trip, a sensation that he had forgotten to pack or do something that was necessary before departing. Anytime he had this suspicion it was usually justified.

But now he had no reason (at least none that he was aware of) to feel this way. It wasn't like he was going out of town. Nonetheless, it lingered. Looking up he noticed a cloudbank forming in the southeast. A chill quaked over his skin and he shivered to discard it -- temporarily allowing the course of the car to lapse into the service lane. He quickly corrected the wheel and decided to ignore his inner ramblings before he drifted back into the water.

And thus, the disturbing game went on.

CHAPTER-EIGHT

The sealed skeleton floated lazily westward until it came to the mouth of the Sea of Marmara. Upon arrival the winds shifted and it took a southern course. Passing through the strait it soon broke through to the Mediterranean Sea. It resumed a western sail and eventually passed by the Rock of Gibraltar and entered the strait that would lead to the North Atlantic Ocean.

The journey took a little more than three months. Sometimes the winds and current fought the floating tomb's destined route but never enough to sway it far off track. The wooden contraption was on a mission and not to be denied. Somewhere, a force had postured the enclosure toward the Atlantic. And it had succeeded.

Adrift in the vast open water it maintained a westerly heading, dipping three degrees to the south. The craft itself was performing beautifully. The sap covering kept the contents inside dry as the wood danced on the surface of the tumultuous sea. The section of tree rode the swells and breakers hundreds of miles, nearly halfway between Africa and North America without incident.

On the one hundred and eighty-seventh day, as the buoyant wood gently rolled with the comber of each widely separated wave, a 12-foot tiger shark lurked underneath. He navigated to a position one dozen feet below the surface as he intently eyed the strange dark shape lingering overhead. Ripples from the vessel cascaded softly in a one-dimensional ever-widening circumference created by the slight movement from the sporadic wind. With escalating interest, the shark wandering a pattern, mirroring the slow course of his prey.

His tail diligently slashed from side to side guiding his position. His dead black eyes tracked the delicacy with apprehension. He had sized up the floating mass and still did not quite know what to make of it. It moved with a certain purpose. Not quite alive but not inanimate either. It was a paradox. The tiger shark had no desire to expend energy just to be fooled. Yet with each pass below the shadowy object, his weariness was overshadowed by a carnal desire to feed.

After a short time the shark glided closer to the surface. He surmised from careful observation that the moving object must be organic. Even if its unusual shape was unrecognizable to the prehistoric predator, it moved too precisely, too life-like. It had drive. Motivation.

With a sudden rush, the ferocious beast lunged upward separating the water with violence. It turned its entire body to the right and opened its jaw to expose the ragged rows of teeth that filled the inside. The carnivorous instinct had been unleashed and the mighty king of the sea was about to swallow the object bounding along the surface with a burst of tenacity.

In a split second it rose upon the floating coffin. Less than two feet away, jaws in position and teeth honed, the shark was violently deflected aside, and its mouth slammed shut. The momentum caused the animal to erupt through the surface. Nearly half its body flew into the air. The shark fell back gliding lifelessly into the water. Its eyes bulged as the carcass went rigid. It somberly sliced through the water and fell without resistance toward the ocean floor six thousand feet below. The vessel seemingly oblivious to the near brutal conclusion of its journey.

The floating tomb continued its path toward what would later be known as North America. Specifically, it was aimed at a tropical peninsula. The relatively thin strip of land, which by definition was surrounded by water on three sides, was connected to an enormous landmass. Thousands of years later when the peninsula matured it would possess extensive vegetation and lavish floral. It would come to be appropriately called *Pascua florida* by the Spanish Explorer Ponce De Leon, which meant "flowery Easter."

But now it was just a desolated area of earth still drying from the deluge.

Eighteen days after the tiger shark had sunk lifelessly to the sandy bottom, two strong hurricanes converged 748 miles to the east of the peninsula. They came as close as 150 miles before the southern storm veered to the east.

The skeleton, still sealed inside, drifted nonchalantly. Miraculously it passed directly between the storm systems guided by some unseen force. It rode the bulky swells with ease, never threatened.

Thirty-four days later the floating coffin was in reach of the coastline. In the last 24 hours two creatures had perished attempting to investigate the tomb slowly gliding mysteriously on the surface of the Atlantic. The first, a Mako shark that had shown only minor interest had made the mistake of passing too close. Its carcass now lay on the ocean floor, soon to be food for the vast array of sea creatures that inhabited the waters. The second was a pelican that had spotted the dark bounding object. It had briefly broken formation and had dipped near the surface to inspect. The two-foot flyby had been an irreparable error. The bird passed the bobbing wood and careened into a swell that had billowed up from the surface. On the relatively peaceful sea, it was as if the ocean had extended a flat hand. It had reached up and snared the bird's feathered torso and yanked it into the pit of its bowels. The writhing, squawking animal dipped below and fluttered helplessly underneath as the last traces of air bubbled up.

As the bird's puffing body, ragged with feathers stretched in every direction, sat perched on a bed of coral, a blue crab eyed the unusual creature that had entered its world with astonishment.

Above, the shipment continued on. A squall shifted the water ahead not far from shore. The journey was nearly over.

CHAPTER-NINE

It was slightly after noon on Sunday when the Seymour's phone chirped and Lindsey answered after checking the caller ID.
"John F. Kennedy Reelection Campaign Collection fund. Would you like to contribute?" she quipped.
"Sorry, I'm a Republican," Curt shot back. "Is your dad there?"
"Yeah, hold on."
A second later Scott was on. "Hey, what's up?"
"You got some time this afternoon. I've got something I want to show you."
"Sure. As far as I know, I'm here for the day. Did you finally get circumcised?"
"Even better than that. I'll be there shortly," Curt said.
"OK. Bye," and Scott hung up the phone.
Curt arrived 45 minutes later carrying a rather tattered shirt box bound by a string. The two sat in the living room, Scott on the couch and Curt in the matching chair. Kay was busy upstairs, although Scott really didn't know what she was doing, and the kids were all out of the house, Lindsey at the mall with some girlfriends and Cody and Katie down the street playing with friends.
"Remember I told you I had a meeting with a man last night?" Curt asked.
"Yeah," Scott responded. "I just thought you were coming out of the closet since you'd had so many rough experiences with women lately," he said with a grin.
"Actually I went to see an interpreter whom I hired to do some work. An old Frenchmen name Pierre." Curt slowly untied the string that secured the box. "Last April, a Frenchman named Jean Luc LeFlore, living in California, passed away leaving an estate riddled in back taxes. Because of the IRS lien, his property and all possessions were put up for sale on one of those internet auction websites. It turns out Jean Luc's great-grandfather, Deure, who was born in 1808, had documented accounts of stories passed down from generations of his great-great-grandfather's adventures in the New World."
"New World?" Scott asked.
"Yeah, the New World. You know America? Home of the free and the brave. God, you're from here, didn't you even stay awake for Florida History in elementary school?"
"I was much more concerned about the present than history. Usually I was staring at the mirror on my shoe to see up the dress of Mary Lou Thomas and her white cotton panties. Please continue. So who was Deure's great-great-grandfather? Is it someone I should know like Ponce De Leon or Cortez?"

"No but you're not so far off. His name was Pinot LeFlore. By shear luck, I bid on Deure's memoirs during Jean Luc's Estate fire sale and for a mere $250 I won out."

"A *mere* $250?" Scott asked.

"Yep. Why?"

"Next time I ask to borrow $250 I'll remind you that's a *mere* amount of money," Scott said with a smile.

Curt continued. "At the time I made the bid, I had no idea what information it contained. But it had been advertised as an account of early French explorations and I just took a chance. It still amazes me that very few people even went after it. Sometimes I guess it's just better to be lucky than to be good. Unfortunately, I don't know French and had to pay a translator to interpret the document. It's taken some time to get that accomplished."

"So what did you learn?" Scott asked slightly intrigued.

"Pinot LeFlore's life reads like an Indiana Jones movie. Born in Valiside, France in 1537, he accompanied Jean Ribault on Ribault's second voyage to Florida in 1565 to help protect Fort Caroline, near the mouth of the St. Johns River, from the Spanish who had colonized St. Augustine some 32 miles south of the French settlement."

"Curt, I'm aware of the history behind Fort Caroline. We both know plenty about it," Scott said sarcastically. "We're also both well versed on St. Augustine's past. I thought you had something interesting to tell me?"

"Patience. Hear me out. This gets good. Deure's writings go on to tell accounts of Pinot's exploits. Because Deure was writing from accounts passed down through generations, he chose to capture the information more in the mode of a historian than a bibliographer, focusing on the important events written in the third person." Curt picked up the notebook and began reading aloud the translated notes verbatim.

> The Huguenots had established the settlement (near present-day Jacksonville) in 1564 on the St. Johns River and called it La Carolina. Translated it means Land of Charles after King Charles IX. It later became known as Fort Caroline. The settlement provided refuge for Huguenots which is another name for French Protestants.

Curt looked up. "I know you know this part but just humor me."

> Having previously laid claim to Florida, Spain saw this intrusion by the Huguenots as a threat to their sovereignty in the New World.

"And if I remember some of my history from grade school, Spain had already claimed Florida by that time," Scott said.

"Very good!" Curt said with a bit of sarcasm. "Mary Lou must have been absent from school that day.

> Phillip II of Spain was none too happy having the Huguenots as neighbors. He subsequently ordered Don Pedro Menendez de Aviles and his armada to attack and capture Fort Caroline in order to seize what he considered to be his land.

"Like gang turf?" Scott asked with a goofy grin.
"Absolutely," Curt said and continued to read.

> And through luck and circumstance, Menendez's force accomplished its mission and killed more than 135 Frenchmen when the fort was attacked on September 20, 1565."

"I know this." Scott commented. "Menendez was very lucky."
"Exactly," Curt said.

> Menendez's expedition of 11 ships and 500 colonists sailed from Spain and on September 4, 1565 encountered a French fleet under Jean Ribault at the mouth of the St. Johns River, which he was unable to provoke into a fight. Ribault, a French Naval officer, was on his second expedition to the New World with seven ships and reinforcements to help guard Fort Caroline. He had previously built Fort Charles at the site of present day Port Royal, South Carolina and then returned to France. Little did he know he would never make it home to see France again. On this particular expedition, there were two brothers accompanying Ribault. One was a 28 year old named Pinot LeFlore and the other was 34 year old Reece LeFlore.

> Menendez subsequently returned to St. Augustine where he began to build a settlement. Hoping to take the Spanish by surprise, Jean Ribault assembled his armada and sailed south to attack St. Augustine.

He looked up again from the page. "This is where the 'luck' part comes in. For Menendez, it was good luck. For Ribault it was shitty luck."

"You still aren't telling me anything I don't know other than two brothers named LeFlore were traveling with Ribault," Scott said. Curt ignore the comment and kept reading.

> As Ribault's forces sailed south to surprise Menendez and the Spanish, a hurricane scattered and wrecked the ships all along the coast just south of St. Augustine. At the same time Ribault was sailing to attack the Spanish, Menendez and his men journeyed over land to Fort Caroline and, being completely unpro-

tected, the earthen fort was seized with little effort. The Spaniards killed 140 defenders while taking 60 women and children prisoner. Forty or fifty others escaped via ship to France.

For Curt, a certain awareness popped into his mind and he took a slow breath as the memory of the dream from Friday night again invaded his thoughts.

"Shit," he said softly as the visions of treading water and then watching the soldiers on the beach now made sense. Of course, it still didn't explain the thing that grabbed him by the ankles with those horrific eyes.

"What?" Scott asked. "What did you say?"

"Nothing," he said, clearing his head and flushing those eyes away. "But think about what really happened way back then. Ribault's luck ultimately determined the fate of history and to this day causes scholars to play the "what if" game to the nth degree. Do you realize that after these events, the French gave up their attempts to colonize the American Southeast? If Ribault had been able to successfully surprise the Spanish settlement at St. Augustine who knows how the past might have been altered."

"Nice history lesson but it's somewhat boring. Remember that I've lived here all my life and most of what you've told me I've heard before on the tour of Castillo de San Marcos in St. Augustine. I assume the interesting part of this story is whatever happens to Peanut," Scott said.

"Be patient. The best is yet to come. And it's Pinot not peanut," he said.

> When the hurricane struck Ribault's armada, several of the ships were lost at sea and many Frenchmen drowned as the relentless storm appeared to have Spanish alliance. The 350 Frenchmen who did survive the gusting winds and slashing waves of the Atlantic Ocean were exhausted and easily captured by the resident Spanish as they washed up on shore or tried to make their way by land back to Fort Caroline. In one of history's bloodiest displays of barbarism, the Spanish soldiers rounded up the survivors and took them to an inlet. When they refused to renounce their religious beliefs, Menendez gave orders to execute them. The Huguenots were hacked to death with knives, swords, machetes, and axes until not a single French soldier was left standing. Ribault himself was decapitated first while his executioner screamed "Heretic!" In the end, the beach was stained with the red of humanity and the incoming waves soaked the bodies, as they lay mutilated on the shore.

Curt looked up from his papers. "This is a pretty thoroughly documented historical event. Not much debate that this is the way it was. I've read other accounts of this incident with some variations but one fact remains consistent--the French prisoners were shown no mercy. Most journals I've read, from Spaniards mind you, depict a bleak picture of the weary Huguenots as they stood on the beach trembling with fear as their enemy relentlessly butchered their way through the congregated crowd. It was an atrocity comparable with Hitler's methods of extermination."

"Well that's quite an uplifting story. Why don't we go eat?" Scott smirked.

Curt continued, "Almost 200 years later, Fort Matanzas was built as part of an important Spanish defense network near the site where the French prisoners were killed. Do you know what Matanzas means Scott?"

"No idea. Cheap souvenirs?"

"It's the Spanish word for slaughter," Curt replied.

"Ouch," Scott replied. "So what about Pinchot and Rice?" Scott asked again.

"I'm getting to them, and it's Pinot and Reece. Up to this point, as I said, everything I've mentioned is well documented in the history books and you were aware of. What I've learned from Deure's diary is there were two survivors from Ribault forces that were not killed at Matanzas. And, you guessed it, they were the LeFlores. He glanced down at the papers and read.

> After swimming ashore, somehow the LeFlore brothers managed to elude the Spanish forces and, from a secure hiding spot on a small ridge near the ocean, watched in horror as their comrades in arms were massacred on the beach that day in September 1565. Fleeing back to Fort Caroline, they were exhausted as they were met with more discouragement when they discovered the settlement had also been captured and most of the inhabitants slaughtered. Vowing to seek revenge for the deaths of their countrymen, Pinot and Reece were able to survive on their own in the woods and somehow eluded any encounters with the Spanish at Fort Caroline. Eventually they made friends with the local Timucua tribe. Learning the ways of the Indians is probably the only thing that kept them alive. But both never lost the passion to avenge the deaths of the colonists and soldiers.

> After years of living with the Timucuas, the two brothers learned of a sacred tribal secret. The Indians had settled the area thousands of years before and the story centered on a fresh water pond several hundred yards across from Fort Caroline. It was small in area, only about 18 feet across, but said to be very deep, so deep that no man could reach the bottom by holding his breath. The pond was completely surrounded by trees and brush and had never been discovered by either the French or the Spanish who now inhabited the fort just a short distance away. It was almost as if the pond itself was hiding from outsiders.

The Indians called the pond at Fort Caroline *Terriousimee*, which means "living bones." The Timucuas believed it possessed an ability to invigorate life where it had been extinguished. To create from that which had been destroyed and to strengthen wills that were mindful and determined.

"Kinda like Ponce de Leon's Fountain of Youth?" Scott commented, slightly intrigued.

"In a way."

"Well I've been there. One of the St. Augustine low points. It's a tourist trap if you've ever seen one. Damn thing didn't work on me, I'll tell you that. I drank some of that gnarly water," Scott said making a comical face.

"That's great, anyway . . ."

Terriousimee was considered sacred to the Timucuas. Once the French Huguenots settled Fort Caroline it was too close to the fort for the Indians. The Huguenots and Timucuas never had any confrontations per se, they generally just avoided each other. The Indians greatly feared the white man and had no desire to challenge them. The pond remained undisturbed. But Pinot and Reece learned of its history and the mysterious nature of its depths by deceiving a young Timucua named Tibu. Tibu was only a teenager, about 16, when the brothers befriended him. Tibu's parents had both died from sickness when Tibu was a baby and the tribe had raised him. For several years, while the brothers lived among the Timucuas, they learned to communicate by teaching Tibu some French and, in turn, learning his native tongue. About the time Tibu was 18, the brothers took him to a deserted stretch of beach on the river away from the Indian Village. After pumping him full of a special blend of wine the brother's concocted, he told them in detail about the legend of Terriousimee and its magical powers. The next day when Tibu's head had cleared he felt very badly for what he'd done. He spoke to the brothers in private and made it very clear to the two Frenchmen that he had violated the strictest of tribal law and pleaded with them never to tell a soul. They assured him they would never speak of this legend to any other white men. When Tibu asked for their word, the brothers agreed to keep silent for as long as their "chest swelled up and down." As soon as they were alone, Pinot and Reece began plotting on how the Terriousimee's powers could be used to fulfill the vow they had made several years before to gain their revenge against the Spanish at St. Augustine.

"So what were the secret powers the pond possessed?" Scott asked impatiently, his interest now aroused.

"This is the part you're not going to like," Curt said. "The manuscript was missing a few pages at this point."

"You've got to be kidding me!" Scott said with obvious disappointment. "You got me hooked and then you leave me hanging?"

"Calm down. There's more," Curt said.

> The next day, Tibu was gone and never seen again. After days of searching in and around the area the brothers gave up hope of ever seeing their young Indian friend again. The two were very distraught. But the tribe seemed unconcerned about the disappearance, it was business as usual. It was almost like he had been wiped clean from the memories of his villagers. Purged, eradicated from existence. No one even seemed to care about the peculiar way he vanished. Some of the elders explained that he was probably not dead but a "young warrior searching for the fields of his manhood" and suggested he had gone off on a self imposed right-of-passage. Pinot and Reece would never find out what really happened to Tibu but they felt a very uneasy feeling about the timing of his abrupt disappearance and the strange tales he had disclosed regarding the pond near the fort.

"So basically," Scott interrupted, "What you have here is a story with a great opening act. Rich in early American History, centered on violence and a couple of brothers who survive the ordeal. Add in a teaser about a pond whose mystery will forever remain intact. That's some script. It'll never become a box office hit but it sounds like a hell of a made-for-TV miniseries. Are you sure your translator didn't make off with the important pages?"

"Positive. I knew they were missing beforehand. Besides, the translator didn't really seem to give a damn about the story. It's pretty easy to see the pages had been torn out. See?" Curt lifted the bound document from under the papers and turned the binder toward Scott. "But I do have some good news."

"Go on," Scott said.

"The manuscript does mention fragments of the plan Pinot and Reece undertook to avenge the death of the French Huguenots at Matanzas. Whatever Tibu had told them about Terriousimee had given them some grandiose scheme." He looked back down at his translated notes.

> The plan involved locating the bones of the slaughtered Huguenots from their resting place and moving them to somewhere near the mouth of the St. Johns' River, 32 miles to the north. The two brothers made numerous trips to remove the remains from the burial site near the Spanish settlement and cart them the distance back, careful not to be seen. It was a grueling effort taking more than six months. They worked relentlessly at the endeavor they had resolved themselves to complete. With each trip's conclusion, the bones were placed in accordance with the legend. For Tibu had mentioned several times "Kentee ibu

sanar". *All waters are joined.* The brothers now accepted the legend without hesitation of truth or doubt.

Scott stared at Curt like a cat watching a fly, concentrating on every move his face made, trying to anticipate that moment when Curt would raise his eyebrows and shoot him that "I got ya" look. But it didn't come.
"Where the hell did they place the remains?" Scott asked.
"I don't know," he said dejectedly. "I bet it's in those missing pages."
"Okay. Go ahead. But the holes in this story are really starting to piss me off."

On their final trip, the Spanish captured the brothers as they unearthed the last corpse. They were brought into town and separated. Reece attempted to escape but was killed by two soldiers as he tried to scale the settlement walls. His body was mutilated by the Spaniards and thrown into the surrounding moat. Although, never informed, Pinot had heard his brother's screams and was sure of his fate.

"Bastards didn't believe in euthanasia, did they?" Scott asked.
"Not at all. But listen to this."

The Spanish soldiers interrogated Pinot to find out what he and his brother were doing. Pinot never did respond and was severely beaten as a result. The orders were given for his execution and he was led into the woods accompanied by five soldiers. But he somehow managed to escape and the five soldiers were never seen again. Pinot was free again. His thoughts were clouded and his sense of direction skewed as he began wandering through the woods toward the north with both hands still tied behind his back.

"He got away from five soldiers with both hands tied behind his back? Did their swords misfire? I'm confused. This story is losing it for me Curt," Scott said slowly shaking his head from side to side.
"I know," Curt replied. "That's what's so interesting to me."
"I want a beer. You want one?" Scott asked. Curt nodded yes.
Scott walked into the kitchen and opened the refrigerator. He reached into the carton which only last night had contained 8 beautiful, 12-ounce Michelob Lights and made a pouting face as he pulled out the last two. He returned to the room. Curt had repositioned himself and was now leaning back in the chair. Still concentrating on the notes, without looking he instinctively reached up and grabbed the bottle as Scott offered it.
"If you thought that was interesting, listen to this," Curt said after taking a swig.

Some time later, Pinot was again captured by the Spanish on the shore near Fort Caroline. This time he was carrying bones in a knapsack slung over his shoulder. The Spanish were very afraid of Pinot, suspicious of what had become of the five lost soldiers, and it required numerous men to subdue the Frenchman. He was then taken to the fort and again orders were given for his demise.

"Any clue on what bones were in his knapsack?" Scott asked.

"The document didn't say. I suspect he was still carrying out whatever plan he and Reece had originally started but who knows. Listen," Curt said.

The captain of the garrison decided to seal Pinot alive, along with his knapsack, inside one of the rooms. It was a very cruel and heinous form of torture, not to mention, very elaborate in a day and time when slashing was the preferred method of execution. But the Spanish felt it necessary.

"Sounds like Menendez and his buddies were afraid of this guy. Hell, he got the best of five. Why not the entire Spanish town," Scott said. "You think they were a little superstitious?"

"I don't know. I'm not a big believer of cults, witches, spells, zombies or other flights of fantasy. I watch *Buffy* just to see the girl snap out some cute one-liners. But I am interested in history and I believe there's something more here."

"But something is amiss with the story," Scott said.

"I know," Curt cut in.

"You know?"

"Yeah, the fact that the story describes Pinot was sealed in the room at the Fort. Fort Caroline was an earthen fort. It wasn't made of stone."

"So how did the Spanish seal him in a room? Did they super glue some trees together?" Scott asked with a morose smile.

"Remember when we took the kids to visit Fort Castillo de San Marcos in St. Augustine last April? It was the day Katie threw up after eating the hot dog in the park and Julie nearly fell off the side of the bridge that crosses the moat to the entrance to the fort?"

"Yep, yep. And?"

"Remember as we walked through the court yard and slowly entered each room and looked around? Remember one room had the anchor to the *Atocha* (which was encased in water to help preserve against the aging process). By the way, every time I think of that ship's anchor it reminds me of Mel Fisher who I enviously refer to as Mr. Gazillionaire. Remember another room had a plaque that described the story of an Indian who at one time was held prison at the fort and literally starved himself to death to escape through the narrow windows?"

"Yep, yep, and your point is?" Scott asked.

"Remember the powder magazine in the back corner of the storage room where . . ."

Before Curt could finish his sentence, a picture flashed in Scott's mind. His thoughts took him back inside Fort Castillo de San Marcos. He could see the very words on a plaque perched upon a cement stand nestled in the corner of the storage room.

"It wasn't Fort Caroline they sealed Pinot inside was it?" Scott heard himself ask the question but was struck by how oddly he spoke the words.

"I don't think so," Curt responded in a low voice slowly shaking his head from side to side. "More likely, Fort Castillo de San Marcos."

They both sat quietly. For the next few moments Scott's mind drifted 40 miles away, walking forward as he crouched under the overhanging wall that led to the small arched room at the back of the storage room in the fort at St. Augustine. He remembered the room was warm, dark and wet and very noneventful. At the ceiling's highest point of the arch it was maybe six and one-half feet tall. It was otherwise a very boring place apart from the mysterious circumstances, which he had read on a plaque at the entrance outside. The room had only recently been discovered in 1997. It had been closed up and, from the authority's best guess, for quite some time. When it was discovered and the room opened up, there were bones found on the stone floor. Human bones. It was unknown to this day as to whose bones they were or the circumstance by which they had come to reside there.

"Do you think it's really possible that some manuscript you purchased on the internet has unlocked the truth about who was found in the powder magazine?" Scott asked with eyes wide open and full of intrigue. "That would be amazing."

"I don't know, but I do know this. I'm taking tomorrow off and going to St. Augustine. And like most of the other tourists who visit the nation's oldest city, I'm gonna visit Fort Castillo de San Marcos. I'd like to take a closer look at that room. You want to come?"

"What exactly are you hoping to find," Scott asked.

"I have no idea. But it's fascinating to me that the document seems to allude to the powder magazine. Think of the historical significance if we can somehow pinpoint Pinot LeFlore to that room. You know you don't want to miss this."

"I probably shouldn't but the truth is, I could really stand a day off." Besides, Scott thought to himself, his work was really at a standstill. As he mentally convinced himself it would be okay to escape the office for a day, he asked, "Have you told anybody else about this?"

"Nope. I'd be a little embarrassed to go public with this unless I can completely substantiate we can identify the remains found in the powder magazine when it was unsealed," he replied.

"And how are you going to do that?"

"I have no idea. And the question is, 'How are *we* going to do it.' Tag. You're now in the game. I can see that interested look in your eyes."

"Well, then. At least we have a plan," Scott said taking a sip from the bottle.

"I have to be honest with you, Scott, before we go off on our wild goose chase," Curt began, "there is one piece of the story which is very inconsistent with history and makes even me question the manuscript's accuracy. If you remember, it mentions Pinot was born in 1537. Construction on Fort Castillo de San Marcos began in 1672 and concluded in 1695."

"Let me get this straight," Scott said, "Pinot was sealed in a room at the spry young age of . . . let's see . . . 1672 minus 1537. You're telling me he was at least 135 years old?" Scott asked.

"That's what I mean. Something's not right," his friend replied.

"Not unless Pinot actually did find Ponce De Leon's fountain of youth," Scott quipped. He took another sip of his beer. "Well, I don't have much faith we're gonna discover anything that archeologists haven't already accounted for but I'll come along for the amusement. What time do you want to go in the morning?"

Since Scott had transportation duties, taking Cody to daycare, and Curt lived on the opposite side of the city, they decided to drive separately. After determining the earliest Scott could get to St. Augustine was 8:30 a.m., he made calls to work and left voice messages to advise several coworkers that he would be off on Monday. Curt headed home after refusing a home cooked pot roast dinner from Kay. His excuse was that his stomach might actually have an adverse reaction to something so good and so healthy. Then he commented to Scott that he needed to make some arrangements for the morning but failed to elaborate.

The remainder of the afternoon was a typical Seymour Sunday with Scott catching the last half of the Dolphins/Patriots game, Kay playing with Austin the cat while preparing supper, Lindsey at the mall and Cody and Katie alternating between playing in the front yard and the back with some of the other neighborhood kids.

Later in the evening when the kids had been bathed and put to bed, Kay asked Scott what he and Curt had discussed. She knew of Curt's interest in archeology and Scott's attraction to anything historical. Not really caring to share the details at this time, Scott explained how Curt might have uncovered some timeline discrepancies in St. Augustine's known history. He kept the response to Kay vague on purpose. He would have felt a little silly admitting he was helping his friend do a little research into a *bones* and *mysterious pond* story. He would meet Curt at the fort in the morning and see what they could determine. The exploration of the powder magazine and any attempt to link Pinot LeFlore, as its sealed corpse, was a long shot at best. Yet the historical diary was intriguing and filled with enough factual data that he wasn't about to pass up even the smallest opportunity to solve the mystery. For one day, work be damned.

That night Scott dreamed he was sitting in a large deserted church. It was a magnificent building with towering stained glass windows on either side. There was a massive pulpit centered near the front with dozens of red candles lining the altar. Behind, a huge white cross hung eloquently on the wall, pressed against a mauve tapestry. The wooden pew was unusually comfortable.

Scott reached forward and opened the hymnal. Oddly, the pages were blank. He thumbed through it with the same result. Eventually, Scott found writing on the book's last page. On the left side, there was a message written in ancient Aramaic. Somehow, Scott was able to translate it.

"Suspended until belief."

He would not remember the dream in the morning.

CHAPTER-TEN

Scott woke up to the ringing of the alarm clock at 6:00 a.m. Monday morning and promptly hit the snooze button. But instead of drifting back to sleep for the extra nine minutes, his mind began churning Curt's words and phrases from the day before. "Five soldiers never returned . . . sealed alive . . . Terriousimee means living bones . . . Kentee ibu sanar . . . all waters are joined . . . 135 years old . . . massacre at Matanzas . . . revenge . . ." Around and around the thoughts migrated in his clouded mind.

At 6:08, Scott made a preemptive strike and turned off the alarm before the next minute arrived. He rolled out of bed throwing on his robe, then awkwardly traversed the stairs, somehow avoiding the family cat that took great pleasure in darting between his feet with each downward stride.

Scott entered the kitchen and fed Austin, who greedily gobbled the goodies as Scott made a cup of coffee and then proceeded into the den and settled on the couch. He grabbed the remote and switched on the big screen TV. The screen brightened just in time to catch the beginning of the weather report. The morning meteorologist was reviewing the current weather patterns across the United States and then focused the pointer on the lower portion of Florida and the Keys which, as he described, were in the direct path of Tropical Storm Damon. The storm was expected to become Hurricane Damon by midnight with possible sustained winds of 115 miles per hour. This would make it a Category 3 on the Saffir-Simpson scale of 1-5. If it continued on its expected course and current speed it would reach the southeastern coast of Florida by Thursday afternoon. He went on to explain the danger in this particular storm was not only its strength, but also its size. It had the capability of being the largest storm within the last 100 years.

"Oh, great. Here comes another one," Scott said out loud, thinking about how close Cindy had come just last week. Actually he had heard about this new tropical storm while driving home from work on Friday, so he had already mentally prepared himself for the possibility of another hurricane bearing down on Florida and another evacuation.

As the weather report continued, Scott thought back to last September when Hurricane Donya had been advertised as just as dangerous to the northeastern Florida coast. Within 30 hours of its possible landfall at Jacksonville, the beaches had been evacuated and Scott had taken Kay and the kids to Atlanta to help man a disaster recovery site for his company. The trip had been one he'd never forget. Packing the family, some clothes and supplies, they'd left the house at 1:00 p.m. on a Tuesday afternoon, six hours after the Beaches had invoked a mandatory evacuation that morning. Scott chose to journey the back roads, hoping to outguess the three-quarters of a million motorists also trying to leave the city and avoid the absolute gridlock on I-95 and I-10. As it turned out, several hundred thousand other evacuees also had the same idea of driving the back roads.

By the time Scott and his family had left, every road out of town was a parking lot. What would have normally taken about 30 minutes to get to nearby Green Cove Springs, took more than 3½ hours of stop and go driving with Kay, the three kids and Austin. They had made Starke, Florida by 9:08 p.m. that evening. The weather reports by then were giving a much more predictable forecast that Donya would slide by, barely touching the coast with its outer reach and Scott seriously considered turning around and going back home. Instead, he had elected to push on. It was 3:45 a.m. before they reached Atlanta. A trip that would normally have taken 7 hours took more than 14. On top of that, Scott had to be up at 6:30 the same morning and drive through Atlanta during rush hour to find the company's Disaster Recovery Center. Three days later, Scott drove the family back to Jacksonville. Donya had missed the city but the employees who had made the trip to north Georgia used the opportunity to test the recovery site so it was not a completely wasted effort, at least as far as the company was concerned.

After last year, Scott vowed not to wait so long to evacuate if the situation arose again. He'd keep a close eye on Damon and make contingency plans well in advance.

After polishing off two potent cups of coffee and watching the conclusion of the weather report and the morning sports update, Scott got the kids up and running for their day at school. About the same time, Scott could hear the master bedroom door opening, signifying Kay's entry into the morning.

Scott prepared the kids breakfast consisting of cereal and toast accompanied by the ever-popular glass of whole milk. They had run out of Cody's favorite food yesterday morning so he was in a bit of a mood. A delicacy found at most grocery stores and always mispronounced by the five-year-old thereby giving it a humorous sounding title. "Top Parts," Cody called it. As in "Toastem Top Parts."

As Kay sat down in the den and began to drink her coffee, Scott updated her on the potential hurricane and they both agreed that there would not be a repeat of last year's turmoil. If they thought there was a 50 percent probability of it making landfall in Jacksonville they would be on their way.

As the topics of conversation changed, from Katie's upcoming school Open House, to Cody's latest Christmas present request, to Lindsey's pleading for a tattoo, Scott was glad to see his wife harbored no resentment for his decision to take the day off without her. Moreover, she seemed relieved he had elected to slow things down and encouraged him to enjoy his day.

As they talked, a little voice in Scott's mind reminded him this was just another example of why he loved Kay so dearly. And as he left that morning to take Cody to daycare, he planted a resounding kiss on his wife's lips that left her somewhat dazed, yet pleasantly pleased.

From the doorway, she waived goodbye to Cody and then gave Scott a naughty wink as he backed the SUV out of the driveway.

After dropping Cody off, Scott headed south, eventually catching US 1. He sat back and relaxed listening to the music pulsating through the speakers. As the Blazer moved methodically down the four-lane highway, Scott's mind drifted over Curt's comments about Pinot and the knapsack full of bones he was toting on his back when captured by the Spanish. Were the bones those of the last Huguenot at the burial site in St. Augustine? Was Pinot attempting to complete whatever plan he and Reece had begun before being caught? Maybe they were the bones of Menendez? Surely Pinot didn't live to be 130 or 140 years old. Back then, it was unusual if someone lived to be 60 let alone 100 or more. But the reference to the sealed room was intriguing. And what was the pond's secret? Scott had meant to ask Curt if there was a fresh water pond near Fort Caroline. He'd do so when they met in St. Augustine.

When he was just a few miles outside the city limits he suddenly remembered a dream he'd had. At first he wasn't sure if it was from the previous night or some night long passed. It was very disjointed and rather frustrating because he could only remember bits and images. The entire picture would not come into focus. The best he could recall was that he was up on top of some structure looking through a doorway as a cool breeze washed against his face. Darkness surrounded him. Every few seconds the distant ground and scenery below became extravagantly lit up, illuminating the area with a sweeping motion, and then darkness again. This light continued to pulsate keeping him confused and off balance. As he looked out over the landscape, he could see the ground swelling and heaving in a churning motion, rising to glisten its white tips and then falling back to darkness. Beyond this motion in the distance he could make out a shaggy paper-like substance dancing to and fro in the wind. The only noise Scott could hear was a whippoorwill crooning and the faint sound of water being slammed into something unknown. The wind at his face intensified and it became increasingly difficult to see. The sporadic lighting was making the situation more and more uncomfortable. Then he had the feeling he was not alone.

Something was coming. He could sense it.

Rising from below, within the structure, making its way upward step by step. His body began to sway as he braced against the strong breeze. Scott squinted into the misty air and, through the continuing strobe effect, he saw the shaggy paper-like substance still waving in the distance. A great noise bellowed and he saw the mass begin to part.

With this, he shivered in fear. His eyes briefly closed and then reopened in an attempt to clear his cluttered vision and clarify the reality. But the waving image on the horizon continued to part very slowly. His trembling subsided somewhat as he realized the distance from the disturbance and his position to be quite extreme. Watching intently, the disturbance continued to his left and then broke into three parts with one wave heading toward him. Chills shot through his spine and dangled in his eardrums, pounding a multitude of beats as the wind pounded his face. Scott instinctively sought to run. But where to? He could move outside the doorway onto an outer deck but he would have to struggle against the fierce wind. As his mind raced he turned around and looked down. In the circular view, he could see straight through to the bottom of the structure and at the series of winding spiral staircases rising upward hugging the wall. Simultaneously he heard a methodical *clank* . . . *clank* . . . *clank* of someone or something traversing the iron steps. Each time the noise was more distinct and audible. Scott's lungs burned, as he gasped loudly and suddenly.

Still peering downward into the abyss, the clanking sound became more prominent and in the dim light, Scott could see the shadow of something coming up to the fourth landing. It continued almost robotically to the fifth and then sixth landing as Scott watched the thing's shadow in horror. He was unable to get a clear view because of the harsh angle. As it approached the seventh landing, the last before reaching the top, there was silence. Looking across the wall from where the thing was, he could see the humanlike shadow with both arms extended over its head. In one hand it held a thick elongated object that gyrated like a helicopter propeller, making a low humming sound as it cut through the air.

Scott could recall no more. By now he was just outside the city gates of St. Augustine where statues of Pedro de Menendez patiently stand on either side of the road marking the entry into the historic district of the town. He was grateful for the distraction.

St. Augustine is a small town with a large tourist draw. Immersed in history, its past is beset with European settlements claiming ownership since the origin Spanish settlement in the 1500s. Today, the heart of St. Augustine retains the distinctive look of an early colonial walled town, with many buildings displaying architecture from the early 1700 – 1800s. The city has also been home to some of America's most rich and famous. Henry Flagler, railroad tycoon, built the Ponce de Leon Hotel in 1885. Names like the Rockefellers and Vanderbuilts were carried from the north to St. Augustine in their personal cars on Flagler's Florida East Coast Railroad. The city proved to be a comfortable winter home for the like.

Veering left Scott passed under the St. Augustine Historical District sign and continued on San Marco Boulevard. The street that paralleled Matanzas Bay was full of tourist attractions all contained within a three-quarter mile stretch. Famous spots such as The Old Jail, The Fountain of

Youth, The Nuestra de la Leche Shrine and cemetery, and Ripley's Believe it or Not lined the road.

Scott didn't favor this stretch in a city so rich with history and grandeur. The single lane was generally very congested with traffic and horse drawn buggies. Four-tenths of a mile past the Shrine and cemetery, there was a large green field to the left and the Fort Castillo de San Marcos sat majestically on the edge of the Bay. To his right, a road that led to a parking area and Welcome Center. The majority of tourist parked in and around this area to venture down St George Street, which was blocked for vehicular traffic and only accessible on foot. St. George Street began adjacent to the fort and stretched two city blocks paralleling the bay with San Marco Boulevard sandwiched between. The street was an attempt to emulate the town as it appeared hundreds of years ago when the Spanish colony ruled the day. The section nearest the fort was a mixture of red cobblestone and stone slabs with Spanish designs. But a short ways in, the look of 20th century man was evident by the smooth cement walkway.

Scott drove by the Castillo de San Marcos and turned left into the fort's parking lot, where he spotted Curt's Mustang. Curt was sitting patiently on the trunk and jumped down as Scott pulled the Blazer in the slot next to him. It was 8:22 a.m.

"What took you so long?" Curt asked as Scott got out.

"Gimme a break. I'm eight minutes early. Besides," Scott continued, "it doesn't even look like this place is open to the general public yet."

"You're right. It's not. I made arrangements with one of the park rangers to get in early. He's a friend of mine," Curt said, pausing to grin. "The fort opens at 9:30 a.m. so we have to be out by 9:15. That gives us less than an hour to explore the powder magazine."

"A friend of yours? You don't have any friends besides me," Scott shot back.

"OK," Curt said. "He's a fifty-dollar friend. Does that make you happy?"

"Yep," Scott smiled.

"I have a question," Scott said as they began walking. "The Huguenots who were killed by the Spanish at Matanzas, does anyone really know where that burial site is? You described it as somewhere near the Spanish settlement in St. Augustine."

"No one knows. It's strongly believed they were buried at a plot of land somewhere inland away from the beach. Substantial research has been done trying to answer that very question. Manuscripts from a Spanish priest suggest the bodies of the slain soldiers were transported to a burial site just outside the settlement on Matanzas Bay. Many digs and excavations by archeologists over the years have yielded no success in locating the burial site though. Others believe there's a fair probability that Fort Castillo was constructed directly on top of the Huguenots' final resting ground. I don't see how this is possible since it was difficult enough to build the fort with the incoming tide each day filling the construction area. The notion of the Spanish covering up the remains of the French with some type of structure does have merit though. Documentation from this era supports a strong superstition and general belief in things that go "bump in the night."

"Wasn't that the title of a porn flick? I think I saw that movie. Every Tom, Dick and Hairy Dick starred in it," Scott said with a smile.

Curt ignored the comment. "As I was saying, the Spanish tended to believe in things such as the boogey man, spirits and ghosts. Building a structure on top of the Huguenot resting place may have been their attempt to seal in the slain French."

"What the hell do you mean 'seal in'? As in, 'they might come a callin' lookin for those who done 'em in?' " Scott said, in his best redneck accent. "Besides, if your internet auction diary is accurate, the LeFlores moved most of the bodies anyway so it's really a moot point. I was just curious."

"You're just a curious kind of guy," Curt remarked.

"Yes, I am," Scott admitted as they continued up the walkway. Before them was the Castillo de San Marcos.

The fort, located on the west side of Matanzas bay, was originally built as protection from pirate attacks and to defend Spanish territory from assault by the English at Charles Town in South Carolina. Governor Manuel de Cendoya had been sent to Florida by the Queen Regent of Spain, Mariana, to oversee construction of the fortification. The site had been agreed upon in 1671 by Cendoya, the town officials, sergeant majors and captains of the current wooden fort in St. Augustine, and the skilled experts recruited by Cendoya. On October 2, 1672, at 4:00 p.m. ground was broken.

Due to its close proximity to the water, clearing the site was difficult. With each high tide, the dug out area would fill with water and work could not be continued until the tide rolled out. On November 9, 1672, the first stone was put in place but neither Cendoya nor Ignacio Daza, the Spanish engineer who designed the fort, would live to see its completion. Cendoya passed away on March 8, 1673. Two weeks later Daza died of an unknown sickness as had many of the laborers. Coquina, a type of shellstone indigenous to the area was quarried from Anastasia Island, which is located east of the bay. (Today, the Bridge of Lions connects the half-mile between St. Augustine and Anastasia Island.) Stone masons produced the blocks, working where the parking lot is located today. The mortar to bond the blocks was created by baking oyster shells in vats until they fell apart into a white powder called lime. Combining water and sand with the lime made the mortar that still holds the fort together today. Many Governors, builders and stone cutters worked on the fort over the years and it was finally completed 23 years after the ground had been broken, on August 31, 1695.

Once complete the castillo was never conquered despite several attempts. Cannonballs were no match for the unusual consistency of coquina, which absorbed the blast rather than crumbling. In addition, artillery positioned along the top walls of the fort had the ability to send cannon fire over a distance of two and one-half miles.

The fort's design by Daza was simple -- A hollow square with diamond-shaped bastions on all four corners and a triangular shaped ravelin opposite the sally port. The ravelin, constructed with a six-foot wall and no roof, was designed to shield the sally port from enemy fire. A 75-foot walkway extended from the ravelin to the drawbridge at the sally port. The fort's simplicity was even more exemplified by the fact there was only one way in or out at the sally port. That is why the ravelin was so important. Inside the fort was a series of storage rooms around a central courtyard. The entire structure was surrounded by a moat.

The fort has seen many historically significant events over the last 300 plus years. It helped St. Augustine endure sieges by British, Georgian, and South Carolinian forces in the mid-1700s. In 1763 when Florida was given to Great Britain, the bastion was renamed Fort St. Mark. In 1783, the Peace of Paris recognized the independence of the United States and returned Florida to Spain. Then in 1821 Spain ceded Florida to the United States. In 1825, Castillo de San Marcos was renamed Fort Marion. In 1924 the fort was proclaimed a national monument and in 1933 transferred by the War Department to the National Park Service (U.S. Department of the Interior). In 1935 the National Park Service began exclusive administration of the monument, and in 1942, the original name of Castillo de San Marcos was restored.

As Scott and Curt approached the fort's National Park Service administration office, they were met by Curt's fifty-dollar friend. Robert Bruin was adorned in the usual light brown Park Service uniform, looking very official. His forest green baseball cap bore the initials NPS and, even though it was going to be a warm day again, Mr. Bruin wore a pair of driving gloves as if he planned to head south and take a few laps around the Daytona International Speedway before beginning his shift.

"Shame on him for accepting a bribe," Scott leaned over and said into Curt's ear quietly. Of course it wasn't that he and Curt were known felons. They weren't looking to do any malicious spray painting on the inside walls, just some investigative work. Curt had ensured Bruin of that. Without stating a word, the park ranger motioned for the men to follow him as he moved down the cement walkway toward the drawbridge at the sally port. As they neared the entrance, Scott saw the ravelin to his left had been sealed off for repairs. Continuing across the drawbridge, Mr. Warm and Fuzzy still had not said as much as "good morning" or "where's my fifty?" Scott suspected that Curt had made an advance payment to guarantee their private entrance and exclusive examination of the powder magazine and, therefore, no words were necessary.

For all the fort's history, the discovery of the powder magazine in 1997 had created quite a stir with local historians. It was connected to a storage room thought to be an artillery depot on the bottom floor, just off the garrison's courtyard. At one time it appeared to be a connecting room to the depot but the entranceway was only three and one-half feet high and led into the 22 x 10-foot enclosed space with an arched ceiling no greater than six and one-half feet at the crest. It reminded Scott of a mini quonset hut with no windows. It was believed to have been an ammunition holding area, hence the name powder magazine. Because of the lack of any ventilation, the room was very warm and moist, contrary to what would be expected in an area for storing gunpowder. It was believed to be a design flaw by Daza and historians suspect its use as a powder storage room was short lived by the Spanish.

As Scott and Curt reached the end of the drawbridge and proceeded through the sally port, Robert Bruin turned and walked in the opposite direction toward his station to prepare for the park's opening. The man never said a word. As they stepped out into the courtyard and followed the walkway along the left, Scott realized he'd never been inside the fort when it was so uninhabited. Typically, on any given day, several hundred tourists were milling around, walking in and out of the storage rooms and examining artifacts on display inside.

"So tell me more about the powder magazine." Scott said. "I remember reading it had only recently been discovered and bones had been found inside but that's about it. Do you know any more than that?"

"It's pretty intriguing." Curt said. "There are no accounts of this particular room in any of the documentation regarding the fort since its inception. It was really discovered in a fluky way. The State Parks Division had sent a man out to inspect the fort's construction as they do every few years to check for any structural problems, erosion or cracks. While using a very scientific method of lightly smacking a screwdriver along the wall at the back end of the storage room, the inspector noticed a distinct hollow reverb and notified the park officials. After a weeklong investigation by utilizing sonar type equipment, a small hole was drilled confirming the open space that lay beyond. Several months later, after gaining final approval from the state, an entryway was carefully chiseled out and extended to what was believed to be its original size, which is very short.

"As the first state park representatives entered the opening with flashlights there was considerable excitement as to what they might find. They were not disappointed in the least. The men entered the room with a sense of adventure but were completely baffled by the array of human bones scattered along the rock floor."

"Yeah, I remember it was a mystery as to who was sealed inside and why," Scott said. "Isn't it amazing to think you've discovered documentation that could validate Pinot LeFlore lived here? A man who sailed with Ribault. A soldier who had inhabited Fort Caroline and sailed to attack the Spanish in St. Augustine."

"And don't forget," Curt added, "a man who had survived the hurricane, eluded the Spanish at Matanzas, watched his countrymen get executed on the beach and then lived to be 135 years old before finally being put to death."

"That's the part I'm having the most trouble comprehending," Scott said as they neared the storage room that connected to the powder magazine.

"I hear ya. I reviewed my notes again last night and there's no mistaking the dates. I described them as they're written. I know it stretches the imagination but sometimes you just have to have some flexibility in rational thought processing. Besides, you're a fan of the X-Files." He stopped short of the entrance to the storage room and pointed. "The truth is in there."

Curt entered the room closely followed by Scott. They moved to the back where another doorway cut through the rock at a 45-degree angle into a small area Scott determined was about the size of his upstairs bathroom. Without the lighting provided by the Park Service, it would have been completely dark. As it was, the lighting was minimal, as if to provide an eerie presence to the place. On the left, the wall hung down from the ceiling and stopped 42 inches short of the floor. This opening led to the room they were anxious to investigate.

"Age before beauty," Curt cracked, motioning Scott inside ahead of him. Scott bent down and turned on the flashlight he had brought from the Blazer. As he cleared under the wall, he raised upright and instantly felt discomfort. He had been in the powder magazine before and had known human bones were discovered upon its unveiling. But this time the uneasiness was stronger, not so much claustrophobic as it was unearthly. It was something he couldn't have explained to anyone. He was glad to see Curt enter immediately behind him. A few more seconds alone in this place and he might have called it a day. Curt flipped the switch on his halogen Ultra-Beam and the room was filled with light. This helped ease Scott's apprehension until he caught Curt shiver out of the corner of his eye.

"What's the matter?" Scott asked.

"Nothing. Why?" Curt replied.

"You just shivered," Scott said.

"Just cold," Curt lied.

"Yeah, I know what you mean," Scott said. "Must not be more than 86 degrees in here."

"Okay. So I got a little spooked when I first came in. I'm fine now. You okay?"

"Just peachy," Scott replied. "Let's get to it."

With that Curt began to slowly walk around and examine the walls. Neither had any idea of what they were looking for but for the second time in two days Scott felt a certain excitement.

Curt pulled out a magnifying glass and examined the smallest details on the ceiling. Scott moved to the far wall and ran his hands over the surface while lighting the area. He continued walking for several feet, feeling the wall, when he happened to look down and noticed the rock slabs on the floor, which measured approximately one foot square. The layout reminded him of the tile job he had had done in the kitchen of his previous house, prior to putting it on the market. He thought back to what Mr. Jenkins of J&H Tiles had said several times about shoddy tile work and how you could tap a piece with your foot and tell how secure it was.

As Scott surveyed the room, he shined the flashlight on every square inch of the floor looking for some anomaly in the design or height of each individual square. Nothing noticeable presented itself so he decided to conduct a "tile craftsmanship" test. Starting in the left back corner and proceeding forward, he gingerly walked in a straight line on each piece of stone slab, one step at a time. Because of the curvature of the ceiling, the first few passes and the last few would not be possible without bending over in an awkward manner. He didn't know what he was hoping to discover but it seemed like a good idea. Besides, Curt was surveying the walls and ceiling and what else was there to look at in the room?

After traversing one row of tile, Scott caught Curt's attention. Curt watched with amusement. "Why are you taking a sobriety test at 8:45 in the morning?"

"Just inspecting the ground," Scott replied. He continued as Curt refocused his attention on the ceiling. Scott walked until he met the wall again and then turned to head in the opposite direction. He continued this exercise and on the third lap his concentration drifted from listening to the sound of his steps to personal matters such as the bills he needed to pay and the yard that desperately needed cutting since he had not attended to it over the weekend.

Five steps out and his mind suddenly snapped back to consciousness. He focused on the quietness that surrounded him. Curt had turned and stood motionless, staring at Scott's left foot. Scott was wandering in the past. They were both standing in a 300-year-old room last inhabited by a human who had probably been sealed alive. They were creeping around in someone's tomb. He and Curt were walking across the same area, the same pattern of stones that once bore the weight of a trapped and terrified soul. Scott began to imagine the fear the man had experienced, closed in alive in this warm and damp place, and left to die . . . in complete darkness, cut off from fresh air . . . in a room where it was almost impossible to move without striking your head on the ceiling.

Attempting to clear his head, Scott retraced his thoughts and recalled the last sound he had heard. It was a distinct muffled sound now echoing in his memory. Curt raised his eyes to meet Scott's. Scott had never seen such an expression from Curt and it sent a chill down his spine. It was a combination of excitement, surprise and fear. As Scott stood in place he shined the flashlight down to the slab where his left foot still resided. He slowly lifted his leg and tapped the stone with his heel. The stone slab made a *clank*. He extended his leg to the next square and performed the same exercise as a litmus test. This time the sound was more of a *clunk*. Testing several other tiles, he got the same *clunk* each time. Only this one stone had a distinct *clank* that suggested hollowness beneath.

Scott could feel his heart pound. Curt moved toward him and squatted at his feet. Scott backed away from the slab and his expectations caused him to shiver. Curt gently tapped the stone with his knuckles, and then tested the squares around its border to confirm the tone.

There was no doubt. This one slab was different, or, maybe the way it was supported was unique.

"What do you think?" Scott asked.

"I think you've found something. God knows what. But you've found something," Curt answered.

By now it was 8:50 a.m. They had 25 minutes to decide what they were going to do.

But Curt had already made up his mind. Retrieving a pocketknife he had had since ninth grade from his jeans he opened the blade. Scott looked at him with bewilderment.

"You're not going to do what I think you're going to do?" he asked tentatively.

"I sure am. Aren't you the least bit interested? Of course you are. I know you too well. If we walked away from here right now without trying you'd be bitching for the next two months."

Scott sighed. Then hesitated in his response. "Okay, but I really don't want to go to jail for destroying a national monument so take it easy will you. Kay might not bail either one of us out if we get caught for something like this."

"I'm not going to damage anything. I'm just going to try and pry this piece up."

With that Curt began scratching the blade along the edge of the slab. The process was slow and time worked against him. After 15 minutes of scraping, the gritty residue in the crack wore down well below the surface level. Curt then began wedging the steel blade in and slowly prying the stone upward. Initially, his efforts appeared useless. The tight formation and the settling of the rock over such a long period of time seemed to create an impenetrable seal. Several times Scott was certain the blade was going to snap.

But after about five minutes of wedging and prying, the slab popped and gave way as if opened like a sealed Tupperware container. Curt fell back surprised as his breathing quickened. Scott almost let out a scream.

As the two regained their composure they stared at each other briefly before turning their attention back to the ground. The slab had been dislodged and then fallen back precisely in place. But the surrounding restraint and the airlock formed over the centuries had been broken. It was now just a matter of using the knife to lift the lid and see if there was anything beneath.

CHAPTER-ELEVEN

Two months after Jesus was crucified, in a land far from the Roman Empire, a teenage girl strolled the beach on the flowery peninsula foraging for firewood. She was a member of the Calusa, one of the four original tribes of Florida.

Not far from the beach, she looked to the east and saw the pristine waves calmly rolling in and the silvery glow of the sun beaming off the distant surface. The water shaded from a subtle green to vibrant blue against the horizon. The beautiful scenery had managed to divert her attention from the task at hand as she stood in admiration. It was a beautiful summer day and she could not resist making her way to the shore for just a few minutes to enjoy the sight of all that nature cared to present to the 15-year-old girl.

She placed an armload of branches and limbs upon the loose sand and walked into the reaching tide, wiggling her toes in the salt water. Incoming waves spilled over her ankles and then receded. The soft sand tickled as it flowed out from underneath and her feet gently settled in the sinking mud. She looked out on the seascape somewhat astonished at the breadth of the waters before her.

It was endless, a continuous body of motion that engulfed everything before her eyes.

Her tribe believed the gods of all nature resided underneath the surface not far from shore. In her childhood this knowledge had terrified her. But as she matured, she understood the water was not a place to fear, but a place to be respected, shown due reverence. The gods were there to protect. And as long as the Calusa understood and appreciated the land and water, they would remain at peace.

As the young woman playfully kicked at the waves a smile broke across her face. The sun felt luxurious on her tan skin and she suddenly gained an urgent need to feel the water against her body. She walked back to the shore just past the waterline and, after checking in both directions, quickly disrobed. She returned to the gentle waves and the sun cascaded upon her body and warmed her entire soul. Her long black hair waved behind and then flew to her chest and down to her breast as the wind mischievously swirled. Her long firm legs never pausing, yet continuing farther out until the water rose above her pelvis.

There she stopped and squatted down to feel the liquid movement on every inch unexposed to the fiery ball of light in the heavens. Now beyond the breakers, the tantalizing motion of the incoming swells kept her body riding blissfully up and down. A swaying, relaxing pleasure ensued and her mind began to drift.

She suddenly felt an extreme loneliness unlike any she had ever known before. What if the gods were not pleased? She rapidly made her way back to the hard sandy shore and quickly dressed, eyeing the crystal blue water that met the sky far away. How could she have been so stupid, so greedy to invade the waters?

She turned and spotted the wood not far away and quickly retrieved it. With each passing second she was becoming nauseated at what she had done. For her, fear from godly repercussion was a reality.

As she was leaving the soft sand of the high beach she happened to glance at a lone palm tree standing well off the high tide mark. There was an object at its base that caught her attention.

Initially, she wanted nothing more to do with this place and was content to make her way quickly back to the tribe with her bundle of wood. But she was strangely attracted to the coarse shape nestled in the sand, its dark color in contrast to the light trunk of the palm, the white surrounding sand, and the light brown sea oats sparsely scattered nearby.

She cautiously approached. But even as she stood over the object, she was without the slightest hint of what it might be. It looked harmless enough. It vaguely resembled a piece of tree but a coating of sorts that masked the top seemed foreign. It was very odd.

Yet it appealed to her. Inexplicably and without reason she was immensely intrigued. She put the firewood to the side and knelt before the object. She could see it was partially submerged in the sand. But now that she was closer, she had a better view of what it might be.

It was a piece of tree after all, weathered and old, but unmistakably wood.

But the sheath on top was strange. It appeared very tightly stretched. She hesitantly reached out and touched the layering, quickly retracting her hand as her fingers made contact.

It was taut and rigid.

An unearthly feeling rose from her knees. It invaded her body through the clean sand and shot past her chest through the top of her scalp. She was momentarily dazed as the sordid heat glazed over her eyes and consciousness waned back and forth. Seconds later it was over.

It was as if she had suddenly been consumed by an angry god and then spit out. Rejected. Expelled.

An odd calmness cradled her soul. She felt strangely invincible and, without thought, grabbed the long cylindrical object from the sand. She draped it across her shoulder and made her way past the palm tree and far away from the beach. Eventually she entered the woods and angled to the northwest, away from her tribe and family.

Unlike the landscape two millenniums later, the coast and inland areas were saturated with underbrush and heavy vegetation. As the young woman made her way through the thick foliage, she instinctively held course, sometimes going around unapproachable patches of thicket but always keeping the same northwest bearing. And she did so with a relentless pace, seemingly growing stronger as the scorching summer sun bore down, creating a stifling mask of humidity. As a Calusa she was accustomed to the heat and intolerable cloaking air.

And on this day, holding the section of aged tree upon her supple shoulder, she seemed to thrive on it.

In time she arrived at the place she sought. She had no idea how long it had taken but she had been moving for some time. The blazing ball had crossed the sky and was falling on the far side away from the great water. Soon, it would be dark and she felt the need to move quickly and be done with her task.

She had not fought the instincts that compelled her to pick up the object on the beach and walk. She understood it was some sort of punishment for her actions. The gods may not have been able to steal her soul but she knew their powers were capable of extreme pain. When the desire overcame her to journey through the woods with the object she had graciously accepted the penalty. Whatever it was *they* wanted she was willing to oblige if it meant being done with her penance. The sooner the better. Then she'd go home to her family and never go near the shore again or venture into the water, which had caressed her body.

Before her now was a small body of water. It was perfectly round, no more than 25 feet in circumference. She bent down and placed the section of tree on the light brown grass that bordered the pond. The stretched covering faced up.

Without knowing why but proceeding as she knew she must, she found a thick branch on the ground and began stabbing and scraping the covering. It was not an easy process. The seal was secure and it took nearly an hour to create the smallest hole in which she was able to thrust yet another thick stick inside.

Using this leverage, she eventually pried the covering off. Inside she found a strangely white, fully intact skeleton of a small creature. But she was not surprised.

It was what she had expected to find.

The carcass had been talking to her through the covering since she had knelt in the sand below the palm and felt the god briefly invade her body.

It had instructed her to come to this pond.

And it was telling her what to do next.

She gently retrieved the skeleton from its housing. The vehicle, which had propelled it from faraway lands thousands and thousands of years before, crumbled into dust and then disintegrated leaving a burnt stain on the grass. The smell of musty air rose from the ground, like charred animal fur.

But the Indian girl never noticed. She had already turned and was standing on the bank. Raising the skeleton high over her head in her right hand she spoke in a low grainy voice "eity onuey accos." *Revenge the soul.*

The water of the once still pond began to bubble and the wind escalated bringing the young woman out of her trance in a horrifying instant before she fell forward. In that millisecond, confusion reigned. It was as if she had fallen into a nightmare from a perfectly awakened state, a nightmare so heinous her heart nearly burst from the terror.

She pitched forward into the water. Somewhere, amidst her agony, she felt the bony object in her grasp slither away.

In the moment before she was consumed, when she understood her fate, all she could ask was to die mercifully, without pain. *The gods had been outraged.*

The churning water seethed into her body and the excruciating torture sent a chorus of chilling contractions through her chest. The ripping and shredding left her organs scattered about, briefly suspended in the murky domain and then gobbled up. Her head violently separated from her neck and shot upward into the air, temporarily leaving the insanity of the water below. It had barely cracked the surface on its way down when it was dispatched into more consumable fragments and ransacked. A coagulated pool of crimson quickly spread over the surface as the sloshing water slowly subsided.

Seconds later the pond calmed to a flat mirror of the trees and clouds hovering high above. The setting was docile again, concealing the events that had just transpired beneath the watery surface.

To the west, the sun teetered on the horizon. The humidity clutched the landscape in total domination as the heat of the day hospitably invited the night to join the party.

And the creature once again lived.

CHAPTER-TWELVE

Pierre Couperin had not slept well the last two nights. He had never suffered from insomnia in his life and he was confused why it would suddenly occur at the ripe old age of 78. Maybe it was the American climate, although, truthfully, it was not so different than Grenoble where he had lived the first 61 years of his life.

An architect by profession, he had moved to the states and settled in Florida in an effort to escape the past. On his 58th birthday he and some friends had celebrated with one too many glasses of champagne at the *Bourgeois Chotel*, an exquisite restaurant on the outskirts of town, and had driven home alone along the winding mountainous streets at 2:30 in the morning. That night would be the last time Pierre would ever put alcohol to his lips.

Blinded by the bubbly he was unaware of his actions until the next morning when the local police arrived to arrest him. While a splitting headache relentlessly pounded away, Pierre listened as the police described how he had swerved into a moped traveling in the oncoming lane at the top of the hill just two miles from his house. With nowhere to turn, the driver had laid the bike down and slid under the chassis of his car, instantly crushed to death. Pierre spent many waking hours trying to recall the event but never could. He was even convinced that morning they had accused the wrong person until they walked him around to the front of his car and showed him a long piece of material flapping from the underside of the front grill and the blood-soaked undercarriage in front of the axle housing.

After a short trial in which he pleaded guilty to manslaughter, Pierre was convicted and spent six months in jail. His license to drive was permanently revoked. What made matters even more devastating for Pierre was that he knew the victim. She was Piana Franco, the 29-year-old daughter of one of his coworkers at LeBaaum. Pierre had been employed at LeBaaum for 32 years but did not attempt to get his job back when released from prison. He knew he could never face his coworker.

Fortunately, Pierre had planned more than adequately for retirement and by the time he had reached 55 he didn't need to work. Now he had nothing but free time on his hands to dwell on what he had done. As the days began to wear him down he became a hermit, seldom leaving his house for fear of meeting someone who knew of his dark crime. He eventually sank into severe clinical depression and, at the urging of his parole officer, began psychological counseling. Upon the advice of his physician, Pierre decided a change of scenery was necessary to try and rebuild the remainder of his life. Being single with no family ties (his older sister had died from a heart attack when he was 52) Pierre headed to the states in search of a new start.

Now, some 20 years later, he still spent time each day thinking about Franco's daughter and asking her for forgiveness. For some reason he had thought of her often the last two nights. He decided it was because he couldn't sleep and didn't have anything else on his mind that he cared to ponder about . . . especially the manuscript that Lockes man had him translate. What an odd read that was. It sounded like some grotesque fairy tale. Pierre was not much up on the history of St. Augustine. He'd only been through the town once in a cab ride and never visited any of the tourist spots or taken in any of the local history. The stuff Lockes asked him to translate didn't really have a lot of meaning to him even if he was French. His people had plenty of land in France, why would they need to sail part way around the world for more in the 1500's? If they'd just been patient, they could have gotten a passport and come over to America as he had. Hell, no Spanish tried to whack him when he stepped off the 757 at Jacksonville International Airport in 1980.

But the more he tried to flush the story of Pinot out of his mind the more it came to the forefront. Even as he dozed on Sunday morning, Pinot had filtered into his dreams along with other sites and events that caused him to awaken abruptly more than once.

Sunday night had been a sequel. Part Deux, the sleeplessness continues. For most of the night he studied the ceiling fan slowly turn. The glow of the moon cut through a slight separation in the vertical shades, just enough to cause the reflection to bank off the blades as they slowly spun. Pierre hoped watching the fan would have a relaxing effect, similar to that of counting sheep. But it was useless. With each passing minute he recalled vague bits and pieces of Lockes' document. The French being slaughtered on the beach, the brothers escaping, the secret of the pond, the plan of revenge. Lockes had specifically asked Pierre to translate on paper in English and not to make any copies, which he had found unusual. But he really didn't care, that is until now. The story had become transfixed in his thoughts over the last 36 hours and now he had a strange urge to refresh himself on the exact details.

He did remember one thing very clearly about the document. It was one passage he could visualize with astonishing acuity as he gazed at the slowly rotating blades. A part he had elected not to translate to Lockes. He didn't know why he had skipped it but he had gotten an odd sensation upon reading and instinctively glossed right by. It was a series of four sentences that seemed so full of nonsense he chose not to disclose them. Now he had an eerie feeling his decision was a mistake.

On Monday morning Pierre arose just before 5 a.m. at his home in Ponte Vedra Beach. The two-bedroom flat was located a block from the ocean at the intersection of Turner and Shackle Avenue. In 90 minutes or so, the sun would be creeping above the water to the east and the shrimp boats and recreational fishermen would be scattered along the horizon. Pierre Couperin would traverse through the morning, drinking his tea and reading the Florida Times-Union on the wooden deck in his backyard. He was literally exhausted, as his insomnia had not allowed a decent night's sleep since Friday. After preparing a light breakfast of corn flakes and milk, he turned on the Weather Channel to get the latest on Tropical Storm Damon. Living on the coast, Pierre kept a close eye on such storms and had first seen updates on this weather pattern Friday evening. Now the updated prediction that the storm would gather strength and soon reach hurricane force made him uneasy, especially since it was reportedly angled toward North Florida. He had lived here long enough to know these things were as predictable as the weather itself and he wasn't immune to evacuation if warranted. He would keep a close eye on this one over the next few days.

By the time the sun shown brightly and the air had begun to heat up, the sounds of beach-goers invaded Pierre's backyard as they did every morning around 9 a.m. Swim suit-wearing locals and tourists strolled along Shackle Avenue carrying surfboards, towels, beach bags, radios, folding chairs and other assorted sand and surf paraphernalia. Pierre didn't mind having the serenity compromised. If he did, he would have moved inland to a nice quiet neighborhood or retirement community years ago. But that was not his way. He preferred to live out the rest of his days enjoying life. As far as he was concerned he had the perfect spot for watching beautiful young females strutting by in bikinis and G-Strings.

When he had first settled at the beach, these sites would frequently remind him of Franco's daughter and he almost did move inland. Many times he was sure he saw the face of Piana Franco pass by. But on this particular morning the pedestrian traffic was light. As October approached, the beaches lost appeal and the crowds wouldn't return again until March when the first spring breakers heading to Daytona Beach would stop by for a dip in the Atlantic.

As Pierre sat in the chair on his porch, newspaper folded in his lap, he turned and looked through the screendoor leading inside and saw the clock over the livingroom sofa said 8:55. Reflecting back on his hours staring at the ceiling fan earlier that morning, he got up and went to the kitchen and removed the tablet of paper hanging by a magnet on the refrigerator door. He turned and opened the middle drawer under the counter and found a pen. Returning to his chair in the sunshine, he jotted down some sentences and then read them aloud. At 9:12 a.m. Pierre put down the pad and pen and closed his eyes as he laid his head back to rest. In the distance he could hear the voices of those passing by and the faint sound of the waves caressing the shore. The seagulls were squawking as they rode the gentle wind brushing along the coast. It all mixed like a symphony in tranquil concerto and for the first time in three days Pierre felt relaxed and faded into sleep.

The dream, or so he thought, began immediately and was vivid. It started with Pierre leaping up and quickly moving toward the chain-link fence and opening the gate to the dirt driveway. Moving through the gate he stopped as a man dressed in ragged clothes ran toward him screaming, blood dripping from his forehead with his hands clutching his chest. Pierre estimated the frantic man to be in his early 40s and could see the material of his shirt was tattered underneath his hands. As the man drew closer, Pierre could also see blood gushing from the man's chest, coating his strained fingers. The man headed straight for Pierre and Pierre quickly moved to the side just in time for the man to pass by as he fell through the gate opening. Rolling around on the ground, the bleeding, screaming man continued to clutch his chest as his eyes rolled back in his head. All of this happened so fast, Pierre stood there dumbfounded. He was frozen, paralyzed with indecision as the man tossed on his lawn from side to side, shouting words, which Pierre could not comprehend. It wasn't that he had a problem with the language, it was just in the manner the excited man was babbling. In fact, Pierre recognized the dialect immediately. It was French.

Clearing his head, Pierre raced inside and picked up the receiver hanging on the wall phone with such force it flew out of his hand and crashed into the crossed swords mounted on the far den wall. The swords and phone fell to the floor with a clank as the elongated cord, now stretched to the other side of the room, lay at the base of the wall. It was pinned there by one of the blades resting upon it. Pierre rushed over to retrieve the receiver, almost tripping over the cord. He kicked the sword aside as he grabbed the phone and punched 911. Holding it tightly to his ear he could hear the pounding of his heart echo through the room while he waited for the connection. Anxiously gripping the phone, pulse racing and sweat trickling down his cheek, he suddenly felt a near presence and whirled around to see the screen door propped open.

He immediately dropped the phone as the bleeding man, now calm and sedate, slowly walked into his living room and sat down on the suede sofa with his eyes fixated upon Pierre. Pierre stood motionless, stifled in fear. The blood was no longer flowing from the man's forehead but continued to gush from his chest. With his hands removed, Pierre could see there was a gaping wound that would surely be fatal if unattended. With a trembling hand, Pierre reached down for the phone but lost his balance and fell back against the wall as the man bellowed harshly, "PINOT! PINOT!". The words sent an electric jolt of panic through Pierre and his legs became appendages that could not be counted on for support. He couldn't believe what the man had said! Pinot! Pinot! The character from that story. It was just not possible. It must be a dream! A very terrible dream!

The bleeding man was silent as he sat motionless on the couch hemorrhaging. His gaze remained fixed on Pierre. The old man could feel his chest ache as the muscles contracted and then tensed into gripping agony. Pierre realized immediately what was happening but was so dazed by the events, he struggled to think clearly as he slid down into a sitting position. His back was propped against the living room wall opposite the couch. The pain in his chest increased with each passing second and he struggled to endure between each horrific contraction. He tried to scream. He wanted to beg the man on his couch for help since obviously, even though injured, the man was in better condition than he was. But no words were audible. The pain was so intense it had stolen his ability to speak. The riveting bolts shooting through his upper body left his head spinning and his vision clouded. Through bleary eyes, Pierre saw the bleeding man in the tattered clothes slowly rise from the couch and make his way methodically across the den. He took slow, deliberate steps toward the middle of the room and reached down to pick up the sword. The one Pierre had kicked away. With a red hand, the man grasped the handle as blood dripped on the blade and trickled to the floor. Standing upright, he glared at Pierre and moved toward the old man who held his hand over his heart, struggling to fill his lungs with air.

The last thing Pierre Couperin witnessed was the bleeding man lifting the sword high over his head with two hands. The sword rocked backward and the man stared directly into Pierre's eyes. Then he hesitated as if having second thoughts. Suddenly the eyes widened and a devilish grin burst onto the face as it quickly brought the sword forward sending the blade slicing through the air. In the split second before it was over, Pierre realized there was something wrong with the bleeding man's left hand.

And then the overwhelming pain that he would endure but an instant and the effect that would last an eternity occurred simultaneously before darkness shrouded Pierre's existence. Fading, a chorus of shrieks and screams ripped through his head.

The next thing Pierre Couperin saw was Piana Franco standing by a café on a remote street corner. She was talking to a stranger and laughing. Laughing deep and heartily as if she had just heard the funniest joke of her life.

The two men moved in closer with flashlights in hand and stared at each other in anticipation. Curt eased the tip of the knife into the crack again and gently pried up one side as Scott slid his fingers underneath to guarantee the slab did not fall back. He withdrew the knife and moved around to the other side and repeated the process, this time holding the side up after it was raised.

In unison, Scott and Curt lifted the stone and moved it to the side. As they did, a rush of dust rose from the opening and slowly dispersed around them. Both men choked on the thick granulated air and their eyes watered from the foreign matter. Momentarily, Scott was able to refocus after wiping his eyes clean with his shirt. He shined the flashlight into the opening. The 12-inch square hole now revealed a flat sandy surface, its depth about three inches below the bottom of the surrounding stone edge.

Initially there had been a deluge of excitement when the men had cracked the seal. Now there was disappointment.

"Nothing," Scott said, "but enough dust to give us both black lung."

But Curt was still eyeing the area intently. Because of Scott's position, the beam from his flashlight was coming at an angle and precluded a visible view of the area on his side. It was immersed in the shadows. But through the darkness, Curt's thoughts were bouncing together like neutrons as he was sure he could make out some form flush against the side. Picking up his flashlight, he quickly drove the light into the darkness. He stared in amazement as the glow came to rest on what appeared to be the skeleton of a small animal.

"What is it?" Scott asked as he leaned forward and caught sight of the object.

"I have no idea," Curt replied with an obvious tone of excitement. "Only one way to find out."

"Be careful, as old as this place is, it's bound to be very brittle." Scott responded.

Curt leaned forward and with his left hand touched the object briefly and then pulled away.

"What's the matter?" Scott asked.

"Nothing. Just checking," Curt replied.

"Checking what? For a pulse?"

"Very funny. Here, hold the light," Curt said laying his flashlight down.

Scott positioned the beam on the skeleton as Curt again reached inside the opening. He grabbed what he assumed was the head and lifted very slowly. Once it was clear, he positioned his other hand under the main body. The skeleton had a very smooth texture and, to his surprise, appeared completely intact. Even more amazing was how sturdy it was. He could have lifted the entire thing out holding the head with no support from underneath. Yet it was relatively light. Curt estimated maybe two ounces. As he held it in his hands, he gently wiped the sand away from the lower section that had been buried in the dirt. The entire remains were roughly 12 inches long, including a four-inch tail section.

"What in God's name is this thing," Curt said.

"No idea. But check out those teeth," Scott responded. "This little guy could have used a good orthodontist." As the words left his mouth he shivered and recalled the odd cloud from Friday morning. This damn thing oddly resembled one of the formations.

Just then they heard a voice outside the entrance moving closer. Curt instinctively placed the small skeleton inside his shirt and cringed, as the sand residue seemed all at once to shake itself loose and fall, coating his stomach. Scott quickly reached over and grabbed the dislodged tile and placed it back over the opening. It fell neatly into place.

"Wait a minute," Curt whispered louder than he meant to.

"What?" Scott asked.

"Open it back up for a second."

"Why? That's probably your buddy coming to kick us out. Time's up. We're going to get caught," Scott said.

"No we're not. Just open it back up and go delay my $50 friend. I just need a few seconds. We probably won't get a second chance at this."

Scott didn't like the idea but he also knew Curt was right. He reached for the knife that Curt had left on the ground and pried up the tile one more time. He removed the slab, laid it to the side and left the room in such a hurry he scraped the top of his head as he escaped through the diminutive opening. As he came through the other side he was startled to meet Robert Bruin, who was preparing to enter. Scott grabbed the ranger by the arm and spun him around in the other direction.

"We know it's time to leave," Scott began, "Curt is just gathering his things and we'll be going." Again, Robert Bruin never said a word but looked at Scott with a solemn glance as if to say, "Hurry the hell up."

The two men reached the outer doorway, which emptied into the garrison courtyard. The fort would open for business soon and the tourists would come meandering in to bask in the historical presence.

Scott stepped out into the daylight and noticed a look of uneasiness on Robert Bruin's face. Bruin turned around apparently disturbed by Curt's lack of urgency to come out. He began to walk back toward the powder magazine. Just as Scott was about to call for his friend as a warning signal, Curt appeared from the opening.

"I know, I know, I'm coming," he said looking almost apologetically to the man who had taken money as a bribe to allow him to be here. "Had to get my things."

Scott and Curt left along the stone walkway that surrounded the courtyard. Robert Bruin walked around in the opposite direction. When they arrived at the southeast corner, Curt quickly turned left.

"Where are you going?" Scott asked.

"Bathroom."

Curt turned the corner and had his hand on the men's room door when Bruin came running toward them. Curt did not see the ranger and continued inside. Scott was speechless, as the ranger approached at full speed. He had no idea what the man was doing. Bruin sailed past Scott and hit the door, slamming it against the wall. Bruin rushed inside. A moment later, Curt was being forcibly escorted out.

"Okay! Okay, I'm going," Curt shouted at the park ranger. "Can't a guy even take a piss?"

Bruin was silent as he followed behind them.

As Scott and Curt made their way back through the sally port, Scott sensed Curt's excitement. He also had a feeling that Curt was carrying more in his shirt than just the small skeleton.

"Did you find anything else?" he asked Curt with a whisper as the two men walked out of the fort and across the drawbridge toward the ravelin.

"Shhhh. Just wait," Curt replied. "We'll talk in the car."

CHAPTER-THIRTEEN

Marvin Sellon was a resident of St. Augustine and a retired archeology professor from Florida State University. Scott had met Marvin in Tallahassee during his junior year while taking an elective course on Florida history. The two instantly hit it off. Marvin was the type of professor who was not afraid of making friends with his students and Scott admired his incredibly dry sense of humor and zealous passion for discovering the mysteries of the past. Scott was so influenced by the man, he nearly changed his major from business management to history. But Scott's parents didn't have a true appreciation for his new found passion and since they were his money source, the idea was promptly overruled.

Nonetheless, Scott took two more courses as electives taught by Marvin and continued to build their friendship. Through the years, Marvin and Scott had stayed in touch and he was overjoyed when the professor decided to move to St. Augustine following his wife's death from cancer in 1992. Since then the two, along with Curt, had become "weekend archeologists" participating in any excavations they could. The banks of the St. Johns River proved to be a haven of Indian pottery and flint arrowheads. In areas where the earth was cleared and the ground turned over for new home construction, even amateurs could find interesting artifacts with minimal effort. Marvin frequently commented there was probably no better place to explore early American history than northeast Florida. Various Indian tribes and European nations had occupied the area at one time or another and the landscape was littered with remains of these civilizations. In addition, Marvin was absolutely intrigued by the mysticism and cultural folklores embedded with the artifacts.

Marvelous Marvin, as Scott liked to refer to the 66-year-old Cornell graduate, seemed to have connections everywhere. Whenever the professor needed to obtain some obscure information or knowledge outside his field of expertise, he always had resources at his disposal.

It was Marvin who had placed Curt in contact with Pierre Couperin to help translate the French document. And the only reason Curt hadn't invited Marvin to explore the powder magazine was because he knew the professor was somewhat of a purist and would never have approved of tampering with a national monument. Although unspoken, Scott knew this as well. Curt and Scott knew prior to exploring the powder magazine that any secrets would only be discovered by less than ethical means. But as with all discoveries, there is a time and a place to bend the rules.

As Curt and Scott walked quickly toward their cars, Scott was somewhat exasperated. Even outside the fort and well away from NPS Administration Office, Curt did not utter a word. They reached the Blazer and Scott motioned for his friend to get inside.

"We'll pick up your car later," Scott said.

Upon the concurrent slamming of the doors Scott turned to Curt. "Out with it," Scott said.

Curt excitedly reached into his shirt and withdrew the skeleton of the fish (or fishlike creature) still perfectly intact. It had been discolored by the sand but was much whiter now in the daylight. "This thing is amazing," he said, "It's as hard as a rock! You figure, at best it's been in there about 300 plus years right?"

Scott nodded his agreement. "Well feel this thing," Curt said. Scott reached over and held the remains. Curt was right. It felt hard as cement, yet exceedingly light.

"What the hell is it?" Scott began. "It feels petrified. But that would take hundreds of thousands of years. And if petrified, it would be completely black. So what are the bones of some fishlike animal doing in the fort? You think Pinot put it there?"

Curt didn't respond. Instead, he reached into the front of his shirt and seemed puzzled as his hand roamed. He leaned forward and untucked his shirt, allowing an object to fall into his hand. "What's that?" Scott asked in an excited tone.

"I don't know yet. While you were diverting our friend I felt around in the sand and found two other things."

"Two? Where's the second?"

"I don't know. That's what I'm looking for." Curt said still searching under his shirt and down the front and then back of his pants. "That's odd. I had that skeleton and one object in front and the other in back. I was trying to distribute them evenly so the ranger wouldn't notice the bulges anywhere."

"No worries. I've known you for awhile. You never bulge."

"Thanks."

"So while you're searching through your shorts, what is the object you're holding?" Scott asked.

"It could be a clump of dirt or a scrap of wood for all I know. I will tell you this though, I could have sworn that damn skeleton started squirming around in my shirt." Curt paused as he leaned forward and pulled his shirt over his head, removing it completely and then shaking it out over the floorboard. Still nothing. He undid the top snap on his jeans and yanked the zipper down. He arched his back, lifting his pelvis into the air and shoved his pants down to his knees. A woman in a white Ford Taurus who had pulled into the parking space next to them gave Curt a disgusted look.

Scott caught the lady's expression and laughed.

"What?" Curt asked.

"I think you made a friend," Scott grinned pointing to the car next to them.

"She'll get over it," he replied pulling his pants back up after checking down each pant's leg. "Dammit. Where did it go? I'm starting to wonder if it's hiding up my rear."

Scott looked at Curt. "If it is, I really don't need to see it."

Scott took the dirt covered object Curt had laid on the dash and attempted to rub it clean. The soil and grime were attached so firmly it was useless. "Better keep these things down," Curt said. "Remember Mr. Bruin's probably somewhere nearby."

Frustrated, Curt snapped his pants and pulled the zipper up and began looking in his seat and on the floorboard. Having no luck, he put his shirt back on and leaned back. "I know there was another object. It must have fallen out. Dammit, I can't believe I did that." He rolled the window down and stuck his head out to look down at the pavement. As he did, the woman in the Taurus got out of her car and hurriedly made her way to the sidewalk towards the fort's entrance.

"I think she really likes you. It must have been your bulge." Scott chirped as he started the engine and backed the Blazer up. He steered the SUV toward the parking lot exit. "It's time to go see Marvin," Curt said. Scott nodded and picked up the cell phone.

Marvin was halfway through a cup of decaffeinated coffee when the phone rang. He was watching a series on the Learning Channel that depicted biblical events and how well they could be substantiated with historical facts. Marvin found it quite interesting. He personally found it challenging trying to tie some of the Bible stories he'd learned in Sunday school with the factual evidence his profession demanded.

Initially he considered letting the call go to the answering machine but decided to answer on the fifth ring when he saw Scott's cell number on the caller ID.

"Sellon residence," he answered.

"Yes this is Barney Fife. I'm calling from Mayberry. Is Andy there?" Scott joked.

"Funny." Marvin quipped with a slight chuckle.

Scott laughed. "How've you been?" He asked.

"All right for a Medicare-eligible guy I guess," he said. "I had the TV on ESPN's *Body Shaping* earlier and confirmed I don't need Viagra."

"Good to know you have matters well in hand. It'll save you a fortune. Not that I would know," Scott replied with a grin. "Hey, are you going to be at the house for a little while? Curt and I need to see you. We're in town about 15 minutes away."

"I'll be here. Does this have something to do with Curt's manuscript that Pierre translated?" he asked with curiosity. "And by the way, why aren't you at work supporting that beautiful family of yours?"

"It's a long story, Marvin. Yes, it involves the manuscript, I think. We'll explain when we get there."

"I can't wait," he responded as Scott hung up.

Sherri Falco slowly strolled through the Winn Dixie Supermarket pushing a shopping cart with a bad wheel Monday morning. Her shift at the Nuestra de la Leche Gift Shop began at 11 and she was rushing to get this lone chore accomplished before heading into work.

She had been working at the shop for the last month and loved it. Of course it wasn't a career, but then again she didn't need to worry about such things. Six months ago while still living in Pensacola, she'd bought into a lottery pool with some colleagues at the office and they'd hit it big. After splitting the grand prize eight ways, she and the other winners each netted a tidy sum of $400,000 per year, before taxes, for 20 years. Not a bad salary for a single woman. And being an intelligent woman, as well as attractive, she had immediately enlisted the services of a certified financial planner who helped devise a plan for her and her daughter Tina to live comfortably now and in the future.

At the end of the school year, Sherri felt a change was in order and had moved to St. Augustine. She adored the quaint picturesque town. Besides, she had no ties to the Florida Panhandle, only moving there upon marriage. On the eastside of the state she'd be considerably closer to her sister who lived in Cocoa Beach. A mere two-hour drive and the siblings could be sipping wine and catching up on old times.

For the first couple of months upon moving to St. Augustine, she and Tina had the time of their life visiting various places downstate such as Disney World, Universal Studios, Busch Gardens and Sea World. But once the school year had started back and Tina began second grade, Sherri had become somewhat bored. Her job at the gift shop was merely a way to break the monotony. She only worked four hours a day but it was a welcome diversion while Tina was learning the three Rs. Sherri arranged her schedule so that she could pick Tina up from school at 3:30 p.m.

Finishing the shopping a little after 10 on this day, she rushed home and quickly unloaded the groceries, cracking most of the eggs as she accidentally put the carton down on the counter with more force than she had intended. This brought an outward chuckle at her own stupidity. After depositing the mixture of yoke, egg white and shell fragments into the kitchen trash can and making a mental note to pick up some more eggs after work, she jumped in the car at 10:35 and barely made it to work on time.

Like Castillo de San Marcos, the Nuestra de la Leche Shrine was a significant piece of St. Augustine's past. Located four-tenths of a mile north of the fort, it was a combination of three interesting attractions with historical ties: The cemetery, the chapel and the cross.

The most significant relevance of the Nuestra de la Leche was its claim as the spot where Pedro Menendez first landed in St. Augustine in 1565. In dedication, a sign in the cemetery proclaims:

THIS SITE HAS OFTEN BEEN CALLED "AMERICA'S MOST SACRED ACRE." TRADITION HOLDS THAT THE FIRST MASS IN THE NEW COLONY WAS CELEBRATED HERE

Like the garrison to the south, the plot of land sits on an inlet off Matanzas Bay. At the waterline, a five-foot bulkhead protects the cemetery from the tidal waters. During the day it is a serene setting with sailboats frequently moored just off shore. For some it is their permanent home. The cemetery grounds contain a large amount of oaks, palm, and other types of indigenous trees, which created substantial shade. Visitors wander the winding sidewalks throughout the venue to explore the gravesites. The appeal was the over-all age of the setting and its historic significance. This was evident by the dozens of headstones of St. Augustine residents from the late 1700s and 1800s.

On her first day working at the gift shop, on her break, Sherri had wandered the winding sidewalks admiring the peaceful nature of the grounds. Occasionally she had stopped to read the inscriptions deeply carved into the markers. One in particular that caught her eye read:

THE REMAINS OF 17TH CENTURY CATHOLIC NATIVE AMERICANS WERE REINTERRED AT THIS SITE IN APRIL 1997

But she never knew where they were "reinterred" from and didn't care enough to ask. But for some reason, the words stuck with her since.

On that same afternoon she also noticed a plot that bore a large granite slab with an inscription of a man who had died earlier in the year. Until that moment she had assumed the cemetery was closed to new admissions.

In addition to the various tombstone and gravesite markers were an assortment of other structures such as statues (one was of St. Francis of Assissi), rock altars, a sarcophagus, a water fountain and a gazebo.

The centerpiece of the cemetery, facing to the left of the bay, was a small stone chapel almost entirely covered with ivy. A plaque near the entrance read:

THE PRESENT BUILDING WAS THE FOURTH ONE CONSTRUCTED ON THE FOUNDATION. THE FIRST HAD BEEN ERECTED IN 1615 BUT FELL VICTIM THREE TIMES TO WAR, PIRATES AND STORMS. THE LAST RECONSTRUCTION BEGAN IN 1918

Inside the double doors of the chapel, the ceiling formed an archway. The room was small and probably held a maximum of 40 patrons when in commission. There were 12 wooden benches in perfect alignment on either side of the thin middle aisle. An altar was at the front. On the left and right walls, high up, were small stained glass windows. But because of the surrounding trees, only fragments of light got in. The chapel was no longer in use but represented a shrine for the thousands of visitors each year to see.

Besides the cemetery and the chapel, the third tourist draw was the *Beacon of Faith Cross*. It was a 208-foot stainless steel cross erected in 1965 to mark the place where Christianity was first planted permanently in the United States. It stood at the back right-hand side on a strip of land that jutted into the bay 175 feet past the cemetery bulkhead. A cement walkway allowed visitors up-close access and the opportunity to read the names inscribed on the base of those who contributed to its construction.

The Nuestra de la Leche Shrine Gift Shop and parking lot was located on the front left of the grounds. Access to the cemetery could be obtained by going through the gift shop and out the back door or by walking over the bridge that spanned the large saltwater fed pond directly in front of the acre. The gift shop was unlike the typical "touristy" ones found on San Marco Boulevard. Items sold were religious in nature. It was really more of a church supply outlet containing many different versions of crucifixes, religious books, cassette tapes and rosary beads.

In the back right-hand corner of the shop was a small room. Built into the left wall was a glass encased three-dimensional model reenacting Menendez's ships landing and conducting mass for the first time in the New World. On the right wall, propped on a long stand was the original outer casing of the coffin Menendez was buried in at the time his body was shipped to France. It had been presented to the mission by the French government in 1956.

Sherri avoided this room and there was no reason for her to ever go in. The room held no inventory and seemed strangely out of place. She had only been inside three times but never felt comfortable. The coffin covering was very ominous. More than that, it was evil looking. Lying under glass it had three very distinctive skull and crossbones etched along the top edge and a series of symbols and letters distributed in a cluttered pattern. She had wondered why a man who had done so much for his people would have a burial covering that appeared so menacing. The site of the bony heads alone were enough to keep her away. As one of the other clerks so aptly put it, "just seeing the thing gives me a case of the creeps."

But there was more. Each time upon entering the small room, she felt a distinctive awareness, a form of deja vous. Something in her past had crossed paths with some element of this tiny enclosure. But she was never able to identify the core of her feelings. The *thing* that set off her shivers. All she knew was that the sensations ran rampant. It was almost like a forgotten dream was trying to forge to the surface.

What Sherri would learn later was that the *feeling* was not of her past. It was from her future.

Marvin lived across the bay on Anastasia Island. His residence was roughly six miles southeast of the fort in a quiet neighborhood four blocks from the ocean. The 1,700 square-foot ranch-style home made for a nice, simple dwelling for the retired professor.

On the drive over, Curt placed the items in a shoebox he found in the back seat of Scott's SUV.

"You know Cody was going to make a lizard carrier out of that," Scott said.

"I'll buy him another one," Curt said placing the box on the floorboard at his feet.

"What kind of skeleton do you think this is? I've never seen anything like it. I'm not even sure it's real," Curt remarked, looking down at the closed lid.

"Beats me. I'm hoping Marvin can shed some light on it." Scott paused. "You want to hear something weird? I've seen that skeleton before. Not *that* one, of course. But I've seen an image just like it. Don't ask where," Scott said thinking back to Friday morning, sitting in the Blazer looking up to the sky and the strange cloud..

Curt gave his friend a puzzled look. "So is it a fish?"

"I think so."

The two friends left the topic for the rest of the ride and reverted to the occasional sophomoric comments they were prone to make to keep themselves amused. As they crossed the intersection of Union and Westcoven, Scott pointed to the "Stop Ahead" sign.

"You know, translated that means 'reform a drug addict.' "

The two laughed. Scott got his turn when he singled out a car with a dealer tag and commented, "Interesting. Most drivers don't list their occupation on their plate."

By the time they reached the neighborhood where the Sellon abode was located, the skies had become clouded. Scott turned the Blazer into the gravel driveway and saw Marvin sitting on the front porch, slowly rocking his wicker chair back and forth with a newspaper in hand.

"About damn time," Marvin quipped.

"What did you expect? Scott was driving," Curt replied as he smiled at his friend.

Marvin rose from his chair and extended a handshake to Curt as the visitor scaled the three steps. Scott followed and gave the man a gratuitous hug. As the men broke, Marvin pointed to the paper now lying on the rocker.

"Now that's my definition of an inept terrorist," he began. "There's a story in there about a man who sent a letter-bomb and was killed when the thing came back returned undelivered."

The three men laughed before Marvin spoke again. "C'mon inside. I'm ready for whatever it is you want to share with me. It's been a slow morning, other than Body Shaping, that is."

Scott and Curt followed Marvin into the dining room where the three sat at the formal table nestled between the china cabinet and the wine rack.

Curt gently laid the shoebox on the table.

"Do you have some paper or cloth I can lay this stuff on?" he asked looking at Marvin.

Marvin gave him an inquisitive look then went into the kitchen and returned with a complete copy of the St. Augustine Record from the previous Friday.

Curt took the newspaper and spread it on the table to his left. He removed the box lid and shuffled the objects to retrieve the skeleton. Lifting it from the box, he carefully shook off the dirt remnants that had collected from the other item. He placed the remains on the newspaper directly in front of Marvin.

"Christ, what is this?" Marvin asked in a bewildered tone.

"You're the expert," Scott said "We thought you'd know."

"I'm an expert in artifacts, not zoology," he said still studying the remains. "This thing is hideous. Where'd you get it?"

"It's a long story. But before we start, we have another item that needs to be cleaned," Curt said.

"Now that's something I can help with." Marvin took the box and walked into a back bedroom. A few minutes later he returned. "I've got it soaking in hydrogen oxidite. It's not a strong solution. Even if the object is brittle it should be okay."

"So what's the story with this skeleton? Where'd it come from?"

"This is going to take awhile" Scott began.

"Scott, look at me. It's not like I have anything better to do," the ex-professor said with a smirk.

For the next 26 minutes Scott and Curt retold how Curt had acquired the manuscript and how it had been translated. Of course, Marvin was aware of this since he was the contact with Pierre. They described the story of the LeFlore brothers and how they had learned the secret of the pond and invoked some bizarre plan of revenge, utilizing its powers. They went on to mention how the human remains found in the powder magazine might be those of Pinot. Of course, that is if the Frenchmen had lived to a ripe old age well past one hundred, Marvin was quick to point out.

They described their exploration of the powder magazine that morning. During this part of the story, they kept waiting for Marvin's reprimand about violating the archeologist's Code of Ethics but to both men's surprise, it never came. Lastly, they recounted the discovery of the skeleton and the other artifact (at least they hoped it was an artifact) below the slab and how they smuggled the goods out of the fort in Curt's shirt.

"You know you're reaching with this story about Pinot. The dates don't match. I wouldn't get too excited," Marvin said when they had finished.

"Yeah, we know. But, and I can't speak for Curt, I have a gut feeling Pinot was in that room. And honestly, that's all it is, just a feeling." That and the fact I saw some strange cloud that gave me a glimpse of that fish, Scott thought to himself. "Is there any real way to substantiate it was him? Probably not," Scott added.

"We may not be able to make positive identification, but there are some directions we can go," Marvin said.

"Such as?" Curt asked.

"First we need to determine what the other item you found is. Of course you know it will be six to eight hours before it comes clean. With the weak solution, it could take longer. Next, we need to find out what kind of animal has or had this type of skeletal structure. That really shouldn't be difficult. What's really amazing is how the teeth have remained intact. Generally, they decay relatively rapidly after death," he said as his eyes sparkled beneath the gray eyebrows. "That alone makes your finding quite intriguing. Then again, it may also send you to jail."

Finally, the remark came that the two men had braced for earlier.

"OK dad," Scott said sarcastically. "We know we went beyond the rules. No more criticism."

"Gentlemen, I hate to break up this fun, but I got a phone call after you called and I need to go help a friend with something. When I return in a couple of hours I'll see what I can do about determining what kind of animal this was," he said pointing to the fish-like object still sitting atop the newspaper.

"We'll get going," Scott said turning to Curt. "You owe me lunch, don't you?"

"Hell no. Remember, I'm down fifty dollars today. This one's on you."

Scott and Curt said their goodbyes and headed to the nearest McDonald's. It had been an eventful morning and they had both worked up quite an appetite.

When Sherri finished her shift, she made her way through town to the Shaft Point Elementary School. She arrived 10 minutes prior to the final bell and patiently waited in the long line of parent cars. As the alarm sounded and the kids spilled out from the school, she anxiously searched for Tina's sandy blonde head and Pokemon backpack that would be draped across her right shoulder. How she loved Tina, she thought. Loved her like she never thought she could love anything. It was a hard thing to describe to someone, especially if they didn't have kids. It was also the thing that had kept her from dating most men she was attracted to. If they didn't have kids there was no way they would understand. Like most parents, she wouldn't think twice about sacrificing her own life in order to save her daughter's if ever the situation arose. She'd once had a Philosophy professor at the University of Central Florida describe love as something or someone you're willing to give your own life for. She had never quite understood the concept until Tina came along.

When her daughter was three, the biological father had abandoned them. (Even though Sherri was married to him for six years, she always referred to him as the biological father out of spite.) For two years, Sherri mentally beat herself up for staying with Patrick for so long. For the life of her, she couldn't figure out why she married the man. He was a cable line installer with no clear ambitions in life and was frequently on the road. Sherri would only admit recently that it had been a purely physical attraction with no deep emotional ties. When he finally left, she was certain he had been cheating on her for several years. More than likely, he had found some floozy in another town to shack up with. Since leaving, he had not attempted to contact her about seeing Tina. The thought of the man repulsed her and she was glad not to have him around to interfere in their lives.

Sherri's appreciation for her daughter grew exponentially one month after Tina's fifth birthday. Sherri had taken her to the pediatric center because of a severe headache that had lingered for 36 hours. Motrin had little effect and the waves of pain that would come every 30 seconds caused Tina to cry out as tears would run down her cheeks. The doctor immediately referred Tina to the emergency room. After a CAT scan and an MRI, which was excruciatingly uncomfortable since Tina had to keep her head perfectly still for nearly an hour while the constant flushes of pain hit her, she was admitted to the Scanlon Children's hospital. The results left the neurologists somewhat baffled. The good news was that there was no brain tumor.

What made Tina's case so unique was that, typically, swelling happens near the top of the brain. This is known as encephalitis. But Tina was experiencing inflammation and fluid buildup in the base of the cerebellum that resulted in the pressure and the subsequent head rushes. The doctors referred to the source of the problem as an unusual form of postviral infection. Or, as Dr. Norman had called it, encephalitis of the lower cerebrum. Tina began receiving doses of Lortab for pain and Dexicron, a form of steroid, every six hours.

On the second day, the doctors performed a spinal tap and were able to rule out any forms of meningitis and leukemia. In any case, the placement of the swelling was most unusual but since it was determined to be viral and not bacterial, the only action was to let it run its course and continue to administer medicine for pain. Depending on Tina's immune system, it was expected to clear up within a few days.

After three days, the pain had not subsided as the doctors had hoped and the steroid was changed to a stronger form. Three days later, Tina was released from the hospital. She was still suffering from an occasional minor headache, but with medication it was manageable from home. Within a week, the pain was gone altogether. For the six days and five nights Tina spent in the hospital, Sherri never left her side except to take an occasional stroll around the floor or to get something from one of the hospital stores or cafeteria.

Sherri had a friend go to her house and pack clothes and toiletries so she wouldn't have to leave. Each night she slept with Tina. Each day she bought her precious little girl something new from the gift shop. Her emotions rocketed up and down, depending on the amount of pain Tina experienced. Initially, before the doctors had determined that Tina was safe from the nasty things, such as the big "C" or a tumor, Sherri had often gone into the bathroom to weep as Tina slept from the medication. The last thing she wanted was for Tina to see Mommy crying. Mommy had to be the statue, the rigid concrete figure that kept convincing the child she was going to be fine and to hold on when the "ouchies" came. (That was the term the nurses used to refer to the painful headaches.)

Since the scare two years ago, Sherri valued every moment with Tina as more precious than life itself. Sherri constantly reminded herself how easily the doctor could have come back into the hospital room after the MRI and informed her about a brain tumor lodged in her little girl's head that would result in a minimal life expectancy. Or he could have informed her about the cancer detected from the spinal tap.

But Tina had been spared. And that's exactly how Sherri felt about it. God had saved her little girl. A little girl that would never, ever be taken for granted by her mother, not one single second from now till eternity. From the moment she received word Tina would be all right, Sherri cherished life. More than that, she absolutely craved the time spent with her daughter.

As the steady stream of children trickled from the school's main doorway and the cars ahead of her gathered their young ones and moved on, Sherri slowly eased forward. Within minutes she was directly in front of the school doorway.

A glimmer of worry invaded her mind. Tina was never this slow exiting the building. This is unusual. As the procession of small bodies slowed, and there was no sign of Tina, she became more and more nervous. It had been at least a full eight minutes since school had let out. Her motherly instinct was about to force her to pull the car out of line and settle in the first available parking space when she saw her adorable seven-year-old pop through the opening. Tina was carefully carrying a piece of work she had created in art class that afternoon, tentatively holding it out so not to damage it. As she spied her mom and approached the Camry, Sherri leaned over and pulled the handle. The door opened in perfect timing with Tina's arrival. Tina slid into the seat smiling with an innocent glow.

"Hey baby, how ya doin'?" Sherri asked as she leaned over and kissed Tina on the cheek.

"Good, mommy. Look what I made today." Tina handed her mother the 8 ½ by 11-inch piece of construction paper. It was adorned in various colors of the artist. Items were detailed in a picturesque array to form a very fluorescent scene. "Do you know what it is?" she asked as her mom began to pull away from the curb.

Sherri looked down at her lap where she had placed the paper. It took her a moment to recognize the setting. "Of course I do, honey. It's an underwater scene. These are the waves on top and these are the fish below. There are also crabs and starfish on the bottom." It truly was an interesting picture.

As Sherri stopped before turning out of the parking lot onto the main road, she studied the picture for a few seconds, admiring the detailed effort Tina had put into the creation. The starfish were multicolored and the fish, mostly very small, hovered near the sandy floor. On the surface, seagulls and pelicans (at least that what Sherri assumed they were) rode the waves, basking in the sun beaming from the upper left-hand corner of the paper. Strangely, there was an absence of anything occupying the center of the picture and Sherri considered asking her daughter if she ran out of time to finish it. She thought better about making such a comment, in case this *was* the finished product. The last thing she wanted to do was hurt her daughter's feelings. Besides, if Tina wanted to add more to the picture, she could always do so at home. For now the masterpiece would find a permanent home on the Falco's refrigerator.

CHAPTER-FOURTEEN

Marvin drove across town to help a friend with a minor PC problem and, while out, used the opportunity to pick up some groceries and mail a birthday card to his niece. All the while, thinking about the unusual skeleton back at his house. He returned home at 2:30.

After stowing the groceries, he sat down at his desk in the front corner bedroom and booted up his Compaq. Once Windows initialized, he launched Netscape. After the Internet connection was made, he navigated through the *Find* area of his Yahoo Home Page. He began searching various zoological and aquatic sites looking for a match to the odd skeleton sitting on his dining room table. He viewed countless websites dedicated to animal types and origins, mammals, fish (prehistoric and present day) and a multitude of other sources of information from such prestigious places as the Indiana State University Library and the Smithsonian with no results. Not one near match.

By 4:45 he was ready to concede. He had conducted well over a hundred failed searches and was about to call it a day when an idea came to him. His fingers changed direction and he calmly typed in new search criteria.

At 5:52 he had what he believed to be a perfect match. And it bothered the hell out of him.

After lunch, Curt and Scott retrieved Curt's Mustang and dropped it off at Marvin's. The professor was still out. They decided to drive back into Jacksonville and visit Fort Caroline, and to find out if the pond described in Curt's manuscript still existed, or for that matter, ever did. In all their excitement and enthusiasm to explore the powder magazine they had overlooked the implications 32 miles to the north. The bottom line was that if the pond didn't exist, there was no basis for the legend.

As they drove along Highway A1A they hit a section between St. Augustine and Jacksonville Beach that was clear for miles. No homes, no people, just woods to the left and small sloping sand dunes to the right, which occasionally separated to display the beach just beyond. As a matter of fact, the only vehicle they saw for several miles was an old Ford truck, which had seen better days, parked to the left in a sandy area. The owner was probably enjoying an afternoon of fishing or sunbathing.

"Curt," Scott began, "what's your take on this pond legend? Not that I'm insinuating there's magic at work or anything preposterous like that."

"The LeFlores wanted to exact some measure of revenge. They were obviously despondent. When they heard the legend it must have been a desperation attempt," Curt said with hesitation. He had been giving this some thought since the day before. "I have to be honest, Scott, I really don't believe in some so-called secret powers. I really don't even believe they had any intent of taking on the Spanish. Two Frenchmen against a town full of soldiers is somewhat less than a fair fight in my eyes. What I do find interesting in the story is that they were transporting the dead French soldiers' bodies. If that's true, I'd sure like to know where they took them and what they planned to do with the bodies. It's intriguing that Pinot may be the poor soul who was sealed inside the powder magazine since no one else has a clue to who it is. But that's a long shot, at best. The dates are just too screwy to coincide with known history. The man would have been 135 years old. I'm assuming if those are Pinot's bones, someone just embellished the story. It makes for a nice story to mention the LeFlores in the same breath with Ribault in the 1500's. All that 'witnessing the massacre' stuff just makes for a better read. A more probable scenario is that Pinot and Reece were born in the 1600s and were never a part of the doomed French attack on St. Augustine. But as for some legend about magical powers, I think that's just a fairy tale."

"I agree, but I've been thinking about the brothers. Their motivation. You're right about Pinot. If it was he that was found in the sealed room then the brothers obviously did not sail with Ribault. But maybe their father did. Or an uncle. No doubt the brothers were bitterly angry by what the Spaniards had done to their countrymen even if before their time. The heinous method by which the French soldiers were put to death. Butchered on the beach in cold blood. That's why I'm leaning toward the possibility of some plan of revenge."

"But it's just a story, Scott. There's nothing to back it up. It reads like a well constructed tale. Which in retrospect, is all it can be."

"I know, but you have to admit it grabs you," Scott continued. "And think about what we found today. That skeleton, which I'm relatively certain, is some kind of fish. Is it just a coincidence the story mentions a pond? Ponds are known to occasionally contain fish."

"True, but last time I checked, the Fort Castillo de San Marcos was a pretty far stretch from Fort Caroline. Unless that was a flying fish, I think you're reaching"

"Am I? OK, why else would Pinot, or whoever was closed up in that room, have placed the skeleton below the slab. The man must have known he would die the minute they closed him in, yet he took the time, the effort, to pry up the stone and hide the fish underneath. Doing so in total darkness. He must have had one hell of a good reason."

"Well, I do agree it's strange but in the first place, he didn't place a fish underneath the slab. He placed a carcass. Second, we have no way of knowing when the skeleton was put there. What if it was placed there prior to his incarceration?" Curt said looking at Scott.

"Maybe. It's just the tie between the pond and that fish could be in the missing pages to your manuscript. At least it makes for a good mystery," Scott said looking out at the sand dunes racing by on his right.

"For the sake of humoring you, let's pretend the fish was placed under the slab by Pinot. What good would a dead fish do? If, as you're implying, it had lived in the pond near Fort Caroline, and possessed magical powers, didn't Pinot pretty much end the story and any hope of avenging his comrades deaths by killing the creature?"

"I don't know, Curt. I'm just trying to think out of the box," Scott replied. "I've had some strange visions and dreams lately and something is just not right. For whatever reason, and don't ask me why, I think its all connected. It's gotten me a little jittery."

Curt heard Scott but did not reply. He was thinking back to his dream and those eyes that had embedded themselves in the back of his mind. They had become like gum stuck in the crevices of a tennis shoe. No matter how hard he tried to clean it off by scraping on the grass, some pieces stick, virtually undisturbed, visible, yet unreachable. Like the gum, the eyes would remain in Curt's thoughts until time itself purged them away or he found some other method to cleanse the memory. As of now, they were ingrained.

The drive from St. Augustine to the Fort Caroline National Memorial on the banks of the St. Johns River took well over an hour and 30 minutes. Traffic was unusually heavy on Third Street through Jacksonville Beach. They pulled into the parking lot just after 3 p.m. The two men proceeded to the Visitors Center hoping to find a park ranger who could validate the existence of a small body of water nearby and aim them in its direction.

They entered the double glass doors as a family of four was exiting to walk the quarter mile nature trail to the nearly full-scale interpretive rendering of the fort. Today, nothing remains of the original, small earthen and timber fortification originally know as la Caroline. The site itself contained within the Timucua Ecological and Historic Preserve.

Inside the building, there was complete quiet. Scott recognized that clean, historical smell that every museum seemed to have. It was a virgin aroma of the past locking pieces with the present. To the left was a glass counter containing souvenirs. A cash register was perched on top. To the right the room spread out into a vast opening. Various artifacts were positioned around the room on display. Items included a full length Indian dugout canoe, a coat of armor with a matching sword behind glass and an assortment of other historical trinkets such as utensils and farming tools of past inhabitants of the area. An elderly woman stood in the left corner with an apron, cleaning off the glass of a display case.

"Shall we ask her?" Scott whispered to Curt.

"Go ahead. I want to look at something," Curt said softly never removing his eyes from a sign he had focused on upon entering. As Scott walked toward the lady, Curt eased closer to the exhibit that had caught his attention. It was actually a collection of exhibits that, he learned later, had just recently gone on display. As he drew close, he felt a twinge of excitement. With the impossibilities and speculations he and Scott had been discussing, he wanted to be sure what he now saw. As they say, reality is fleeting and his seemed to be racing along at the speed of light. This latest dose had him more confused than ever. Yet there it was, in plain English, scripted for everyone to see:

"All Waters are Joined"
An Exhibit by the Timucua Indian Foundation

Curt stood in place and stared at the letters, making sure they actually formed the words his brain comprehended. Scott walked up behind him.
"She's just a clerk. She had no idea . . ." Scott stopped short as he saw the title and it registered instantly. "Hooooolllly cow," Scott said sounding more like Gomer Pyle than a college educated white-collar manager.
"Kind of coincidental, don't you think?" Curt said.
Scott began reading the storyboard aloud:

These exhibits tell how the St. Johns River meets with the Atlantic Ocean, where salt and freshwater converge to form a well-adapted environment capable of sustaining a variety of life, including human.

"Human, huh?" Curt remarked as the levity of what Scott read began piecing nicely with the manuscript back in the trunk of his car sitting at Marvin's.
Scott continued reading. They learned the series of exhibits cataloged the history of the St. Johns River, including the time frame of French colonization in the 1500s. The presentation was achieved mainly through the sketches and writings of LeMoyne and Laudonniere, two survivors of the ill-fated colony.
But it was the last exhibit that really struck the attention of Curt and Scott. It was entitled "The Domain" and featured a satellite picture of the Timucua Preserve with close-up photographic images of various natural landscapes. As the two men studied the picture searching for a small body of water, they spotted Spanish Pond southeast of the Visitors Center. The accompanying text described it as part of a freshwater wetland that had derived its name from the probability it had been the site at which the Spanish soldiers camped the night before they attacked Fort de la Caroline in 1565. Curt placed his finger on the casing where the water appeared on the photograph and turned to Scott.
"What do you think?" Curt asked with a gleam in his eye. His excitement was obvious.
"I think it's too convenient," Scott replied.
"What do you mean?"

"Remember the story said it was well hidden. This thing's right in the open for everyone to see. Besides, you and I both knew about Spanish Pond. It's no secret. It's featured just across the road with wooden walkways and a nature trail. Not exactly obscure. It's basically marsh. I don't think that's what the manuscript was referring too. It doesn't feel right.

"There you go *feeling* again". Curt said enunciating *feeling* as if it was a six-syllable word. "Don't you know men don't have feelings?"

"Funny," Scott responded.

"Anyway, Spanish Pond is the only water visible in this photo besides the St. Johns River. And this is a high-tech shot. With NASA technology, it's possible to spot a stain on your underwear through your Dockers from 50 miles above the earth. It'd be kind of hard for Mother Nature to hide a body of water under those circumstances, don't you think?"

Scott looked back at the picture of Spanish Pond. The size of the pond itself did seem to fit the description in the manuscript. It was small and it was located near the fort, but not too near to be seen if dense cover prevailed.

"Scott, let's go check it out," Curt said. I know it's been awhile since I've been over there. And I've never ventured from the nature trail that surrounds it. Maybe there's more off the beaten path."

Scott nodded and, as the two men turned, they were face to face with a mountain. Before them was a man nearly seven feet tall. He had broad shoulders, dark skin and darker, well cropped short hair that hugged his head. He looked to be in his fifties. His age made for an unusual contrast with his dark hair, which gave no hint of ever graying. Grecian Formula, Curt would think later. As the two startled men quickly took a step backward and looked up, a deep voice bellowed, "Can I help you gentlemen with anything?" Although friendly, it still caught Curt off guard and he choked on his saliva as he attempted to respond. Scott started whacking his friend on the back.

"Yes. Yes you can," Scott said as his shaky voice regained its composure. He continued to peer upward, noticing the man's sullen brown eyes and leathery skin. This guy was no stranger to sunshine.

"Well, what can I . . . do for you," he returned. As Curt finally dislodged his own spit and began breathing correctly again, Scott saw the park ranger's nametag. Charlie Tatterhorn.

"This body of water on the picture," Scott began as he turned back and pointed. "What can you tell us about it."

"Not much else than what you probably . . . read," Tatterhorn replied. His voice now seemed more human and his face gave a glimmer of a slight smile as if he was hiding the fact he enjoyed something. "It's really not much of a pond. You probably caught . . . the information on how it got its name."

As the big man spoke, Curt focused on his words. They were spoken clearly enough. Almost too clearly. His English wasn't broken but it also wasn't fluid. His sentences paused with sharp uneven cuts. Every word was delivered slowly and precisely but the unusual breaks left you hanging. Curt remembered his dad would speak like this sometimes and then get frustrated when his young son would attempt to finish his sentences for him. "Hey Curt. Can you hand me the . . ." After several seconds of silence, Curt would jump in "Socket wrench, hack saw, butter knife?" "No," his father would say with some degree of frustration. "I need the . . ." "Pot holder, shoe horn, TV set, tampon?" Curt would respond. Needless to say, dad didn't always appreciate the comments.

Now, as Curt stood looking up, he had no ambitions of pulling the same tactic with Charlie Tatterhorn. Curt wasn't even sure this man really knew how to form a complete smile and he wasn't ready to test his sense of humor. But the man did speak with authority and it wasn't just that he towered above most of the rest of mankind. He had a strong confident face, with tight eyes that lacked any give. These stern features backed the sentences that came from his mouth. Whatever this man said, you were going to listen, even if you had to be patient. So as the park ranger continued talking, the audience of two listened attentively.

"Yeah, we read the Spanish may have used it for a campsite the night before attacking the fort in 1565. Is there any physical evidence of this?" Scott asked, now more at ease.

"Well," Tatterhorn began after a long pause, "there's no physical evidence, but documented accounts from several of the . . . Spanish soldiers suggest it."

"Does the pond have any other significance?" Curt asked.

"No," Tatterhorn responded with an assurance that seemed odd. But his next sentence was unexpected. "May I now ask you a question? Why are you interested in the pond? It's a small . . . freshwater body of water that may have been utilized as a water supply for the French. The fort is where the historical . . . significance is. The pond may have seen soldiers for a day, but the fort was the . . . cornerstone to the settlement."

"No particular reason," Scott replied, not wanting to give the man any more information.

"Do you men realize," Tatterhorn began with his usual hesitation, "that the battle of Fort Caroline was the first armed conflict between European nations for control of the North American continent? If the French had won, Fort Caroline, not St. Augustine, might have become the nucleus of the oldest settlement in North America."

It seemed to Curt that Tatterhorn was trying to turn the conversation. Of course he and Scott knew the historical significance of the battle. Tatterhorn was feeding them a line of "park ranger information" that was probably preached to him on the first day of the job.

"Yeah, we're aware of the area's significance as it relates to St. Augustine," Curt said. "We're pretty well versed in local history. But are you familiar with any legends that might relate to Spanish Pond? We've heard of some crazy stories coming from the Timucuas that we're trying to gather some background information on."

The comment surprised Scott and he turned to look at his friend. Curt remained focused on Tatterhorn's eyes, which became slightly enlarged. Obviously, the question had hit some internal chord. There was a brief moment of silence that felt like a day and a half to Scott. Tatterhorn, who never lost visual contact with Curt, had drifted into some desolate place where he was floundering about, searching for the proper way to respond. But the words eluded him for a moment.

"Exactly what Timucuas did you hear this from?" Tatterhorn finally asked with a sarcastic tone that instantly made both men wonder about the ranger. It was the way he emphasized Timucuas, like their use, or misuse, of the term offended him.

Since Curt had already started construction on the road, Scott decided to lay the asphalt. "We've seen some documented accounts of a nearby village of Timucuas that was here around the time Fort Caroline was established. The information mentions a legend. A pond that held a secret power. It is referred to as . . . um . . ." Scott rummaged through his front right pocket looking for the scrap of paper on which he had jotted some notes after he and Curt had first talked.

"Here it is," he went on withdrawing the crumpled note. "It was called Terriousimee. It means . . ."

Tatterhorn interrupted. "It means *living bones*," he said in little more than a whisper. As the silence again prevailed, he stared right through Scott. His mind was searching through the vaults of all that he had learned and experienced in his lifetime. There was a bizarre glow coming from his face but it was not of happiness but of discomfort. It was apparent the man knew volumes about what Curt and Scott yearned to understand. It was also apparent this knowledge disturbed him. He had been perfectly content keeping the secret buried in the caves. Now these two had caused the legend to be retrieved and brought to light again.

"Mr. Tatterhorn, what do you know about the pond?" Curt asked politely.

"I know that Spanish Pond is not *the* Pond," he said reluctantly. His mannerism indicated he didn't want to reveal any more. His eyes looked down and to the side avoiding both men. It was then, Curt noticed that Tatterhorn was no longer speaking in broken sentences, just in a slow, laborious monotone dialogue. As the man realized his suggestive body language, he altered his gaze back to Curt, but it was too late. They were on to him and he knew it.

"Look, in case you haven't figured this out yet, I'm of Timucua descent," the ranger said. "I've heard many stories and legends about things. But that's all they are. This is the 20th century. I don't think a thousand-year-old tale about a pond is the least bit relevant to anyone."

"So tell us what you know," Scott said out of frustration.

Tatterhorn turned to the side shaking his head back and forth looking at the floor. "No!" he said. His voice bellowed out with force and then he turned and looked Scott dead in the eyes. "Some secrets should never be told. Knowledge can be very dangerous. You couldn't even begin to understand. Your minds are contained, trapped within preconceived walls between tangible things and imagination. Once something travels beyond the walls of reality, it plummets over the edge into the waters of fantasy. Except this is not always the case. The line is not always so defined and the consequences not so bountiful. Apparently, even your God makes mistakes."

Scott realized the struggle to get the man to talk had turned into an exercise in futility. He reached into his pocket and retrieved his wallet.

"Here's my business card," Scott said handing it to the large man. "It's got my work and home number. Please think it over. We're only asking these questions to solve a historical mystery, not to disrupt anyone's life or betray a Timucua secret. But as you said, it is the 20th century. Isn't it time we put some things to rest?" Scott's tone was friendly but deliberate. He didn't want to further upset the man.

For an instant Tatterhorn looked at Scott. Then he snatched the card and placed it in his shirt pocket. Without another word, he turned and walked away, leaving the center by swinging both glass doors open simultaneously. The metal release bars made a loud *clank* upon the impact. It was the equivalent of a wife slamming the bedroom door after getting into a fight with her husband. Except this wife was 6'10".

"Well, that went nicely," Scott remarked sarcastically.

"Quite the information storage depot," Curt added.

The men left the Visitors Center and make their way back to Scott's Blazer. It was 10 minutes till four and the heat of the early afternoon was continuing to blaze the landscape. On the way out Curt stopped Scott abruptly and motioned toward a sign. It was a historical marker set on their right at the start of the quarter mile dirt trail that led to Fort Caroline. After reading it, Scott turned to Curt with an inquisitive expression.

"You know, I had forgotten about that," Scott said.

The marker gave a brief history of the Fort, mentioning Ribault and Menendez and the significance of the area. More importantly, it contained a disclaimer regarding Fort Caroline itself.

On their way home, Scott and Curt decided to continue their exploration for another day. The situation had gotten too interesting to stop now. They made plans to leave Curt's car at Marvin and retrieve it in the morning.

Once the decision was made, the information on the marker became the topic of conversation. Unlike Fort Castillo de San Marcos in St. Augustine, Fort Caroline had been unable to stand the rigors of time. In fact, no physical evidence of the earthen fort with the wooden walls had ever been found. As they drove on, Curt repeated the wording on the marker "The National Park Service preserves the probable area where this early story of European colonization of northeast Florida occurred."

"Probable," Scott said, "but not conclusive."

"Yeah, and that translates into speculation as to whether or not this is the actual site. Of course if it's off, the pond, if it really exists, won't be near there either."

"You're very intuitive for a man in his late thirties," Scott said.

"Mid-thirties," Curt replied. "Don't start that age crap again. Remember, you're older than me."

"So what's our plan now?" Scott asked as the SUV sped down Butler Boulevard.

"Let's get on a three-way call with Marvin at 8 p.m. and see if those artifacts have come clean. Other than that, I'm open for suggestions," Curt said.

"I sure wish that Tatterhorn had told us what he knew. If he wasn't a park ranger I'd have beat it out of him," Scott said in a Sicilian accent, faintly resembling a line from "The Godfather." Then he began humming the theme song.

"Yeah, and then I'd be explaining to Kay why your asshole was sticking out of your ear."

"Maybe we can track down some other Timucua descendents. Let's ask Marvin's advice this evening when we talk."

For the remainder of the drive, the men chatted about the various events throughout the day and then the conversation turned to Curt's single life, Julie, and Scott's fish, or whatever it was, he'd hooked in the pond on Friday night that snapped his line. Traffic had just started to get heavy as Scott pulled the Blazer into the apartment complex. He stopped in front of Curt's building and the two said their goodbyes.

On Scott's drive home the traffic was beginning to show the familiar signs of rush hour. It was now 4:30 p.m. Scott suddenly felt very fatigued. The day seemed to have lasted a week. He was enthused yet drained at the same time. As he pieced together all they had encountered and learned, there was something hollow. An unclosed circle. An imperfect solution was all their discoveries had handed them and he started to question himself.

Why was he so intrigued by the so-called legend? Sure, there would be bragging rights to other archeologists and historians if they could prove the skeletal remains in the powder magazine were those of Pinot LeFlore, but it was more than that.

Much more.

Proving the identity of the poor soul would be interesting. More than that, it would make the front page of the St. Augustine Record. Hell, it might even be substantial enough to be a cover story on National Geographic, since more than 400 years of history were involved.

But as important a discovery as it would be, it was overshadowed in Scott's mind by the turbulent need to know and understand the secret of the pond. He had not mentioned this to Curt, at least not as assertively as he could have, but he knew there was breadth to the legend. Something about the body of water they sought contained a force, an entity, a calling, which was drawing him to it.

He felt it as sure as he had ever sensed anything. There was absolute certainty.

A cold chill crisscrossed through his chest as he thought about the skeleton of the fish-like creature he had last seen lying on Marvin's dining room table. It was so unnatural. He even wondered for a moment if it could be extraterrestrial. The next vision that fluttered through his mind was the creature circling aimlessly in a small pond. A swimming skeleton with teeth extended. It was hungry, craving a taste of its desired source of nourishment. Scott saw the picture as if he were watching it on his big screen TV. Then, it was gone.

His stomach churned and he thought for an instance he was going to be sick. Reaching over he flipped on the radio. The music seemed to settle his nerves and gastric unrest. Three more miles and he'd be home.

At 5:52 p.m. Scott was watching Katie flip through the channels of the 52-inch Panasonic. He was standing in the kitchen listening to Kay vent about work. He and Curt had reasoned it was best to keep their findings a secret at this time so her day occupied the conversation. Of course they didn't know what they had found and it would be silly, based on the evidence so far, to convince his wife they were hot on the trail of some great discovery. But the image of the skeleton continued to flash in front of his eyes as Kay's lips waggled slowly, losing volume.

In the background the screen popped with a new picture every second, prompted by the trigger finger of his younger daughter. In an instant, Scott caught a glimpse of a news flash.

"Katie, flip back to channel 33 please!" Katie turned to look at her father and he motioned at the TV with his forefinger. Katie hit the controls and backed up two channels. Kay was silent.

"Sorry honey," he said to Kay but never looked in her direction as he walked toward the TV and sat on the couch beside Katie.

"What is it dad?"

"Shhhh," he said.

The interruption to the regularly scheduled programming was to update the position, speed and projected landfall of hurricane Damon. It was still tracking a strike path just north of Daytona Beach. Its sustained winds were now pushing 97 miles per hour. The frontal system expected to divert it northward had not appeared. At its present pace, it would slash the coast of northeast Florida Thursday morning around 10:30.

"This is not good," Kay said slowly walking up behind her husband. She wore a here-we-go-again look.

"If this thing is still headed our way tomorrow, we're leaving," Scott said. "Why don't you give your sister a ring and see if they'd put us up for a day or two." Kay's sister Leila and her husband Barry lived in Pensacola with their two kids. They'd been after the Seymours for two years to come visit. Now seemed like the perfect opportunity.

As Scott climbed the stairs to his bathroom he thought about the pond, the bones and the fish. It was something he was anxious to explore further but he would not put his family at risk. The search for the truth would have to wait. So he and Curt would be delayed a few days. Big deal. It wasn't like the fish was going to swim away or the centuries-old legend would be altered. A category 4 hurricane, that stood a chance of turning into a category 5, was nothing to play chicken with. He'd inform Curt during their call later in the evening.

CHAPTER-FIFTEEN

At 6:08, Officer Loren Tankersley responded to a call at Ponte Vedra Beach. A surf fisherman had reported seeing what he believed to be a body in the tall grass just over the dunes in an area of land that separated Highway A1A from the shore. Probably a wino Tankersley thought. The homeless were known to make camp near the water and sometime sack out along the beach. There were few homes on this two and one-half mile stretch of coast and that meant no one to run them off.

As the officer pulled up to the site, he spotted a brown Ford Ranger partly decorated in rust parked in the sand just off the pavement. A man stepped out of the passenger side. He appeared to be fortyish with dirty blonde medium length hair under a Skoal baseball cap. His skin was dark as if he spent a considerable amount of time outdoors. He was wearing old blue jean shorts and a tank top shirt, and raggedy high-top tennis shoes that he'd probably bought in the late eighties. Officer Tankersley followed standard procedure by radioing dispatch of his position as he brought the squad car to a halt. He killed the engine and grabbed his nightstick as he opened the door and stepped out. The man slowly walked toward the officer.

"Are you Mr. Beam?" Tankersley inquired.

"That's right," the man replied. "First name's Jim."

Tankersley looked at him somewhat amused for a few seconds. "You're kidding," he finally said.

"Nope," Beam replied. The man obviously had little sense of humor as Tankersley stared at him waiting for the punch line that never came.

"So what did you see?" Tankersley asked.

"There's a man's dee-id body o'er that way," the man replied pointing to the sandy hill that blocked the view to the breakers smacking the beach on the other side.

"Are you sure it's a body?"

"Yep."

"Are you sure it's a dead body?"

"Yepper to that too."

"How do you know he's dead?"

"You ever seen 500 flies sniffin' around a live corpse?" Beam said with a solid dose of twang.

You stupid-ass redneck, I've never seen a *live* corpse, Tankersley thought to himself.

"Sir, would you show me where?"

"I reckon."

Tankersley followed Beam across the road and onto the sandy mound. Even though the dunes were only 10 or 11 feet high, the loose sand made the climb arduous and the officer, with his slick shoes, slipped twice. The second time he nearly slid back to the base.

94

"You need to git ye some good shoes liken these," Beam said kicking his left foot backward and accidentally pelting sand into Tankersley's face as the officer struggled to ascend the hill. "Sorry 'bout that."

Tankersley made no reply as he thrust his tongue between his lips and abruptly spit with his mouth still tightly closed to flip the sand off the tip. He wasn't so sure Jim Beam hadn't kicked sand in his face intentionally. Maybe the redneck didn't like the way he questioned him about seeing the corpse. Or maybe Mr. Beam just wanted a story to tell his friends down at Shorty's Bar and Grill about how he'd tossed sand in a cop's face and got away with it. Either way, Tankersley was more than a little annoyed as he reached the top of the hill and turned to question good-old-boy Jim when he spotted the shape that lay folded in the grass and brush eight feet below.

The body was bent at the hips and neatly compacted with the legs drawn up underneath. It was as if someone had made a Z and then smartly compressed it. The head was unseen, hidden by a clump of sea oats several feet above the body. Clothed in dark green shorts and exposed from the waist up, the multitude of insects stirred as an ocean breeze blew in. The wind suddenly cascaded the rank air over the mound into Tankersley's face. The putrid smell caused the officer to gag.

"Oh God," Tankersley exclaimed, covering his mouth with his hand.

As the officer took a step forward to gain a closer look, he lost his footing and began to slide. He desperately tried to gain his balance but failed and landed on his back, still flowing on a downward path straight for the corpse huddled near the base. The view was sickening as he quickly approached the mutilated body and realized the man was headless with dried blood caked about the neck and shoulder area. At his current angle and speed, his right foot, which he was attempting to use as a break, was about to plunge directly into the hollowed-out pus-ridden cavity where the head once resided. His left foot was sprawled in the air and useless to help avoid the collision. Acting more out of reflex than premeditation, Officer Tankersley picked his right foot out of the sand and lifted it into the air to match his left. To Beam, the cop looked like one of those stupid break dancers that spun on their back with their legs coiled up. An instant later, Tankersly crashed into the corpse as he let out an embarrassing scream that he would later deny when asked about the incident.

"It was the funniest goddam thing ye ever heared. I thought a tom cat had just hooked up with a stray that had chopped his balls off!" Beam would later tell a bevy of officers and reporters.

But at the moment, Tankersley was screaming from a combination of grotesque fear and unimaginable pain. The adjustment he had made to assure his foot didn't bury itself all the way from the body's neck through its chest had one very negative effect. It left Tankersley's testicles on a straight line with the torso's crimson red shoulder blade. As he made contact, the feeling was immediately excruciating and his vision blurred from black to white as colored spots danced all around. In his agony, he saw the flies scurry about.

Then he passed out.

He lay there motionless with his legs spread to either side of the corpse's shoulders. To Jim Beam, the image was priceless. If he'd had a camera, he could have convinced his buddies that the officer was hiding the man's skull up his dumper.

"Talking about gittin' hee-id," Jim Beam chuckled as he proceeded back to his truck to find a pay phone and call the police again.

At 8 o'clock, after informing Kay he would be taking the next few days off with or without the hurricane's arrival, Scott phoned Marvin.

"Hello!" Marvin answered as if he was annoyed by the interruption.

"Gee . . . did you wake up on the wrong side of the city?" Scott asked.

"Oh it's you. I was wonderin' when you were going to call." Scott could tell instantly that the man was not himself. His speech was slow and dull.

"Are you okay?" Scott asked with earnest concern. "You don't sound well."

"My ulcer's acting up. Of course the three shots of Captain Morgan probably didn't help." Then his voice went low and serious. "Scott, I got something to tell you."

Scott was surprised at Marvin's tone. He was not sure he *wanted* to hear whatever the professor had to say.

"Hold on a moment. Let me bring Curt on." Scott activated the three-way calling function and dialed the number. Curt picked up on the first ring.

"Jeez, I thought you forgot about me. You're late."

"Hold on, Curt. Let me bring Marvin on. He's got some news for us and he doesn't sound particularly happy about it."

Scott clicked the receiver down and then released. "Marvin? You there?" Scott asked.

"Yeah, I'm here. You got Curt?"

"Yeah, I'm on. What's going on Marvin?"

"After you two left this afternoon and I finished my errands, I came back home and started researching the Internet for any information that might help determine what kind of skeleton you found. Searching the normal sites related to mammals, reptiles, and fish proved useless. So on a whim, I started looking up Indian legends, based on what you told me. I came across something unusual. You boys know I'm a man that believes in fact not fiction. I've devoted most of my life to proving what was and how it was. For the most part archeology is an exact science. Cultures live, they fade away and, if they're not well documented or preserved, they have to be rediscovered by future generations with shovels and pick axes. Of course with technology, we have sophisticated sonar equipment available as well."

Scott could tell the Captain Morgan was making Marvin a bit more talkative than usual. But he also sensed Marvin's seriousness. The professor was not himself.

Curt's patience was not as lengthy as Scott's and he broke in, "Marvin, what exactly are you trying to tell us?"

"I found your fish."

To Scott, the words were surreal. The impact must have jarred Curt as well. Except for the high-pitched background hum that seems to live in every phone line, there was absolute silence.

Marvin continued speaking very slowly. "There was a picture of a fish, with meat and skin of course, that is a perfect match. I've studied it for the last several hours and I'm sure of it."

"Well don't keep us in suspense," Curt began, "What kind of fish is it?"

"It's called the Kilgotian. I found it within the context of an Indian legend." Marvin's tired words trickled out. He sounded like a man who had just finished the Boston Marathon and needed a good night's sleep.

"Marvin, are you all right?" Curt asked.

"Yeah, I'm fine. Just a little shook up."

"Kilgotian," Curt began, "what kind of species of fish is that?"

"It's not any kind of species!" Marvin said, as if each question was an annoyance.

"Marvin settle down," Scott broke in. "We just want to know what we've got."

"I'm sorry," he replied with true sincerity. "What I mean is this isn't a species. It doesn't even really exist! It's a character in a myth. There's no substance, no reality. Certainly, no basis for such a creature." The men could hear Marvin make a deep sigh. "But there's no denying what you've found."

"Marvin, tell us about the myth." Curt said.

"It seems to fill in some of the gaps in your manuscript. Not all, but some. The Kilgotian is described as a one-of-a-kind. The myth mentions how it was created by the white man's god to help maintain the earth's varying species during a time when the world was covered in water. But afterward, it took up affiliation away from God. Aligned with other forces."

"Any idea what the hell that means?" Scott asked.

"Think about it, Scott. Think about Sunday school lessons. Covered in water. Doesn't that sound like the Great Flood?" Marvin replied.

"So this was Noah's pet fish? Do you know how absurd that sounds?" Curt asked. "Besides, you make it sound like this thing is a beast. God wouldn't have created such an unholy thing."

"What are you talking about? He made diamond back rattlesnakes, great white sharks and black widow spiders. He's responsible for tornadoes, famine, and flesh-eating diseases. Heart attacks, Alzheimer's and cancer. God seems to have wandered away from the controls while mankind bitterly presses on with all kinds of dangerous horrors lingering just beyond the horizon," Marvin snapped.

"OK Marvin, take it easy. What has you so unnerved?" Curt asked.

"I told you. It's this goddamn fish. The fish is described as the lone inhabitant of a pond. A fish capable of bringing back *Soulful Ones*."

The recognizable term instantly rattled in the ears of Scott and Curt. "Marvin, Soulful One was a phrase mentioned in Curt's manuscript, but it's not defined. Does your information describe what it is?" Scott asked.

"Not in detail," Marvin's words sounded a bit more confident and secure. "It seems to be a living being who, for whatever reason, died an unnatural death."

"Like a French Huguenot sliced and diced on a secluded beach," Scott added.

"So, what you're saying, is this fish somehow assists with reincarnation," Curt asked.

"If that's how you interpret 'bring back'. For all we know, bring back might be a spiritual awareness, not a tangible entity. I only offer that because of the term Soulful One," Marvin added. "Somehow your LeFlore brothers factored this fish into their revenge strategy. I'm sure of that now."

"So how does the myth describe this power? How exactly does the Kilgotian bring someone back?" Scott asked.

"The myth is unspecific about the process or the outcome. But it offered strong warnings."

"Again, I don't understand what you're worried about Marvin," Scott said. "It's just a legend. A story. For the sake of argument, and forgetting rational thought, let's say the fish was real and had certain powers. The damn thing's pretty much lifeless now. It's a series of connected bone structures lying on your dining room table." But even as Scott spoke, he wasn't sure if he was trying to convince Marvin or himself.

"Yeah, that's what I told myself, too. But then a thought occurred to me. About an hour ago I went into the kitchen and filled a glass half full of water. I poured the contents on the spine near the tail. Not more than four or five ounces I tell you. I swear to you, as crazy as I know this sounds, the water had no sooner touched the bone than flesh formed across it. Before my eyes, I watched the underlying meat build and then the scales develop on the surface. About a three-inch square patch. I promise you I had not had a damn thing to drink when this happened. I sure as hell have now," he said with a trace of nervous amusement in the words.

There was a brief silence.

"And then the most amazing thing occurred," Marvin's voice was trembling. "The fish, or at least the part that had materialized wiggled! It was moving its tale! I don't know how else to describe it." Marvin's tone was disconcerted and his energy fading.

There was utter quiet. Neither Scott nor Curt knew how to respond.

"One more thing that just occurred to me," Marvin said. "Funny, I hadn't even remembered this until now. There was a distinctive odor when this happened. That is, when the fish seemed to almost come back to life. It was a familiar fragrance. The smell of aged fluid. Kind of musty smelling. It had the scent of water in a glass left by your bed that had been there for a while. You know, that smell your nose picks up just before you take that nasty sip in the middle of the night. The smell that says "put this water down the drain and get some fresh stuff." I didn't remember that until just now."

"Marvin, I don't know what to say," Scott began. "This just sounds so unreal."

"I wish it was, Scott."

"What happened next?" Curt asked in an excited tone.

"About 15 seconds after it started it stopped. Then the flesh faded and it was all skeleton again. It looks just like it did when you saw it last."

Again there was silence.

"It's not that we doubt you but this sounds like something out of the Twilight Zone. I keep waiting for Rod Serling to jump in." Curt said.

"I know, Curt. I've sat in my recliner for the last 35 minutes questioning what I saw. But it was real. I swear to you both. I have to admit it. It scared me so bad I have the damn fish in the oven right now."

"Please tell me you're not cooking it," Scott said trying to ease the tension all three felt.

"No. But I have it on warm. I don't want to take any chance on a shred of moisture touching this thing."

Curt nearly laughed, barely covering his mouth. But it was too late. Marvin picked up on the snicker.

"You might think it's funny but you didn't see what I did."

"Marvin, we took a trip over to Fort Caroline this afternoon and ran into a park ranger who seemed to know more than he let on. A towering man named Charlie Tatterhorn. You ever heard of him?" Scott asked, still trying to digest Marvin's story about the skeleton.

"Nope."

"He said he's of Timucua descent," Curt said.

"Then he's probably a liar," Marvin responded bluntly.

"Why's that?" Scott asked curiously.

"Because the Timucuas were wiped out by disease in the 1700s. When Spain relinquished Florida and St. Augustine to the British in 1763, only a single Timucua Indian is listed on the manifest of the natives shipped to the town of Guanabacoa in Cuba. I guess it's possible he's a descendent, just not probable. Even so, he wouldn't have much Timucua blood."

"Interesting," Scott said.

Again there was silence before Marvin spoke up. "Boys, I'm going to go. I think I'll drink about half the bottle sitting in my liquor cabinet while I get up to speed on Damon. I didn't watch the six o'clock news but I did record it. I want to catch the latest update. It's got me a little worried. Almost as much as that damn fish."

Scott now had more questions for Marvin on exactly what had happened with the fish, but he decided to leave the subject until the man was more rational. "I can tell you this," Scott said "Damon's still heading in our direction. The Seymours will be leaving town tomorrow night if there's no change in its course."

"I heard that," Curt chimed in. "By the way Marvin, did that artifact come clean yet?"

"I checked it a while ago and it still needed to soak some more," Marvin replied. "I placed it in a fresh batch of solution. It should be ready when you guys get here in the morning."

"Sleep well, Marvin. We'll see you in the a.m.," Scott said in closing.

"Sleep is not something I suspect I'll get much of this evening," Marvin said in a flat voice and then dropped off.

"Scott? You still on?"

"Yeah."

"What do you think?"

"I think Marvin had a bad dream," Scott responded. "He's never said anything so absurd before. It bothers the hell out of me. This man's not some whack."

"I know, Scott." Curt could tell his friend was extremely concerned and with good reason. The professor's disposition was not simply odd, it was extreme. "We'll clear things up in the morning. I'm sure there's a very good explanation for all this. See you tomorrow."

As Scott placed the phone on the receiver he was struggling with the notion of the Kilgotian fish and the sanity of Marvin Sellon. This was a man who based everything upon facts. In Scott's mind, for Marvin to go off on such an obvious fictional fling seemed to indicate some sort of mental disorder.

Yet, Marvin's account seemed strangely within the parameters of Scott's reality on this Monday evening, and that bothered him to no end.

Twenty-two minutes later Scott's phone chirped and Marvin's number flashed on the caller ID. Scott had logged into his company's LAN and was busy responding to work e-mails.

"Hey Marvin," he answered as he finished typing a response to the Chief Financial Officer's question about the fourth quarter financial outlook.

"Scott, I don't even know how to say this." Marvin's voice was littered with cracked words. "He's dead."

"Who? Who are you talking about?" Scott asked excitedly. His mind suddenly jolted from work to the more horrid truth of a person's demise.

"Tucker Chalet."

Scott was dumbfounded. The words hit him the way humidity slams your face on a July afternoon in Florida after leaving the comfort of an enclosure cooled by central air conditioning. It's a brutal, deflating feeling that zaps energy from every cell of your body.

Tucker. He and Curt both knew Tucker. He and Curt *had* known Tucker. Tucker Chalet was a fellow novel archeologist. But more than the weekend variety. Tucker loved the field of science with such passion, he would have made a living out of it if he felt it could sustain his lifestyle. The four men had participated in the San Luis dig last fall in Tallahassee. Mission San Luis de Apalachee was the western capital of the mission system in Florida from 1656 to 1704. At one time, it had a population of more than 1,400 Apalachee Indians. The community was described as having the appearance of a small Spanish city. The settlement had been forced to evacuate in 1704 after numerous raids by the British and their Creek Indian allies. Fortunately, the San Luis location was never lost. In 1820, officials visited the site and recorded descriptions of the ruins. Ongoing archaeological digs at the site have surfaced many aspects of the populace.

The men had spent four days together at the site. During daylight they excavated Spanish and Indian residential areas. Each evening they were out on the town, a new restaurant every night. While their time on the dig turned up few artifacts, it did allow Curt, Scott and Tucker time to become friends. Marvin had known Tucker for a number of years, first becoming acquainted at a National Archeologist Society Meeting in Delray Beach in February of 1997.

The man was a true optimist who shared their passion for uncovering the past. He had taken up the hobby in his late twenties as a diversion from the hardship of his wife leaving him at the altar on his 26th birthday. On his thirtieth birthday earlier this year, Marvin, Scott and Curt pooled their money and had a stripper appear on Tucker's doorstep at dinnertime. Tucker had a strong wit and was amused with the ploy declaring himself a "very bad boy" to the lady in the short black dress.

Because Tucker lived in Orlando, the foursome had gotten together only 5 times since the San Luis de Apalachee dig. The most recent, a social event involving beer and oysters in the spring when Tucker had arrived in town unexpectedly on business for his financial consulting firm. Scott and Curt had come to embrace Tucker as their third amigo. No offense to Marvin, but the professor's age difference kept him somewhat distant from some of their distasteful humor and liberal thinking.

But Tucker had fit right in. And now, from Marvin's information, he was gone.

After an endless pause Scott spoke up, "Marvin. What happened?"

"I don't really know. I saw the news and they had a late breaking story of a man found just off Ponte Vedra beach by a surf fisherman. It was horrible . . . just horrible." Marvin was losing his composure again. Scott could hear the tears forming. His voice was ragged and ranged in and out. Scott suddenly felt his own emotions give.

"What did the news say?" Scott asked with a kindness not displayed earlier when asking about the Kilgotian fish.

"He was cut up. Oh, God help us, he was cut up and then . . ." Scott could hear Marvin pull away from the phone. No words were spoken. There was no need. Through the distant buzz he could hear the man convulsing and then coughing. It was a slurpy, gutting sound that Scott hadn't heard since he had had a wicked case of influenza in the spring. As Marvin heaved and groaned, Scott waited patiently on the line.

After about two minutes Scott spoke up, "Marvin, are you okay?"

Marvin replied immediately, "Yeah, I'll be fine." The professor was resting with his mouth on the microphone silently building courage to continue without buckling to his emotions. Now Scott had jump-started him back into the conversation and he was ready to give it another try.

The words strained out of his mouth, momentarily lodging in his throat and then expelling with a burst of air. "Tucker was decapitated."

Again there was silence. It was as unexpected as anything Scott had ever experienced. Run over by a bus, killed in a plane crash, even gored in the running of the bulls, all of these would have been within the realm of predictability. But decapitation? This was unthinkable. It was the most heinous of outcomes.

Scott finally broke the silence, "What happened? What was he doing in Ponte Vedra?"

Marvin didn't so much answer the question as he made a comment, "I didn't even know he was in town. Don't you think he would have called? God, maybe if he had, this wouldn't have happened."

"Marvin, what happened?" Scott asked again very slowly.

"He was near the beach. On the small dunes that border the shore and A1A. He must have been looking for shark's teeth or some nonsense like that. Goddammit, why didn't he call me?"

"Keep going," Scott interjected, urging Marvin on.

"They found his body on the inside of the dunes and his . . . his head about 30 feet away in a bed of sea oats."

"Are you sure it was him?" Scott asked.

"Yeah, they immediately notified his mother after making positive identification and, therefore, were able to release his name. I replayed the tape several times. I watched it hoping I had misheard the name but as they removed his body, I saw the gold bracelet he always wore on his right wrist. It was him. Why the hell didn't he tell us he was in town?"

"Did the police say if they think it was premeditated?" Scott asked.

"They didn't speculate. They did mention there were unusual circumstances."

No kidding, Scott thought.

"I got the impression they meant something unusual besides the way he was killed. But they didn't say. Whatever it was, wasn't disclosed to the press."

"I don't know what to say. I'm in shock," Scott said. "Marvin, are you going to be all right tonight?" Scott wasn't actually sure if *he'd* be all right but he tried to be strong. "Between your simmering fish and now this news, you've had a pretty tough evening."

"Yeah, I'll be fine. I'm taking a few more sips of whiskey and then I'm going to bed. I still can't believe Tucker is dead. I just spoke to him last week on the phone and he didn't say anything to me about coming up here this week. Dammit why did this happen? Who would do such a thing?"

"I don't know," Scott replied. "I can't imagine."

"I'll talk to you guys in the morning when you get here. Goodbye."

Scott said goodbye with a shaky voice. The butterflies in his stomach had turned into condors ripping their way through his intestinal tract.

After Scott hung up, he immediately called Curt and broke the news. It was not a long conversation. Curt's reaction mirrored Scott's. By the end of the call, they reconfirmed that Scott would be by to pick Curt up by 8:30 a.m. the next morning. Then Scott went upstairs and climbed straight into bed. He had considered taking a beer and the half-full bottle of Jack Daniels into the bedroom but didn't want to answer any questions from Kay or his kids. Such action would surely have aroused interest and concern. Right now he wanted neither. What he sought the most was quiet. Kay later went upstairs to see what her husband was doing but after three words from Scott she returned to the children downstairs. The sentence came bitterly and tearfully from Scott's lips and Kay felt his sorrow. Not so much for Tucker, whom she had met only once, but for her husband who was grieving for a lost friend. After hearing the words she closed the bedroom door behind her and cried silently in the darkness as she descended the stairs.

"What's daddy doing?" Cody asked beaming up with that innocent face from the bottom of the stairs.

"He's resting honey. He's had a hard day," Kay said with a stoic expression.

For Scott Seymour, the next few days would not get any easier.

CHAPTER-SIXTEEN

Scott was already downstairs continuing to contemplate the senseless death of Tucker and the day's activities when the phone rang at ten minutes after six. Kay was in the shower and the kids, with the exception of Lindsey, who was in her room applying face paint, were still snuggled in their beds.

As Scott stood at the kitchen counter sipping his coffee, the phone rang and he reached for the receiver on the wall. He did so with some trepidation as the last few experiences with Alexander Graham Bell's invention had brought both unbelievable and disheartening news. Now the combination of caffeine and sugar pinged off the floor of his stomach lining as he answered. "Hello" he said hesitantly.

"Is Scott Seymour there," a man's voice asked.

"Yes, this is he."

"This is Charlie Tatterhorn. We met yesterday at Fort Caroline. I'm the park ranger you talked to."

"Yes, I remember" Scott said encouraged the man had called.

"Have you seen the morning paper regarding the man killed at Ponte Vedra?"

"No," Scott replied feeling his stomach tumble. "But I know about it. It was on the news last night. He was a friend of mine, Mr. Tatterhorn." A quick image shot through Scott's mind. It was a picture of Tucker looking up from a hole at the dig site of San Luis Mission. His face was covered with sweat and the attached dirt. It had reminded him of a distasteful imitation of Al Jolsen's *Mammy*. The thought had always brought a smile to Scott's face. But now it was replaced with a barren expression.

"I'm sorry to hear that," Tatterhorn said hastily and with little sincerity. "But I have to ask you something?"

"Go ahead," Scott said, half-paying attention, half-staring at the image of Tucker's dirty face. In a grim thought, it was bitterly ironic that the man's face would now be placed in a casket and covered with a ton of dirt.

"What do you really know about the legend you questioned me about yesterday?"

Scott hesitated as he absorbed the question and shed the image of Tucker's face. "All I know is my friend and I came across some documentation that described a pond near Fort Caroline that contained some magical power."

"What else do you know? Did you find something?" Tatterhorn spoke the last word with an escalating tone.

"That's all I know. What do you mean find something?" Scott said, trying to conceal his false innocence. Scott had never been a good liar and he was thinking about the fish skeleton.

"Don't patronize me! You're lying!" Tatterhorn said firmly.

The man's directness temporarily caught Scott off guard. A moment later he was on the offensive, "Mr. Tatterhorn, this conversation is about to end unless you want to tell me why you called."

"Don't hang up," Tatterhorn said in a manner that made Scott suddenly understand the man was scared. "Your friend who was killed. I know more than the news released."

Scott kept his mouth shut. He had Tatterhorn backpedaling and wanted to keep him off balance. Each millisecond of silence bought Scott more control. "What do you know?" he finally asked in a slow, confident tone.

"I have a friend who's a deputy with the St. Johns County Sheriff's Department. Tucker Chalet wasn't killed in a very conventional manner."

"I'm aware of that Mr. Tatterhorn."

"Here me out. Not only was his death a result of being slashed about the chest and stomach, he was also decapitated in a fashion that could only have been accomplished with a sharp heavy object."

"A sword?"

"A sword similar to what you may have seen yesterday on display in the Visitors Center at Fort Caroline. My friend tells me, based on the medical examiner's autopsy, there hasn't been a murder by such means in over 33 years anywhere in the United States. The last occurred in Arizona when a thief broke into some eccentric weapon collector's home in Tucson and was surprised by the owner returning from an out of town trip. The thief had grabbed the closest available weapon, which happened to be a 17th Century Manchurian sword hanging on the wall, and had run the owner through before chopping his head off."

"So what are you trying to tell me?" Scott asked. "This type of death is rare. I understand that."

"What I'm saying," Tatterhorn replied as if his patience were being challenged, "is this was a very unusual choice of murder weapon. And there's something else. Something you won't see regarding this case on the nightly news."

"And what's that Tatterhorn?"

"The marking carved into your friend's back."

A chill ran across Scott's shoulders and down his left arm. As the tingling subsided, Austin the cat slid between his legs barely running its extended fur across the hair on Scott's leg. Scott leapt into the air.

"Jesus Christ cat!" he yelled as he settled back down. Austin turned and glared at the lunatic human before sitting down and nonchalantly extending a back leg for grooming.

"Seymour, are you all right," Tatterhorn asked sarcastically.

"Fine, fine. Just the family feline attempting to induce heart failure."

"What?"

"My cat, Tatterhorn. Go on. What markings?"

Scott sat down on one of the three bar stools on the side of the kitchen island counter. He reached for his cup and had just taken a sip when Kay surprised him from behind.

"Who are you talking to?" she asked with a whisper.

Again he jumped. "Dammit!" he said. The remark was not aimed at Kay but it was taken that way. She gave him a dirty look and went about making a cup of coffee. Again Tatterhorn spoke up.

"Seymour, what's wrong there. Are you in a three-ring circus?"

Scott ignored the comment.

"The medical examiner found strange markings on Tucker Chalet's back," Tatterhorn said. "It was determined they were inflicted after death. And not just random slash marks. It was a precisely detailed symbol. My friend faxed me a sketch of it."

"What exactly was it?"

He could almost hear Tatterhorn swallow hard. In the background, Kay clinked a metal spoon, swishing the water, milk and instant coffee together. For a few seconds, it was the only sound coming through either of Scott's ears.

"Tatterhorn? What was it a picture of?" Scott asked again a bit louder. Kay turned to stare at her husband and mouthed the question, "Who are you talking too?" she had not slept well and Scott's failure to answer was sending her toward a bad mood.

Finally Tatterhorn spoke. "It wasn't a picture. It was a symbol. The symbol of the French Huguenot cross."

As the words sunk in, the mental images over the last several days cluttered Scott's brain. Assembling the puzzle was not an easy task and it was too early for his mind to be functioning well enough to be efficient.

"Are you sure?" Scott asked.

"Of course. It's a pretty common symbol when you work at the only French Huguenot historical settlement in North America. I recognized it in an instant. Why someone would carve it into a corpse's back is what bothers me. To my knowledge, this was never a practice of the Huguenots. I would feel better if it had been. Then we'd probably just be dealing with a copycat murderer. Someone who read some history books and replicated the crime. But that's not the case."

"Just curious, Tatterhorn," Scott said. His mind was becoming clearer. "Did your friend contact you, or did you contact him?"

"I called him when I saw the news. He faxed the sketching to me late last night. There's something very evil about Tucker Chalet's death, Mr. Seymour."

"Why would someone link an ancient French sect to such a grizzly deed?" Scott asked.

"Your guess is as good as mine. Unless . . . Tatterhorn caught himself before he disclosed more than he wanted Scott to hear.

"Unless what, dammit? We played this game yesterday. What is it you're not telling me?" Scott demanded. The combination of the story, yesterday's discoveries, Marvin's fantastic account of the fish and Tucker's death all pressed down on him like an anvil.

"Well, it's almost like there's a strong proponent of the French Huguenots on the loose," Tatterhorn replied. "It's just a little coincidental that you and your friend are asking me about the pond.

"Tatterhorn, I will admit this," Scott said, "we discovered information that describes a fish that inhabited a body of water next to Fort Caroline. The Kilgotian. The documentation mentions it has the ability to bring back Soulful Ones. But I have no idea what *bring back* means. Nor do I know what a *Soulful One* is. I don't know if that means it can reincarnate something that is dead or some other fictitious nonsense. Our sources also don't describe how the fish does whatever it does." Scott still did not feel compelled to disclose to the ranger that he and Curt may have actually found the remains of the Kilgotian. He surely wasn't going to mention Marvin's story from last night.

"Mr. Seymour, you do know quite a bit. In light of your friend's death, doesn't any of this information bother you?"

"Based on what you've just described about the cross on Tucker's back, it sure as hell does." Scott paused. "Tatterhorn, be honest with me. Do you know where the pond is? The one described in the legend?"

There was no delay. It was as if the time for piece-meal sharing of information had passed. The big man feared few things in life but the notion of a vengeful Soulful One resurrected after 400 years was enough to cause concern. He, like Scott, really didn't know what a Soulful One was, but he had heard the story from his ancestors since reaching adolescence. They always spoke about the topic with reverence and fearful tenacity. Soulful Ones were presented as entities brought back to earth that were not supposed to exist at this time. They reeked of ominous fortune and calculated terror. As these thoughts circled inside Tatterhorn's mind, he shuddered and answered Scott in a distressed voice, "Yes, I know where it is. Meet me at the Visitors Center at one o'clock this afternoon."

Scott was amazed the man had given in so easily. "Well OK. We'll see you then."

"One more thing," Tatterhorn said, "be prepared."

"Prepared for what?" Scott asked inquisitively as the phone clicked and he was left listening to an off-key dial tone. It suddenly occurred to him that Tatterhorn's speech pattern had been crisp and clear. The stuttering so noticeable yesterday was gone.

Scott hung up the receiver and was met by Kay's concerned gaze. "What was that all about? Who is Tatterhorn?" she asked before taking a sip.

Not wanting to go into much detail, Scott responded. "A park ranger that Curt and I met yesterday. He has some crazy ideas about Tucker's death."

"And you're going to meet him somewhere to discuss? What exactly is all this about?" Kay asked.

"Obviously the man is some kind of lunatic. I have no intention of meeting him. I only said that to get him off the phone," Scott lied.

A look of relief flowed over Kay's face as Scott made his way back upstairs.

Two hours later Scott picked Curt up at his apartment. The sun was already beaming brilliantly and the morning had begun to heat up. Curt climbed into the Blazer carrying a thermos full of coffee and two plastic non-spill cups.

"Can I hook a brudder up?" Curt asked in a gruff New Jersey tone after fastening his seat belt.

"You have the worst Mafia accent I've ever heard. But I will take some coffee," Scott replied as he backed the vehicle out of the parking space.

Curt unscrewed the lid and began pouring. "I still can't believe what happened to Tucker. I caught the story on the news this morning. It's just terrible. The man couldn't have had any enemies. There's no way it was premeditated. I think he was in the wrong place at the wrong time. God, this world has gone beserk."

Scott ignored Curt's comment. His mind was elsewhere. "Guess who I got a call from this morning?" he said as he turned at the red light and picked up speed. He didn't allow Curt a chance to respond. "Charlie Tatterhorn. He started asking me some odd questions and then wanted to know what we really knew about the legend. Something's bothering him."

He took the coffee from Curt's extended hand and carefully placed it in the console cup holder. The steam rose above the surface. "He even asked me about the death of Tucker. Of course he didn't know we knew Tucker until I told him. He commented about how strange it was for someone to be killed that way, with what appeared to be a sword. He said it had been 33 years since anyone else had been murdered in such a manner in the US."

"So what was he getting at?" Curt asked. "For a man who said very little yesterday, he sure opened up to you this morning."

There was a distinct hiatus in Scott's response, which allowed Curt time to take a sip. Then he looked at his friend who remained fixed on the road ahead. "What I'm going to tell you is what Tatterhorn told me. I spent the entire ride over to your house trying to determine a reason he might lie to us and I came up empty." Scott's tone was extremely serious.

"What is it?"

"He told me he has connections with the St. Johns County Sheriff's Office. They sent him a drawing of the markings on Tucker's back."

"Natural markings?"

"No. Carved markings. Apparently by the attacker." As Scott spoke, he turned to face Curt and saw the strange vacant emotion wash over his friend's face.

"Oh my God," Curt whispered. "What was it? What did it say?"

"It wasn't words. It was the French Huguenot cross. Tatterhorn is positive. And here's the capper, I honestly think the man believes we may have a revenge-minded 16th century Frenchman among us."

The sound of the radials skirting the road and the wind whipping off the windshield filled the otherwise audible void.

"He actually said that?" Curt looked at Scott in complete amazement.

"Not in so many words but it was implied."

"Scott, what if some or even all of the legend is true?" Curt said, gazing out the window at the passing cars on the highway. "What if a soul man, or whatever the hell it's called, could be brought back. Haven't you felt a little uneasy since Sunday when we discussed this whole thing? I know I have. I almost wish we hadn't gone in the powder magazine yesterday morning. What if something we've done had some adverse effect? Kick-started some chain of events? A lot of shit has happened to us in the last 48 hours."

For a moment Scott was quiet. He wanted to tell his friend how preposterous he sounded. How completely ludicrous his ramblings were coming across. They were two blue-collared professionals, securely locked in reason with logic as their ally. He wanted to tell Curt this, even laugh out loud. But he couldn't. As irrational as the man sitting to his right was this Tuesday morning, Scott could not deny that he had spun the same absurd rhetoric through his thoughts. The truth was he had felt strange ever since Curt had chosen to let him in on the manuscript. It was an ominous feeling. But it was also a sense of incompleteness, of unanswered questions. What could or did the Kilgotian Fish really do? Could it possibly come back to life as Marvin had described? Where was the pond it had once inhabited? Were the bones found in the powder magazine those of Pinot LeFlore? What was the unknown artifact they had discovered with the skeleton? What was Tatterhorn so paranoid about? And most important, what happened to Tucker? What *really* happened to Tucker.

"A lot has happened in the last couple of days," Scott finally said. I'm counting on today to get some answers. Tatterhorn wants to meet at Fort Caroline at 1 p.m. I think he's going to show us the pond."

"What'd you do? Threaten him?"

"Nope. As I said, I think he's scared."

"Well, I got a secret for you Scott. So am I."

The Chevy glided along US 1 enroute to Marvin Sellon's house. It would be another 35 minutes before they arrived. The skies were suspiciously clear and the sun sparkled in the distance. It was a beautiful early fall day in Florida. A slow, yawning breeze trickled through the trees lining the highway and the wheels of the Blazer made a melodic whistle as they spun.

Out in the Atlantic Ocean, 638 miles to the southeast, the force of Hurricane Damon was ripping apart the coastline of a small, uninhabited island called Teandria. With sustained winds now topping 124 miles per hour, the storm had developed a life of its own. With gritting teeth and a tremendous overhand punch, it bashed the shore and inland areas destroying everything in its wake, and threatening to tear the small island off the face of the earth and dump the patch of sand and rock hundreds of miles away. The destruction was infinite and unspeakable.

Soon the eye would pass over the tiny island. What once had been a lush and tropical forest of palms, sycamores and teistras would be replaced with a barren terrain as tree trunks and limbs floated off shore gathering in clumps in the surf.

When Damon finished with the island's demise, its torture complete, it would gather its lethal talents and head back into the open sea, settling into a 12 mile per hour pace, its course transfixed on the eastern seaboard of the United States.

By Thursday morning, St. Augustine was targeted as the likely recipient of Damon's distasteful hospitality. By then, it would be a force so strong, some wondered if God himself could stop it.

CHAPTER-SEVENTEEN

At 9:15 a.m. Scott steered the Blazer into Marvin's driveway and found the man where they often did, sitting on his front porch chair. But today Marvin was not reading the paper or easily tapping his feet to some internal music. Today, he was sitting very still, eyes intent on watching the street traffic. His hands folded across his lap and his feet anchored flatly on the wooden deck. Scott suspected Marvin was nervous, anxious to have some friendly visitors.

"Hey Marvin, are you all right," Scott asked, climbing out of the Blazer.

"Hell no. Poor Tucker's been murdered, I got a skeleton that really takes to water and I hardly slept a wink. When I did, that damn fish was chasing me. It was the worst nightmare I can ever remember having. And I mean EVER!" his words were so loud they unnerved Curt.

"It's okay, Marvin," Curt said, placing his arm around the professor's shoulder and turning him in the direction of the house as the three men entered the living room through the wide open front door. The air that morning had been cool and as they walked inside the change in temperature was negligible.

Curt steered Marvin to the couch and Scott sat on his other side. "We've got some other things to tell you about Tucker's death and the pond. Do you think you're up to it?" Scott asked.

"No, but go ahead anyway. None of this makes sense anyway so whatever you know may help things fall into perspective." As the man spoke Scott caught the foul smell of the liquor from the night before.

"Don't count on it," Curt said grimly.

Scott recounted his conversation with Tatterhorn, except for the part about a French Huguenot trotting around town. When Scott was done, Marvin leaned back on the couch and let out two heavy sighs.

"Boys, I'm afraid. All of this is spooky. Tucker's death and then that fish." As the word *fish* hit their ears, both Scott and Curt looked away as if not wanting the man to notice the disbelief in their eyes. Marvin's breathing became intense and quick. "I swear to you, that damn thing started to come alive. I know what you're thinking. Old Marvin's flipped the channel. Only got one oar in the water, got one wheel in the sand, whatever other reference to being crazy you want to make. I'm telling you it came alive, or at least would have if I'd poured more water on it."

Scott and Curt were silent. Both looked down at their shoes. It wasn't that they completely discounted what Marvin said but what he described was simply not possible. It defied every moral and ethical constant of life and death. Reading about a legend of reincarnation (if that's what *brought back* meant) was one thing, witnessing such an earth shattering anomaly was truly unthinkable.

Was it possible Marvin had seen such a counter-biblical process? The overwhelming probability was that he had imagined it, or maybe even dreamed it. That would be a better explanation than what the man was suggesting. Besides, he had admitted to having nightmares about the fish. Maybe he had dozed off and had one of those realistic dreams. There had to be a logical explanation.

"Boys, please trust me on this one, Marvin pleaded. I don't have the nerve to prove it to you. I can't watch that thing start moving again. It could give me a heart attack. I'm simply asking that you believe me. As crazy as it sounds, you have to believe me." This time his words were calmer, yet no less filled with passion. His intelligent side had reminded him that yelling would only present an image of a lunatic. As he spoke, his eyes searched out Scott's and then Curt's. Although he didn't see the acceptance he'd hoped for and needed, he did see the possibility of blind faith from his friends' eyes.

"Marvin, we do believe you," Scott said. His words fell on the professor's ears with applause. But the next sentence sent his emotions on a roller coaster ride to the edge of his wits.

"But we do want to replicate what happened."

"Scott, I'm begging you, please," Marvin said as he grabbed his friend's hand and held it between his, "I can't take it!" The ghastly expression on Marvin's face was like no other look Scott had ever seen the professor display. The man suddenly wore a haggard, painful grimace. The lines on his face buckled and shadows fell between. He could have passed for 98 years old. Water pooled in the corner of his eyes and his pupils appeared as if they'd just been dilated. His lips were flat and firm. There wasn't a single joke in the world that could have chiseled a smile on Marvin's solemn expression.

"Marvin," Curt began calmly, "Its all right. We want you to leave the house for a few minutes and let us sort this out. Scott and I discussed this on the way here. We believe you but it's just something we have to do."

"Did I tell you about the sounds? The horrid, demonic sounds that goddamn thing made? Did I?"

"No," Curt said lowering his eyebrows as he thought back to the conversation of the night before.

"Well, I'll tell you this. I never want to hear it again as long as I live. Those sounds killed 10 years off my life and I'm near the end of my rope as it is! I don't want to hear them again!"

"Marvin. Take my keys and go to the store or go to the park. I'm parked behind you. Here, take them," he said to the professor as he placed the keys in Marvin's right palm.

"I'm just stating for the record that I tried to warn you, but you stubborn men have to see and hear it for yourselves. Well you better wait until I've been gone about ten minutes before you get a drop of water near that skeleton. I want to be well out of earshot range. You hear me?"

Scott and Curt nodded in silence.

"Just be sure to have him back in the oven when I return. I'm not coming back for 45 minutes so don't look for me before then. I want no part of this."

"Understood," Curt said.

Scott and Curt stood on the porch and watched the Blazer pull away. As it rounded the corner at the far end of the street, the two looked at each other, gave a small nod, and went inside.

After dropping Tina off at school on Tuesday morning, Sherri had promptly returned home. It was 8:42 a.m. when she pulled in the driveway of her rented three-bedroom, ranch style home. The residence was several blocks from the heart of St. Augustine's historical district yet the neighborhood was relatively serene, magically hidden from the bustle of tourism a short stroll to the east.

As usual, she had to be at work at 11:00. This left the normal hour or two to lounge around reading the morning paper, watching Maury Povich or embracing some form of exercise, which lately she had neglected. The adult responsible thing to do, and what her conscience attempted to persuade her to do, was to take a walk on this pleasant fall morning. But she struggled with the notion and, to counter the voice of reason, opened the St. Augustine Record in search of some fascinating news story or intriguingly decadent scandal to capture her attention. Nothing. Placing the paper on the coffee table, she hit the controls and the TV boomed to life. Too early for Maury. Ten minutes to go before he would be discussing topics such as, "Women who sleep with their brothers but are married to their uncle's sheep," or some other inspiring intellectual conversation. Sherri only watched it for the comedic value. At least that's what she told herself.

Realizing any good excuses had been exhausted, she resolved herself to the obvious conclusion. "Shoot," she said with a chuckle for only the goldfish, Smutley and Penelope, in the 10-gallon aquarium located in the dining room to hear. "I guess I should at least take a brisk stroll." Actually, there was no reason for her to be concerned about her health or shape. Sure, walking a few laps around the block was exercise but she got plenty of that chasing Tina around the park and through their daily routines. She was in the prime of her life. Her figure was shapely and proportionately sound, and her legs were lean and firm. She knew that by wearing the right fitting low cut shirt and tight jeans, she could turn every guy's head in a 200-yard radius. But she was way beyond the shallowness of flaunting her looks. At 33 years old, she had her priorities clearly aligned and they started and ended with Tina. She hadn't even dated since moving to St. Augustine and God knows she was hit-on by a variety of men from all walks of life. Something about a stunning redhead appeals to the male species, her mother had told her when she had turned fourteen. It wasn't that she was immune to her desires. Far from it. She frequently wrestled in the middle of the night with sexual dreams and fantasies that ranged from passionate, caressing sexual adventures with men she knew, to the extreme, down and dirty no-name, no-questions-asked interludes with strangers. But she had kept these needs at bay, deciding instead to dedicate her energies to Tina. Until now she had been quite content with this lifestyle. Yet lately, she had felt the urge for male companionship growing stronger. She knew the time would soon come when she'd be ready to settle down again. But she would make sure it would be the right man. And not just for her.

She clicked off the TV and rose from the couch. Passing the kitchen table she grabbed her keys. She went through the front door, turning to place the key in the lock to secure it. Once done, she bounced down the steps and headed south down the sidewalk as the morning glow filled her with instant warmth. It was days like this that made her wonder why anyone would choose to live in snow country. The light breeze and radiant sun made her feel vibrant. The caressing air flowed over her skin and she smiled. It was a great day to be alive.

Three houses down, she made an absolute decision to take a stroll every morning for the next couple of months or until the weather was not so crowd-pleasing. It was ironic that Damon was bearing now on North Florida, yet today was sunny. She'd heard the climate that preceded a hurricane was typically picturesque. At least that is what the locals who visited the gift shop had told her. It was the proverbial calm before the storm, Sherri thought.

Sherri had already made plans to evacuate. Charlene was coming up from Cocoa Beach to meet her and Tina and the three were going to drive to Tallahassee this evening. In an odd sort of way, Sherri was looking forward to it. They had already booked a room at the Travel Lodge and it would be fun spending a few days with her sister in the state's capital. Being a college and government town, there were plenty of nice restaurants and points of interest to visit. Besides, she'd never been there and welcomed the travel. It would also be an opportunity to spend more quality time with Tina.

As Sherri continued down Ballaton Street she mentally went through the checklist of things she needed to accomplish in preparation for departure. After work and picking up Tina they would swing by the grocery store to get some sandwich meat. Sherri had not planned on preparing dinner. Sandwiches along the way should do. She would also buy a 12-pack of Cokes and a pack of juice cartons for Tina. At home, Sherri would make sure all electrical appliances such as the clocks, TVs and radios were unplugged. She'd need to empty the refrigerator in case power was out for any extended length of time.

After unplugging the house with the exception of the aquarium (shutting off the filter would have killed the fish and there was no way to take them with her), Sherri would secure the windows with masking tape (like it would really help) and load her suit cases and personal items she had packed last night, into her car. Sherri and Tina didn't have a tremendous amount of personal items, so it was not a monumental undertaking. The rented house had come with furniture and Sherri had placed her sofa, loveseat, stereo cabinet and assorted other pieces in storage upon moving to St. Augustine. She had spent about an hour and a half Monday night packing her clothes and Tina's things into empty boxes. Once loaded, they would be ready to roll. Charlene was due to arrive around 5:30 and they planned to hit the road by 6 p.m.

But for now, there was nothing for Sherri to do besides finish her walk, go home and get ready for work. As she made her way left on Girrand Avenue, she approached a young couple pushing a baby carriage with twins. She smiled at the infants as she passed. For an instant, the motherly twinge hit her and she felt a mild sadness. Tina would always be her baby, but she wouldn't mind becoming a mother again someday. But she had already decided it would only happen in wedlock. Sure, she had friends who had chosen to become single moms. It was just not a decision that suited her. She was old fashioned in that she believed in the unity of family. These thoughts began to depress her so she changed mental topics and again focused on the activities she needed to accomplish before leaving town. She wanted to make sure she hadn't neglected any important checklist items.

At the intersection of Girrand and Maitland, she cut through the parking lot of the Gate convenience store and gas station and happened to overhear a couple bantering with the counter clerk at the island between the pumps. The station was empty with the exception of the Plymouth Breeze with the Hertz Rental Car sticker on the back bumper at pump number three. The couple seemed to be having difficulty communicating with the attendant and Sherri instantly recognized the language. She walked up to the counter behind the elderly man and woman. They appeared embarrassed and the lack of compassion from the attendant annoyed Sherri.

"I'm sorry," the clerk said, "I just don't understand what you're saying!"

As the man looked at the clerk and sighed, he prepared his next attempt at communication. Sherri could see the lines of concern creeping upon the forehead of his wife as she turned her head sideways.

Before the elderly man could speak, Sherri tapped them both on the shoulder.

The couple turned to face Sherri. They instinctively knew she was there to help. They looked at her as if she was their savior. Relief darted over the face of the woman and the man smiled.

"Attends un instant, je vais expliquer au préposé. *Hold on a minute and I'll explain to the attendant*," Sherri said.

"Oui, merci. *Yes, thank you,*" the man responded.

Sherri turned toward the man behind the counter. "They were asking where they can get on the bus tour for the city. It's on Westwide and Ring Blvd right?"

"Yeah. I'm glad you came along. I couldn't make heads or tails over what they were askin'. They're French, right?"

"Yeah. I'll tell them how to get there."

"Thanks," the attendant said as he admired Sherri's smile . . . and more.

Sherri looked at the couple and motioned for them to head back to their car. On the way she began talking. "Vous recherchez le tour guide de la ville en autobus, n'est-ce pas? Je vous ai entendu que je passais près de vous. *You're looking for the City Tour Bus, right? I overheard you when I was walking by.*"

"Oui. *Yes we are,*" the man replied as he withdrew the keys from his pocket and stared intently into Sherri's eyes.

"Vois-tu lumiere de circulation un quartier plus loin? Va jusque là et tourne a dronite. C'est Westwide. Le tour guide demarre à partir de la deuxième lumière que tu appercevras. Ca Sera l'intersection de Westwide et le boulevard Ring. *See the traffic light one block up? Go there and take a right. That's Westwide. The City Tour bus departs from the second light you'll come to. That will be where Westwide intersects with Ring Boulevard.*"

The couple thanked her and went on their way. Sherri turned down Maitland and headed home quickly. She felt good that she was able to assist. Those six years of French came in handy, especially in a town full of tourists year round. As she approached her front yard the sky became overcast and the air very still. The sound of traffic three streets over could be heard as the clouds gathered above in rapid succession, stacking to form a blockade on the horizon. She entered her house considering the dramatic difference in the weather since she'd departed.

As Sherri crossed over the foyer into her living room the temperature in the house caught her by surprise. It was cold. Very cold. She made a beeline for the air conditioning control panel in the hallway and checked the setting. It was aimed at 76 degrees but the temperature inside was 57! The unit was not running, but she flipped the switch to off anyway. It must have malfunctioned, she thought. Even with the cloudy skies, the temperature must be at least in the mid- to high-70s outside.

She moved to the hall closet and found a light pullover turtleneck sweater that she donned. That was better. It didn't do much to warm her but at least she felt better covering the pointed nipples beneath her shirt. Not that anyone else was there, but she had an image of the 10-year-old paperboy stopping by to collect and getting an eye full. Or possibly his eyes poked out. Sherri chuckled out loud at the thought as she walked into the kitchen to check the answering machine and make a cup of instant coffee.

She walked past the refrigerator and checked the machine on the counter. Five messages.

"Gee, I must be important. Let's see how many handsome professional gentlemen called today," she said to herself with a coy smile. She hit the play button and then turned to get a mug from the coffee tree to the right of the sink.

> *Click.* "Hey, this is Nora. Can you bring your grandmother's recipe for lemon meringue pie to work today? OK. Thanks." *Click.*

Sherri turned on the cold water, filled the cup and placed it in the microwave on high for 1 minute and 30 seconds.

> *Click.* "Hey Sherri, its Charlene. Just wanted to confirm I'll be there by 5:30. I'm bringing an extra large cooler so we can take some drinks. I even got some juices for Tina. Ok? Well, I'll see you this afternoon. Oh, I almost forgot, Cindy Woodson, you remember Cindy from high school? She just recently had triplets. I can't even imagine. I think I'd have a nervous breakdown. Feeding time must be a circus. Well, got to get ready. See ya later." *Click.*

God I love my sister, but the woman sure can ramble, Sherri thought staring at the microwave as the cup slowly rotated inside.

> *Click.* "Hello, this is Jeremiah with United Pest Control. We need to schedule your annual termite inspection. We'll try reaching you again this afternoon." *Click.*

Jeremiah? A bullfrog is gonna take care of my bugs? That's pretty amusing. The bell sounded on the microwave and Sherri reached in to retrieve the cup.

> *Click.* "Hello, this is Tracy Steele, Tina's homeroom mother. We're looking for volunteers for the fall festival coming up in November. I'll try you later." *Click.*

She placed two spoonfuls of sugar and one spoonful of coffee in the cup and then turned toward the refrigerator to get the whole milk.

> *Click.* "You are in the water." *Click.*

The voice on the machine was queasy and grainy. It was not spoken so much as it was sung in a haunted warning manner. At the exact moment she heard the words, Sherri gasped as her eyes fixated on the refrigerator door where the scenic ocean artwork of her daughter hung proudly. As before, the small fish were swimming along the bottom and the starfish and crabs were still clinging to the sea floor. The seagulls and pelicans (if that's what they were) glided just above the surface, basking in the bright glow of the big yellow ball. But what startled her was the image that now filled the void she had almost questioned Tina about yesterday afternoon.

It was not very large, but its arched back and meat-shredding teeth bore the signs of a killer. Its brown scales and fins accentuated its large, glossy white eyes that seemed to roll in the two dimensional picture.

As Sherri began breathing again, she realized the magnificent detail in which the creature had been added. No accessories such as glitter or buttons were used, but the drawing itself appeared to be done in chalk or charcoal. Sherri had seen similar pictures by artists along St. George Street. Some of these street artists, who made a meager living drawing portraits of tourists, were rather good. The fish now residing in her daughter's picture matched their professional work.

Sherri stood gazing at the picture. On one hand she was uncomfortable that Tina would add such a carnivorous entity to the tranquil scene. Yet, on the other hand, she was impressed by the sheer talent behind the artwork. Then realism struck her. There was no way Tina did this. As much as I'd like to think she could, it just didn't happen, she told herself. But how did it get there? When did it get there? Sherri reflected back to the morning's activities and tried to recall seeing the picture. She couldn't. When did it get there? Was someone in the house now?

The thought paralyzed her. Then she recalled the last message she'd heard on the machine. The shock of seeing the fish had almost caused her to forget the voice and the words. Sherri nervously walked over to the caller ID as blood dispensed erratically through her veins. She shivered. The house was remarkably quiet. Checking the answering machine she was amazed to see the final call had not registered. The last number she saw was for Tracy Steele. She checked it again, running through the series of calls.

    1 - Clayton, Nora – 8:52 a.m.
    2 - Charlton, Charlene – 8:54 a.m.
    3 - United Pest Control – 9:01 a.m.
    4 – Tracy Steele – 9:04 a.m.
    End of Messages

She moved her hand back to the answer machine and pushed the play button again. As the messages played in order, she walked back to the picture pinned on the refrigerator by the magnets; two Coca Cola, one Shaft Point Elementary School and one Budweiser frog magnet. Relocating the holders, she freed the picture and sat down at the kitchen table examining it. In the background she heard Nora, her sister, Jeremiah, and Ms. Steele leave their messages. When the homeroom mother finished, she raised her head to prepare herself mentally for what would come next. She uncontrollably held her breath as she listened to the silence.

And silence.

And more silence.

The machine clicked and shut down automatically.

What the hell? She rose from the table and walked over to the device on the counter and played the messages again. This time she concentrated intently on each word. As Ms. Steele ended her sentence with " . . . you later," she felt her body tighten waiting for *those* words. Nothing. A few seconds later, the machine cut off again.

Sherri slowly backed away from the counter staring at the machine. A charge thought went through her. Did I really hear a voice say, "You are in the water?" Maybe I said it. I heard it at the same time I spotted the toothy fish that magically jumped into Tina's 2nd grade art class assignment. Maybe that's it. It came from me. I was so stunned at what I saw that I blurted it out. Sure. It was plausible. It was a little spooky to think her mouth had submitted such words without her brain authorizing their release. But what about the tone? The raspy, ominous tone. Where the hell did that come from?

Sherri stood in the middle of the kitchen in a daze. Again the notion that someone else might be in the house struck her. *How else can the picture be explained?* Fear eclipsed her and she ran to the table. She grabbed the picture and her keys and bolted out the front door. Once outside, she turned quickly to secure the dead bolt and, out of the corner of her eye, saw a shadow flash through the high window on the door. In panic, she struggled to remove the key. It jiggled loose and she sprinted to her car. Climbing in, she fired up the engine and was off, screeching the tires as she drove down Maitland 25 miles an hour faster than allowed. A small bead of sweat ran down her forehead as she glanced at her wristwatch. It was 10:08 a.m. So she'd be a little early for work. She'd left her smock at home but Nora would loan her one even if she had forgotten to bring grandma's homemade recipe for lemon meringue pie.

She didn't stop breathing heavy until she turned into the Gift Shop parking lot.

As her shift began and customers streamed in and out, Sherri occasionally looked at Tina's picture. She kept it partially hidden under the counter where the large item bags were kept. She had elected not to share the events of her morning with Nora or any of the others for fear she'd sound ridiculous. And it was ridiculous. Clearly, there was not a message from anyone stating, "you are in the water." She had imagined it. As for the picture, well, there had to be a reasonable explanation. Pictures just don't draw themselves.

As the morning passed, more acceptable answers came to mind. She finally singled out the one with the most promise. Tina must have traced the picture from a book or magazine. That was it. What a simple answer. And I'll confirm it at 3:30 p.m. when I pick my daughter up. I'm so stupid. In my panic, I wasn't thinking right. God, am I really a blonde? She grinned at this inner comment.

As the day wore on, she mused several times about what had happened and how she had allowed herself to became so afraid.

Scott and Curt stood in Marvin's kitchen looking at the oven door. The dial was set on "bake" and the oven temperature at 200 degrees. Scott flipped the switch and the interior illuminated. He bent down to take a look. There it was, nice and dry.

The creature was on a huge, dark green oval plate. It reminded Scott of the fish skeletons he had seen on *Tom & Jerry* after the cat had eaten the good parts (which was everything but the bones). This one was nowhere near as white as the cartoon version but it was intact and clean.

Scott examined it through the glass searching for any trace of skin, scales or flesh. Anything to substantiate Marvin's claim of the extraordinary event from the previous night.

But the creature was lifeless. No epidermal covering, no motion. Nothing, but the skeletal structure looking as sturdy as it did yesterday afternoon when they'd left it on the professor's dining room table.

"How exactly do you want to do this?" Scott asked standing erect and grabbing two potholders.

"All the way."

"Are you sure you want to go there? We could just sprinkle a few drops and then see what happens. You know, kind of a pre-test?" Scott said looking for his friend's concurrence.

"Huh uh," Curt replied, shaking his head from side to side. "I want to see the whole thing." Deep down, so did Scott. He did not attempt to dissuade Curt any further.

Curt leaned forward without hesitation and slowly dropped the door. The warmth rapped him in the face. He momentarily leaned away to avoid the heat. Then, using the potholders, he proceeded to pull the middle rack out and reached for the plate, holding firmly to each end. He turned and laid it on the counter beside the sink. The skeleton was peaceful and dormant, as residual remains should be. It was hard to believe this thing would do anything but lie there when he and Curt applied water.

In an odd visual, Scott could see the creature's soul in some remote, unexplained place, laughing at the two humans playing with its bones. What they were preparing to do, the experiment they were prepping for, was, by every measure of humanity, insane. Scott actually had a brief notion that he was dreaming. Surely his conscious self wouldn't be performing such an act.

But here he was. Standing in Marvin's kitchen with Curt about to conduct a surreal test. This type of scientific endeavor only occurred on the SciFi channel. But Scott felt he owed it to Marvin to proceed. In some ways he hoped the beast would flap around like, well, like a fish out of water. At least it would vindicate the professor's claim. He would hate to think his old friend was slipping away, possibly from a combination of age and senility.

The two men stood perfectly still staring at the plate.

Scott was waiting on Curt to do something.

Curt was waiting for Scott. At the same moment, they turned to look at each other and started laughing. The absurdity of the situation had struck Curt as well. Scott put his right hand up to his forehead and then ran his fingers across his closed eyes as if to straighten up. This was no time for humor. It was a time to be serious. But damned, if it wasn't funny at the moment. As Scott gained his composure, he looked back at the skeleton and clenched his lips closed. Then he spoke.

"So what do we do? Sprinkle some water on him?" he said as he opened up the top drawer below the counter and found a basting syringe scattered among the various kitchen utensils. As he retrieved it from the drawer, a spatula and a can opener fell loudly to the floor. He held the syringe up to Curt for concurrence.

"Nope," his friend said with an absolute tone as he bent down and gathered the fallen items. He rose and returned them to their place.

"How then?"

"The tub."

"The tub?"

"Good idea. I never thought of that," Scott said with enlightenment. "We'll baste him in the tub and then stand back and see what happens. If the damn thing really does materialize, it should be contained there. Remember, Marvin said it made some horrific sound. This way, we could get out and close the door." All of this seemed very rational to Scott. He was pleased that Curt had arrived at this solution -- until Curt spoke again.

"No. I want to fill the tub and drop him in it.

"Curt, you know I'm having a difficult time with this. I want to believe Marvin but the other side of me keeps screaming it's impossible. But if this goddamn thing is capable of coming back to life, I'm not so sure submerging him in water is something we should do."

"If we're going to do this, then let's do it right," Curt said. "These last couple of days have been too weird to dick around now. I want to know the truth. With each passing hour I have this irrational gnawing at my gut. I can't even begin to describe what that means. I just know something's not right."

Again, Scott couldn't argue with Curt. He dropped his eyes and looked down. Scott too felt the foreboding. There was no other term to describe it.

He sighed. Still donning the potholders, Scott firmly grasped the plate and turned toward the hallway that led to the bathroom. As he spun, the remains glided off the platter as if they were practically weightless and gracefully fell to the floor like a piece of notebook paper, fluttering one way and then the other in a zigzag pattern. The skeleton slid to a halt on the vinyl floor at their feet.

"I keep forgetting how light this thing is," Scott said as he knelt down and placed it back on the plate lifting it by its skull. Curt clamped a hand over the top, careful not to make contact with the warm plate, and the two awkwardly made their way to the bathroom in a straddling, waddling motion, Scott moving forward and Curt backing up.

Once inside, Scott placed the plate to the left of the sink on the counter after Curt cleared away Marvin's shave cream, a toothbrush in the holder and a can of Right Guard. Scott sat on the closed toilet seat lid as Curt bent down and turned the bathtub knob to cold. The water blasted forth hitting the drain and splashing back up into Curt's eyes. He briefly shook his head and then wiped the water away.

"Nice shot. No water pressure problems in this neighborhood," Scott said with a smile.

Curt gave him a dead pan look and reached down to stop the drain. Slowly, the water began filling the tub. The sound was nearly deafening.

"Are we just going to chuck him in when it's filled?" Scott asked loudly.

"You're askin' me like I'm some sort of reincarnation expert," Curt replied. "But yeah, basically I thought we'd just toss it in. How stupid are we going to feel if this thing just sinks to the bottom?"

"Much better than I'll feel if it starts swimming around."

"Good point."

As the water gushed from the faucet, the two men waited patiently. On the counter, the Kilgotian sat quietly waiting its turn.

CHAPTER-EIGHTEEN

At a small patch of woods near the Nuestra de la Leche Shrine, Reece LeFlore sat panting in rapid succession. A wild, disturbed look cascaded across its hollow face. The pupils danced madly in the white background. The confusion was overwhelming as he latched a hand to the side of his head and his skull trembled like a Magic-Fingers bed. He tried to muffle a tortured moan, but the suppression increased the pain surging through his head and chest. Beside him lay the sword that had hung on the wall of the residence of the first enemy he had slain. He still remembered the satisfyingly horrific expression his victim had provided prior to slumping lifelessly. Since then, Reece had successfully managed to slaughter three other enemies on his way to the Spanish settlement that beckoned him to the south. Two men and one woman. For him, there was no guilt. Man, woman, child, it made no difference. The enemy was the enemy. And every chance he got he would run his sword through or decapitate them, commonly taking his time and making the event linger on. With each death, there had been a strangely satisfying resolve that made him want more. And his hunger for revenge was insatiable, growing by the minute.

Starting with the first, he had made a decision to carve the French Huguenot cross into each corpse as a declaration of victory, an arrogant signature. *Let them fear the Huguenots. Revenge is upon them*!

Now as he sat on the hard dirt, scattered memories since he had arisen soared through his thoughts.

So many things seemed bizarre. He thought about the odd fortifications he had seen while traveling south along the shore. There were numerous structures positioned on the beach, apparently guarding against sea attacks. The roads were made out of some sort of flat, solid stone instead of dirt and the vegetation was sparse. Machines glided on wheels rapidly along the strips of stone. The clothes of his victims had also been very queer, like none he had ever seen. The material was foreign to him, some foul Spanish invention, to be sure. Although, all of this was highly unusual, he was not dissuaded. A compelling motive carried him on. The part of the brain that would normally have kicked in, to question such abnormalities and to caution him, had not returned.

Earlier in the morning, while hiding behind a wooden fortification, he had overheard a lady saying the first words he understood. Since coming back, he had not heard any language he had been able to interpret. Certainly, the Spanish tongue was unfamiliar to him. But on the other side of the wooden barrier, where the machines were moving about (the machines he had seen often since returning and assumed were Spanish war creations), he had heard the woman with the red hair speaking French and this confused him in several ways. He was surprised to hear anyone speak his native language and she had used words he was unaccustomed to, like *toor bus* and *interseckshon*. But the woman could not be trusted for she spoke a combination of French and another tongue, Spanish to be sure. She was, no doubt, a spy.

He had carefully followed the red haired lady and watched her go into the structure not far from where he now was resting. As the aches swelled and then subsided in his skull, he leaned forward and glared at the ground. The realization was that this place was overrun with enemies. For the moment, he was one against many. But that would change.

There was a strong sense of urgency. A will that ruled his thoughts. He felt it as much as he felt the hatred for those who had massacred his people. Those who had mercilessly driven their swords through the mass of defenseless French compatriots lined on the desolate beach.

The force drew him like a homing signal. Beckoning him on. Calling him to raise the sword of vengeance and continue the morbid denial of Spanish infestation.

As his mind spun in turmoil, indecisive about his next move, he filed the image of the red haired lady and the importance she might lend to his efforts in the lone section of his mind still within his control. The remainder of his head was bustling with a saucy yellow fluid flowing among the conduits and nerve endings. Reality for Reece LeFlore had ended in the 16th Century. What now occupied this vessel was a creation that mankind could never conceive and God would never acknowledge.

CHAPTER-NINETEEN

The tub was full of cold water and Curt closed the spigot.
"Should we say a prayer or something? "Scott asked in an attempt at humor.
"Dearly beloved," Curt began, "we are gathered here today to witness this unholy matrimony of skeletal structure and flesh. A meeting of skin and bones. A union of not only legend but of insanity. If anyone objects to this, please speak now or forever hold your peace."
"Thank you Reverend. And yes, I object the hell out of this."
Scott looked at Curt and then picked up the plate. The potholders were no longer necessary but he could still feel the warmth radiating. The skeleton slid easily to the side almost falling off but Curt quickly pushed it back toward the middle. It made a high pitched scraping noise as he did.
"Ouch!" Scott shouted. "Why don't you just run your fingernails on a blackboard."
"None available," Curt said.
Curt shifted against the wall and promptly backed into the towel rack. It tagged him in the small of his back.
"Crap!" he said softly as he took a half step forward and reached around trying to rub the sore spot.
"Now I know why Kay sometimes refers to us as two-thirds of the Three Stooges."
"Nice," Curt replied still attempting to massage the area.
With a sigh, Scott looked down at the fish's skeleton on his lap. In a moment they would know whether to package up Marvin for the funny farm or throw out everything mankind knew about life and death. Either way, the complications would be extreme and the resolution challenging to accept.
"What are you waiting on? Dump him in"
"I'm scared. I'm scared, Curt. We don't know what this thing is. We don't know what's going to happen." Scott could feel his intestines tighten and grip relentlessly.
"But we have to know."
"Why?"
"Because I'm scared, too. I'm afraid we've already gone too far to stop now."
"Too far to stop what? What are you talking about?" As the words leaped from Scott's mouth he already knew the answer. Tucker. Tucker's death was too damn coincidental. And the fact that the symbol of the Huguenot cross had been scarred into his back just made it all the more conclusive. Somehow, what they had discovered, maybe even actions they had taken, had awakened a force. Scott was sure of this. As sure as he was that Professor Marvin Sellon was sane.

Curt stared at Scott and then Scott looked down at the plate again. "I know, I know," he said giving in to the silence.

"Let me do it," Curt said. He took a step forward and lifted the skeleton from the plate. Scott sat on the commode.

"Oh," Scott said. "I almost forgot. Marvin thrust this in my hand as he left." He stood up after putting the plate on the counter and reached into his jeans and removed a small plastic case. Inside were four off-white semi-round objects. He popped the lid open and removed two and handed them to Curt.

"What's this?"

"It's wax. Remember? Marvin swore this thing made some God-awful noise. Put them in your ears." Still holding the skeleton in his left hand, he used his right to insert one wax ball into his left ear and then one in the right. Scott did the same."

"Can you hear me?" Scott asked.

"Of course I can. These don't make you deaf."

Scott placed his middle finger back to his left ear and sunk the wax in deeper. He was not satisfied it was working effectively. After the adjustment, he mockingly mouthed some words to Curt without speaking.

"Very funny. I know you didn't say anything. Enough foreplay. Let's get this over with," Curt said turning to sit on the edge of the tub. The tub was an oversized garden variety with rose colored ceramic tile bordering all three sides that extended to the ceiling. On the back wall, 18 inches high, started a series of opaque window squares that formed a large X. This pattern allowed a considerable amount of light to enter the bathroom during the day.

Curt held the fish by the spine and took a deep breath as he shot a quick glance at Scott and then back to the water. In his mind, his plan was to slowly submerge the skeleton, guiding the tail in first. If the thing did develop flesh and an attitude, he would prefer those teeth would form last and be farthest away from his fingers. Those protruding shredders looked too damn menacing to play around with. He wanted no part of them.

As he stretched his arm over the surface, he began to lower the fish slowly into the still water. It was within four inches of the surface when it began to hum and quiver. It was like holding an electric razor. Subtle, constant vibrations. Curt hesitated, startled by the noise and movement. Then there was another sound. A distant jingle. Closing his eyes and slowly opening the heavy lids he continued lowering. He had prepared himself for oddities such as this and was not about to stop. Two inches from the surface, Scott grabbed his arm.

"Stop!" he shouted so Curt would hear through the wax mufflers. "The phone's ringing!" Curt lifted the skeleton and placed it on his lap and took a series of deep breaths. Scott had startled him.

Scott ran from the room removing the wax from his left ear. The portable phone was on the kitchen counter. He remembered seeing it there earlier and got to it by the fifth ring. The built-in caller ID told him it was a familiar number.

"Hello."

"Scott? Is that you? Your voice sounds funny." It was Marvin calling from his cell phone.

"Yeah, it's me. What's up?"

"You haven't put any water on that thing have you?"

"No. You interrupted us." Scott almost blurted out they were putting *it* in water – not water on *it* but decided that might set off further objections from the professor so he pushed on. "Why?"

"I was thinking about a couple of things. First, did you remember to put your ear plugs in?"

"Yes, sir," Scott said not particularly happy with the question and slightly annoyed with the professor's concern at the moment. He was treating Scott like an elementary school student and not a grownup. "Marvin, let me get going so we can do this. Don't come back for at least a half hour."

"Wait! Wait! There's one other thing I wanted to mention."

Scott didn't say a word.

"You still there?"

"Yeah, yeah. What is it?"

"The fish seems to possess a natural energy. A very volatile power. In the information I found yesterday, it described an enormous force the Kilgotian was able to cultivate and channel. Some of the wording almost made it sound as if it was combustible."

"Combustible?" The word caught Scott's attention. "As in explosive?"

"Who knows?"

"So what are you telling me?"

"I'm telling you to be careful." His words were sincere. He spoke with a grandfatherly tone that made Scott regret his impatience with the man.

Scott took a breath. "We will, Marvin. I promise. Now let me get back to Curt. We'll see you soon." There was a click on the other end of the line.

Scott returned to find Curt still on the edge of the tub staring into the water. The skeleton was back on the plate sitting at his feet. "Combustible?" Curt asked with raised eyebrows. He had overheard part of the conversation.

"Marvin's just worried."

"So am I. Before you stopped me I could feel that thing shaking. You heard the humming sound, didn't you?"

Scott nodded.

"Just to be on the safe side, let's modify our strategy." Curt came off the ledge and passed by Scott. He took a right and strolled down the hallway to the closet at the far end. Scott followed. Upon opening it, Curt was faced with an assortment of jackets, windbreakers and suits. On the floor there were several boxes sealed with masking tape, a stack of National Geographic magazines (Marvin use to quip he only bought them for the nude pictures of the natives in New Guinea), a pair of snakeskin boots and an old set of golf clubs. The clubs, consisting of a full set of irons and four woods, were in a brown rustic looking bag nestled in the back left corner. Curt wondered if they were antiques. He reached in and pulled out a nine iron.

"What are you doing? You going to chip him into the tub?"

"Just want some distance between me and the vibrator when it hits the wetness," Curt responded.

The two walked back to the bathroom. Curt propped the club against the outside doorframe. Scott stood back and watched his friend enter and then followed. Looking down he immediately noticed the water level had dropped, maybe as much as two inches.

"Looks like Marvin has a slow leak. Should we add some more?" Curt asked.

"There's enough."

Curt reached down and lifted the skeleton. With his left hand he grabbed the maroon towel from the rack and wiped the edge of the tub dry. No need to let this thing get moist and have a head start just in case the impossible does happen, he thought. Throwing the towel on the floor he carefully placed the fish on the edge of the tub, laying it long ways. "Back up," he said to Scott, motioning his hand in an up-down manner. Scott retreated into the hallway. Curt came out of the bathroom and then reached in to pull the door to, leaving it halfway open.

He turned and clutched the handle of the golf club and slid the head along the carpet of the bathroom until it reached the base of the tub beneath the skeleton. He sat just outside the doorway flush against the wall with his right arm extended inside holding the club. Scott stood over him watching intently through the opening. Curt reached for the doorknob and pulled it toward him, leaving a gap of about six inches for his arm to stretch through. Scott moved to his left to get a clear view of the Kilgotian.

"Are you ready?" Curt asked. He was focusing on the position of the iron's head in order to align it directly below the fish.

"No. But do it anyway," Scott responded breathing quickly. His head was beginning to churn and his thoughts scattered. For a millisecond the light in the bathroom seemed to vanish. It was replaced by blotchy darkness and purple dots that careened madly through the air. This kaleidoscope image lingered and Scott felt lightheaded. He realized he was hyperventilating. He leaned back against the hallway wall to steady himself and hit it harder than expected.

"What's the matter?" Curt turned and looked up. He had raised the nine iron up to the skeleton and was about to shove it in when the sound drew his attention.

Scott paced his breathing and his head cleared. Colors came back into normal perspective and he wiped the sweat from his forehead. He let out a sigh and blinked several times. "I'll be fine."

Curt turned to look back at the tub through the opening where his arm was inside. He raised the club head again and angled it up to the middle of the skeleton. He had positioned the spine of the fish toward the outside so it would fall in right-side up. He had no idea if this mattered.

His tactic was simple. He would push the fish into the water and then drop the iron inside and slam the door shut. Curt didn't have to explain any of this to Scott, as it was obvious. The word *combustible* had alarmed both of them.

The club head hovered in the air as Curt attempted to control his outstretched arm and take precise aim.

"You going to knock it in?" Scott asked.

"This isn't as easy as it looks," Curt said. He could feel his arm getting tired as the club head volleyed in the air. He finally decided to just take a shot. He abruptly thrust forward with his arm and cleanly missed the skeleton. The metal head passed over it by more than three inches.

"Nice shot," Scott said, now feeling a little more like himself.

"Shut up," Curt said almost laughing. "This is hard!"

Curt focused his attention back on the metal head. After the miss, he had dropped the iron on the carpet in disgust. He picked it up by the rubber handle and now steadied for a second attempt. Scott moved forward and stood over Curt holding the doorknob and gazing at the skeleton.

This time Curt would not miss.

Curt postured the clubhead in the center of the spine but his forward push sent the angled metal toward the back half of the fish. The skeleton spun counter clockwise and teetered on the ledge. For a moment, the weight was perfectly balanced and it rocked like a seesaw. Then, as if pulled down toward the surface, it fell in with the head and ghastly teeth pointing straight up.

Because of Curt's lower line of sight, the skeleton was shielded as it hit the water. But Scott's stance gave him an overhead view. In the instant Curt dropped the nine iron and retracted his arm, Scott pulled the door closed with a loud *slam*. Scott was relieved not to hear Curt scream. He had not waited for an indication from his friend that he was clear.

As the thump of the door faded, Scott saw the fish in a flashback. Just before he had sealed the entrance, he had registered a visual that now had his mind buzzing. He could see the skeleton sliding into the water, head up. In the instant it fell, the teeth had grown larger and jutted out of a developed mouth! A head now whole with features reflecting light as it skipped off its slimy exterior. But the eyes, were the main attraction.

They were glazed, oversized and despondent. Just the thought of those bulging water balloon globes with the swaggering pupils sent a shuddering sensation through Scott.

Scott could not shake the image. It was burned inside, etched near the base of his brain, and it wanted attention. It wanted to be revered and remembered with astonishment and utter disbelief.

He backed away from the door pressing his fingers against his temple. "It's in there," he said very plainly.

"I know it is."

"No!" he shouted. "I mean *it's* in there!"

Curt began to speak but was distracted by a loud abrasive noise emanating from inside the bathroom. It sounded like the buzzing of a swarm of bees multiplied by a thousand. Each man placed his hands over his ears to filter the distasteful sound. The raw trembling hum seemed to glide in and out, increasing then decreasing in volume. As it did, it echoed with a sour reverberation until the noise was nearly deafening even with the wax implants. Curt squeezed his face and shut his eyes in pain. Scott, although feeling the waves of a splitting headache, seemed to weather the noise better. With his eyes still open he looked at the light sprinkling through the door jam and watched it manifest into a deep blue glow. As it radiated brightly, it suddenly changed to a light yellow burn filtering through the framing of the door.

Thirty seconds later, the noise ceased and the outlining light faded until it was gone. Curt was crouched against the wall cringing, eyes still shut. Scott had never looked away from the door and was still standing two feet away.

For Scott, the silence was interrupted only by the pulsating flow of blood pinging his skull. The headache was not the gradual, building kind that he was used to. It burst into his head the second the awful noise had begun and now almost made him believe his brain was melting and the liquid would drop into his spinal column.

Curt opened his eyes and rose. He apparently wasn't suffering the same crippling aftereffects. He looked at Scott and knew his friend was not right.

"Scott . . ."

"I'm okay," he lied cutting Curt off.

The two looked at the doorknob. Their thoughts were aligned. Should we go in? There's no sound coming from inside.

Curt was the first to reach out. But before his hand got within a foot of the knob, the door swelled and bowed outward. They could hear glass shattering on the other side and felt a slight breeze flush through the edges of the frame. There was a plethora of clinging and clunking sounds. Immediately, Curt thought of the scene in *Twister* when the axes, blades and sickles launched into the wooden insides of a farm shed as the forceful winds engulfed it. Curt had a strong compulsion to get away from the bathroom in case the objects inside went airborne and the door gave way.

"Get back!" he yelled.

He turned and grabbed Scott's arm, dragging him down the hallway. They had taken four steps when the bathroom door ripped off its hinges and smashed into the hallway wall on the opposite side. It briefly stood erect and then, from the top, leaned forward until it caught on the left side of the doorframe and spun inward. It landed with a thud and slightly bounced as it continued its roll to the right. It finally braced itself against the right side of the door jam. Half the length of the door was now inside the bathroom as it lay on its side.

But Scott and Curt had not turned around to watch. They kept right on running and didn't slow until they were in the front yard beyond the sidewalk.

"What the hell just happened?" Scott asked as he labored for air.

"I have no idea," Curt responded huffing like he needed an oxygen mask.

"I know this," Scott said between gasps, "Mr. Sellon is of sound mind."

Curt just nodded and watched the front door of the house as if he expected it to swing open and the Kilgotian to burst into the front yard and go for his jugular. Both men were ready to sprint at the first sign of movement. Scott wiped the perspiration from his right cheek.

"Yeah, but are we?" Curt finally asked, never looking away from the front door.

Twenty minutes later, Marvin pulled into the driveway with a slight grin on his face. He knew his friends had doubted him. Now they were standing on the sidewalk keeping a watchful eye on the front of the house.

"Hello boys," he said exiting his vehicle. His mood was lighter than when he'd left them. "What's the matter? Seen a ghost?"

"My nerves are doing the three-minute mile," Scott said. Although his headache had vanished, he was still experiencing flashbacks of the Kilgotian.

Marvin smiled a little more. "Why Scott, what's the matter?" he said very politely.

"You heard Scott. We're a little unnerved at the moment," Curt replied not content with Marvin's sarcasm.

"Yes Curt, I'm hearing just fine. What about you gentlemen?"

Suddenly, Curt realized his own hearing wasn't optimal. Marvin's words sounded muffled and weak. He reached for the sides of his head and then remembered the wax was still in place. He felt stupid and Marvin just smiled as he removed the small round objects from his ears. Scott did likewise.

"So what did you conclude from your experiment?" Marvin prodded with an annoying amount of pleasure.

"You're acting very crotchety. Do you know that? Don't make me call you crotchety. I hate that word. I always feel like a pervert when I say it," Scott said taking a breath. "We concluded you're sane. In the widely accepted definition, that is."

"Very funny. And?" Marvin replied.

"And that the fish in your house defies all known science. It breaks every notion of life and suggests the absolute concept of reincarnation. At least for one animal. The whole thing seemed like some special effects scene in a movie. It also has some strange power. Either that or it didn't appreciate how dirty your bathroom is."

"My bathroom?" Marvin said with surprise. You had him in my bathroom?"

"To be exact, in your bathtub," Curt replied.

"He was in my bathtub?! Curt, tell me you didn't place him in a full tub of water."

"OK."

"OK?"

"OK."

"Ok what? Did you place him in a full tub of water."

"Yes."

"Christ."

"And it's still there," Scott said.

"Who's still there? The fish?" Marvin sighed.

"The fish," Curt responded.

There was a pause in the conversation as Marvin's mouth dropped opened but the words ceased.

"Marvin, how attached to the hall bathroom door are you?" Scott asked turning to look at the front door and ending the awkward silence.

"Why?" Marvin asked, trying to understand the question.

"Because it's not very attached to the hall anymore," Curt said, kicking the ground and looking away.

CHAPTER-TWENTY

Charlie Tatterhorn was busy educating some tourists from South Carolina on the historical significance of the French Huguenot settlement. He stood lecturing the party of four just inside the visitor's center at Fort Caroline along the banks of the St. John's River.

"Huguenot was derived from the term *Huguena*, a word that meant *people who walk at night*. Their only safe place to worship had been dark caves. The struggle between the crown of France and the Huguenots was at its pinnacle in 1450. Their adoption of the Bible as the mainstay did not sit well with the priests and monks of those days. During the next hundred years the new belief flourished, as did their persecution. In May of 1562, Jean Ribault led two ships several miles into the mouth of the St. Johns River and claimed the area for France. In June, 1564, more than 200 French settlers established a colony. Many of these settlers were Huguenots who wished to escape the tyranny of the crown."

Tatterhorn went on to describe the concurrent settlement in St. Augustine by the Spanish. He described the attempted French attack of the southern Spanish settlement (thwarted by a hurricane) and the eventual capture of the earthen Fort Caroline by Menendez's forces. He concluded by stating Fort Caroline was the last effort by France to build a permanent settlement in Florida.

The tourists seemed duly impressed, save the 14-year-old with the Walkman surgically fitted to his ears. As they exited the building and headed toward the natural path that would lead to the near full-scale interpretive rendering of the fort, Tatterhorn glanced at his wristwatch. It was 11:18. Seymour and his friend would be here at 1 p.m. He needed to get ready soon.

The last words he had told Scott Seymour on the phone that morning were to "be prepared."

Tatterhorn really wondered if the men were prepared to die.

At midday, the park ranger went to his car in the parking lot and indiscreetly opened the trunk of the '94 Chevy Lumina. He fumbled around in a milk crate on the left side next to a spare tire. He grumbled out loud as the object he sought eluded him among the clutter of tools and oil cans. Burying his fingers under some rags, he felt the outline of the leather sheath. Content he had what he needed, he wrapped an old tee shirt around the long thin covering and quickly walked the path in the direction of the earthen fort. As he made his way, he could see the front gates of La Carolina in the distance. The entrance was framed by a wooden archway with the seal of the French Huguenot cross on a large oblong piece of wood mounted at the highest point. All those who entered or exited the fort would pass beneath it. Tatterhorn himself had looked up at it hundreds, maybe thousands of times.

Shortly after passing the fort, he departed from the trail to the left, heading northeast into the thin underbrush.

After considerable debate, the three men decided to reenter the house. Scott slowly opened the front door with Curt and Marvin close behind. They resembled Moe, Larry and Curly, fearfully stacked one behind the other. The first bit of good news was the silence that prevailed. But the lack of sound also made them uneasy.

Once inside they saw that a saturated layer of white, chalky dust had settled on the furniture and floor. The air was stale and thick.

"My god," Marvin said softly.

They crossed the living room and crept into the hallway. The bathroom was on the right just past the kitchen. The door was still lying on its side, resting lengthwise on end, propped against the inside door jam and sticking out almost the entire width of the hall.

The three stared at the fallen door and then looked at each other.

The men moved cautiously toward the bathroom at a reduced pace. As they approached, the damage to the door became more visible. The long edge angled upward with the doorknob assembly had been sheared two-thirds of the way to the top. The door jam where the bolt had been secured was shredded, with splintered wood pieces jutting out. On the other side of the opening, the hinges still remained but were precariously dangling in a mangled fashion pointing in different directions. Where the force had slammed the door into the hallway wall, there was a near perfect, two and one-half-inch round hole representing the knob's intrusion. The carpet around the doorway was littered with pieces of wood, plaster and a thick coating of the white dust.

The house remained eerily silent. Upon reaching the bathroom doorway, Scott leaned against the outside and slowly brought his head through the opening to peer inside. He was prepared to regress upon the first sign of movement. Curt and Marvin were positioned behind, watching Scott's body language, ready to dart at the least hint of trouble. Scott made a quick scan of the bathroom. The fish was nowhere in sight but the entire bathroom was a combination of a yellow hue offset by black dust, thickly coating the carpet and tub.

"It's not here," he whispered.

"What do you mean its not here?" Marvin asked impatiently.

Scott noticed that most if not all the water had drained from the tub. There might still be a minimal amount but he couldn't tell from where he stood. The X pattern windows had been blown out and were letting in a healthy dose of sun and fresh air. The beams of light illuminated the dust particles floating in the air. The medicine cabinet mirror to the left of the sink had shattered and the fine fragments of glass lay just beneath the dust with the pieces reflecting the unusual lighting. The countertop items were in complete disarray and were strewn about, some in the sink and some on the carpet. The toilet paper roll, which Scott remembered being new, was gone and the cardboard holder was singed to a blackened crisp. The green ceramic plate, which had held the Kilgotian, was partly embedded in the drywall just above the towel rack. It appeared completely intact.

Then he spotted it.

It was lying between the toilet and the tub. The skeleton of the Kilgotian. It was motionless. Just a lifeless formation of bones. It had gathered a small amount of the black dust resulting in a zebra-like appearance, with stripes in a random pattern. "I see it," Scott said breathing a sigh of relief.

"What's it doing?" Curt asked. "Is it still in the tub?"

"Nope"

"It's not in the tub?" Marvin asked in a loud whisper.

"It's okay," Scott said, "It's just a skeleton again. But your bathroom is going to need an interior decorator."

"Dammit," Marvin said, pushing by both Scott and Curt. "You two owe me a new bathroom. I told you to believe me but noooooo. You had to see for yourself." As he caught sight of the inside he was flabbergasted. "My God. Do you see what this thing did?" he asked in awe.

Curt stuck his head into the doorway beside Marvin and cautiously stepped over the door and retrieved the Kilgotian. His shoes crunched the debris on the floor. After wrenching the plate from the wall, he placed the skeleton back on it. While Scott and Marvin stared at the remains of the bathroom and the destruction, Curt walked into the kitchen and returned the fish to the oven. He turned the dial to *bake*. The temperature setting was 200 degrees. He didn't want any possibility that moisture would reach the skeleton.

He bent down, flipped the light switch on and looked at the creature through the window. By now, Scott and Marvin had joined him. Marvin walked to the refrigerator and grabbed a sixteen ounce plastic bottle of Coke from the second shelf. Scott knelt down beside Curt and looked at the dial setting. He reached up and rotated the temperature to 300.

Marvin took several manly gulps. He recapped the bottle and placed it back. He strolled toward the oven and stopped, standing just over Scott and Curt looking down through the glass.

"Excuse me," he said as he leaned forward between the two and cranked the dial to 450.

"My God. What have you guys discovered? This is way beyond archeology, beyond anything I've ever heard of," Marvin said later as he plopped down on the couch, raising his feet to rest on the coffee table. "That fish is nothing I can even begin to describe. If it doesn't kill us first, we're probably all going to be famous. So you're meeting with that fella . . . what's his name?"

"Tatterhorn," Curt replied.

"Tatterhorn. This afternoon, right?"

"Yeah," Scott said.

"And what exactly is the purpose? Show you where the pond is, or used to be that this godforsaken creature came from?" he said pointing in the general direction of the kitchen.

"Yes," Scott responded as Curt rose and went into the kitchen.

"And you said he told you Tucker had a symbol carved in his back. The Huguenot cross?"

Scott nodded his head.

"What does all this mean? What do *you* think it all means? As unlikely as this is going to sound, I do have a theory. Being a man of reason, it goes against everything I believe but when I was out earlier I had some time to think and I came up with a wild one. You want to hear it?" Marvin asked as Curt returned with a glass of water and sat down.

"Marvin, after that fish just trashed your bathroom, my mind's an open book," Scott responded and Curt nodded.

"Understand I'm not blaming you and Curt. If it weren't you two, it would eventually have been someone else. But finding that fish was not a good thing. It's evil. I know that sounds melodramatic, especially coming from me, but hear me out."

As Marvin spoke there were no surprises to his audience. At heart, Scott and Curt both felt responsible for Tucker's death. Intuitively their consciences charged them with finding the answer.

"I think somehow, someway, you guys have accidentally revived a force, maybe human, maybe not," Marvin started. "I know that sounds ludicrous and its hard for me to even say this with a straight face but the facts are there. That fish in my oven is clinically dead. As dead as Abraham Lincoln, JFK or Elvis. But it has a distinct advantage. Unlike the King, who will never taste another jelly donut, the Kilgotian can be reincarnated with simple H_2O. If it can be brought back from beyond the grave then maybe it has the ability to reincarnate others. If, as I presume, you've inadvertently reincarnated someone, he may or may not be connected to the French Huguenots of 1565, but for some reason feels he is."

Scott stared hard at Curt and saw the expression he expected. There were clearly no objections to Marvin's hypothesis. The fact that a scholared, well respected, history professor was commenting and speculating on such a paranormal circumstance caused Scott to realize what a bizarre situation this had ballooned into.

"The fact that this Tatterhorn knew of the pond and seems intrigued by your interest worries me. What's his angle?" Marvin asked.

"I'm not really sure. But he's definitely interested in what we know. I didn't tell him we had the fish," Scott said looking from Marvin to Curt to ensure his friend understood not to mention the Kilgotian when they went to Fort Caroline.

"Just be careful when he shows you around," Marvin warned. "His agenda may not include your safety. Remember, there's a killer on the loose."

"We will," Scott assured him. "Marvin, if we have done something wrong by discovering this fish, we plan to make it right." Curt nodded his head in agreement and the old man smiled.

Scott and Curt departed from Marvin's just before 11:40 a.m. The professor would have joined the boys on their field trip to Fort Caroline but had made arrangements with Simon Pillar, curator of the St. Augustine Museum to have the sealed remains of the human skeleton found in the powder magazine delivered to his house. Since it had been discovered several years ago when the room was first opened, the skeleton had been on continuous display in the museum. Recently, amidst renovations and the addition of a new wing, the facility had been closed. It was not scheduled to reopen till mid-October.

With this temporary shutdown, and Marvin's connections, he was able to secure the remains for a day. In order to make sure he was home to take delivery, Marvin stayed behind. The museum had told him the skeleton would be dropped off sometime between 1 and 5 p.m. He couldn't risk missing its arrival. Although still nervous about being in the same vicinity as the Kilgotian's skeleton, Marvin diverted his thoughts to cleaning up. The white coating of dust had settled everywhere leaving the furniture and carpet layered in powder.

Scott and Curt decided to take both vehicles and drop Curt's Mustang off at his apartment later that afternoon. With Damon approaching, they would have no choice but to leave town and deal with these unusual circumstances afterward. Curt would need his car to evacuate if the need arose.

Scott had already jumped in the Blazer and fired up the engine when Marvin came out holding a manila envelope. Curt was about to slam the door of his Mustang.

"Scott!" Marvin shouted and then realized it would be easier to get to Curt. "Curt, do me a favor. Drop this off at the Nuestra de la Leche Gift Shop. A friend of mine named Nora told me they have a woman, I believe her name is Cheryl or Sharon, who can translate these." He held the envelope out for Curt to grab.

"What is it?"

"It's some information I pulled off the Internet. I think it pertains to our buddy in the oven and the legend but it's hard to tell. It's in French. I know just enough French to get me in trouble. Nora said this woman at the gift shop wouldn't mind translating."

"Why don't you take it to Pierre?"

"I've been trying to reach him since yesterday and there's no answer."

"OK. Will do."

The two vehicles backed out of the driveway and were off. Heading west down Anastasia Boulevard, Curt pulled beside Scott and waved the manila envelope. Scott seemed puzzled. There was no way to communicate the need to make a quick stop so he took the lead. They drove over the Bridge of Lions and veered north along the water. Fort Castillo de San Marcos was directly ahead. The road wound left at the entrance to the fort's parking lot and then right heading north again once beyond the large grassy perimeter. (This S pattern allowed tourists to see the fort from three sides while traveling on San Marco Boulevard.)

Several blocks later, Curt saw the familiar massive steel cross to his right, rising into the sky near the shore. He passed in front of the large parking lot where visitors entered the cemetery across a small wooden bridge that spanned the saltwater pond. Just beyond, he turned right into the small parking area of the Nuestra de la Leche Gift Shop. Scott followed his friend and they parked in adjacent slots.

"What are we doing here? What'd Marvin give you?" Scott asked once Curt had walked around to the driver's side and the Blazer's window came down. He'd seen the two chatting before they left.

"He wants me to drop this off to a friend that works here." Curt said and walked toward the entrance.

"Anything I should know about?"

"Just something Marvin needed done."

"I'm going to get going. We'll be pushin' it to get there by one as it is. I don't want to miss Tatterhorn. Besides, I need to call Kay and see what's going on with this Hurricane and her work."

"Okay, I'll catch up with you at Fort Caroline."

As Scott backed up and pulled away, Curt entered the shop with all intentions of finding Nora or Sharon, dropping the package and leaving within the span of about thirty seconds. As he approached the counter he noticed a strikingly beautiful woman assisting a customer. She had stunning red hair and an extremely cute figure. She was probably in her early 30s but could have easily passed as mid-twentysomething. She glanced up and saw Curt walking toward her and briefly smiled. It was a warm confident smile that instantly captured Curt's attention. She resumed attending to the elderly man buying the packet of postcards, continuing a friendly conversation and never missing a beat. As Curt waited patiently for the man to leave, a second clerk arrived. She was an elderly lady who was surely someone's grandmother. Seeing he had nothing to purchase and was carrying the envelope, she offered to assist with a slight look of bewilderment.

"Sir, can I help you?"

Damn! Damn! Damn! I wonder if this lady would be upset if I told her I prefer to speak to the attractive woman? The red-haired woman again looked up and smiled at Curt as she bagged the elderly man's souvenirs.

It was as if she'd read Curt's mind. This time he was prepared and grinned like a little boy.

"Um yeah . . . yes, I hope so," he said now looking at the older clerk. "I'm looking for Nora." The words had no sooner left his mouth than he spotted her nametag. It was not the typical displayed moniker you might see on a bag boy at Harris Teeter or a salesman at Barnes & Noble. This one was just shy of being a billboard. The letters N O R A were profoundly displayed across her chest like the serial numbers on a felon's mug shot. The large letters probably helped the elderly clientele who frequented the shop.

Curt blushed slightly as he put his hand to the side of his mouth. "Boy do I feel stupid." The woman just smiled and the whiteness filled the room. Curt nearly ducked. Dentures for days. No one has teeth that perfect, he thought. Meanwhile, the beautiful red haired lady pretended to busy herself with something under the counter. Curt was certain she was just looking for a reason to laugh at him.

"You must be Curt," Nora said.

Curt looked at her puzzled for a moment and then realized Marvin must have called.

"Not bad, huh? You're not even wearing a nametag and I got it right," Nora smirked.

The younger woman was now adjusting the stock of bags under the counter and kept smiling as she paid close attention to Nora's comments and the man's replies.

"Marvin asked me to give this to you. It's the info for Sharon to translate," Curt said handing Nora the envelope.

"You mean Sherri. Her name is Sherri," Nora said as the attractive clerk rose behind her and crossed her arms on her chest, eyeing Curt. He couldn't help but return the gaze and then followed her hand as she pointed to the nametag across her shirt.

"Maybe we should chip in and buy this gentleman a pair of reading glasses," Sherri said with a laugh as she turned toward Nora and then shot a seductive smile at Curt.

Curt chuckled as he watched the woman's eyes and got exactly the reaction he'd hoped for. She offered a handshake. "I'm Sherri Falco."

"It's nice to meet you," he said, easily taking her hand. The texture of her skin was silky smooth. "Are you a friend of Marvin's?"

"No. But I've seen him in the shop before. He seems like a nice guy."

"He has his moments. So how much are you charging him for the work? He's worth millions you know," Curt said with a straight face.

She laughed and gently bit her bottom lip. "Nothing, it's a freebee."

A little girl about 9 or 10 approached the counter and Sherri looked at her, indecisive whether she should break off her conversation with Curt or wait to see if Nora would assist. As if on cue, Nora stepped over to ring up the girl's order. She was buying a small silver cross. It was the store specialty. Hundreds of them donned the wall to the right of the register. Crosses on necklaces, chains, collector spoons, postcards, bookmarkers, can openers and on an assortment of other tourist staples. Most were a memento of the 208-foot stainless steel *Beacon of Faith* cross watching over the cemetery in back.

Curt and Sherri temporarily suspended the conversation to watch the little girl whose mother was standing by the door patiently waiting for her daughter. She had jet-black hair and bangs that stopped just above her eyebrows. Her expression was warm and sincere. She was obviously shy as she placed the necklace on the counter for Nora to see and kept her eyes fixed on the counter.

"Oh, honey, that's a precious necklace," Nora said picking it up and entering the amount on the keypad. The little girl was quiet but Nora continued to smile and chat away.

"Is that for you?" Curt asked as he found a brief opening between Nora's run-on sentences.

The little girl looked up and grinned.

"She reminds me of my daughter," Curt said looking back at Sherri.

"How old?"

"Thirty-six," Curt replied with a smirk.

"No, your daughter."

"She's six. The love of my life."

"Mine's seven. And the love of my life," She said coyly.

"Oh," Curt said hoping to determine her marital status in the next few moments. He'd already noticed she was not wearing a ring. "Does your husband work here in town?"

"We're no longer married. He was on the road more than he was home anyway so I don't really miss him." Sherri had already noticed the barren finger on Curt's left hand but these days a lot of men go without wedding rings. At least that is what she had experienced. "And yours? What does she do?"

"Anyone she wants to. We're divorced," Curt said with a sarcastic tone.

Sherri's smile widened.

As Nora finished another customer's order Curt suddenly ran out of things to say and felt extremely awkward. It was highly unusual for him to freeze up like this, especially around a woman he found so appealing. She was so confident and exuded a crisp, witty intelligence.

"Well, I guess I should be going. It was a pleasure meeting you," he said staring directly into her eyes. Her gaze never waned. "When can I tell Marvin you'll have this translated for him?" he asked grasping for anything to continue the conversation.

She picked up the envelope Nora had laid under the counter to the right of the gift bags. She undid the metal clamp and reached inside removing three pages.

"Oh this won't take long. Will you be coming by to get them when I'm done?"

"I'd love to . . . I mean yes."

She smiled. "I might get them completed before I head out of town tonight."

"Taking vacation?"

"Running from a hurricane."

"Oh yeah, I forgot. I might be doing the same in the morning."

"Here. Hold on a second." She reached forward and pulled a section of register tape out of the slot. Turning it over, she scribbled something on it. "Here's my home number. Call me later and I'll let you know how I'm coming with it. Just make it before 6:30 or you won't hear from me for a couple of days." She handed him the note.

For Curt, the seal had been broken. He now felt at ease and the words were ripe to leap from his mouth. "You know, since you didn't ask for a fee, I've been approved to buy you an all expenses paid dinner at the restaurant of your choice upon completion of this task."

"Gee. That sounds great. Can I bring a date?" she said very seriously.

Curt bit on her shrewd acting. "Well, I guess," He said disheartened.

She turned to assist a patron with his order and then cut her eyes back at Curt. "What night's good for you?" Her eyes sparkled and the corners of her lips angled upward.

Just before 1 p.m. Scott pulled into the parking lot, and spotted Tatterhorn standing by a large oak near the trail leading to the reconstructed Fort Caroline. He was wearing his usual light brown ranger attire and blocking out more sun than the tree he was next to. Scott parked the Blazer and walked toward him. Still a good ten yards away, Tatterhorn turned and began down the path.

"Hey, Tatterhorn. Wait up. My buddy's not here yet."

Tatterhorn continued on. "Tatterhorn!" Scott yelled, now trotting to catch up. The man never slowed. When he came alongside, Tatterhorn spoke.

"I don't have time to wait on your friend. You either come now or forget it." His voice was stern and fixed. From the man's tone, Scott knew a discussion would be ineffective. As the large man blazed down the trail, he fell into pace behind and slightly to the left.

They proceeded down the quarter-mile dirt path that led to the earthen fort. After several hundred yards they broke through the woods into an opening with a grassy field to either side. Ahead, the path made a curve to the right and led under the wooden archway to the fort. The symbol of the Huguenot Cross centered at the pinnacle.

As the path turned, a second path forked to the left away from the fort into the woods. The sign signified it to be a one mile nature trail. Scott continued on the heels of Tatterhorn, whose long gliding steps made it difficult for him to keep step.

"Could you slow down just a bit? I don't see the smoke so there's really no rush."

Tatterhorn turned to briefly scowl at Scott, never breaking stride. He peered to the right scanning the fort and then behind to the trail where they had just come from. Being a Tuesday, tourist traffic was light. Scott had never been to the fort except on the weekend. Unlike St. Augustine, it didn't have quite the draw and therefore was relatively quiet during the weekdays. Today was no exception, and the last humans Scott recalled seeing were a young couple leisurely walking the path back near the visitor's center. They'd blown by them like they were standing still and Scott suspected they were probably 300 yards behind. The couple seemed more intrigued with the color of each other's eyes than they were about exploring the historical significance of the surrounding area. Scott wouldn't be surprised if they never made it to the fort.

Upon reaching the fork, Tatterhorn cut sharply left onto the nature trail. He again glanced backward and Scott got the distinct impression Tatterhorn was nervous about being seen. Marvin's warning popped up in his head like an oversized flashcard. *Just be careful when he shows you around.* He could hear the word *careful* spoken in the professor's voice and it lingered in his mind like an echo. Small beads of sweat broke out on Scott's forehead as the path made a gentle uphill slope and the muscles in his legs felt the change. He pushed on, suddenly aware of the intense quiet and solitude of the woods that surrounded him.

Tatterhorn was like a robot, never speeding up nor slowing down. Just constantly lifting and swinging those gunboats in a forward, mechanized motion. His pace was relentless and Scott pleaded with the man more than once to slow down. There was no way Curt would ever catch up. And even if he got to the fort in time, he'd never know where to go. As they rapidly progressed, Scott began keeping a watchful eye in all directions.

The woods on either side of the trail were not thick. The undergrowth was sparse and the oak and pine trees dominated the landscape. Along the sides of the path there were downed trees in different phases of rot. It would have been a very serene setting under normal circumstances, a great place for a field trip or outdoor discovery lesson for an elementary school class. Every so often a small plaque positioned on a ground stake gave some obscure fact about the indigenous vegetation. But Scott was in no mood to admire the landscape.

As Tatterhorn kept the wheels churning and remained strangely silent, Scott could feel the perspiration slide down his back and under his shirt. The day was not a scorcher, somewhere in the mid-seventies, but the workout was intense. Scott estimated they had gone 500 yards and, for the most part, the journey had been uphill. It was not a tremendously steep incline, but it was enough to make the average thirty-something-year-old winded.

"Tatterhorn," Scott gasped, hoping to get an answer as to how much further they had to go.

No response.

"Tatterhorn!" he yelled.

No response.

Scott lowered his head slightly and picked up speed and found himself running. He passed the large man by 10 yards and turned around. He planted his feet in the middle of the path and held his palm out in frustration, signaling Tatterhorn to stop.

"Goddammit. Why don't you answer me? I want to know how much farther we're going," Scott said panting. Tatterhorn stopped within two inches of the outstretched palm as he glared down at Scott.

For a moment he said nothing. Then his lips parted and he pointed to his left. "It's over there. Not far."

The large man was hardly breathing. Scott briefly marveled at the physical conditioning Tatterhorn must be in. "How far?" Scott asked, but the man had already turned left and was hiking through the woods. Scott began to pursue and then stopped. He bent down and dropped three pennies on a barren area of sand just off the path. He quickly stood erect before Tatterhorn noticed what he was doing and then followed, at the moment, at least, content that they were close. A short distance beyond, the underbrush became considerably dense and Scott began watching his steps closely. With the numerous fallen trees, it was an ideal nesting area for the eastern diamondback rattlesnake, with its two-inch fangs and poisonous venom. In the aftermath of summer and the onset of fall, it was a prime time for the species to be active.

Scott estimated they had traveled about 40 yards when Tatterhorn finally slowed down to a legitimate pace. Ironically, this bothered Scott more than the speed walking. Tatterhorn scanned the ground, moving tentatively. The terrain had remained constant but something caused the big man to observe each step with a high degree of caution. Maybe the man was also fearful of snakes but it seemed to be more than that. It was as if he was a soldier picking his way through a minefield. Slowly the two proceeded.

Ahead there was a cluster of massive trees spanning 25 feet across. A few steps closer and Scott could tell the base of the middle section of trees was positioned outward. Together with the adjoining trees, the section formed at least a half circle on the side that was visible. The trees were so tightly stacked, and the limbs stretched out so thickly, they formed a solid convex wall.

As far as Scott knew there could have been an African elephant behind the natural (or at least he assumed it was natural) cover. It was certainly large enough and it was impossible to see through. As Tatterhorn gingerly approached the barrier of trees, he moved around to the left. Scott followed gazing at the wall. Now he could see that the unusual alignment continued around the sides, apparently spiraling into a full circle. They walked around the perimeter and came to a stop at the opposite side. The formation was perfectly symmetrical and as round as a water tower. It was uncanny. Tatterhorn pushed aside a limb hanging down and, between two trees leaning slightly away from each other, Scott could see inside through a two-foot opening.

Although the sun was shining with the effervescent glow of an early autumn day, what Scott saw was dimly lit and covered in a gray veil. The trees circling the area had brilliant green foliage reaching into the sky. This covering formed a dense cloak, closing out most of the light to the inside. Initially, all Scott could see inside was the backside of the tree line they had first approached. This view was even stranger than the outside. The trees appeared to blend into a seamless wall. For a moment, Scott thought there was a manmade structure inside the circle.

Tatterhorn leaned forward sticking his huge head through the opening turning left, then right. Content, he cautiously proceeded forward, swiveling his oversized frame sideways and squeezing through. Scott followed with less effort.

Inside, Scott smelled the scent of bark mixed with a touch of dust. The cover overhead did not completely encase the area. Some indirect light funneled in from gaps in the leafy branches that angled in all directions above. Beyond these openings, Scott could see the top of taller trees growing nearby. They were responsible for shielding the reclusive spot from the direct sunlight.

As Scott took another step, Tatterhorn immediately stopped and held a hand back to halt him. Scott looked down at the ground. The two men were standing on a five-foot wide section of light brown colored grass that ran in a circle along the inside base of the trees. It reminded Scott of a track encircling a football field. Farther inward, the ground turned to near perfect white sand. The sand was rippled and capped with small swells every foot or so. Scott estimated the area to be about 15 feet across and was bordered completed by the strip of dry grass.

Pushing Tatterhorn's hand down, Scott walked forward to the edge of the grass.

"Stop!" Tatterhorn ordered.
"What is this place? Where's the pond?"
"In front of you."
"That's sand."
"This is where the pond is. You can't see it, but it's there."
"It's there?"
"Yes."
"Who made this place?"
"No one made it. It just is."

"Dammit Tatterhorn, why can't you just respond with some direct answers instead of talking in code."

"This place is beyond what your mind can conceive. The Kilgotian lives here. It and nothing else. When it was taken away, the pond went dormant. It's in hibernation. But even as it sleeps, it craves to have the fish returned. To gain the fish it will direct the actions of others, if given the opportunity. That is why you must not step away from the shore."

"The shore? This patchy brown stuff is the shore?" Scott asked, pointing to the ground they stood on.

"Yes."

Scott looked at the white mounds and swirling designs washed on the surface just beyond the dingy grass. In an odd way, it resembled the restless surface of water. But the resemblance could also be attributed to Tatterhorn's subliminal suggestion that this was somehow a pond. Scott knew the difference between water and earth.

But what a unique mark of nature this place was. A perfectly round area of sand, surrounded by a circular strip of grass, all secretly contained within a perfect ring of trees. For the most part, sheltered from the outside elements. Sheltered from man.

"So why can't I step on the sand? Is it like quicksand in the old Tarzan movies?"

"No."

"But if I step in, it might *order* me to go get the fish and bring it back?" As soon as he completed the question the alarm rang out in his head.

Tatterhorn glared at Scott. "You have the fish? You told me you didn't. You lied to me, Seymour!"

Thinking fast, Scott mentally recounted his words. "Calm down, Tatterhorn, you're going to pop a blood vessel. I was joking that the pond would make me go get the fish. I didn't say I had it. I assumed I'd get instructions where to locate it." Not a bad cover-up, he thought.

Tatterhorn stared hard at Scott then looked away. "The thing is not a toy. At one time it was a tool of mankind that ensured continued existence. Now it needs to be sent back."

"Tatterhorn, what's your deal? I mean why are you so interested in some damn fish?"

"The Kilgotian has evolved into pure evil. Being of Timucua descent, I have carried on the efforts to find the thing and destroy it as my ancestors had. It was taken from the pond by a madman. If it gains power in this day and age, the loss of life will be unfathomable."

"How does it gain power?"

"Once brought back to life in fresh water, it has the ability to resurrect the dead. These unfortunates are called Soulful Ones."

"I've heard the term."

Tatterhorn looked at Scott then gazed toward the white sand before continuing. "With each Soulful One the fish commands a larger army. Initially, the resurrected attend to their own earthly needs -- sex, greed, revenge -- but ultimately they belong to the fish and it will direct their actions. The fish directs its own will and God has washed his hands of it."

"Didn't you just tell me the sandy pond right here would also direct my actions if I stepped into it?"

"Yes."

"So not only does the fish have control, the pond commands as well?"

"You don't understand," Tatterhorn began as he reached behind and seemed to adjust his belt. "This is the Kilgotian's pond. It will always be the Kilgotian's pond. Even though the water evaporated when the fish was removed, the pond is here and it still holds its essence, understands its needs. And its primary need is to be returned."

Scott looked back at the sand as Tatterhorn continued fidgeting with his hand behind his back and pulled his shirt out of his pants. Scott bent down near the edge where the white sand bordered the brown grass. Reaching to the side he picked up a small twig and cast it on the sand. It landed gently, cushioned by the soft grains. As it rested on the surface, Scott stood up and turned toward the park ranger.

Tatterhorn was three feet away and holding a large hunting knife in his right hand by his side. His left hand dropped the sheath to the ground. At the sight of the serrated edge, Scott was stricken with fear. Tatterhorn had never been normal as far as Scott was concerned and always seemed to have a psychotic glint in his eyes. Now it was a terrifying look of anger.

"What are you doing?" Scott asked with obvious nervousness.

"The Kilgotian must not be released in this world again. It has no place here." He raised the steel blade. "I'm going to ask you again." A trickled line of sweat ran down either side of Tatterhorn's face and raced to his chin. "Have you found the fish?"

Instead of responding, Scott pressed to have his question answered and his voice quivered. "What the hell are you doing with that knife?"

"Answer the question!" Tatterhorn screamed. The man had no patience and the words hit Scott with a chilling tinge.

Scott became instantly nauseated and hesitated in his response. His first inclination was to deny that he and Curt had the Kilgotian's skeleton. But the seedy, irrational expression of the towering man wielding the sharp deadly object was enough to make him realize Tatterhorn was in no mood to be jerked around. For him to deny it again would take a steady voice, confident tone and secure body language. Faced with the degree of fear that had invaded his body, this would not be possible. Scott decided to be straight.

"Yeah, we found it," Scott said softly with a trembling voice. "Tatterhorn, put the knife down."

"Seymour, you're a fucking idiot. You and your friend. You're fools. You think you can play with that thing. It'll rip your goddamn organs out." He raised the knife to his chest with the blade pointing upward at a 45 degree angle. "Where is it?" he asked firmly, clenching his teeth and barely separating his lips.

Scott stared at Tatterhorn. Tatterhorn took a step toward him and Scott took one step back. His heels rested an inch and a half from the border of the sand. "What do you want?" Scott screamed as Tatterhorn glared at him with disdain.

Tatterhorn spoke in a deliriously calm voice. "I want anyone who knows anything about that fish dead. Where is it?" he said as his eyebrows arched down and the sorted lines in his brow crinkled into a pattern of white lines between red gaps of flesh.

"We're not going to revive the fish! We just want to make sure it hasn't already done something!"

"Done something? You mean what happened to your friend on the beach?" Tatterhorn's pupils swelled. "You bastard!"

"Hey, we didn't do anything with the fish. We're not to blame!" Of course, Scott did hold guilt about Tucker's death. He was positive it was somehow linked to the Kilgotian.

"WHERE IS THE KILGOTIAN?" Tatterhorn bellowed as his face turned crimson red and the sweat poured down his cheeks and glossed his thick neck.

"If I tell you," Scott said, struggling to regain his composure, "you'll kill me." Scott's own words sent a chill through his body.

Tatterhorn raised the knife and with his left hand, grabbing the blade by the flat side. He took his right hand and grasped the handle and positioned it as if he was holding a javelin. "I'll kill you anyway. Remember, I told you to be prepared."

The blade was extended toward Scott and terrifying reality shot through his veins. *I am going to die in this godforsaken place. This gigantic lunatic with the sharp metal object pointed at my skull is strong enough to bury the knife in my brain up to the handle and there is little that I can do. Maybe I can avoid him for a few seconds but no more. He's blocking the only exit to this cursed place. Now my bones will be left for some future archeologists to find!*

The physical dominance of the man compared to Scott was staggering. At most, Scott weighed 185. Tatterhorn probably went 350 plus. Scott's only chance was to try and kick the huge man square in the groin. He'd probably only get one clean shot before the blade ripped through his head, chest or stomach. Scott's mind flushed with fear and he almost passed out as Tatterhorn moved forward. There was complete silence. It was as if the birds had stopped and were perched among the high branches to watch the massacre. Tatterhorn's gaze burned a fiery red as the blood vessels appeared to have exploded around the pupils and slid out in all directions, merging with the creases flowing across his face. Tatterhorn drew closer and Scott completely abandoned his strategy of attacking the man's testicles. He repositioned out of fear, strategy gone, by lifting his arms into the air to shield his head. He acted out of a natural defense as he dropped his head.

As he moved his eyes from Tatterhorn's, with his arms extended to intercept the assault, or at least slow it down, he caught sight of an object moving toward the giant's right side. It was coming from somewhere behind the crazed park ranger and moved silently and swiftly. Tatterhorn had lifted the blade in the air above his head and the next motion would send it penetrating some part of Scott's body.

The giant screamed as he prepared to plunge the steel into the outsider. "AAAAAHHHHHHHUUUGGGHHH!

Scott closed his eyes and opened them as Tatterhorn's tone abruptly changed from aggression to one of startled pain. The object from behind had collided with the man's lower right side, catching him in the kidney. Tatterhorn was caught completely off guard and was now angling past Scott to his right. The blade still high in the air but falling rapidly as he dropped his hands to break his fall. Scott quickly leaned to his left, narrowly avoiding the steel as it whisked by his face and shoulder and Tatterhorn stumbled onto the sand, desperately trying to gain his balance.

In front of Scott, Curt held the tree branch, still firmly in his hands, and was panting loudly. Both men were perspiring profusely and the contained area now held the aroma of sweat. Scott was speechless as Curt somehow managed a smile. Both men focused on Tatterhorn who had landed in the middle of the sandy area flat on his belly. From what Scott could tell, the man had lost the knife somewhere in the loose earth and was in no rush to find it.

Tatterhorn was motionless. If his head hadn't been propped up, they would have thought he was dead.

Very slowly, he turned his head back to his right and looked at the men standing on the grassy area. He had a look of sheer terror. The big man was petrified. Scott remembered how Tatterhorn had warned him about the sand, how he respected it and had been careful to stay off. Now he was *in* it, surrounded by the white stuff and too scared to move.

But what is he afraid of? Scott wondered. Here Tatterhorn is, lying on the sand and nothing's happening. As the sentence scurried though his mind he turned toward Curt. What the hell am I thinking? I have a chance to get out and I'm standing here like an idiot watching to see what happens to Tatterhorn. What will happen is he's going to come to his senses, shake off the pain from Curt's home run and kill us both. Knife or no knife with his bare hands if he has to.

Without a word, Curt read his mind and turned to make his way between the two separated trees. Scott quickly followed, never looking back.

The blow had left a searing whelp on Tatterhorn's lower back. But that was the least of his problems. It was an afterthought. He remained still. So still he barely breathed. His head faced directly down, merely inches from the surface as he strained to keep it raised.

He closed his eyes tightly and begged not to die. Begged and pleaded. The stinging pain made him wonder if Seymour's friend had cracked open his skin with the limb. Taking the hit was not that bothersome. He'd been in more pain than this before. But what sent his thoughts rattling and his breathing into deep, labored draws was the fact he might be bleeding from the wound. And bleeding on the sand would surely be the trigger. As it was, any movement would be sensed. He really wondered why he was still alive. Everything he had ever heard guaranteed death by now. Here he was smack in the middle and the earth had been quiet. No noise. No disruptions in the sand. Nothing.

He began to temper his breathing in easy inhales and long exhales to minimize the movement. His rocketing pulse was settling somewhat and he lifted his head just enough for his eyes to see the grassy area seven feet ahead. He had fallen completely away from the two men into the center of the sandy area. Since landing he had not heard any sound from behind and was sure the men had left.

His hands were sunk to the knuckles. Embedded in the bright white sand, the contrast with his dark tanned skin gave the appearance of paws lying on the surface. Contrary to what Scott had assumed, Tatterhorn still had a grip on the hunting knife. Moving only millimeters at a time, he slowly lifted his right hand still clutching the blade. In slow motion, his hand came out of the sand, first his fingers, then the knife followed. As it all broke through, he realized with utter horror he was no longer holding the knife by the handle but by the serrated steel. What Tatterhorn feared most had occurred. He quickly dropped the knife as his hand leaked a stream of blood that pooled between his fingers, the dark red ooze mixing with the fine white grains of sand on his dark skin.

"No," he whispered in agony. But it was too late. Casually, the glob of granulated blood drifted down onto the white floor producing three large spots before Tatterhorn frantically rolled on his back and placed both palms on his chest. The bloody right hand first, covered by the left. He had been so shocked and it happened so fast, there was nothing he could have done to prevent it. A sickly feeling overcame him and he closed his eyes.

Scott and Curt left the circle of trees in a full bore run. Rattlesnakes or not, Scott wanted to get as far away as humanly possible. The earth seemed to glide under their feet as adrenaline kept them moving. They made their way through the underbrush and quickly came upon the nature trail and turned right, never slowing. Curt could feel his side cramping about 200 yards down the dirt path but continued, knowing his friend was not about to stop. Besides, slowing down and waiting for Tatterhorn to catch up was not a good idea. He'd just landed a stunning shot to the big man's back with part of a tree and Tatterhorn might be a little upset, even mad enough to uproot one of these centuries-old oaks near the fort and drop it on both men.

 They reached their respective cars in the parking lot and jumped in. They would talk once down the road but now was not the time.

CHAPTER-TWENTY-ONE

The delivery of the package from the museum occurred as planned. Shortly after one o'clock Marvin rose from his Lazy Boy to greet the knock at the door. An unfriendly butch-looking woman in shorts and a Harley Davidson tee shirt stood on the porch holding a large box.

"You Sellon?" she said gruffly.

"Last time I checked," the professor replied.

"Where do you want it?" she asked impatiently.

"Are you from the museum?"

"What do you think Einstein?" she replied.

Not waiting for Marvin to move, she came through the door nearly rolling the man off his feet. Upon Marvin's directions, she turned toward the dining room and placed the box gently on the table. At least she understands the term "Fragile," Marvin thought. The box stretched nearly the entire six-foot length of the surface.

"Hey Mac, you gotta sign for that," the woman said with a gravely voice as Marvin attempted to shut the door behind her. She was obviously a two-pack-a-day smoker for quite sometime. Her facial features exaggerated the look of a disgruntled union worker. Her black hair was buzzed and bristled on top, tinted with blonde at the tips. She had a deep tan that Marvin suspected stayed dark all year, as if her body had been stained with lacquer. Both ears were riddled with at least a dozen silver, small hooped earrings that went from the lobes to the top. She was holding a clipboard with some official papers stacked slightly out of alignment. Marvin noticed her massive biceps and thick forearms with an elongated tattoo of a scorpion running from her right wrist to the crux of her elbow.

This is no woman. At least not from this planet, Marvin decided.

Even in his prime, and Marvin had been a scholarship athlete on the wrestling team, he doubted he could have taken this woman in a best two out of three falls.

She handed him the clipboard and a BIC pen that she grabbed from behind her left ear. Marvin looked down studying the paper.

"Jeez dude. Right there!" she said pointing to no particular spot near the bottom of the form. Marvin signed his name as the woman smacked her gum and sighed impatiently. At this point, he didn't even care to know what the document said and returned the clipboard and pen to the man-woman.

She turned and walked away and Marvin saw her jump into a gray Isuzu Trooper parked on the street. "What in the hell was that?" he asked himself, shaking his head.

Marvin closed the door and returned to the dining room table. The box upon it was neatly packaged in brown paper secured with light yellow packaging tape. It measured 5 ½ feet long, 3 feet wide and 6 inches thick.

In the top upper right hand corner was the inscription, "Property of St. Augustine Museum." The phrase, "Fragile – Handle with Care," was displayed in three-inch capital letters on each side of the box as well as each end.

Marvin retrieved a steak knife from the kitchen and went to work slicing open the edges. Once the packing tape had been severed, he was able to easily lift off the top lid of the thick cardboard box revealing an extensive amount of newspaper bundled in tight balls.

"High tech packing," Marvin chuckled.

He cautiously lifted each roll until the plastic cases underneath came into view. He was unsure exactly how the items had been packed and was taking no chances of damaging any of the artifacts. Once he could see the remains were intact within secure casings, he was able to proceed with less apprehension.

The phone rang. It was Curt. "Has Scott checked in with you? I'm in the parking lot at Fort Caroline. His Blazer's here but he's nowhere around."

"Nope, haven't spoken with him. But, the remains arrived from the museum. I'm getting ready to unpack them."

"I guess he and Tatterhorn couldn't wait," Curt responded as if he didn't notice Marvin's comment.

"Why don't you call him on his cell phone?" Marvin asked.

"Because it's sitting in his Blazer. I can see it. I guess I'll go looking for them. Talk to you later."

"Bye."

Marvin returned to the dining room table and carefully unloaded the contents of the box. Each casing was labeled with its skeletal remains. The first one he removed was a long thin plastic case containing the leg bones; the femur, patella, tibia, fibula and tarsals. A second box held the humerus, radius, ulna and carpals also known as the arms. A third, wider box housed the pelvis, spine, rib cage, sternum, clavicle and skull. In each, the bones were positioned against a Styrofoam backing as protection. The bones were a dirty shade of pale and Marvin noticed how fragile they appeared. He gently laid the three casings across the table after placing the shipping box on the floor. Marvin had seen skeletons often over the years but had never gotten to a point where he was perfectly comfortable examining one. More times than not, he felt a slight case of the willies. It was hard to make the disconnect most archeologists could achieve. For him, it was always personal. There had been a soul, at one time long ago, embedded within the flesh and bones before him. Now, more than ever, he was cognizant of this fact. Maybe it was because youth had evaded him and it posed a subtle reminder that the body is only the shell . . . and the soul is the essence of what we are.

As was usually the case, Marvin wondered how the man spread out in pieces on his dining room table had died. Had it been a painful death or a case of going quietly into the night? Heart attack, stroke, aneurysm? High blood pressure, gunshot wound, knife slashing? Fallen off a cliff, food poisoning, trampled by a horse? Of course there were usually telltale signs of someone's demise. But most times, archeologists, unless trained in pathology, are unable to ascertain the cause of death. Marvin knew from initial examinations by such experts that the cause of death was not certain for the man found sealed within the powder magazine.

As Marvin stepped back and scanned the table he felt *the* twinge. An unsettled feeling. Before him, were the remains of a man. A man similar to himself. Well, maybe not as educated. But a man nonetheless. If this was who he believed it was, it was a man who walked the earth four centuries before Bertha Louise Sellon had given birth to Marvin. A man who had traveled from France to America not on a luxury liner or the Concorde but on a wooden ship with the most meager of accommodations. A man who lived without the comforts and convenience of air conditioning, debit cards, incandescent lighting, telephones, washing machines, dishwashers, automobiles, clocks, mass transportation, toasters, microwaves, refrigerators, TVs, stereos or Sony Playstation. He was a man who lived in a time of turbulence and frequent despair. When nations sought new lands. A soldier who had chosen to leave his homeland to journey far away to aid fellow Huguenots in their attempt to establish a colony in La Florida. A man who had sacrificed everything for his beliefs. Such strong convictions had steered him to an exciting, wonderfully strange New World full of palm trees and flowers where death was only a sword swing or a bout of smallpox away. Where native tribes roamed the area and existed with nature.

What an intriguing life these earlier adventurers must have lived, with their actions defining early American history. Marvin wondered if they had any idea how their deeds would be noted, how their struggles and hardships would be remembered.

This was a man who had experienced it all. What an exquisite resource of information he would be if he were alive today. Marvin thought about the stories and adventures the man could tell. The historical perspective of life in the New World during the 1500s. What if this skeleton, these remains, really could be reincarnated? Just think of the information to be gained from this man. Someone who experienced life first-hand during this period. A true explorer. Just to spend an hour interviewing the man would fulfill the dream of any historian or archeologist.

Marvin cleared his thoughts. The brown stained bones were lifeless inside their cases. He walked back into the corner bedroom carefully avoiding the wreckage that had been his bathroom door. The bedroom was his hobby room and where the boys' artifact was soaking, still undefined. After searching through the top four drawers of the bureau, Marvin found a large magnifying glass and returned to the dining room. The remains were not to be removed from their plastic containers. That was the agreement he had made with Simon Pillar, the man who was breaking the rules as a favor to Marvin.

And Marvin intended to respect the stipulation. The last thing he ever wanted to do was damage such a rare piece of history. His only intent was to view the remains. He was looking for something, some malformity, some indication that this was Pinot LeFlore. Something that would connect this skeleton to the story of the brothers. But even Marvin realized this was a shot in the dark.

As this thought went through his mind, he let out a mental sigh. He could see the bones without the aid of the magnifying glass. Did he really expect to turn up anything new with it? He wasn't Sherlock Holmes and Marvin, although enthralled with having access, began to temper his expectations.

Tatterhorn's last conscious memory was of lying on his back in the soft sand with his hands folded on his chest and looking up at the ceiling of branches and leaves intent on blocking the sunlight. Minutes, maybe hours, passed as the noise of the outside world had faded and he began to hear a faint rustling within his prison. As immeasurable time passed, it grew louder. It was a sound no man should have been able to perceive, a sensory experience reserved for Mother Nature alone.

It was the sound of the trees growing, stretching their massive frames and slowly extending their branches to seal him more tightly inside. Above, the jutting limbs and flocking leaves resembled a spider web that was slowly closing. Each quadrant sealed. *No way in Hell for the fly to pass through.* Every conceivable avenue of escape was being manipulated to create a solid barrier. From where he was, Tatterhorn could not see the separated trees where he had entered and Seymour and his buddy had escaped, but he was certain it was sealed as well.

As the light was stolen from him, he was sure death was imminent. But death was not what he feared.

This small area of ground, that until yesterday morning had been nothing more than sparse bushes and patches of grass, had locked his fate. The same place he had been in awe of Monday morning when he'd left the visitor's center after chatting with the two outsiders and saw the precise circular rim of trees. A patch of earth that he had never been sure was the location of the pond even though it was where the legend had said it was.

Now he believed. Deep down he had always believed.

As the branches reached out and intersected, Tatterhorn became aware of a second sound he prayed was just within his tortured mind. It was a silky, grinding churning sound. Like the sound of roller blades gliding along a wooden floor. A soothing yet disturbing feel of sand traced his body. It started at his right elbow and moved down his thigh to his feet, then back up to his left thigh, left elbow, arm, around his shoulder, to the side of his face, over his head and back around. The swirling pattern didn't stop upon completion of its lap, but continued. A grim picture of police chalk outlining a corpse came to him.

With each completed cycle it gained speed. Tatterhorn tried to lift his head to see what he felt, but something firmly held him to the ground and he opted not to fight for fear of upsetting the force. A force he was all too sure controlled him. A force that he knew would soon dominate him.

As the sand circled up the left side of his face on the fourth pass, he cut his eyes hard to the side to try and see but to no avail. His fright escalated.

Tatterhorn's heart pounded in his chest and his breathing became rapid and sporadic. For a moment, he was sure he would hyperventilate. Thirty or forty more times around his body and he realized the ground below him was giving way. He could feel the sand moving aside and see it begin to close in as he sank level with the surface. As the sand engulfed his body he became light-headed. He tried to move his hands but they were paralyzed.

Moments later he was in darkness.

When the blackness left, everything around him was composed of shadows and translucent images. There was no more feeling in any part of his massive frame and he wondered what was supporting his weight. Then he began to drift. The suspended feeling bewildered him. Up, down, right, left, north, south, east, west had no meaning. He was no longer contained.

He just was.

And then calmness pervaded his soul. He knew he was at the entryway to heaven.

It was peaceful. Death had become an ally, and the horrid fear was gone. His life had ended rather quickly and virtually without pain. Time itself had no parameters, as he seemed to flow in one constant direction.

Watching the maze of colors he suddenly felt a stinging chill. Then rapid heat traveled the length of whatever his body now was, starting at his feet and racing to his head. It was intense and he tried to scream and release his pain. His mouth would not respond.

Then the cold shuttered through what he had become. Horror embalmed his thoughts. Maybe he had not gone to heaven!

Utter fright eclipsed him.

As the frigid numbness continued, his soul shook violently and his consciousness sailed away for good, abandoning him to the elements.

Scott followed Curt to his apartment. When they arrived, he jumped out of the Blazer and caught Curt with a hug almost knocking his friend over.

"Hey, don't get all emotional and everything."

"Shut up. You saved my life."

"You would've done the same for me. So what'd you do to piss Tatterhorn off and what in the hell was that place?"

"I'll explain on the way back to Marvin's. Jump in."

Curt locked the doors of the Mustang with his remote key chain and climbed in the Blazer. "Scott, we've got to call the police."

"I thought about that. But what am I going to tell them? That Tatterhorn and I were in search of a legendary pond? Even though the lunatic turned on me he's the one with the huge whelp on his back. Maybe even broken ribs. It could turn into his word against ours. The man's a respected park ranger. I just don't want to get into that mess with the cops."

"Tatterhorn might hunt us down," Curt replied.

"I'm more concerned that he will die in those trees. I think you hurt him bad, Curt. He never did move after he hit the dirt."

"I think you'd agree that he deserved it," Curt said.

"Yeah, but what if he died from your blow? Do you really want to get into that right now with the police?"

"It just seems wrong not to report him but I see your point. You still haven't told me why he attacked you?" Curt asked.

"Before I begin, tell me how you found us?" Scott asked inquisitively.

"Well," Curt began, "I give you credit for being a brilliant individual."

Scott gave Curt a questioning look as he put the vehicle in "Reverse" but held on the brake.

"When I arrived at the parking lot I found your truck," Curt began.

"Sport Utility Vehicle."

"Whatever. Anyway, I called Marvin to ask him if he'd heard from you. When he said he hadn't, I decided to go look for you. I had an odd feeling it might be best to catch up. I was pretty sure he was taking you somewhere off the trail so I headed that way. I came upon a couple and they told me two men who fit your description had passed by walking quickly. When I came to the fork where the path veers right into Fort Caroline and left on the nature trail it was a pretty easy decision. But as I moved down the dirt trail I had no way of knowing where you might have exited. I started closely scanning the ground looking for any footprints. That's when I saw it."

"Saw what?"

'It."

"It?"

"The sand drawing of the fish aimed south just off the path. It was very clever. I suspected you had stopped to tie your shoe and used a stick or your finger to draw it as a sign for me. You're quite the artist. I have to say, I was most impressed. It looked just like the Kilgotian's skeleton. Right down to the protruding teeth."

Scott looked at Curt dumbfounded.

"What was really ingenious," Curt continued before Scott could respond, "is how you placed the three pennies around it so it'd stick out. I caught the reflection of sunlight and then saw your drawing. I figured you pointed the head of the fish in the direction you were going and, sure enough, went that way and found the clump of trees. As I approached, I heard you and Tatterhorn inside. You know the rest."

After hearing Curt's explanation, Scott returned the Blazer to "Park." He was struggling to assert his next thought into words. When he did, the words came out slowly as if making sure his tongue didn't say anything his brain hadn't approved.

"What the hell are you talking about a fish?" Scott asked.

"The drawing of the Kilgotian. Among the pennies on the ground."

"I do admit to dropping the coins. It wasn't so much for you to find me as it was for us to be able to find the pond without Tatterhorn, if we ever wanted to go back."

"Nice thinking."

"But I didn't draw any picture."

"Think hard, Scott. You're making my skin crawl. The picture was within the triangular placement of the coins. The fish itself was a good ten inches long."

"I didn't do it. When I dropped the coins they weren't more than a few inches apart. As a matter of fact, I really thought I screwed up because I placed them in an area of sand with enough grass so that two of the pennies weren't that visible. I didn't have time to adjust them because I didn't want to raise suspicion with Tatterhorn. But I didn't draw a picture of the fish."

Curt stared at Scott. In his mind he could see the three pennies positioned around the image of the Kilgotian skeleton traced in the sand. It was a picture so perfect, so precise in detail, he had even questioned whether Scott had drawn it. His rational side had convinced him it was the only alternative.

Curt was silent for a moment as he thought through the possibilities. "Maybe it was already there. You just happened to drop the pennies around it?" Curt said, not believing his own words but hoping to arrive at a conclusion that didn't border on the supernatural.

Scott placed the vehicle in "Reverse." The Blazer moved backward and came to a halt. Scott shoved the gearshift into "Drive" and mashed down on the gas. "I didn't draw it," Scott said as the vehicle moved forward.

"Maybe you got help," Curt said, trying to lighten the moment. "Somebody up there likes you. It's good to have important friends in high places"

"Don't go there," Scott warned keeping his eyes on the road.

Curt shook his head slightly from side to side. "How strange these last two days have been. When I finally wake up its going to be Monday morning and I'm going to realize this all never happened. And guess what? We're not going to start it off by going to the powder magazine in the Castillo de San Marcos at St. Augustine this time. We're just heading straight to the beach."

Scott forced a smile as he drove out of Curt's apartment complex and onto the main road. On the ride back to Marvin's, Scott went into complete detail about Tatterhorn's comments and their verbal exchange within the confines of the trees. How the big man seemed to be ghastly afraid of the sandy area and how he flipped into a knife-wielding psychotic. Scott mentioned how Tatterhorn referred to the sand as *the pond* and mentioned that a madman took the fish from it. Scott also told how Tatterhorn had rambled about the power of the pond, describing it in such a way it led Scott to think the pond was somehow craving the Kilgotian.

After 20 minutes of talking, Scott took a break.

"All of this seems so unreal," Curt said. "You realize this fish could turn out to be one of the greatest archeological finds ever?"

"If it doesn't kill us first," Scott replied. "Something I forgot to tell you. Tatterhorn mentioned that with each Soulful One, the fish commands more."

"More what? More attention? More money? More M&Ms?"

"I think his words were, a larger army."

"Oh, that's comforting."

"Tatterhorn said one other thing that disturbs me. He said God has washed his hands of it. He was referring to the fish," Scott said in a serious tone.

"Do you really think God had anything to do with something supposedly so evil?"

"I wouldn't give anything Tatterhorn said much credence. He sounded completely insane. It was just the way he said it. Like a higher being was responsible," Scott replied.

"Well, God did create everything on earth. Therefore it stands to reason he created the Kilgotian," Curt said.

"Look Curt, I really don't think we should get into a conversation about God and creation." Curt knew Scott was right.

Although Scott had always believed in God, they had gotten into some recent debates about the Bible and the feasibility of various biblical accounts. Scott took a more analytical and judicious approach these days. More and more he questioned his own belief and the stories surrounding the miraculous events described in the Greatest Book Ever Written.

Why should he accept something that had never been proven to exist, at least to him? He'd never seen God. Never heard him talk or felt his presence. It was just something he had believed in as a kid. Like Santa Claus, the Easter Bunny and the Tooth Fairy.

So why did he still believe in God? How old do you have to be before reality hits you square on the head and makes you wonder how come you've been believing in something that has no basis other than millions of other believers who, themselves, have never see him? Seen it? Seen whatever the heck God is supposed to be?

He had recently determined it might be time to grow up. But when faith has been your guide for so many years it's a hard thing to release. It's a security blanket. Ironically, most choose to believe in God for fear of his wrath upon the nonbelievers. Scott's opinion on this was simple yet direct. If God only wanted us to believe in him, then it would have been preprogrammed into mankind's brain. It would have been a hereditary trait. A genetic hard code. Of course, purists argue that belief is voluntary for a reason. The acceptance of the unseen is our key to get into heaven.

Scott had a visual of God standing at the desk of the Holy Holiday Inn. As guests check in, he eyes their Lifetime Report Card. *Mr Parker. Pleased to meet you. I see you got an A on belief. Very, very nice. What an outstanding human you are. I guess I can overlook this 'D+' you got in Marriage (there's some notation here about adultery?) and the 'F' in Political Science (something about lying to the Grand Jury?). These little indiscretions can be overlooked since you believe in me.*

On the other hand, Scott was struggling with the notion of a godless existence. This led him to concede the possibility of a godlike higher power. But the belief had recently taken a serious hit and was waning. Someone, or moreover something, had created mankind. As an amateur archeologist, Scott knew man's inhabitance of the earth had only been during the last 2 million years. A mere speck on the timeline of mother earth, estimated to be 4.5 billion years old. In comparison, as we all found out in Jurassic Park, dinosaurs had been around for more than 200 million years. So for man to believe in God was a way of justifying his existence. We'd be really upset if scientists were able to discover someday that the human species was born out of elephant dung. The whole story of Adam and Eve would have to be junked.

But what really made Scott lose faith (if that's what you call becoming a "realist," he had argued with Curt) was his questioning of the biblical stories. It seemed that back in those times, a miracle occurred about every three or four days. As far as Scott could recall, he'd never witnessed a miracle. He was thirty-seven. Now granted the world's a big place, and maybe they occurred where he wasn't. But with mass communication the way it is, and the use of the Internet, it was strange there had been none reported. You'd think a miracle would create quite a stir.

Oh, yeah. There were the interesting and absurd stories in the *Star* and *Daily Ledger*. Front-page articles about the statue of Mother Mary in some church in South America bleeding from the eyes, numerous Elvis sightings in Wisconsin and the half-man, half-woolly mammoth babies found in some African jungle. But none of this was proof positive. No confirmations of a bona fide, 100 per cent, absolute miracle. It was so disappointing. Scott jokingly estimated that in his lifetime alone, there should have been 4,320 godly events, give or take a couple hundred. Why hadn't any occurred? It seemed very convenient that the headman had elected to show himself long ago but stayed away from modern man.

Why was that? Why had God elected to take the Fifth Amendment when there was so much need for His abilities? When children and adults are dying from cancer and AIDS? When turbulence and war continue to desecrate the lives of millions? When poverty and homelessness have become an accepted way of life, even in the United States? Why? Scott thought he was beginning to understand why. There was really no mighty-one perched on high watching over us that cared. No Supreme Being called God to wave his wand and cause miraculous endings. No entity to turn horrid misfortunes into happily-ever-afters. The whole concept was just that. It was a fairy tale. Man's fiction to make things better. Something to turn to in times of need. A desperation plea. A crutch, if you will. The entire cause, was actually a sham. A charade. *They* had been fooling Scott since he was three. Now in his mid-thirties, he struggled to conjure up enough sensible answers to explain the being everyone calls God.

With all of this incentive and justification for nonbelief, Scott still occasionally talked to God in times of need. He just wouldn't admit it. Even to himself. Usually he did it unconsciously.

The last conversation Scott and Curt had on the subject ended without ending. On that particular day riding home from the movies, Scott had gotten Curt exasperated and the two separated that afternoon not as close friends, but as opponents on either side of the ring. It had left both men with an unpleasant feeling and they later agreed to keep their distance on the topic. Friends should never discuss politics or religion. After their lively discussion that day, Curt understood the sense in this rule. He planned to adhere to it.

"Hey, guess who I ran into at the Gift Shop?" Curt said in an obvious ploy to change the direction of the conversation.

"Your mother?"

"Nope."

"My mother?"

"Nope. I was with her last night in the Jacuzzi. She's probably still sleeping in."

"I give up."

"My future wife," Curt said as his mouth turned up at the corners.

"Isn't one alimony payment enough?" Scott said laughing.

"I'm serious. Her name's Sherri. She's the woman Marvin is using to translate those French documents. She's incredibly cute. Got a great personality and she's smart."

"So when's the wedding?" Scott asked as he turned the Blazer onto U.S. 1 heading south. They were 30 minutes from Marvin's.

"It'll probably be delayed by Damon. She's leaving town this evening."

Curt opened his mouth to say more but was interrupted by the ringing of Scott's cell phone.

Marvin carefully examined the rustic bones as best he could through the plastic covering. His anxieties had settled for the moment. He started with the case containing the torso and head. The skeleton itself was in an amusingly pristine state. Having been sealed in the powder magazine for centuries enhanced an extraordinary job of preservation. The features were crisp and defined. But nothing unusual appeared to Marvin.

Running the magnifying glass the length of the chest to the skull revealed no glaring anomalies. Marvin sighed. His thoughts raced back and forth.

"Think, Marvin, think." He had started with little inspiration but now, for some unforeseen reason, he felt invigorated. There is something to be found. I know it. I can feel it. Marvin was not generally a man concerned with psychic vibes or premonitions, but this one was strong. The skeleton on his dining room table had a message to convey. But he hadn't figured out the language. But there it was. It was in front of him. Dead and still. The last earthly pieces of a man.

As Marvin examined the second enclosure with the leg bones, his thoughts scurried back to Curt's manuscript and of the pond the young Indian had told the brothers about. How Pinot LeFlore had been locked away in a fort. Marvin's findings on the Internet. The information about the Kilgotian fish and the legend of its power. In a flashback, he recounted the terrible noise and the improbable partial recreation of the fish when it had come in contact with water. All of these memories over the last 48 hours wound in his head like a chaotic ball of yarn, continuing to wrap tighter and tighter.

It was the same feeling he had when he was flying out of town and sensed he'd left something behind. Something he forgot to pack. Every damn time he had that feeling it had been correct. A pair of shoes, a belt, his glasses. The feeling was never wrong. Someone standing near the back of the shop in his mind always took inventory. Unfortunately, he was a meek and soft-spoken man whose voice was not always heard clearly in the control room. The man running the show could hear the shouts from the back but the words were often unrecognizable. Just sounds that barely made it to the front. In essence, the controller knew something had been left off the list just because the distant man was making noise. But that's all it was. No detectable words.

Marvin had that same feeling now. The man in the back of the shop knew what he was missing and he was screaming his lungs out trying to draw attention. But the man wasn't close enough to the control room to make sense.

Frustrated, Marvin sat down at one of the table chairs and laid the magnifying glass down. He rubbed his eyes with his hands in an attempt to block out light and any and all distractions. "Come on Marvin. Something's here. Something that's not right," he told himself.

He removed his fingers from his now watery eyes and allowed them to focus on the third and last plastic container. The case that held the humerus, radius, ulna and carpals.

There it was.

Of course.

He was looking for the not-so-obvious and there it was. Right out in the open. He rose and almost lost his balance as the chair teetered back and then fell with a hard thud on the dining room floor. Six inches farther and it would have dinged the china cabinet. Gathering control, he walked excitedly back to the spare bedroom, stepping around the debris littering the hallway. In his rush, he cut the entryway into the bedroom too tight and slammed his right shoulder into the door jam.

"Ouch," he muttered as the pain creased down his arm and into his elbow. Once in the room he proceeded to the desk where the deep round glass bowl contained the artifact the boys had brought him yesterday morning. The object lay peaceful at the base immersed in the cleaning agent. The hydrogen oxidite was working, the fluid was stained from the dirt coating, but the item was still unrecognizable.

"It's time to rush the process," Marvin whispered as he grabbed a set of forceps from the lap drawer and retrieved the object from the bowl. He allowed it to drip dry for half a minute and then laid the object on a folded towel on the right side of the desk. He felt his pulse quicken as he grabbed several small instruments from the drawer and began slowly scraping off the debris.

The solution had been more effective than he initially thought. The outer corrosion was easily stripping with each pass. Several minutes later, as he ran the metal scraping tool over the length of the object, he heard a very familiar sound.

An unmistakable sound.

The sound of metal on metal.

He quickly dropped the metal object back into the hydrogen oxidite and, using the forceps, shook most of the remaining aged decomposition off.

It was a small knife.

He was not surprised. He had actually expected it.

The handle was mostly decayed but the steel blade was distinctive. Marvin placed the object back on the side of the folded towel. His heart was thumping. He realized the room was filled with intense silence as he worked. A small shiver traced his spine. It was still not completely clean.

He plopped the object back into the hydrogen oxidite faster and from a farther drop than he meant. The solution kicked up and caught him with a single drop in his left eye, somehow circumventing his glasses. A stinging burn pierced through his cornea. The pain was immediate and intense. He had never really understood the term *climbing the walls* but it had true meaning for him now. If he'd had longer fingernails, he would've been on the ceiling by now. As the package said, "Avoid swallowing or contact with eyes."

Marvin pulled off his glasses and placed a hand over the eye and stumbled into the kitchen. This time he caught his left knee on the out-of-place protruding bathroom door.

"Ouch!"

He moved to the sink and bent down as far as he could. He turned on the faucet and flushed the eye with cold water. Good thing he had decided to do the dishes piled in the sink this morning or he'd be laying his head in half of a bowl of Campbell's Chicken Noodle Soup. This brought some relief but even after five minutes of rushing water and several minutes of wiping his eye with a clean dishtowel, he could still feel the residual burning.

"Nice move, stupid," he said as a commentary to himself. It sounded like a comedian putting a drunken heckler in his place. He sat down at the kitchen table after grabbing a mirrored magnet off the refrigerator door. He removed the dishtowel from his left eye as the nerves began to settle. He was worried about the damage. Even when he had concluded the rinsing his vision had been blurred, and not the type of blur that glasses can correct. It was a distorted blur. But after holding the towel on for several minutes his eye had regained strength and seemed to be adjusting. He looked down into the mirror and was pleasantly surprised to see the red swelling corpuscles had subsided. Although he had not seen his eye immediately after the splash of the hydrogen oxidite, he was sure it must have resembled an all-red fireworks display on Independence Day.

He used the towel to wipe his nose. The moment the pain set into his eye, fluid had begun streaming out of his nose. It streaked straight down and hovered on his top lip but the dishtowel saved the day. He tossed it on the counter beside the sink making a mental note to place it with the dirty clothes later.

Scott took the cell phone from the middle console of the SUV.
"Hello."
"Scott, it's Marvin. Did Curt catch up with you?"
"Yeah. He's here with me. We're on our way back to your place. We've got quite a story to tell you."
"Tatterhorn?"
"Yeah. We'll tell you what happened when we get there. Did the skeleton arrive from the museum."
"Oh boy! Did it ever!"

"What do you mean by that?"

Curt turned to look at Scott's inquisitive expression.

"Even before it arrived I had a feeling it would reveal something interesting. I kept looking over the bones but almost didn't notice something quite obvious?"

"And what was that?"

"Well, after the skeleton arrived I decided to check on the artifact you brought to me yesterday. It was still soaking and didn't look like much. I hurried the process with some manual intervention. I did some careful cleaning. I'll tell you a secret. Never get hydrogen oxidite in your eye. It's not a pleasant experience."

"I'll catalog that one for future reference. Now what about the artifact?"

"It turned out to be a knife. I matched it against pictures of other knifes from the time period of 1585 – 1690 and it seems to fit the description. Crude but effective."

"What is it?" Curt asked Scott.

"A knife?" Scott whispered.

"What'd you say?" Marvin asked.

"Nothing. Go on."

"Yeah, but here's the interesting part. The skeleton found in the powder magazine is missing the ring finger of the right hand."

"Are you sure?" Scott asked.

"Of course I'm sure."

"Sure of what?" Curt asked.

"Marvin, hold on."

Scott placed the cell phone in his lap. "Marvin says the artifact you found by the Kilgotian is a knife. Curt think hard. Remember the second item you picked up and placed down your shirt. The one that never made it out with us."

"Yeah."

"Could it have been a human metacarpal?"

Curt paused, thinking back to the powder magazine and briefly examining the object in the dim light. The thing had been about 2 ½ to 3 inches long and, as he recalled, had two bumps at just about even intervals down the shaft.

"It's possible. It's very possible," he said excitedly.

Scott lifted the phone. "Marvin, remember us telling you yesterday Curt had removed one other object from beneath the slab that was lost. It's quite possible it was a finger bone."

Marvin's response was very articulate. "I think that Pinot LeFlore, if that's who is lying on my dining room table, used the knife to cut off his own finger and then hid it under the slab."

Scott didn't know how to respond to Marvin's notion but, based on the physical evidence, it did make sense. What was intriguing was the why?

Why would a man sever his finger in the first place? Even more confusing, why would he hide the detached appendage?

Scott did know one thing for sure. The Kilgotian was intimately involved.

"Marvin, we'll be there shortly. Just sit tight. What happened with Tatterhorn is very bizarre."

"Don't come to my house," Marvin said suddenly. "Meet me at the Nuestra de la Leche Cemetery."

"Why?" Scott asked, expecting the answer to be somehow related to the information he was having Curt's future wife translate.

"I want to show you something."

"Did your translator come up with something?"

"No. It has nothing to do with that. Just meet me there. I'll see you in the parking lot. Just tell me this. Did you find the pond?"

"I think so."

CHAPTER-TWENTY-TWO

Scott and Curt arrived at the cemetery just after 3 p.m. Marvin's car was parked and empty. They proceeded up the walkway toward the gift shop. Curt had been on cloud nine since Scott had informed him they were coming back. He was hoping to catch Sherri. Since he had no idea of what hours she worked he tried to temper his anticipation.

Scott saw the moonstruck expression come over Curt's face as the woman, who could only have been Sherri, strolled out of the door toward the men, her red hair floating in the wind and framing her face with a model's appeal. Her walk was easy and confident. Scott could instantly see what had drawn his friend's attention. If she had a mind and wasn't arrogant, he understood Curt's wedding plan preparations. She was carrying the envelope with Marvin's documents and shot a flirtatious little grin when she saw Curt.

"Nice," Scott said softly under his breath as he and Curt continued up the walkway.

"What a coincidence meeting you here," Curt said returning her grin. "You come here often?"

"Every weekday," she said. "I also leave everyday at three o'clock to pick up my daughter from school. Were you coming to see me?" Sherri asked.

"Truthfully? No, but I'm certainly not disappointed I did."

"Isn't that sweet," she replied.

The bantering had become too soppy for Scott. "You two are making me ill. This is like a conversation out of a Harlequin Romance novel," he said with a chuckle.

"Who's your ill friend?" Sherri asked.

"This is Scott Seymour. But don't mind him. He's been sick ever since I've known him."

"It's a pleasure to meet you," she said extending her hand. "I'm Sherri Falco. Part-time gift shop clerk and translator extraordinaire."

"It's a pleasure. Have you seen Marvin Sellon? He's probably inside."

"To be honest, I've never met the man. I only saw him one time so I probably wouldn't recognize him if I did. Sorry."

"Sherri, you would've known him," Curt cut in. "He has this big fluorescent nametag across his chest that blinks in split-second intervals with green and red lights. He resembles a Christmas tree."

Scott looked at Curt as if he'd just downed a fifth of Bacardi. Sherri smiled wryly. For a moment Curt really thought she was offended until she spoke.

"Those are reserved for Gift Shop employees on their 25th anniversary of employment. Now wipe that grin off your face," she said laughing. "Scott Seymour it was nice to meet you. As for you, I expect to hear from you soon," she said, giving Curt a glance that set his pulse racing.

With that, Sherri Falco walked to the parking lot and got in her car. She backed-up and waved goodbye as the men stood on the sidewalk watching.

"I think I'm in love," Curt said.

"C'mon," Scott began, "let's find the Professor."

The two entered the gift shop. No sign of Marvin. Curt moved to the counter where Nora was propped on a stool reading a John Grisham novel.

"Hello, Nora."

"Well hello. Didn't expect to see you back so soon. You just missed Sherri."

"I'm looking for Marvin. Have you seen him? His car's out front."

"No, I haven't."

"We're going through the cemetery. If you happen to see him, please send him our way."

"Will do."

"Thanks."

Scott and Curt moved to the back of the store where a door led out to the cement path. Once outside they scanned the immediate area. The day had turned out beautiful and the sun was at full bore. But underneath the cover of the oaks that filled the area, the grounds were shady and cool.

There were two ways for the public to access the cemetery; one was through the gift shop and the second by way of the bridge that spans the saltwater pond at the north end of the parking lot. In distance, the two entrances were only about 50 yards apart since the cemetery itself was not large. It was unusual that Marvin would have parked at this end of the parking lot but then may have entered by the small bridge. It was obvious he was nowhere near the back of the gift shop so the men walked down the winding sidewalk toward the chapel in the middle of the cemetery.

A slight breeze kicked up as scattered patches of visitors walked the grounds. Beyond to the east the bay was tranquil. A few sailboats sat quietly off shore.

As Scott always liked to do, he read the dates on the tombstones in between searching for Marvin. The graves were not clumped together but distributed unevenly and sparsely in no particular order. Scott had always thought they could have buried four times the number here if necessary.

Scott and Curt approached the north side of the small chapel. Two wooden doors with an arched stone covering marked the entrance. Ivy engulfed almost the entire structure.

Still no Marvin.

"Maybe he's inside praying after his experience with the fish," Curt said.

"Maybe we should be after our experience with Tatterhorn," Scott replied.

They stood near the entry to the chapel and stepped aside as an elderly couple came out. The older man was wearing Bermuda shorts with a bright flowery short-sleeve, button-up shirt. The white socks and hard black shoes put an exclamation mark on the entire ensemble. Even his wife, dressed in more conservative attire, seemed embarrassed to be walking around with her neon husband. Curt and Scott glanced at each other with the same thought and had to fight back the laughter.

"If I ever become that senile please shoot me," Scott said laughing after the couple was out of distance.

Scott signaled right and they continued around the west side of the small chapel. Ahead, just to the left, stood Marvin Sellon. He was reading a notepad and then scanned the ground to his right as the men approached.

"You're a hard man to find," Scott said.

"I've been right here. It's not like this is a large cemetery. I'm going to start calling you two eagle-eye."

"Whatcha got? Why are we here?" Curt asked, barely beating Scott to the question.

"After determining the finger you found was probably from the skeleton in the powder magazine I got to thinking. This whole thing's one big mystery. I normally would take my time and research each fact carefully but Tucker's death has me unnerved. I feel a sense of urgency to all this."

"As do we Marvin. As do we," Scott said.

"I got back on the Internet and started researching the one thing we hadn't concentrated on."

"Which is?" Curt asked.

"The source of your document, Curt. Where it came from."

"I told you. I got it from an estate sale. I can't recall the man's name at the moment."

"Jean Luc LeFlore. It was the manuscript created by Deure, his great-grandfather based on stories of Pinot and Reece passed down through generations. How did you happen to come across this particular document?"

"Just luck or unluck, depending on your perspective," Curt responded. "I had heard about the estate sale from . . ." His words died as he looked up into the high branches of the trees covering the area. His speech was frozen as he checked his recollection.

"I heard about it from an e-mail advertisement."

The three men stood silent as the gentle wind blew and tourists grazed the historical grounds.

"Where's this leading, Marvin?" Scott chimed in.

"I think Tucker was in town for a specific reason. I did some research on Jean Luc LeFlore and discovered he was in St. Augustine when he died of natural causes. And get this. He paid good money to be buried here."

"Here where? Here?" Scott asked pointing to the ground.

"Here, there." Marvin replied, aiming to the right.

The tombstone, not more than eight feet away, was a light shade of gray and obviously much newer than those in the immediate vicinity. The words were sunk deep in its surface.

> *Jean Luc LeFlore*
> ***Born 1926***
> ***Descent to the French Huguenots***
> ***"Water Transcends Time"***

"Another reference to water. I feel like we're in the middle of a Mickey Spillane mystery with a Stephen King twist," Scott said. "This is so strange. Curt, did you know about this?"

"Nope. I assumed he was buried somewhere in California where he lived. "Hey," he said inquisitively, "where's the date of death?"

"I wondered the same thing. I asked a groundskeeper and he said he had no idea either but it was not a mistake. It was listed with only his birthdate at his request prior to his death."

"And the burial plot thickens," Curt said.

"And get this. He was buried with some of his personal effects."

"Anything of interest?" Scott asked with raised eyebrows.

"Some jewelry; a watch and a bracelet, a favorite hat, a bible and a family manuscript," Marvin replied.

"A family manuscript, huh? Any idea what words of wisdom it contained?" Curt asked.

"Nope. But I know where you're going because I thought the same thing."

"Damn, I'd sure like to get a look at it," Scott said.

"Well, it's too late for that. Now tell me about Mr. Tatterhorn." Marvin asked.

The three men walked back to the parking lot, this time traversing the bridge, as Scott and Curt depicted the events that transpired at Fort Caroline earlier that afternoon.

In the distance, back toward the bay, the huge Beacon of Faith Cross soared into the sky, it's massive steel frame stretching up and out at the intersecting pieces. The sun beamed off it, reflecting in several directions as the calm water sat below. The clouds were juxtaposed in the background as the happy visitors caravaned through *America's Most Sacred Acre*.

On the ride back to Marvin's house, the voice on the radio foretold the weather in a flat, emotionless, monotone voice.

"At 3:30 p.m. eastern time, Hurricane Damon is positioned 538 miles from the Florida coast keeping its steady aim and methodically plodding along. The winds are now up to 134 miles per hour. The storm has gained intensity as it flourishes over the open Atlantic. Although still a Category 4, this has become a hurricane of such magnitude and potential that forecasters and emergency planners have begun to prepare with the highest degree of caution. There are still 41 hours until Damon is expected to slug the shores of northeast Florida with nothing in its path but open water. Damon should become a Category 5 by early Wednesday with sustained winds in excess of 155 miles per hour. If it goes as predicted, it will make landfall Thursday morning. Experts are comparing this storm to Hurricane Camille whose sustained winds were estimated to be in excess of 175 mph. Some of Camille's winds exceeded the 205 miles per hour velocity found in most tornadoes."

"Son-of-a-bitch," Scott mumbled.

Curt just shook his head.

Scott knew if Damon hit as a Category 5, the storm surge would be in excess of 18 feet. He had learned from living in Florida that this is the most devastating effect of a hurricane. The surge would coincide with the storm's contact with land and cover the low-lying areas with one to five feet of water. The crushing waves would continue to ride in, tearing at the coast and new found waterways. Any structures less than 12 feet above sea level would suffer major damage. All beachfront homes would be devastated.

Each year, about 60 intense storms come to life in the Atlantic. On average, only 10 reach tropical storm strength and only six become hurricanes. Florida sees its share with almost 40 percent hitting the Atlantic or Gulf of Mexico shores. In this part of the world, a hurricane reaches Category 5 intensity, on average, once every three years with only two striking the United States in the last century. Recently, the closest in strength was Hurricane Andrew, a strong Category 4. In August of 1992, Andrew blistered South Florida with sustained winds of 145 miles per hour and gusts over 175 miles per hour. The destruction was colossal, prompted by a seventeen-foot storm surge.

At 3:42 p.m., the mayors of St. Augustine and Jacksonville were conducting emergency meetings with their respective City Council members, linked via conference phone. The latest update on Damon's position, strength, wind speed and estimated time till landfall had just been received from NOAA, the National Hurricane Center on the campus of Florida International University in Miami. The mood in the rooms was anxious.

It was one of those rare times when politicians were in complete agreement. When two cities were in complete agreement. The councils passed unanimous decisions to evacuate the area's beaches and the entire town of St. Augustine at 7 a.m. the following morning if there was no change in Damon's direction. There was no choice. The First Coast held over a million lives. A direct hit might be unavoidable, but the loss of life could be kept to a minimum if the areas were properly evacuated.

CHAPTER-TWENTY-THREE

At 3:33 p.m. little Tina Falco came bouncing through the doors of the elementary school, her eyes scanning the line of cars for her mommy's. Once found, she ran to the door. Sherri reached over to the passenger seat and threw the envelope in the back. Tina climbed in the car and, as always, was greeted warmly by her mom.

For the better part of the day, Sherri had put the events of the morning out of her head. It had been a nice day with pleasant customers. In particular, one patron stood out. Meeting Curt had created quite a distraction to the sea picture incident. Now she was anxious to get some answers from Tina and put the issue to rest.

"How was your day honey?" Sherri asked.

"Good."

"Did you do anything fun today at school?"

"We saw a movie about the ocean."

"Oh really," Sherri's stomach turned slightly. "Are you studying the ocean this week?" She asked the mute question even though she ached to ask another. The one that was burning a hole in her thoughts.

"Uh huh. Can I have a snack when we get home Mommy?"

"Of course, honey." Sherri barely heard the question. "Tina, I have a question."

"Yes?"

"Remember the beautiful picture you drew for me yesterday? The underwater scene of the ocean I put on our refrigerator?"

"Uh huh."

"After you gave it to me, did you draw any more on it?" Sherri asked the question praying for her daughter to respond positively.

"Yeah, mommy. Did you like what I added?"

Sherri let out a lung full of air that almost whistled between her oval shaped lips as she sighed. "It's a little different sweetheart."

"I thought the picture needed something more."

"Well it sure added something," Sherri said as she turned and smiled at her daughter. Tina beamed back.

The remainder of the ride home, Sherri was upbeat discussing the details of Tina's day at school, the recent Buffy the Vampire Slayer episode, and singing a rousing rendition of Brittany Spear's "I'm not that Innocent" along with the radio. It wasn't until Sherri pulled into the driveway that the uneasiness settled upon her again.

"Honey, what you added to your picture," she said turning the ignition and killing the engine, "it was a fish, right?"

"What?" She gave her mom that childish baffled stare. "Oh yeah. It was a fish."

The momentary lapse of confirmation created a lump in Sherri's throat that slowly began to fade.

Sherri swallowed. "Where'd you get the idea for such a fish?"

"We were studying about pre . . . prehic-storic fish. I tried to make it look like one of those."

"Prehistoric huh?" Sherri cut her daughter a grin. "Well I'd say you accomplished your mission. Come on. Let's go get that snack. Hey, Aunt Charlene will be here later. We're all driving to Tallahassee this evening so we have to make sure we have everything packed."

"Is the hurricane still coming?"

Before taking Tina to school this morning, Sherri had discussed the possibility of leaving town. But Tina still didn't fully comprehend the situation. Sherri knew this was still the case by looking in her eyes.

"I'm afraid so. But we'll be long gone before it gets here. It's not arriving for two more days."

"What's it called again?" Tina asked.

"Damon."

"Why's it called that?"

"Hurricanes are given people names. And they're in alphabetical order. Each year a new list is created that alternates boys' and girls' names. Since this one's called Damon, that means we're on the Ds. So there have already been three storms before Damon this year. One beginning with A, one B, and one C. Does that make sense?"

"I guess. But what happened to the first three storms?" Before Sherri could respond, Tina changed the subject. To her, there was a more pressing topic. "Can we go in and get my snack now?"

Tina had quickly lost interest in Hurricane Naming 101, Sherri thought to herself. "Of course sweetheart."

Tina leaped from the car with her Pokemon book bag in tow dragging the ground.

"Honey, pick that up or you'll ruin it."

Tina walked briskly to the front door with her mother trailing behind. Sherri placed the key in the lock and opened the door for her daughter to enter. Just then, she remembered the envelope in the back seat.

"Tina, I forgot something in the car. I'll be right back."

"OK. Are there any cookies?"

"Check the jar," Sherri said, referring to the big orange cat cookie jar to the left of the stove on the counter.

Sherri strolled back to the car and grabbed the envelope. It was a gorgeous day and the warmth from the sun was comforting on her skin. She paused in the yard for a few seconds to soak in the rays and removed the document from the envelope. She was somewhat curious about what it was and had barely looked at it at the Gift Shop. The glare off the paper was blinding so she returned the document inside. As she slammed the back car door shut, she suddenly remembered her experience in the house this morning and the strange shadow she saw, or thought she saw, through the glass windows at the top of the door. An overwhelming urgency for her daughter's safety bit at her and she broke into a full run back toward the house. She ran onto the porch and glided through the front door at full speed.

"Tina!" she screamed coming to a halt just inside and then remembered the quest for a snack had taken her daughter into the kitchen. She raced through the living room and into the kitchen but it was empty. Her heart nearly exploded.

"TINA!" this time she screamed out of fear. She shot into the hallway and toward her daughter's room. Her chest was heavy as terror draped her mind. She was moving fast but the world seemed to be churning around her, limiting her ability to travel in a straight line. She slipped and ran into the bathroom doorjam but kept moving forward to Tina's room at the end of the hall on the left. The door was almost completely closed and Sherri could feel her mouth go instantly dry as horrifying images of what lay behind the door cascaded before her eyes in a mental kaleidoscope. She reached the door in a full gallop. Her shoulder ached but she was oblivious to the pain. With one quick push she was inside Tina's room. She scanned from left to right and spotted Tina stretched out in bed on top of her comforter with her little hands folded in a perfect arc over her chest. Her eyes were closed and her tiny body was limp.

Sherri ran to the bed and instantly dropped to her knees and hugged her daughter. Tina was so startled, she raised up and smacked Sherri's forehead with her own, sending her headphones flying through the air and landing at the foot of her bed after bouncing off her Mom's backside.

Sherri continued to squeeze Tina and Tina hugged back although not really knowing why or what was going on. The little girl's eyes were as big as saucers.

"Mommy, you frightened me!" Tina said.

"Oh, baby. I'm sorry. Mommy didn't know where you were. You had me scared to death."

"I'm here, Mommy. I was listening to my Brittany CD." She glanced past her mom toward the end of the bed. "I hope my headphones aren't broken."

"If they are, I'll buy you new ones." Sherri said still holding Tina in her arms. Her pulse was returning to some semblance of normalcy. She moved up to sit on the bed beside her daughter.

After a few quiet moments of cuddling, Tina looked up at her mother. Sherri noticed an innocence in her expression that only a child could possess. A purity that is somehow lost as we become adults. What a shame it is she has to grow up, Sherri thought. Tina nestled closer as Sherri felt a spasm of pain radiate through her shoulder. There would be a bruise. A big bruise.

Tina's next words hit Sherri like a bolt of lightning. It was a sentence she would forever remember.

"Mommy, I like the fish you drew on my picture, too."

As intense as the situation had become, the storm had to take precedence. It had formed into a particularly dangerous combination of wind, rain and attitude. All three men were aware of this and as soon as they made it back to Marvin's the conversation alternated between the events of the last few days and their respective evacuation plans. Scott phoned Kay to acknowledge he'd be coming home soon and that they would leave town after securing the house and packing the SUV.

Curt made arrangements to pick Marvin up after a brief visit with his daughter in the morning.

As much as the men wanted to pursue answers to the fish, Tatterhorn, the powder magazine skeleton and its detached finger, they were realists. The legend of the fish was becoming more of a possibility. But Damon was real, and it couldn't be ignored.

So the men tabled the mystery of the Kilgotian and Scott and Curt drove back to Jacksonville reflecting on the preparations for departure. On the ride home, they infrequently mentioned the fish. This was neither by design nor intention. It had become a secondary agenda. In a macabre way, Scott was pleased to have something else to occupy his mind. Since Sunday, the story of the LeFlores had dominated his thoughts. Tucker's death had brought the whole week to a stale, vile standstill and he continued to feel strangely accountable. He knew it was easy to justify his feelings as an absurd case of connect-the-dots, but nonetheless the guilt lingered. And it gnawed at him regardless of his attempts to rationalize it away.

Scott was sure Curt felt the same way.

A few minutes before reaching Curt's apartment, and after nearly ten minutes of silence, Scott spoke. It was an attempt to lighten the atmosphere.

"If a bunch of cows are called cattle, then . . ." he said with a slight hesitation "are a bunch of cats called cowels?"

"Good point." Curt said with a straight face. "But you know what I've really been wondering about?"

"What's that?" Scott bit on purpose.

"You know how new cars are built so that their lights are on all the time?"

"Yeah." Scott responded.

"How will motorists ever determine if a funeral procession is in progress? Maybe the shift will be to turn the headlights off. It would seem to be a more symbolic relationship with the lights out and all."

"I think you're on to something. Either that or you're *on* something. You been working on that one long?" Scott said with a smidgen of humorous sarcasm.

"Nope. It just came to me."

"And I think that's where it should remain."

Upon reaching Curt's apartment, the men had a quick conversation as Curt got out of the Blazer. They both mentioned returning to town Friday afternoon and, depending on the damage, would be back at Marvin's on Saturday morning. Although unsaid, neither had an idea of the next steps. Closure to the situation was something they couldn't get their arms around. For all they knew, they might never understand the legend of the pond or who murdered Tucker but they were unwilling to concede just yet.

As Curt stood outside the passenger side of the vehicle with the door wide open, he looked hard at Scott. Then he seemed reflective as he gazed to the sky. "It's funny, this hurricane coming now."

"What do you mean?" Scott asked.

"It was a hurricane that destroyed the French Huguenots as they sailed to attack the Spanish settlement of St. Augustine in 1565. And now a massive storm is once again on the horizon. It just seems coincidental since we are in the middle of uncovering something that seems so intimately related to this piece of history."

Scott had pondered the same thing, yet tried to dismiss it to his friend. "True, but this is Florida. It's not like hurricanes are uncommon." Even as Scott said the words he didn't believe them. There was another force here at work. He absolutely felt it.

"I know, but still . . ." Curt said as he closed the door. "Hey, good luck. Go get your family out of here," he said to Scott through the open window.

"You too. Take care."

Curt closed the door and waved goodbye as Scott drove away. Curt turned down the sidewalk and climbed the stairs to his apartment.

Sherri stared at Tina. "What fish?" Sherri asked in a shaking voice.

"The other fish in my ocean picture. The one not on the bottom or top. The one in the middle," Tina responded.

Sherri's stomach turned and twisted as she stood up. At that moment the room seemed to illuminate and Tina's face went to stone.

"Didn't you draw it?" Tina asked.

"Of . . . of course honey," her mom stuttered trying to mask her emotions.

Tina's eyes reflected the light again and all was well in her little world.

"He's got really big teeth. I like him."

"Oh," was all Sherri could muster. Her brain again went through all the possibilities of how the fish got in the picture. None she could accept.

"I'll be right back, honey. Just stay here."

"Okay," Tina said innocently.

Sherri left the room and moved down the hallway toward the kitchen. She had often used the term *white as a ghost* and at that moment felt she represented a pretty good interpretation. The walls of the hallway appeared to breathe as she moved toward the kitchen, expanding in and out, somehow, full of life. Now the irrational explanations invaded her brain. Poltergeists? The house was only 12 years old. She was pretty sure there was not a graveyard underneath.

She passed through the entrance to the kitchen and gazed at the refrigerator door. The picture was gone. She searched the room and found it lying on the kitchen table next to the newspaper and several bills. She approached the table with trepidation. The picture looked as it had this morning. The fish positioned in the middle was as angry and vicious as ever. But now Sherri spotted another addition to the scene. Something she hadn't noticed this morning. It was a small round object sitting on the ocean floor. It had abbreviated fins and both eyes were on the same side of its body. It was Tina's new fish. Although crude, Sherri knew it to be a flounder. The eyes gave it away. That's what Tina had meant by prehistoric. Flounders were thought to have been a species of fish that, millions of years ago, had resigned themselves to live on the ocean's bottom. In order to exist as a bottom dweller lying flat on its side, evolution had administered both eyes to one side of the head. This gave it complete upward vision. In essence, it was a funny looking one-dimensional creature with an all white underside. Tina once commented that God had taken a break during its creation and had never gotten back to finishing the job. It was an excellent example of nature's adaptation but the flounder did look like an incomplete product.

Sherri lifted the picture from the table examining it further. She desperately wanted to ask Tina where the vicious looking fish had come from and who was responsible for it. But since she'd already told a white lie, she decided against it.

She walked to the counter and opened the second drawer that was packed with Tina's miscellaneous school papers, treasures only a mom would save and cherish but with little value to anyone else. In one motion, the picture was shoved inside and the drawer quickly closed.

Sherri walked back to the kitchen table and sat down. Suddenly she felt like she was six years old and had just awakened from a terrible nightmare, very alone and insecure. Sobbing and crying in bed, her mom would eventually come to comfort her. But until then, it was a very desolate feeling. Exposed and unprotected, easy pray for anything evil lurking in the darkness. She would lie motionless in bed trembling with the covers above her head perspiring.

But her mother was not here to comfort her.

No one was here to comfort her.

Tina was down the hall but Sherri would never allow her daughter to see fear in her mother's eyes. This would be a secret Tina would never learn.

Sherri wiped her brow and cleared the warm moisture that had pooled above her left eye.

In the silent house, she could hear the distant sound of Tina singing and the faint swish of water cycling through the aquarium pump and back into the tank.

She wondered what Curt Lockes was doing at that very moment.

Scott arrived home at 5:45 p.m. after picking up Cody from the daycare. Kay had left work at 5:30 p.m. and, with the traffic more congested than usual, wouldn't arrive till after six.

Scott had considered stopping by the grocery store to pick up some items but the overflowing parking lot convinced him otherwise. Bottled water, batteries and Sterno were flying off the shelves faster than they could be stocked. It was the normal course of human behavior. He and Kay were prepared for hurricane season and because they were evacuating and not trying to ride this one out, any supplies they needed could be acquired along the way.

Katie and Lindsey were busy packing their personal items. Mom had called and gotten the ball rolling. The plan was to leave by 7:30 so there was little time to waste.

"Cody, go to your room and pack some toys in the small suitcase in your closet," Scott said as they made their way upstairs. Cody went bouncing off and Scott headed to his bedroom to pack.

Thirty minutes later Kay arrived home, somewhat frazzled. What Scott was about to tell her would not be taken well. In the last 15 minutes his personal plans had changed.

As soon as she walked through the door he motioned for her to go upstairs. She followed wearing a puzzled expression but without asking, assuming it was something not for the kids to hear.

"Kay, I need to stay behind until the morning," Scott said.

"What? Why?"

"I need to help secure the office. Taylor called me a few minutes ago and asked if I could lend a hand."

"Scott, we really should leave tonight. Otherwise we'll get caught up in the traffic like last year."

"And you will leave tonight. You and the kids."

Kay looked at him and was about to argue but saw a steadfast determination in her husband's eyes. "You really should leave tonight with us," she said with a hint of bitterness. "You're going to get caught up in the same bullshit we did last year. You'll be sitting in one spot on I-95 for 15 minutes and then move five feet before stopping again. If you remember, we averaged about three miles an hour for the first four hours. You're also leaving me in a car to deal with three kids tonight. I hope you don't think I'm happy about this."

"I know, Kay, but I have responsibilities."

"You have a responsibility to your family as well."

"And I wouldn't do anything to put you guys in danger. That's why I want you to leave this evening."

There was really no point in arguing. Scott was not budging and her attitude shifted several minutes later as she quietly accepted the situation. "Do you want to take the Blazer? I'd really feel more comfortable in my car." She had given in almost too easily. Scott was relieved she hadn't continued to push the issue.

"That's fine. I'll leave in the morning as soon as I'm done at the office. Were you able to get the reservations at the Holiday Inn in Valdosta?"

"Yeah. They only had a few rooms left so we were lucky. I just can't believe the one time we get an opportunity to visit Sheila, they're in Las Vegas."

"I'll meet you guys there, hopefully in the early afternoon." Scott made the statement with no clear notion of whether he'd be there or not.

"Scott is there something else? I know Tucker's death is not easy. It's just you and Curt seemed so wrapped up the last couple of days in your archeological whims."

"Whims?" Scott replied with obvious dissatisfaction in her choice of words.

"You know what I mean. I didn't mean it to sound trivial. But it is just a hobby. It's not like you're getting paid for it."

"Kay, there are other motivators in life besides money."

"I know. But this hurricane is a monster and we better make sure our attention is focused on it," she said, removing another Samsonite suitcase from the closet and tossing it on the bed.

"Don't worry. I have my priorities straight," he said.

At 10 minutes till eight, after hugging Scott and saying their goodbyes, Kay drove the stationwagon out of the driveway. She played the tough, I-can't-show-emotions-in-front-of-the-kids, type to a tee. Scott respected the hell out of her for it, too. Cody was half-heartedly waving from the back, sitting beside the car carrier where Austin was meowing nervously. Tears fell on the little boy's cheeks. He was crying because his daddy was not coming with them. No matter how many times Scott told his son he'd be with them tomorrow, Cody begged through a face streaming with tears for daddy to come. Cody's pleas tugged at his heart and it was all Scott could do not to cry. He continued waving as they drove out of sight and then turned toward the doorway. He reached down and grabbed his shirt pulling it up to his eyes and wiped the moisture away.

"Goddamn that fish," he muttered as he went back in the house slamming the door behind him.

CHAPTER-TWENTY-FOUR

At 20 minutes past six, Curt picked up the phone. He held the crumpled register tape in his hand as he dialed. Before the end of the third ring a woman's voice answered.

"Sherri?"

"No. I'm sorry. She's not here at the moment. Can I take . . . maybe it would be best if you called back later," the woman said with obvious concern.

"Excuse me. She asked that I call before she went out of town. Is she still leaving at six thirty?"

"Well, that was the plan," the woman responded.

"What do you mean?" Curt asked.

"May I ask who you are. How you know my sister?"

"My name is Curt. She's helping me with some information."

"Oh, right. She said you might call. I'm her sister, Charlene. Sorry for the interrogation. It's just that I'm worried. She left as soon as I got here, around ten minutes after five. She went back to work to pick up Tina's rag doll. One of the arms was about to fall off and a woman there repaired it for her. Sherri forgot to bring the doll home so she went back to get it. It's just that she should have been back about 20 minutes ago. She was the one so insistent we leave at 6:30. She's afraid if we're late arriving in Tallahassee that the hotel won't hold our reservation."

"The gift shop is probably closed and locked up tight. Does she have keys to get in?" Curt asked, trying to hide his concern.

"Yeah. She said she has full access. I even tried calling her on the cell phone but it just rings and then goes to messaging." Charlene's voice again wavered with concern. Then it lowered. Curt could hear what he assumed to be Tina singing in the background. "I just saw the news about that poor girl who was killed near St. Augustine. I would go looking for her but I'm afraid she'll return while I'm gone. Besides, I don't want to upset her daughter."

Curt had not seen the news and knew nothing about a murder. The words landed but he didn't allow them to soak in. He was more concerned about the woman he had met that afternoon with the sweet smile and charismatic personality. "Charlene, if she doesn't show up by 6:45, call me. Even if she does, have her call me. My number is . . ."

"I got it. It's on the caller ID. Where are you calling from?"

"Just up the road in Jacksonville. I could be there in thirty minutes. OK, call me at 6:45."

"Goodbye." Curt heard the distant click and began pacing in his kitchen. He made a cup of instant coffee and sat on one of the barstools at the counter. The minute hand on the wall clock made a small jagged move and was now angled directly south. It would make this move fifteen more times while the apartment retained the silence. Curt considered calling Scott but didn't want to bother him. He was sure Scott was busy preparing his family to leave.

At 6:47 by Curt's clock, the phone rang. It brought him out of a semi trance as he had fallen into deep remembrance of the events with the Kilgotian fish in Marvin's tub that morning.

"Hello," he said hurriedly.

"Curt? This is Charlene. Sherri's still not here and still not answering her phone. I'm really worried," her voice was now audibly shaky.

"Charlene, I'm driving to the Gift Shop. I'll be there by 7:20. I'll call you every ten minutes from my cell phone in case she shows back up at the house."

"OK. Thank you. Thank you so much. God I hope nothing has happened to her."

Curt hesitated responding as he thought about her plea to God. He considered making a similar silent request but for some reason refrained. "Talk to you soon," he said. He hung up without waiting for her response.

Curt was out of his apartment, down the steps and into his Mustang before a minute had passed. He cranked the engine and whipped the car out of the parking lot and onto the road. This would be the shortest time it would ever take him to reach St. Augustine.

Scott sat on the couch and rewound the tape in the VCR. He punched the play button and settled back.

Katie loved to record prominent news events. She'd started a couple of years ago and had quite a collection of video tapes. Scott thought it was noble for a pre-teen to take such interest in current events. Of course his definition of news differed from his daughter's. She considered the birth of a panda at the San Diego Zoo, Tu Pac's death and Freddie Prinze Jr.'s latest movie to be lumped in this category. But at least she understood the significance of Damon and had primed the VCR to record as soon as the evening news aired.

At the time the news came on and Scott was watching it live, he had every intention of driving Kay and the kids out of harm's way. Several minutes later, everything had changed.

Now, he was watching it again, thanks to Katie's diligence and he could feel his emotions stir.

As expected, the lead story surrounded Damon's approach and the local plans to prepare. But after a brief commercial cut away, the second story was about a gruesome murder just north of St. Augustine. The body of a young woman believed to be around 17, Lindsey's age, whose name was not released, had been discovered in the bushes on the west side of Highway A1A. Although not decapitated, the teenager had been thoroughly mutilated. Since death, estimated as early that morning, the corpse had been a snack for the local buzzards. The reporter also made reference to Tucker's body and how authorities would not go as far as to admit they had a serial killer on their hands but did express concern about the nature and proximity of the murders.

The story was given less airtime than usual for a crime so heinous, for today there were bigger fish to fry. The hurricane was more prominent news. The scant 40 seconds the network allotted to the murders seemed to downplay the crime and make it resemble something as trivial as a case of shoplifting gumballs from a grocery store. But the prevailing undertone could not be ignored.

At least not by Scott.

The coincidences were bounding back and forth and now began slamming together in Scott's mind. But it was the reporter's last sentence that altered Scott's decision about leaving town. Nine words that meant nothing to almost anyone else watching besides the police. But the connection to Tucker's death was unmistakable.

"There were strange unknown markings on the deceased's back."

The story itself had bothered Scott. The fact that the girl was a teenager in the hey day of life. The horrid way in which she had been killed and then pecked on by those disgusting birds. The fact that somewhere, a mother and father were grieving over the senseless death of their daughter. A girl just like Lindsey.

But the moment Scott heard the reporter's last words he knew he had to stay to resolve whatever he and Curt had started. Somehow they were responsible and Scott was certain of what had been carved in the poor girl's back. The thought sickened him.

He turned the VCR off and leaned back, closing his eyes. In more ways than one, his future had been predetermined. He was slowly coming to this realization. The message the clouds had tried to convey to him on Friday had all but been ignored.

Now he was forced to listen.

At quarter past eight, Scott called Curt's apartment and got the answering machine. He left a message regarding the murder. Scott figured Curt was probably out taking care of chores. He desperately wanted to discuss this latest development with his friend.

As Scott meandered through the house, too upset to sit, his mind swirled. Maybe I'm being irrational about this, Scott thought. Dammit, I should have gone with Kay and the kids. There's a massive hurricane headed straight at me, the whole area is probably going to be evacuated in the morning and I feel the need to stay! Am I out of my mind?

But Scott knew he had made the right decision. Now he needed to talk to Curt. He tried his friend's cell phone but it wasn't on. The call went straight to messaging.

Curt made the entrance to St. Augustine in twenty-four minutes. Traffic on U.S. 1 had been light heading south but he noticed a consistent line of cars streaming along in the northbound lane. Many had already begun to evacuate as a result of Damon's slow but concerted effort to reach North Florida.

As promised, he called Sherri's house every 10 minutes. Each time he hoped to hear her voice. Both times he heard Charlene's. Still no word from Sherri.

Curt angled his Mustang down San Marco Boulevard toward the historic district. He arrived at the Nuestra de la Leche Cemetery three minutes later and turned into the Gift Shop parking lot. The sun was slowly departing and within an hour would leave this day in the hands of the night.

A Toyota Camry was parked on the left in the nearest space to the building's entrance. He pulled in directly beside it. There were no other cars in the lot. The make and description matched Charlene's definition. The license plate was a St. Johns County tag. Unfortunately, he didn't know her tag number. Charlene had been unable to find anything at Sherri's house with this information. He chastised himself for not paying more attention when he and Scott had seen her leave work earlier.

He climbed out of his car and felt the hood of the Toyota. It was warm but not scalding. He guessed the engine had been off at least an hour. This correlated with what Charlene had said.

He strolled around to the driver's side of the car and immediately spied the rag doll lying on the passenger's side floorboard. The door was unlocked and ajar. He opened it delicately in case the alarm had been set.

Silence.

He instantly detected a subtle, sweet perfume fragrance embedded in the cloth seats. It was Chloe. He knew it to be Sherri's from this afternoon, when the same smell had blended with her visual beauty and charm. All these ingredients had melded together in his mind to form the backdrop of her appeal.

He reached down and grabbed the doll. It was intact. Sherri's cohort had done a fine job of mending little Tina's friend. There was no doubt this was Sherri's car.

He closed the door, locking it behind him, and placed the doll in the passenger seat of his Mustang. Then he walked to the back and opened the trunk. He reached in and removed a large flashlight. It resembled one of those police issue versions, long and thick. When Curt had purchased it, Scott had kidded him that it was an attempt to make up for his sexual inadequacies. In reality, Curt viewed it more as a weapon than a source of light. This time was no exception and he felt a tad more comfortable with the flashlight firmly in his grasp.

Curt searched the immediate area. He attempted to enter the Gift Shop but found it locked. He could see through the glass door that all lights were off with the exception of a small lamp that created a dim glow in the back. He reasoned it was possible Sherri was inside and had locked the door behind her. He knocked furiously for five minutes before giving up. He circled around back to the cemetery and casually scanned the area. It was completely barren of life.

As the shadows set in, the headstones bore a misty gray appearance and he became uncomfortable moving down the winding desolate sidewalk. Nonetheless, he was not about to leave without conducting a thorough search. She was here somewhere. Her car was the proof.

The tree cover caused the darkness to accelerate and the quietness began playing on his mind. Each little noise gave him reason to abruptly stop and tighten his grip on the flashlight, as the sound of his breathing magnified. His eyes had trouble adjusting to the dark. Fading shadows and images danced out of the corners, sending his mind reeling on more than one occasion.

He softly began calling Sherri's name as if afraid to wake the inhabitants nestled below the surface. Soon his words became bold and he found comfort in hearing his own voice, as long as no one besides Sherri answered.

"Sherri!" he yelled as if calling to someone in a crowded mall thirty feet away.

No response.

"Sherri!" he intensified, hoping to penetrate farther into the dusk and beyond the confines of the treed area.

No response.

"Sherri! Are you out here? It's Curt Lockes!" he screamed as if conversing with someone while standing near a MD-80 Jet engine chalked up and ready for take off.

And yet, there was no reply.

Curt had made one lap around the centrally located chapel before moving toward the grassy bulkhead bordering the bay. He abandoned the sidewalk and cut across the lawn, avoiding gravesites wherever possible. Even as an adult, he had no desire to tread over someone's last remains. He reached the edge and looked down at the rippling water six feet below. It was low tide and there was a small section of sandy beach.

But no Sherri. This was a relief. As he had approached, a horrifying premonition of finding her body sprawled on the muddy area just out of the water's reach had flashed through his mind.

With a sigh, he turned and walked back the way he came, calling her name one last time.

No response.

He passed by the chapel and glanced at the door. It appeared firmly shut and the inside was dark. The stained glass windows on the sides would have surely given away any hint of light.

He walked to the front of the gift shop and stopped at the back of Sherri's car one last time to scan the area. He looked down at his watch and saw that it was 7:45.

He was completely frustrated and absolutely terrified of what had become of Sherri Falco.

Clearing his head he tried to offer more positive reasons for her disappearance. Perhaps she had car trouble. If so, she would leave the car and go get assistance, he thought. But why didn't she use her cell phone to call? Could the battery be dead?

But from Curt's brief interaction with the woman, she didn't strike him as someone who would allow such a thing to happen, especially with a hurricane approaching. She was too intelligent. It would have been fully charged. Something was wrong. As each second passed, he instinctively knew her situation was deteriorating and he was upset at himself for his lack of any strategy.

As the sky darkened above, Curt climbed back in his Mustang and picked up his cell phone. His eyes kept searching the area beyond the parking lot in all directions as he hit the redial button.

"Hello," an anxious voice said.

"Charlene. It's Curt. I found her car but she's not around."

"Oh my God," Charlene sighed as if she had completely given up hope.

"Charlene, I'm sure she's fine. She might have had car problems and left it here." He thought about how unconvincing he sounded. His words were squeaky and uncertain yet they seemed to soothe Charlene to a small degree.

"I guess," she said softly.

Of course, why in the hell would she leave it unlocked, he thought. "Charlene, where are you? What is Sherri's address? I want to come by."

"It's 11764 Ballaton Street." Charlene gave him quick directions.

"I'll be there in a few minutes and we'll decide what to do." He planned to tell her he had found the car unlocked in person. He didn't want to alarm her over the phone.

He could hear Charlene take a deep breath and the voice of a young girl ask if that was her mommy on the phone. There was a pause and a few muffled words as if the receiver had been covered. Then Charlene returned.

"Should I call the police?" she asked in a whisper.

"It won't do any good. They don't consider adults missing until after 24 hours. Sit tight. I'll be there in a few minutes." As he hung up the phone, Curt could feel his confidence growing. He realized he had to be strong in order to get Charlene through this and hide the realization from Sherri's daughter.

As he drove through St. Augustine he had a vision of Sherri running through the woods being chased. It passed through his mind like wind entering his head and exiting a fraction of a second later through the other side. It left him cold and unsure of what he was doing. He questioned going to Sherri's house. Was it really his place to get involved with this woman he barely knew? Hell, he'd just met her this afternoon. He had an ominous feeling his own life would be put in jeopardy if he did. What was he doing? He had a daughter to think of!

But then again, so did Sherri.

He drove on.

Something pushed him beyond his normal tolerance for fear. Perhaps it was the multitude of strange happenings he'd recently experienced or just plain adrenaline. Whatever it was, it made him angry and determined. He became agitated to the point he hammered the steering wheel with the palm of his right hand seven times until the pain forced him to stop. While the skin ached and the blood darted through like pinpricks, his temper remained focused.

He would help Sherri.

In the chapel in the Nuestra de la Leche cemetery, Sherri stood pinned with her back against the far wall with a steel blade wedged under her chin. It had sliced a small divot in her neck and the blood had oozed down her throat and onto her chest. The trickle had begun to dry in a crimson jagged line.

She was motionless. Absolute fear plagued her eyes. Her captor stared at her with glossy pupils that stood out in the darkness.

Death was a twitch away.

At a few minutes before eight o'clock, Marvin answered the door. Before him was a man in dark slacks and a white button-up shirt, dark tie and a dark blazer. He looked like half of "Men in Black."

"Can I help you?" Marvin asked. The man instantly thrust an unfolded piece of leather into Marvin's face. It was so sudden it startled the professor.

"I'm Detective Sean Cowens with the St. Augustine Police Department. May I come in?"

Marvin steadied himself. "What's this regarding?"

"You were an acquaintance of Tucker Chalet correct?"

Marvin resented the word acquaintance. He reserved it for people he'd met once but would probably never have another interaction with. "He was more than an acquaintance. He was a friend," Marvin replied with a bitter tone.

"Can I come in?"

Marvin swung the door open and stood back.

The detective came inside and Marvin directed him into the living room to the couch. Normally he would have led a guest to the dining room for discussion but Pinot LeFlore's bones still occupied his table.

Marvin chuckled to himself at the thought of seating the detective at the formal table just to see the look in his eyes when he spotted the remains. The way Marvin's luck had been running, he'd probably be arrested for killing the 400-year-old corpse.

Cowens took a seat and pivoted his body forward as Marvin took a position in the Lazy Boy, where he had been dozing before he was rudely interrupted by the doorbell.

"Mr. Sellon, how well did you know the decedent?"

"His name was Tucker."

"How well did you know Tucker?" Cowens reworded in a calm, soothing tone.

Marvin was surprised by the man's sudden attempt at sincerity. "About three years. I hadn't seen him since the spring. He lived downstate and came to visit on occasion. We're fellow archeologists."

"I'm aware of that. Did you know he was in town?"

"No. And it was very odd for Tucker not to call." Marvin's eyes gave away his sadness. Talking about Tucker was not easy. "Have you found out anything about his death? Do you have any suspects?" Marvin inquired.

"Mr. Sellon, I really can't disclose that information." Cowens paused and then started again. "So you had no idea he was here?"

"That's right."

"Do you know a man named Jean Luc LeFlore?"

Of all the things that had surprised and shocked him the last few days, Cowen's question had come out of the blue. He paused, thinking quickly. Do I admit knowing the name? I really don't want to go into the whole story of the manuscript and the things that have happened. This man will have me carted off to the mental institution, Marvin thought.

"I believe I saw a man by that name buried in the Nuestra de la Leche cemetery. The only reason I remember it is because I have a friend who works there and they get very few additions to the grounds," Marvin said.

Detective Cowens looked at Marvin a bit caught off guard. Marvin wasn't sure if the detective's surprise was the result of discovering that Jean Luc LeFlore was buried in town or that Marvin knew about it.

"Are you sure of the name?" Cowens asked somewhat bewildered.

"Yep," Marvin said running his hand over his tuff of gray hair. "May I ask what this man's involvement is with Tucker's death."

"I really can't say."

"Look," Marvin said annoyed. "I've just given you some information you were not aware of . . ." Marvin said taking a guess Jean Luc LeFlore's location had been news to Cowens.

"If it's true, I would have found out anyway," Cowens cut in.

"Regardless, all I want to know is why you're asking about this man. A man dead and buried."

Cowens turned his head and looked around the room as if they might be overheard. The walls didn't appear to be listening so he leaned forward and motioned for Marvin to do the same.

At that moment, Marvin realized what a goof this guy really was.

In a low voice, Cowens began, "Jean Luc LeFlore hired Tucker Chalet to do some kind of archeological work for him."

"Archeological work? What kind of archeological work."

"I'm not sure yet. We retrieved a notebook from Mr. Chalet's body. It referenced LeFlore and some information that really didn't make a whole hell of a lot of sense."

"What kind of information?" Marvin asked.

"I really can't say," Cowens said for the third time since the conversation had begun.

"You want me to help? Give me more information." Marvin suddenly felt like he had the upper hand. Cowens looked relatively young and Marvin suspected he hadn't been a detective for long. This was probably his first murder investigation. St. Augustine wasn't exactly a hotbed of violent crime.

"I shouldn't," Cowens said reluctantly.

Marvin just stared at him.

The silence disrupted Cowen's resolve and he finally gave in. "I really do want to catch the bastard that did this. And we all feel this second homicide is related."

"What second homicide?" Marvin asked surprised. He'd napped right through the six o'clock news.

Cowens told Marvin about the teenage girl. The young detective was very disturbed by her death and could not hide his anxieties, nor did he try.

When he was through, Marvin asked again. "Tell me what Tucker was doing for LeFlore and I might have better insight into who might have been involved. You do want to catch the killer don't you?"

Cowens didn't respond but folded his bottom lip underneath his top front teeth as if to stop the information from flowing out. It didn't work.

"As odd as this sounds, his notes mention looking for fingers."

"Fingers?" Marvin said with a fake surprised tone. It was unusual of course, but he immediately thought about the skeleton assumed to be Pinot LeFlore sitting on his table and the knife he had placed back into the solution in the bedroom. Marvin wiggled in his seat uncomfortably. If the detective happened to wander into the dining room, Marvin didn't look forward to explaining why he just-so-happened to have a skeleton that was missing a finger on its right hand. Although he wasn't sure Cowens was astute enough to spot the discrepancy.

"Yep, fingers," Cowens confirmed.

"Did it say why?"

"No. Do you have any ideas why?" Cowens asked.

"No."

"I thought you said you could help. Don't you have any theories? You're an archeologist? What's the historical significance of fingers?"

"The only thing I know about fingers is that restaurants serve chicken fingers and I've never seen a chicken with fingers," Marvin said with a wry smile.

Cowens wasn't amused. He reached into his top shirt pocket and pulled out a business card and handed it to Marvin.

"Let me know if you think of anything," he said as he stood up and walked toward the door.

"One thing," Marvin said as the detective reached the door. "Were there any strange markings or designs on the second victim similar to the first?"

"How did you know about the design?" the detective asked with a look of concern. Marvin had caught Cowens off guard.

"It was on the news after Tucker's body was found," Marvin lied. "So was anything similar done to the girl?"

After staring at Marvin for a few seconds, Cowens turned and grabbed the handle, "Good day, Mr. Sellon."

CHAPTER-TWENTY-FIVE

When Curt arrived at Sherri's house, a little girl was in the front yard playing with a bright pink plastic ball. A woman was sitting in a folding chair on the lawn with a telephone in her hand. A stationwagon was parked at the road.

"Mr Lockes?" the woman said walking toward the Mustang as Curt stepped out. Curt knew it must be Charlene but the differences between the sisters were staggering. Where Sherri was tall, Charlene was short. Where Sherri was thin, Charlene was not so thin. But Curt instantly recognized the attractive features and red hair, which bore a striking resemblance to her sibling. But beyond the familiarity, Curt could see Charlene was weary and looked considerably older than she probably had several hours ago.

"Please call me Curt. Any word?"

"Nothing," Charlene responded despondently.

Curt had the doll in his hand. The little girl stopped bouncing the pink ball when her eyes focused on Ms. Toni. She had named the doll after one of the nurses during her hospital stay several years ago. It remained with Tina through thick and thin.

Since it was getting pretty thin, Curt thought Tina might like to see her old friend.

"Ms. Toni!" Tina shouted happily. You've got my Ms. Toni. And her arm's all better."

Curt held the doll out as Tina approached.

"Here you go honey," Curt said pushing a smile on his face.

Tina grabbed the doll and cuddled it. "Thank you," She said spinning like a top, never letting up on the bear hug.

Curt squatted to eye level with the little girl when she finally stopped. "Did you see my mommy? I thought mommy was going to bring Ms. Toni home."

"Your mommy will be home in a little while. She's at work," Curt lied. It was easy to lie to children. Usually the lies were in their best interest. Lying to adults had more malicious purposes. He had never found those lies quite so simple.

"Aunt Charlene, when's Mommy coming home so we can go?" Tina said as her blue eyes sparkled as only a little girl's can.

"Soon," was all Charlene could manage as she looked up at Curt apprehensively. Changing the subject Charlene asked, "Mr. Lockes . . . I'm sorry, Curt, would you like something to drink." Curt immediately understood Charlene's intention. They needed to talk without small ears listening in.

"That'd be great," Curt said.

As Curt began to walk toward the front door he heard the faint ringing of his cell phone. It was still in the car. He turned back, ran to the car, and answered on the fourth ring.

"Hello."

"Curt, it's Scott."

"Hey, where are you?" Curt could tell he was not calling from a cell phone. "Aren't you supposed to be on the road by now?"

"Things have changed. Where are you?"

"I'm in St. Augustine. What do you mean things have changed?"

"I thought you guys weren't planning to leave until the morning?" Scott asked.

"We're not leaving till the morning. The woman I met this afternoon, the one translating the document for Marvin from the gift shop, is missing." Curt lowered his voice as he spoke. Tina had gone inside with Ms. Toni but he didn't want to take any chance of her hearing.

"What do you mean missing?"

Curt explained the situation. How he'd found her car at the cemetery and then come over to Sherri's house to meet with Charlene.

"Did you hear about the second murder?" Scott asked.

"Yeah, but no details. What did you mean when you said things have changed? What's changed?" Curt asked again.

"Curt, I just spoke to Marvin. A detective investigating Tucker's death paid him a visit. Marvin feels this new murder is related. From what he said and how the cop reacted when Marvin mentioned the graphic knife carving, I'd bet anything that poor girl had similar markings. The symbol of the Huguenot cross." The words stammered out of Scott's mouth in an icy manner. It sounded like he literally choked them out. Finally Scott continued. "I sent Kay and the kids on. I feel very connected to what's happened and I can't leave. You're probably going to tell me how silly this is, but I feel willed to stay."

Curt took a deep breath. His replied somewhat surprised himself. "As do I."

Without hesitation Scott continued, "I'm coming to St. Augustine. Tell me how to get to where you are and we'll look for your friend together."

Curt provided Scott directions and then hung up. Charlene was standing in the doorway holding a glass of ice water. Concern was scribbled on her face.

Curt approached her and spoke quietly. "My friend is coming to help search for Sherri."

"Thank you," she said with a sad smile.

From the time it took Scott to reach Sherri's, Curt had convinced Charlene to take Tina and leave town. Charlene had expressed a concern about the hotel in Tallahassee holding their reservation after 11 p.m., even though it was guaranteed on a credit card. Curt agreed. With the massive pool of people fleeing Damon from the east coast of Florida,

Tallahassee would be inundated. If Charlene left by 8:30, and if traffic was still flowing briskly, she should just make the 170-mile trip in time.

By the time Charlene and Tina climbed in the car it was 8:34.

As Curt stood in the yard, Charlene handed him the house key through the window.

"Normally I wouldn't give my sister's house key to a man I just met but she spoke of you with such warmth and trust."

Curt eased a small smile. "You've got my cell phone number and I've got yours. My battery is low so I'm only going to have it on when I need to call."

"Even though you've already said this, promise me a couple of things," Charlene said as she cranked the engine. She leaned out the window and whispered to Curt, "Promise me you won't leave town until you find her. Promise me that." A solitary tear dripped down the left side of Charlene's face as she stared into Curt's eyes.

"I promise," he said softly. Tina hadn't heard. She was busy calmly adjusting the radio station tuner. And why not? The two adults had assured her that Mommy would meet them in Tallahassee after she finished up some work at the gift shop. For Tina, all was well and the trip was almost under way. Tina loved traveling and staying in hotels. It would be an adventure. Time to get the adventure started. She would see mommy soon. Her world was secure.

How blissful ignorance can be Curt thought as the stationwagon pulled away. Out of view and unbeknownst to Tina, Charlene secretly wiped the tears from her eyes as the adorable little girl to her right sang along to an unrecognizable song.

Curt solemnly waited in the driveway, perched on the trunk of the Mustang, watching the last glow in the western sky. Scott arrived 10 minutes later.

At 9:06 p.m. a man walked through a dark quiet ally in St. Augustine. Ahead a short distance, the narrow walkway would intersect with St. George Street.

Since leaving work that evening at 7:30, after staying late to help secure against the approaching hurricane, he had walked the streets. His mind was a logjam of flowing thoughts and tainted memories.

The evening walk seemed to retrieve the events from long ago. Those images he had rewound and played several thousand times throughout the centuries. He thought back to when he was a young tribal member and had befriended the two brothers. How they had manipulated him to obtain the secret for their advantage. The rage he had felt when he realized what they had done. The anguish he felt for his mistake.

He thought about the recurring dream. The ominous dream he'd had the night after divulging the information so many years ago. The nightmare scenario of the brothers' actions and deeds. A bloodbath of sights and sounds echoing into a realm of concise visions in strange locations and odd surroundings. People running through the streets screaming. Innocents bludgeoned by French swords as cries for mercy were ignored.

He lived with his mistake for four years after that eventful night long ago with the LeFlore brothers - - 1,554 days after leaving the tribe and living on his own with barely a solid night's sleep to count, he was finally driven to the brink. On that particular morning in 1571, he was awakened by the horrific nightmares. Once his head cleared he completely understood the atrocity of his actions.

The pond was the tribe's most highly guarded secret and was only mentioned among the tribal elders. Tibu had found out about its powers when he'd accidentally overheard a discussion one night as a small boy. It was shortly after his mother had passed away from illness when he was playing quietly behind the elders' campfire meeting. As a child, Tibu had always seen himself like the fox and frequently spied on the adult tribe members, hiding behind trees and tents to listen in on conversations and activities. He occasionally got an eye full of men and women performing men and women activities and it had initially scared him into believing that the moon changed people into animals.

On that fateful day in 1571, his guilt had bubbled to the point of becoming overwhelming. For four years he had considered some way to make amends. But as the dreams persisted he was forced to do the unthinkable. That night when he awoke, it was still dark and he was bathed in sweat and trembling. He had slept in an isolated area less than half a mile from the village. Even after deserting the tribe he had never gone far. He had lived in solitude a short distance from his people, careful not to be seen.

As he sat up, he recalled the visions which, moments ago, had flushed him awake. The scenes had been very clear and real. Crafted down to the last detail as they always were. At one time, he had tried to convince himself these ongoing dreams were just *nifiligs* as the Timucua called it. *Not of the earth, water or soul but of the wind. Something that could not harm or help*. But this particular vision had persisted so long and was so intense, he had quickly vanquished the notion of their harmlessness. These dreams were too real. They were too foreboding. And the guilt he felt for dishonoring his tribe, too immense.

On that fateful night, he got up and gazed into the air, inspecting the bright illuminating circular object among the multitude of smaller, sparkling points of light. There was an eerie stillness that echoed his pain. Nature's normal noisemakers were at rest. No croaking, clacking and clicking. Just a slight breeze that helped dry the sweat from Tibu's face. Tibu contemplated the irreparable damage he had done. The severity of dislodging the secret to outsiders. Telling the brothers about *Terriousimee* was an inexcusable offense. As the wind slowly glided through his hair he felt the burden of a man who had the weight of a thousand stones on his chest.

His course of action was now an imperative. There were no other choices.

Tibu arose and slowly made his way to the outer edge of the woods. As he reached the trees, guided by the glowing moonlight, he found the foremost oak. Pulling out a small sharp piece of flint, he carved words into the mighty tree on an area that no longer held bark, a smooth and hard opening seemingly provided for his purpose. The message would be his legacy. Afterward, he proceeded on his journey to the pond to awake the Kilgotian fish.

His ultimate intention was to interfere with the brothers' plan and seal the secret of the pond, thereby gaining some small measure of redemption. He was certain the cursed dreams would follow him after death unless the future was altered. It would be his punishment throughout eternity. By destroying the brothers he might end the horrific nightmares. What he didn't know was that his life would continue so distant into the future. He often wondered what he had done to bastardize the process and elongate his existence.

His plan was simple, yet heroic on that fall morning in 1571. After severing the middle finger on his right hand and wrapping his wound with a tourniquet, he would suspend his red stained finger carefully above the pond on a series of leaves clumped together where the branches of the trees intersected. He did this by carefully scaling one of the oaks, an arduous task with the excruciating pain from his hand, and slowly climbing out on a limb that stretched above the water. Just below, as the moonlight flickered and danced on the surface, the unseen Kilgotian impatiently churned the surface and focused its attention upward. Tibu had to be extremely careful. A slip would be catastrophic. The Kilgotian would show no mercy.

Upon placing the severed finger securely on a cluster of leaves high above the pond, Tibu backed down the tree. Once on the ground, he lay next to the bank and drifted back to sleep. Again the dreams came.

The following morning, before daybreak, he arose. The pain from the severed appendage was boiling and the tourniquet was soaked in blood. In retrospect, Tibu realized he very easily could have bled to death before waking. But that was not to be. It was not allowed to end that way.

Groggily, he made his way to the ocean, following the glow of the rising sun for direction. The walk was long and strenuous and took the better part of the day. At dusk he slept less than a mile from the shore. He awoke early the next morning and walked into the surf. Within minutes, he had drowned.

Tibu understood the changing seasons. He knew the cold time was coming and the leaves would turn brown and break off from the trees within a few months, sending the finger into the pond for the Kilgotian to consume. It might even occur earlier if a strong breeze kicked up or a storm sent cascading sheets of rain down on the branches. Of course there was always the risk the finger would blow onto shore and never reach the water but Tibu had taken careful consideration in strategically placing it well over the pond to minimize the chance of it missing the surface. Nonetheless, there was risk. And he had gambled his life on these variables outside his control.

What he did not know, and never would, was that a female mockingbird had spied his appendage lying dormant on the leaves the morning just minutes before he entered the salt water of the Atlantic Ocean. To the creature, the tan and red streaked object resembled a nice fat juicy worm. The mockingbird flew onto the branch and attempted to lift the morsel in her beak. But the weight was greater than anticipated. The bird fluttered trying to regain its balance and was forced to drop the awkward treat before toppling over. The finger fell toward the pond. In an instant, she dove in an attempt to retrieve it.

The appendage smacked the surface at the same moment the Mockingbird clutched it in her beak. But it was too late. The Kilgotian's grinding teeth seized the finger along with the bird's skull, shredding them alike. The bird's body continued under and was gone in an instant. Blood pooled underneath the surface and feathers glanced off the top and blew onto shore. The fish returned to the bottom, content for the moment, rolling its eyes in appeasement.

Seconds before, Tibu had become part of the ocean. The timing, although not as Tibu had planned, and dangerously close, had been successful.

It was so long ago. So very long. But he remembered it in great detail. He could still recall his fear as he made his way to the beach that morning and stepped into the surf. He could taste the salt water filling his lungs and the intense burning as he gulped the fluid and gagged on it. How the cloudy water had gone from bright blue to black and then he was again walking, this time coming out of the water feeling refreshed and strong.

For years he tried in vain to locate the brothers but was unsuccessful. This was the most frustrating part, not being able to find them, and not knowing what happened or where they had gone. He learned centuries later that there was a line of ancestors related back to Pinot LeFlore but was unable to obtain any information on what actually happened to the brothers. Regardless, they were long dead. That much he was sure.

Still the nightmares continued.

When Tibu invoked the pond's power he had not planned on the longevity he experienced. It was uncommon for a man to live more than 150 years after becoming a Soulful One. But he came to the somber conclusion his longevity was part of a greater design. One guided by a superior force. He resolved to carry out his mission as best he could. If only he knew what his penance would be.

The man, who had 23 names over his lifetime, had lived with these disturbing visions of the LeFlores and their bloody retribution almost every night for more than 400 years. The dreams were just as persistent and real as he remembered on that first night after divulging the secret to the brothers when the scenes had clouded his mind and he awoke, head aching from the effects of the alcohol.

Over the years, he had seen it all. American history was something he experienced firsthand, not something he read from a book. He recalled vividly the transitioning control of the fort at St. Augustine. From the Spanish to the French, back to the Spanish, then to the English. How it had changed names from Castillo de San Marcos to Fort Marion and back to Castillo de San Marcos. He vividly recalled the agonizing extinction of his people by the white man's disease in the 1700s. He had fought in the American Revolution and Spanish-American War and vividly remembered the Civil War, World War I & II, the Korean War, and Vietnam. He could recall the signing of the Declaration of Independence, the discovery of electricity, the first Model T Ford, the Wright Brothers success at Kitty Hawk, Eli Whitney's cotton gin, Albert Einstein's theory of relativity, the 1919 Black Sox scandal, Lincoln, Garfield, McKinley and Kennedy's assassinations, prohibition, Pretty Boy Floyd & Machine Gun Kelly, the connection of the Transcontinental Railroad, the California Gold Rush. And all the while unable to escape the premonitions.

On and on his life continued. It was a void existence, waiting for some kind of instruction. Then in 1947, it all became clear.

That was the year the visions in his dreams began to bare a striking resemblance to modern day structures and roads. The background buildings did not look so different than the dwellings and offices he dreamed about. It was then that he was sure his dreams were not phantom flights of fancy existing only to create agony, not just his sub-conscious playing a game of guilt. They were premonitions of things to come. Events he would be a part of and could possibly alter. It was the time-indicating instructions he had been waiting for.

It was also when he knew that other forces were guiding him, but he didn't understand why and wasn't sure he ever would. He yearned for the day when he might be afforded the opportunity to change what he foresaw and end the nightmares for eternity.

A small mouse startled Tibu as he reached St. George Street and headed right. The rodent scurried through an opening in a corner building.

His slow pace took him past the closed shops and restaurants that lined either side of the cobblestone street. The mouse had awakened him from the trance and his thoughts turned to current matters.

He considered the irony in his encounter with the two strangers Monday morning. Obviously it was his fate to participate in the LeFlore brothers event, but how these two were involved was a mystery. And it deeply troubled him. Were these men allies or enemies? He wasn't sure and only time would tell. They had never been a part of his dreams but maybe they were the answer to averting the disastrous outcome he had witnessed for so many nights. Could they be the missing piece that would prevent the destruction and terror, or would they be the catalysts? The time might come for him to kill them but he could not afford to be too hasty. Patience had to be observed each step of the way. His intuition would be key.

After four centuries, the time had come to lay the nightmares to rest.

CHAPTER-TWENTY-SIX

Scott and Curt left Sherri's house and drove to Marvin's to drop off Curt's car. When they arrived, the professor was busy surfing the web, pecking at the keyboard and donning his bifocals in deep concentration. Marvin did not hear them enter through the front door and did a pretty fair imitation of a man scared to death when Scott spoke up. After taking a minute to explain the situation with Sherri Falco, and once Marvin had caught his breath, the men were off to search the streets of St. Augustine.

On the north side of the bay, the roadways were clear. The night had brought with it a hushed, sedate atmosphere to the small town. St. Augustine was not much of a nightspot to begin with and, in preparation for Hurricane Damon's arrival, many residents had already taken flight. As the Blazer crested the Bridge of Lions, spanning Matanzas Bay, the lights from the structure sparkled in the calm water below. On the far side, the white street lamps lined the bulkhead like a string of Christmas lights. The small shops and restaurants, long since closed for the evening, were deserted and the cars moving slowly along the street adjacent to the bay were at a minimum. The serene setting struck Scott as grotesquely ironic. In less than 36 hours this placid setting could be decimated and under water.

Scott and Curt reached the gift shop at the Nuestra Senora de la Leche cemetery and saw that Sherri's car was still there. Scott parked next to the vehicle and Curt jumped out and touched the hood. Ice cold. They began searching the immediate area, each armed with a flashlight. As dusk had fallen, the moon cloaked behind the clouds causing the night to be unusually dark. The grounds of the cemetery were not well lit under normal conditions and now there was an inert stillness about the place that had both men on edge.

After surveying the front parking lot area and the pond where the short arched bridge spanned to the right side of the cemetery, Scott and Curt separated. Curt was to continue searching the grounds while Scott ventured beyond.

Curt angled behind the gift shop and reached the winding sidewalk of the cemetery. Scott headed toward San Marco Boulevard and crossed the street, moving south in the direction of the fort. As he passed a series of small gift shops, motels and mini-marts, Scott counted a grand total of six people on foot and a dozen or so cars passing in either direction. The town had become deserted.

Curt searched the cemetery grounds as he had done several hours before with the same sobering results.

Not a trace. Nothing.

He shined the flashlight across the grass and was occasionally surprised by the luster of light that reflected off the granite tombstones.

Even after centuries of wear and erosion they sparkled with brilliance when given the proper incentive.

Curt slowed his pace, realizing Sherri could be lying unconscious on the grass and he would probably walk right past. He moved with trepidation, flashing the beam back and forth across both sides of the stone walkway, meticulously covering every square inch.

The night air began to offer a bitter, stale smell and the trees hung over the area creating a solid darkness. Above, their thick, canvassing limbs interlocked forming a seemingly impenetrable roof. Several times, Curt's attention was drawn to a muffled rustling from above. Sharp breaks, scratches and the stressful sounds of bowed branches made him jittery. Just squirrels or birds, he told himself. But he found no comfort in this.

A slight breeze began blowing in from the bay. The incoming smell of salt air was strangely comforting to Curt and his confidence returned.

With each step Curt slowed his pace as the light sought out the ground. He approached the small chapel and shined the light on the structure. To the left of the entrance, the words in white lettering on the marker glowed.

He picked out the second sentence. "Erected first in 1615, this shrine of Our Lady fell victim three times to war, pirates and storms." Curt thought about the last aggressor of the three, *storms*, and thought what Damon might do to this little stone structure. It would surely fall for a fourth time.

Curt decided to proceed on the walkway to the right of the chapel. The beam landed on the four-foot high sarcophagus just off the path. On the arched lid, the inscription read:

DON BARTOLONE OLIVEROS – 1800
CONSORT OF
DONA FERNANDA GONZALEZ - 1799

"What in the hell is a 'consort?' I've never had one of those," he said out loud to himself.

Moving beyond, past the sarcophagus, was a 35 by 10-foot area contained within a 2-foot high stone wall. Inside were six tombstones, each adorned with a small stone cross affixed on top. The inscription on the sign read:

SIX SISTERS OF THE CONGREGATION OF
ST. JOSEPH ARE BURIED HERE. THESE SISTERS
CAME IN 1866 TO OPEN SCHOOLS AND TEACH
CHRISTIAN DOCTRINE IN FLORIDA

Curt shined the flashlight inside the area. The low cropped grass was a dirty brown shade. The combination of the high tree cover and the stone enclosure had precluded proper sunlight and moisture.

Curt angled the light across the length of the site and immediately spied a dark shape between the second and third headstones. The oblong object was approximately six inches in length and two and one-half inches thick. At first he believed it to be a small rodent such as a rat that had died and come to rest, appropriately enough, amongst the dead.

But then he wasn't sure. As he concentrated, he carefully stepped over the low wall. He knelt down and, with better proximity, instantly knew what it was. The black leather casing that had fooled him. He reached down and picked up the Nokia cellular phone. Not thinking about police evidence collection procedures and how he was establishing new prints all over the device, he hit the button to see the destination of the last call.

It was Charlene's cell phone number. Relief and confusion merged, and he knew he had found Sherri's phone.

But as he held the phone pondering the logistics of where Sherri's car was parked and where the cell phone had come to rest, he felt a burning sensation in his hand. When he had picked up the phone from the grass, he was unconsciously aware of how slippery it was but had been more concerned with determining its owner. Now the pain became excruciating and he realized, with chagrin, that his lack of consideration toward the wet substance was complete stupidity on his part.

He immediately dropped the phone and wiped his hand on the dry grass, attempting to disengage the substance. But the awful stinging continued. With his left hand he aimed the flashlight at the phone, which had landed right side up, and saw a slick yellow fluid which, in some places, had hardened across the face, partially covering the numbers. He flashed the beam onto his hand. His red swollen palm was pulsating as the heat radiated underneath his skin and burned as if he were holding his hand in a campfire..

"Dammit! Dammit!" he shouted and his words seemed to awaken America's Most Sacred Acre. Very close, a cricket sang and a frog croaked in a sporadic melody.

Again he desperately wiped his hand on the dry ground and then brushed it off on his shirt, frantic for anything that would dislodge the stinging fluid. Minutes later, after considerable grimacing and several stray tears, the stifling pain ended and his labored breathing began to subside. When it did, he stood up shaking his head. The phone was in front of his feet.

"What in God's name was that!" he screamed at the cricket and frog who went silent.

He glanced down at the phone. Then at his hand, his red, wrinkled palm. Then back at the phone.

"I'll buy her a new one," he said and turned. He stepped back onto the walkway. As his light cut the morbid dark, he suddenly stopped and drew in a large breath. The stark inhale lodged in his inflamed lungs.

He couldn't breathe. Couldn't exhale.

The grounds, which a few moments before were spotted with isolated markers here and there, were now littered with headstones. There were hundreds, maybe thousands cluttering the acre. Haphazardly, meshed together. It was as if they had sprouted from the time Curt had walked over to the Six Sisters of the Congregation. The shadows arced across the setting as Curt stood mortified. Could this be an illusion, he thought as he finally exhaled. Is it the angle of the light?

Mesmerized, he slowly walked back down the path to the front of the chapel and then right toward the bay. The headstones filled the grass on either side of the path as he held the flashlight in front, scanning back and forth. In most cases, the markers were only separated by a few feet, with virtually no room for a body to be buried between.

His heart skipped as the flashlight blinked twice but came back on with full brilliance. It was still dark. So very dark. That's all I need, he thought.

Twenty yards before the bay, the walkway veered to the right. It would eventually lead beyond the cemetery and to the south side of the small cove that nestled against the Nuestra Senora de la Leche. From there, it continued to the Beacon of Faith Cross before circling back and connecting with the far side of the parking lot.

But as the path turned, Curt stepped on the grass toward the bay and the scattered array of granite that now filled the landscape. It was like a dream. The headstones had come out of nowhere and he wanted a closer look. It had to be a mirage. But a quick forefinger on the cold stone of the nearest slab sent his mind sprawling.

This was no optical illusion or bending of light. The headstones were real.

Fighting an overwhelming urge to run, he knelt down. From the sidewalk he had been unable to read any of the inscriptions. Now, with his flashlight directed to the face of the headstone directly in front, he sought the name of the owner. The stone was aged and worn as if it had been there for centuries. For all he knew, it might have. This was a cemetery and there were graves here before this outcrop. There was no way to distinguish the old from the new, or so he thought.

Then he read the first name. Perplexed, he rose and moved to another marker. Then a third. And another and another and another. On the ninth headstone he dropped to his knees as the flashlight remained fixed on the inscription. This is impossible. What is going on? Am I dreaming? He looked down at his hand. There was a residual ache that occasionally flared since his experience with the yellow fluid. It was acting up again.

As he clenched his fist to fight off the discomfort, his mind sought out reason and security.

"How can this be!" he screamed and a faint echo bounced in the distance.

Every headstone Curt examined appeared to have weathered extensive damage, as time tends to do. Every inscription also had a name, a birth year and a death year.

Every death date was the same . . . 1565.

The same year the Spanish troops had slaughtered the shipwrecked French Huguenots at Matanzas Inlet.

And the names were all French.

A gentle breeze crossed his face. He realized how much he had been sweating as the cool wind iced his perspiration. Beyond the grounds and multitudes of headstones the bay glistened as the moonlight shimmered off its relaxed waters. Curt was hypnotized by the effect, easily dancing on the surface, as his mind toiled in confusion.

Sherri's phone of pain was one thing. That was easy enough to explain. Obviously some sort of plant such as poison oak or poison ivy had come in contact with it.

But the growth of countless graves or at least the headstones representing what he assumed were the French Huguenots was a far more tricky issue. He gazed out in the distance and then closed his eyes, desperately wanting these things to go away. He knew in his heart that they did not represent any measure of good.

With his lids firmly shut he suddenly sensed another presence. It was the feeling every human being gets, an undeniable ability to know someone is near. An inherent trait probably resident in our genes from early cave man, when our entire existence was simply to stay alive. To know who was around, or more specifically, who was sneaking up from behind.

Someone was behind Curt. The skin tickled on his spine.

He clutched the flashlight tightly in his hand. Using his aching palm, he quickly pushed himself to his feet and sailed around swinging the plastic cylinder like a club. The swift arc sent the beam prancing off a series of markers and coming to rest on the far side of the chapel.

Curt was alone.

The breeze again flared up this time pushing his hair up and tickling his ears. His skin crawled with anticipation and his arteries channeled enough blood to nearly push his heart through his chest.

"It's just the wind you idiot," he chastised himself quietly. Then something touched his left shoulder. He jumped forward, landing three feet away. His pulse nearly came to a standstill.

"AHHHHH!" he screamed and turned, pointing the flashlight.

Scott dropped his hand and stood in amazement waiting for Curt's brain to acquire recognition.

Curt bent over and held his chest. "Jeez, you scared the holy shit out of me. I nearly messed my pants," he said between deep breaths.

"Hey, have you been planting headstones? I don't seem to remember this cemetery being nearly this overpopulated."

Curt was laboring as he spoke. "I don't know what's going on Scott. These things just appeared. When I first got back here, they weren't here," he said shaking his head from side to side.

Scott pointed his flashlight in a 360-degree radius, examining every reach of the lot. "This is unbelievable," he said in amazement.

"Well, you better believe it. And look at the inscriptions."

Scott approached the closest marker. "Pasques Neore, 1537 – 1565."

He was speechless.

"I checked quite a few," Curt said as he raised up and stepped beside Scott. "Each one is from the exact same time period and appears to be French. Each one also has a death year of 1565. The year Fort Caroline was destroyed and the Spaniards massacred the Huguenots south of here."

"This is all like a bad dream," Scott said.

"Yeah but for what reason. You know we're trapped in the mix?" Curt said somberly.

"I know. That's why I didn't leave with my family. Any sign of Sherri? I didn't see a thing."

"I found her cell phone on the other side of the chapel."

"Really." Scott's eyes lit up, "Are you sure it's hers?"

"Positive. It had Charlene's number programmed in. I left it on the ground over there."

"Why?" Scott asked.

"Because it stung the hell out of me," he said turning his palm up under the shining light. The skin was a glaring shade of red streaked with scratches.

"What happened?" Scott asked in amazement.

"I'm not sure. It must have absorbed some poison from a plant or something. When I picked it up it had some yellow crap on it. I'm not touching it again."

There was a splashing sound in the direction of the bay and both men turned. They each directed light out to the water but saw nothing. The surface remained calm and the moon cut a line from the distant shore across the bay.

The stillness was picturesque. It was also very unnerving.

"Nothing like being in a cemetery in the pitch black darkness, huh?" Curt said.

"Yeah. There's probably not more than 12 billion other places I'd prefer to be right now," Scott responded with a shiver.

The two men stood watching the water in silence without a clue of what to do next. Looking out across the bay to the left, the Francis &

Mary Usina Bridge reached out of St. Augustine and over to Vilano Beach and carried Highway A1A along the Atlantic Ocean. Flickering lights dotted the span periodically, seemingly moving at a snail's pace.

Across the bridge, A1A would continue hugging the shoreline through Ponte Vedra Beach and up to Jacksonville Beach. Because of its proximity to the shoreline, it was a popular road. So well known in fact, it had the distinction of being the title of a Jimmy Buffet album. For Scott and Curt it would also be known as the route a *Soulful* Reece LeFlore had traveled to make his way back to St. Augustine and proceed with his plan of revenge.

When Curt and Scott returned to Marvin's, the professor was sitting on his couch poring over loose papers. There were two neatly stacked piles on the coffee table and three scattered clumps to his left on the cushions. As the men entered, he raised his head and peered at them over his glasses that had fallen halfway down the bridge of his nose.

"Any luck?" he asked encouragingly.

"No. But we did find her cell phone in the cemetery," Curt responded.

"Along with several hundred additional graves . . . or should I say, headstones," Scott added sitting down in the recliner.

"What?" Marvin asked with a curious stare.

Curt explained how he had found the cell phone and had suffered the strange burn to his hand. He flashed his palm as evidence. He described how the markers had appeared out of nowhere and, based on the dates, seemed to represent the massacred French Huguenots.

"Did you touch them? Were they real? The headstones I mean." Marvin asked excitedly.

"Real enough," Scott added.

"I don't even know how to respond. This is all too strange. I'm beginning to think you two are cursed," Marvin said, clearing all but one page from the couch and placing the rest in an unruly stack on the coffee table.

"Gee, thanks Marvin," Scott said as he surveyed the various stacks of papers lying about. "What are you reading anyway?" he asked as Marvin adjusted his glasses higher on his nose.

"I found something very interesting. Remember Scott when you mentioned what Tatterhorn had said? Something about the Kilgotian being from "your God"? Then I read about that Indian legend on the Internet yesterday. That got me to thinking."

"About what?" Scott asked. His interest was piquing.

"About the Bible."

"Oh great," Scott said with a look of disgust that irritated Curt.

"Go on," Curt said.

"After you guys left this afternoon, I resumed my search on the Internet. I was really grasping for straws. Then I remembered the discovery of the Trascent Cave drawings this past July. I hadn't really paid much attention at the time."

"I remember that. They're possibly related to Noah's Ark," Curt said.

"So it seems. Dr. Justin Mollur led an expedition late last year to the Ararat Mountains in Turkey in search of evidence of the Ark's existence."

Scott interrupted the conversation. "I thought Ararat was just one mountain."

"Actually, that's somewhat of a misnomer. Ararat is a mountain range with twin peaks. Although Genesis 8:4 mentions the Ark coming to rest on this mountain, Ararat was probably the term for the region and not a specific mountain peak. Anyway, this led Dr. Mollur and his team to search several mountains away from Ararat, which is where most scholars believe the Ark to be entombed in snow and ice, somewhere above the 10,000-foot mark."

"Wasn't the Ark, or at least a piece of it, found years ago? It was on some TV show," Curt said.

"Hardly. In the late '80s and early '90s there were frequent claims the Ark had been discovered 15 miles away from Mount Ararat. It was called the Durupinar Site. Extensive research and geological data later confirmed that the formation, contrary to a popular fuzzy photograph, was just a rather large rock jutting out from underneath the snow. It was around this time that Ark hunting became popular. With the breakup of the Soviet Union, expeditions were no longer considered a security threat to the Russians," Marvin said.

"That's right," Scott began, "the mountain sits right on the Turkey-Soviet Union border. So what does all this have to do with us?" Scott asked impatiently.

"I'm getting there." Marvin gave Scott a glare that made him feel like a freshman who had spoken out of turn and been reprimanded by the knowledgeable professor. Scott eased back in the recliner and listened.

"Until Mollur's expedition this past summer, there had been few attempts to find the Ark over the last five years."

"So what about the cave drawings?" Curt asked as he squatted on the floor in front of the coffee table.

"Not far from the Durupinar Site, actually the next smaller mountain to the west, Dr. Mollur and his crew were searching for the Ark when they discovered a well hidden entrance to a cave near the top." Marvin paused and his eyes narrowed. "What they discovered inside was absolutely amazing."

"The cave drawings," Scott chirped.

"Yeah. Cave drawings. Pictures that lined a shaft that stretched down into the mountain at an 18-degree angle for several hundred yards. The entire cave itself appears to have been a fissure to vent the flow of magma at one time."

"An extinct volcano?" Curt asked.

"One that went dormant millions of year ago," Marvin replied.

"What about the drawings?" Scott asked, leaning forward in the chair.

"The drawings were pictures of animals. More appropriately, paired animals."

"From the Ark?" Curt asked looking at Marvin for concurrence.

"That's what Mollur believed." The room was silent with the exception of the aquarium filter cascading the cycled water back into the tank.

"The walls of the cave were filled with images on either side. And I'm not talking about kindergarten works of art. These were detailed, meticulously drawn pictures. Very recognizable animals. Zebras, gorillas, kangaroos, buffaloes, lions and elephants, just to name a few."

"So what is it, some kind of passenger manifest for Noah's Ark?" Scott remarked.

"That's the speculation. The drawings have recently been confirmed to date back more than 35,000 years ago. Can you imagine? These pictures may have been created by Noah himself as a record of the animals brought aboard," Marvin said holding his hands in front of him and locking his fingers together.

"How many paired pictures are there?" Curt asked.

"It's hard to say. Mollur estimated 30,000, give or take several thousand. Poor guy was unable to photograph them all. He actually ran out of film. Can you imagine? Possibly one of the greatest biblical discoveries and he didn't pack enough Kodak paper."

"Marvin, correct me if I'm wrong, but aren't there millions of species of animals in the world?" Scott asked.

"Just over one million I believe."

"So Noah didn't bother taking them all," Scott said sarcastically. "And again, I have to ask, what does this have to do with our situation?"

"I'm wondering the same thing." Curt said glancing at Scott.

"You two need to go out and buy a cup of patience. Listen to me for a minute. True, there are more than one million species of animals but Noah would only need to transport those incapable of surviving in water. There are over 145,000 species of water dwelling creatures such as fish, starfish, sea urchins, clams, oysters, coral, jellyfish and sponges that you can wipe off the list. Another 30,000 protozoans can also be eliminated. You can also exclude aquatic mammals, amphibians and reptiles. Most of the 840,000 arthropods such as shrimp, barnacles and crabs would not have needed a seat on the boat. Many of the 30 plus thousand species of worms and many insects could also have made it without riding in the Ark. Biblical scholars have reasoned that as few as 25,000 pairs of animals may have been aboard."

"I still don't know where this conversation is going," Scott said, "but answer this. There's not a ship around today that could carry such a load of cargo. How do you explain that? Especially when you have such animals the size of giraffes and elephants."

"Oh, but you're wrong. Think practically. The bible never states Noah took full-grown animals. It stands to reason that in order to maximize space, it would make much more sense to take the young."

Curt raised his eyebrows. He'd never considered that option.

"And look at the size of the Ark," Marvin continued. "From what we know about a cubit, this vessel would have been over 70 feet wide and more than 450 feet long. It would have also been 50 feet tall. Based on these dimensions it would have been very seaworthy and nearly impossible to capsize.

"But let's get back to the 25,000 pairs of animals. Based on the premise that Noah brought along young animals let's estimate the average animal to be the size of a German Shepherd. Using the dimensions I just referenced, the animals would have filled up less than 40% of the Ark."

"Are you positive?" Scott asked.

"I read it from Mollur's website but I checked the math myself."

"So this cave may actually have pictures of every species of animals Noah took along for the ride?" Curt remarked. "That is amazing."

"That's what Mollur is suggesting. And although he did run out of film on the trip, he's on a second excursion as we speak. A while ago I contacted one of his research assistants who was unable to make the journey because of a broken leg."

"You know this Dr. Mollur?" Scott asked.

"I've met him before through a friend of a friend. With some convincing I asked his assistant to fax me a picture from the cave. Since none are currently uploaded to Mollur's website, I was very curious about one of the drawings he specifically referenced in his field summary."

Marvin leaned back and reached over to the solitary sheet of paper turned face down on the couch. He lifted it and slowly turned it toward the men.

It was a picture of one fish neatly and exactly drawn into a stone wall. Its features were undeniable. Marvin almost chuckled at the startled expression on both men's faces.

"The Kilgotian," Scott whispered loud enough for Marvin to hear.

"The Kilgotian," Marvin repeated. "It looks identical to the one I told you I found last night. See!" Marvin held up a piece of paper he retrieved from the coffee table. Although the picture was a smaller version than the fax, there was no denying it was a picture of the same creature.

"Remember? I told you the Indian legend mentioned it was created by the white man's god to help maintain the earth's varying species during a time when the earth was covered in water?"

"Damn, I was right." Curt said. "It was Noah's pet fish."

"I don't know if I'd go that far but if Mollur is right, and the pictures in the cave represent a visual log of all the animals carried in the Ark, it appears pretty obvious our fish was there."

Scott reached for the fax of the photograph. "This was a drawing in the cave? Then where's the second fish? You said they were in pairs."

"That's what was so unusual about this drawing. Every other picture had pairs. Presumably a male and a female. But when Mollur discovered this one among the others, it was a single creature. At first he thought the second etching must have been worn away but further investigation discounted that theory. There had been virtually no deterioration within the cave for thousands of years. It was hidden well enough from the elements that it was in a remarkably virgin state. It was almost as if it had divine protection."

Scott rolled his eyes as Curt grabbed the one picture still in Marvin's hand and the faxed picture from Scott.

"This is amazing!" he said after a brief examination. "I wonder what the legend meant when it said the Kilgotian helped maintain the earth's varying species?"

"It's pretty obvious to me," Marvin started. "Everything I've read speaks to some form of reincarnation. Curt's manuscript and your buddy Tatterhorn . . ."

"Me and Tatterhorn are no longer friends. Remember, we had a falling out," Scott interrupted.

Marvin continued, "Tatterhorn mentioned the fish had the ability to create Soulful Ones. What if this fish was on Noah's Ark? Maybe it was God's way of assuring that Noah and his family survived the ordeal. None of us can deny that carcass in my oven possesses some odd power. Surely, the three of us can attest to that. I've got a splintered bathroom door as proof." Marvin said as his excitement grew.

"For some reason, for some specific purpose, God created this creature and now you've found it. We've touched it! We've touched history."

"We have history," Curt said in a low voice.

"And we're all going to *be* history if that thing ever gets in the water," Scott said. Then he continued in a low, calm voice, "Don't get me wrong. I appreciate the possible significance of what's stewing in your kitchen. But whatever power it has scares the shit out of me. Sorry to put a damper on your celebration."

The other two were momentarily silent. Scott was right. Although the fish was quite a find, they still didn't have any proof it was the fish in the legend or the one drawn in the Trascent cave. They had never seen the Kilgotian fully clothed with meat and skin. And although they had a pretty good idea of how to get the complete view of the beast, it went against their better judgment to attempt to reincarnate it again. They doubted Marvin's house or their sanity could stand the stress.

Anyway, there was no absolute proof of what Mollur had discovered. Maybe it was just the drawings of someone who had heard the story of the Ark. Maybe they just decided to make up the picture of the fish.

But still. The picture from the Indian legend and Mollur's photograph were a match. Dead on.

"This is all mind boggling," Curt paused and then continued, "But I think it's time I head back out. Something has happened to Sherri Falco and I've got to find her. Marvin, keep an eye on that fish."

"Unless it learns to open the oven door it's not going anywhere."

"I'm going with you," Scott said rising from the chair.

"Don't you guys want dinner? I've got some stew in the oven?" Marvin said with a slight grin.

"We'll pass," Scott replied and closed the door behind him.

Marvin Sellon got up from the couch and stared at the two pictures side by side on the coffee table as he had done for quite some time before Scott and Curt had returned. One was like a copy of the other. Same gnarled angry teeth, same curved backbone, same dorsal fin, same split tail. It was astonishing and disturbing at the same time. It was also an amazingly easy match to the skeleton in his oven. Marvin had no doubt they had *the* Kilgotian. A fish created by God thousands of years ago and given to Noah to carry aboard the Ark. Possibly a tool to help an old man accomplish the Supreme Commander and Chief's work.

Marvin's mind began spinning as he thought about the significance of discovering the Kilgotian. Most myths are just that. Very rarely do they hold substance. Usually they're fabricated stories to explain anomalies in nature or to help justify our own existence. Occasionally, a piece of a myth will unfold some measure of reality. But the Legend of the Kilgotian appeared to have the ability to be much more fact than fiction.

Marvin decided to recheck his houseguest for the hundredth time that day. He walked into the kitchen and moved toward the oven. There appeared to be a light blue glow emanating from within but he quickly realized it was a reflection from the clock on the adjacent wall. He slowly knelt down and flipped the light on.

The skeleton of the Kilgotian sat quiescent on the plate. Marvin turned the oven off. No need to keep wasting electricity.

One of the last things he'd said to the boys before they left began echoing in his mind. He stood up and walked over to the sink. He reached down and opened the bottom cabinet drawer to the right. Spotting what he needed, he pulled out a ball of twine. He returned to the stove and wove the end of the twine through the oven door and wrapped it around the cabinet handles above. He repeated this loop, oven door to cabinet handle, five times before cutting off the twine and tying a neat knot. Then he reached down and flipped the inside light off.

When he finished, he got a glass of milk and sat down at the kitchen table, eyeing the oven.

"Let's see you get out now," he said, raising his glass in a toast.

The ringing of the phone startled Marvin and he nearly dropped the glass. As he picked up the receiver, he smiled thinking how it had spooked him.

It was John Shanis, Dr. Mollur's research assistant, calling from the professor's office at Stanford University.

"Mr. Sellon, this is John. I talked to you earlier and sent you the fax. I'm assuming you got it."

"Yes, thanks."

"A few minutes ago I was in contact with the professor at the site via a short-wave satellite hookup," the man said excitedly. "I mentioned you had called and the professor said he remembered you. He just asked that you keep the picture I faxed to you confidential. Professional courtesy and all."

"Understood," Marvin replied.

"But what I really called to tell you, and he gave me permission to disclose this to you, is two-fold. First, what he's just discovered in the cave and secondly, what I discovered two weeks ago." John Shanis was speaking at an exasperating pace and was almost breathless.

"Calm down, son. I'm not going anywhere. Slowly tell me what you know."

CHAPTER-TWENTY-SEVEN

At 9:19 Tuesday night Ambrose C. Ridden was leaving work. He had just finished closing the Eckerd Drug Store on the west side of San Marco Boulevard, one block south of the Nuestra Senora de la Leche Cemetery. As the store manager, he had authorized an early shutdown at 7 p.m. so that the employees could get home and prepare for the impending hurricane. He had remained behind with two volunteers to secure the premises and board the windows. Now as he locked the doors behind him and set the alarm, he could feel the warm breeze blowing in from the east.

Ambrose had been in charge for just over a month. His predecessor had moved downstate and accepted a position at a store in Fort Lauderdale. But for Ambrose, this was only a job, not a career. He was biding his time while rehabbing his knee in preparation for next summer when he again would attempt to make the Jacksonville Jaguar's roster.

The last few years, luck had been unkind to Ambrose. Two years ago, he had been signed as a free agent cornerback by the New Orleans Saints and then cut seven days before the start of the season. Last year, he got into the Jaguars' camp and impressed the coaching staff enough to earn a spot on the five-man practice squad. But during the third week of the regular season he suffered an anterior cruciate ligament (ACL) injury while turning to defend a receiver running an out route. Surgery seemed like such a distant option. He knew the road to recovery would be long and arduous and delayed his decision for six weeks before going under the knife. In early November, the successful procedure was undertaken to repair the torn cartilage in his knee.

Now the long months of rehabilitation seemed endless. He had hoped to be back by last summer but the knee took longer to respond than anticipated. But he was determined. Nothing was going to keep him from giving football another shot next summer and he hoped the Jaguars would afford him that opportunity. He had been a great corner at Ball State and knew he could play at the next level. Undersized at 5'10" and 172 pounds, he needed to convince the right people.

As Ambrose walked through the empty parking lot to his car he heard the sound of a pleading voice. He stopped and strained to see through the darkness. A man appeared to be forcefully pulling a woman between the ally of the two small stores across San Marco Boulevard. The man wore ragged clothes and carried a long object in his left hand. Ambrose immediately ran toward the edge of the street and, after quickly checking traffic, dashed across and into the front of the alley. He froze as he lost sight of the pair among the shadows. The pleas faded. Ambrose listened intently, but failed to pick up any further sounds.

Now he was indecisive. But moments later, beyond the end of the alley, muffled cries escaped from the bleakness and he cautiously moved toward the sound. He took each step in small strides to minimize the sound of his approach. Whatever the object the man in the alley was holding weighed heavy in Ambrose's thoughts. He had to be careful, had to protect himself. He passed from the light to the shadows and then paused in the pitch dark. He wanted to give his eyes a moment to focus and his pupils time to enlarge. He had no idea how far back the alley extended and he needed any edge in case of attack.

As his eyes became accustomed to the darkness, the shape of two figures dimly materialized against the wall to his left. He had come within several feet of the man and woman without knowing it. One of the figures leaped forward and swung an object toward him. Ambrose reacted and pushed off the ground sailing backward, barely avoiding contact as the object passed by, swiping at neck level. The image of the man's glowing, watery eyes seared the darkness and the grunt from the attacker sounded more choking than air being expelled. At the same moment that the woman screamed, Ambrose crashed back into the wall and slammed his head against the cement. Just before losing consciousness, through blurred vision, he saw the woman escape down the ally.

The attacker slowly moved in for the kill. Lifting the object to his left, he was prepared to swing a fatal overhead blow to the body slumping against the wall. Then he hesitated, looking left, and suddenly took off down the dark alley in the same direction where the woman had escaped.

Scott and Curt returned to the Gift Shop parking lot to retrieve Sherri's car and return it to her house. Charlene had given Curt a spare set of keys and the garage door opener. When they arrived, the car sat alone and abandoned in the lighted parking lot. It gave Curt a sick feeling to see the lone vehicle in desolation but he still held onto the hope that the charismatic woman he had met only this afternoon was alive and safe somewhere.

He climbed out of the Blazer and started the Toyota. Scott followed Curt through the streets of St. Augustine back to Sherri's house.

It was 10:08 p.m. when they secured the car in Sherri's amazingly neat garage and then the two men were off to continue their search. This time they kept the radio on in case of any breaking news, the type of news they didn't want to hear but couldn't avoid. The DJ's chatter focused exclusively on Damon's approach, evacuation procedures and the damage probabilities if a direct hit was sustained. There was no mention of the recently murdered victims. Curt said a silent prayer as they drove down Freon Street and turned right onto Maple.

At the intersection of Maple and Lennis they spotted a patrolman idling in the parking lane. The officer was busy looking down at his lap, probably finishing up the details on a parking violation, which struck Curt odd since there were no vehicles in the immediate area. More likely he's bored and looking at the October issue of Penthouse, Curt thought.

"Let's talk to him," Curt said as he motioned for Scott to pull over.

Scott angled the Blazer into the space ahead of the squad car. The two men got out and approached the driver's side. The officer noticed them immediately and seemed to scurry with the item in his lap before lowering the window.

"Gentlemen," the officer said in a firm yet friendly voice. "What can I help you with?"

Scott thought how smallish the man looked for a police officer. He had dirty blonde hair cut in a crew, tight beady eyes and probably went no more than 155 pounds. Not the typical ominous cop portrayed on TV.

"Officer we're concerned about a female friend of ours," Curt said. "She has been missing since around six this evening. She was to return home by 6:30 to meet her daughter and sister and leave town ahead of the hurricane."

"A missing person report can't be officially filed until 24 hours have passed," the officer responded.

Curt continued, "I know, I was just wondering . . ."

"But in light of the recent homicides, I'll put out a communication to the other officers on duty."

"Thanks," Scott and Curt said in unison. The policeman's nametag was now visible as he turned his body slightly to the left: Sgt Shultz.

"Where was she going this evening before she was supposed to meet her family?" the officer asked as he removed a pen and notepad from his shirt pocket.

"Back into work. She's a clerk at Our Lady de la Leche Cemetery Gift Shop," Curt responded.

"That cute redhead?" The officer's eyes lit up. Curt became instantly defensive.

"Yes," he said. "She's a close friend of mine." Curt scowled at the officer, who shifted in his seat uneasily as he realized he better moderate his comments. For all he knew this man could be her fiancé. The officer's discomfort gave Curt a small measure of satisfaction.

"I need her name and a description," Shultz continued in a professional tone.

Curt gave him the details as requested although he was sure the officer had the information stored in the recesses of his mind.

"I guess as a regular in a small town you get to know the star attractions," Scott commented to Curt as the two men walked back to the Blazer afterward.

Curt frowned but then a glimmer of a smile spilled across his face. "As long as I'm the co-star, I'm okay with that," he said.

"Besides, didn't you notice the ring on Sergeant Shultz's finger?" Scott asked as he grabbed the door handle.

"I see nothing," Curt said before entering the passenger side.

The men drove the streets for another 30 minutes when Scott decided to call Kay. She and the kids were just outside Valdosta, Georgia. Other than a little weary, she sounded in reasonably good spirits. Scott wished he were with them. Again he promised to leave in the morning, continuing to fabricate the "securing the office" lie. He had always felt a good dose of remorse when lying to his wife. But this time, and under these circumstances, his conscience was protected.

As Scott hung up, Curt phoned Charlene and gave her the disheartening news that he had not located Sherri. She took it in stride and surprised Curt by temporarily changing the subject. She informed him they were still 25 miles from Tallahassee. She was not in a good position to make the 11:30 p.m. deadline so she had contacted the hotel to make sure they would hold the reservation and was relieved when they guaranteed the room. As she spoke, he could tell the woman's nerves were becoming frazzled. The initial courage was dissolving quickly. Through quivering speech she fought to maintain her composure. As easy as she could have broken down at that moment, she struggled to keep her watering eyes from overflowing onto her cheeks. The last thing she wanted to do was alarm Tina. As she paused between sentences to fight back the tears, Curt could hear the little girl in the passenger seat playing her GameBoy and giggling.

Curt didn't want to push her but he had to get a few questions answered.

"Charlene, I know you're trying not to upset Tina but I need to ask you a few things. Just give me short answers so Tina won't catch on."

"Okay." Her speech struggling to gain some rigor.

"Has anything recently happened to Sherri out of the ordinary?"

"Huh?"

"Anything unusual or strange?"

"Other than winning the Lotto, no."

Curt turned and grinned at Scott like a man who had just been offered entry into a threesome with Pamela Anderson and Shania Twain. Scott had never seen so many teeth.

"What?" Scott mouthed to Curt.

"Well, that is unusual but I'm referring to anything she might have told you about, such as a dream or a vision."

"No nothing. She did show me the picture Tina drew at school."

"What picture?"

"The ocean picture. Tina drew it in school."

"What about it?"

"The fish."

Curt was speechless. He felt his chest expand and release three cycles before he had the composure to go on.

"You there?" Charlene asked.

"Yeah. What fish? What about a fish?"

As Curt spoke, Scott stared at him with eyes wide open. In the instant he diverted his attention from the road, he ran through the stop sign at Trevor and St. Andrews. One of the few cars on the road, a white Ford Ranger, swerved and barely avoided the back end of the Blazer. The flabbergasted driver administered the proper finger gesture as Scott gained control of his vehicle, swerving hard to the left to avoid slamming into the cross-leg of a billboard. He guided the tires back on the pavement and realigned the car on the road.

"Oh shit! Oh shit! Oh shit!" Curt panted.

"Are you okay?" Charlene asked.

"Yeah. Give me second."

Curt held the phone down as Scott pulled into the Eckerd's parking lot. As the vehicle came to a stop, Scott threw his head back and then brought it forward turning to face his friend. His face was flush. "What about a fish?"

"Charlene, what about a fish?" Curt asked again.

"Well, you-know-who had created the thing I mentioned before about the deep blue."

Curt noticed the quiet background on the phone. Charlene's tactic of talking in adult code was probably because Tina was no longer occupied with the Game Boy. "Go on," he said.

"It had all sorts of pretty aquatic swimmers that a pre-adolescent would normally conceive. That is, with one exception." Charlene paused. "When Sis first got it from little T it was void of anything in the epicenter."

"Hold on a moment," Curt told Charlene.

Curt covered the bottom of the phone and whispered to Scott. "When Tina first brought the picture she had drawn home from school, it was an ocean scene with sea creatures. But it was void of anything in the middle of the page."

"Go on," Curt told Charlene removing his hand.

"Sis put it on the icebox, like all parents do. The next day when TF was educating the noodle, a new finned entity entered the scene. Sis noticed it after coming back from a stroll."

Curt placed his palm back across the speaker and faced Scott. "After Sherri returned from a walk the next day, there was a new fish in the picture that she had hung on the refrigerator."

"Did Tina add it in?" Curt asked lifting his hand.

"There was denial but the mother is suspect," Charlene responded.

"Are you talking about my Mommy?" Tina's innocence chimed in the background. She had picked up on the one word Charlene had effectively managed to avoid until that moment.

"I better go now Curt. Please call when . . . if . . ." Charlene's voice broke off. She was losing it again.

"I will. I promise," he said with less than thorough confidence and the receiver on the other end clicked and went dead.

Curt looked at Scott. He felt sincere concern for Charlene. She was holding up the stone pillar that supported the crumbling roof that dangled over little Tina Falco's existence. He wondered if she was strong enough to continue for much longer.

"I want to see that picture. Let's head back to Sherri's," Curt said snapping out of his concentration.

"Okay. But as screwy as things are going, I bet I know what that fish looks like."

"Yeah," Curt said with a huff. "So do I."

Scott cranked the engine and steered the Blazer back onto the quiet streets. It was now 11:17 p.m.

When they arrived at Sherri's, Curt punched the garage door opener and Scott pulled into the driveway and cut the motor. They entered the house through the garage door, which led to the den. Although some lights in the back rooms had been intentionally left on, the den and kitchen beyond was bathed in darkness. They had no idea where the light switches were located and Scott momentarily considered returning to the Blazer to retrieve a flashlight.

They moved through the pitch-black den, feeling their way around the furniture. In the nothingness that engulfed them, they moved cautiously. Suddenly, Scott placed his hand across Curt's chest. The two men stopped as they simultaneously made out the outline of a man sitting at the small table in the kitchen. His shadowy image was almost translucent as it formed a waving silhouette. As they had approached, the ghostly apparition shifted its weight.

Scott and Curt stood completely still, eyeing the figure from just beyond the doorway into the kitchen. Their hearts raced. Neither knew whether to run back out or charge ahead. Obviously it was an intruder. But was it an armed intruder? A better question that surged through Scott's mind was why did the dark figure resemble smoke billowing upward in the shape of a human?

For a few moments nothing moved. The image remained stationary, barely seven feet away. In the murky blackness it was impossible to tell if the intruder was looking in their direction. Surely he had heard them coming. They had made their way through the den with no intent of concealing their approach. But just beyond the doorway the fragile outline of the man was obvious. And as it repositioned itself, any uncertainty that it was a living presence vanished.

Curt and Scott stood frozen as the image rose, the chair legs making a whining scrape as they dragged across the floor. Now fully erect, its features seemed to gain consistency even in the darkness. It was a man.

Curt gingerly reached his hand forward and gratefully found the switch on the wall near the door. With a quick flip the room was ablaze with light. The man hovering beside the kitchen table did not move. He was firmly fixed in his stance and staring directly at them as he had been the entire time.

Watching. Waiting.

Scott, acting more out of impulse than rational thought, dodged to his left and grabbed a poker iron from the brass fireplace on the side of the mantle. He tried to disengage it from the stand, only to dump the entire ensemble on the carpet before it came free. He quickly returned to Curt's side.

While Scott was in hand to hand combat with the fireplace set, Curt was able to adjust his vision, and identify the intruder. It took several seconds before recognition set in. It was a man he had seen before, but something was very different. Then Curt pictured him in the right attire. The hat, the uniform, the shoes. It was his fifty-dollar friend, now wearing jeans and a strikingly white tee shirt. He wore the same driving gloves he had Monday morning when the men met him at Fort Castillo de San Marcos.

"Bruin, what are you doing here?" Curt barked, his voice filled with more anger than Scott could have mustered at the moment as he held the trembling poker.

Upon hearing the words, Scott recognized the park ranger.

"It's okay. I'm not a thief," Bruin said calmly, his eyes concentrating on the movement of the men. His trust was still not assured and they might attack at any moment but his instincts told him they wouldn't. "I was brought here."

"What?" Curt asked. "What do you mean *brought here*? Brought here by who? This is breaking and entering."

"What about you two? You're in here as well," Bruin said calmly but defiantly.

Curt raised the key after lifting it from his pocket. "We were invited. I'm betting you weren't."

"In a manner of speaking, I was."

"What the hell are you talking about?" Scott asked. He was over his anxiety and becoming quickly annoyed with Bruin's responses. This day had lasted forever and seemed nowhere near concluding. He was way past being a little edgy at this point.

Bruin pointed down at the piece of paper lying on the table. The sheet was rectangular. He turned the page so it was aimed at the men as they moved forward.

"Oh my God," Curt said staring at the picture.

It was Tina's artwork. The Kilgotian was portentously patrolling just below the surface. The professional image of the creature overshadowed the other crayon creations. The precise details and three-dimensional imagery brought the fish to life. The protruding teeth seemed ready to jump off the page and go for the nearest jugular. You could probably throw the paper in a tub of water and it would start swimming around Scott thought as he stared at the image.

Curt broke off his concentration on the picture and glared at Bruin. "You still didn't answer. Why are you here?"

"I told you. I was drawn here. It's my purpose."

Scott looked at Curt. Curt shrugged. Obviously the man had no intention of attacking them. He had adequate time to hide or even leave the house when they had arrived. Surely he would have heard the car pull up or at least heard the garage door rising.

"Why are you interested in the picture?" Scott asked trying for a different angle.

"The fish. It's the Kilgotian," Bruin said.

The men again looked at each other. Then at the drawing. The fish was identical to Marvin's two renderings.

"What do you know about it?" Curt asked intrigued but still angry.

"I know I've regretted ever discovering the secret."

The words were chilling and again Scott and Curt looked at each other.

Bruin was staring into space, eyes fixed somewhere on the wall behind the table. Then he sat down in his chair. Scott and Curt cautiously sat down in the chairs on either side.

"What secret is that, Mr. Bruin?" Curt asked leaning in.

"Don't you know by now? The power it possesses." Bruin shifted in his seat. The movement startled Scott and Curt.

"How are you involved in this?" Scott asked.

"It's a long story."

The night was dragging on and the day had been filled with so many odd occurrences and discoveries that Scott could feel the staggering weariness settle into his bones. But his anticipation of what Bruin had to say forced his zealous response. "Go on!"

But before Bruin could start, Curt changed the subject. "Do you know where Sherri Falco is?"

"I assume you're talking about the redhead?"

"I am," Curt said glaring at the park ranger. "What do you know about her disappearance? Are you involved?" Curt said angrily, rising from the table and staring down at Bruin.

"I promise you I had nothing to do with it. But I do know what's happening. For the moment she's safe. She has a talent her captor values."

"What are you talking about! Where is she?" Curt growled.

"I told you it's a long story," Bruin replied slowly looking Curt directly in the eyes. I assure you, I want nothing more than her safe return. For that matter, I want the killings to cease and all of this to end."

Scott watched Curt's reaction. He believed Bruin. He didn't know why, but he suddenly felt the man was their ally, not their enemy. He wasn't so sure if Curt held the same perspective.

"Then come with us, Mr. Bruin." Curt said as he pushed the chair in place under the table. "It's time to go and hear your story."

Scott watched Curt as he walked to the kitchen door leading to the den. "Marvin's?" Scott asked.

"Yep," Curt responded never turning.

The three men left the house, closing the garage door behind them, and climbed in the Blazer. Curt had Bruin sit in the front passenger seat to keep an eye on him.

Although difficult to suppress the questions, Scott understood Curt's rationale of involving Marvin and the men were silent the entire drive back to the professor's house.

CHAPTER-TWENTY-EIGHT

When they arrived at Marvin's, it was well after midnight and the house was dark.

"The professor must have turned in," Scott said as the Blazer glided to a stop in front.

But as the men approached the front door they could see it wasn't completely closed. Even in the shadows, the gap between the jam and the door was evident.

"Something's wrong," Scott said in a panicky whisper as they moved toward the porch.

The three men strolled to the entrance and slowly pushed the door open. The frame was splintered at the point where the bolt normally held its secure position inside the wood.

"Let me go first," Bruin said. His voice was commanding. Surprised by his demeanor, Scott and Curt stepped to the side to let him pass.

Without hesitation he entered the dark living room and moved forward. Scott followed and began to search for the light switches. He called for the professor. "Marvin! You here?"

Curt brought up the rear and followed in Bruin's footsteps.

"Marvin! Where are you?" A moment later Scott found the dining room switch plate and turned it on. With the light, everything appeared normal. The table was clear and the china cabinet was in order. If the professor had been burglarized, it was not by a very efficient thief.

Bruin and Curt made their way into the kitchen. No sign of Marvin.

"Marvin!" Curt yelled down the hallway toward the back bedrooms. They entered each room and turned the lights on. Scott followed down the hallway as they searched the last bedroom. He was struck with a sickening feeling.

This is wrong, very, very wrong.

"What could have happened to him?" Scott said despondently as they returned to the living room. The concern in his voice was pressing. Curt looked at his friend with an empty stare as he shrugged his shoulders.

Suddenly the men heard a faint moan from the hallway. It came from a tattered, broken voice. Bruin turned and led the way. Stopping at the hall closet he quickly ripped the door open. The speed and aggressiveness of his actions caught Scott and Curt by surprise and they both fell slightly backward as the door slammed into the wall. Inside, a huddled man lay on the floor, tangled among a pile of coats, jackets and plastic clothes hangers.

"Marvin!" Scott yelled, circling to the side of Bruin, "are you okay?"

Marvin was trembling. His eyes wore a terrified expression. Scott reached down to help Marvin up.

"Some . . . someone was here Scott!" he stuttered as Scott helped him up. Then Marvin saw Bruin and fell back into the closet.

"Who the hell is he! Is he the one?" Marvin asked with wild eyes.

Curt looked at Bruin. "Marvin calm down," Curt said. "He's with us."

"Are you all right? What happened?" Scott asked, raising the professor again with Curt's help. Bruin stood back. His expression never changed.

"Someone broke in. I was going to the bathroom and someone came in." Marvin words were quick and sparse.

"What happened next?" Curt asked.

"I crapped in my underwear! What in the hell do you think happened!"

A smile broke across Scott and Curt's faces. Robert Bruin stood to the side, as stoic as a statue.

"What Curt meant is what happened with the intruder? Did he see you? Did you see him?" Scott asked, trying to fend off a grin.

"Scott, you think this is funny? I don't find this amusing at all. And you? You're enjoying this too? He yelled pointing at Curt.

"C'mon, Marvin," Scott said. "What happened?"

"God I need to sit down," Marvin said. The four men walked into the living room and Marvin plopped on the couch. "Have you checked the place to make sure he's gone?"

"We checked every room. There's no one here," Curt responded.

"Who is he?" Marvin asked with a puzzled expression looking at Bruin as if they'd already told him once and he'd forgotten. "And why is he wearing Michael Jackson's glove?"

"We'll get to that in a minute. Now start from the beginning. What happened here?"

"Let's see. Where to start. Oh yeah, I was on a phone call with Mr. Mollur's assistant." He paused. "Have I got some news for you boys," Marvin's tone was returning to normal and his excitement had changed from terror to elation.

"One thing at a time, Marvin," Scott said with a calming hand on the professor's shoulder.

"Okay, okay. First the intruder. After we were done talking, I went to the bathroom. The next thing I knew there was a crashing sound coming from the living room and all the lights went out. I could hear someone or something making noise throughout the house. I considered staying in the bathroom but with no goddamn door on it, I decided to get out. When I did, the house was still. I thought whatever had entered was gone. I came down the hallway but about the time I reached the hall closet, I saw a shadowy figure moving through the living room. What was so odd was that it glided more than it walked. It's hard to describe. God, it was strange."

"Shadowy, huh?" Curt said turning to look at Bruin suspiciously.

"I told you I'd explain," Bruin said.

"We'll get to you in a minute," Scott said impatiently. "Marvin, you better look around and see if anything is missing."

"I can tell you now one thing that's gone."

"What's that?" Scott asked.

Marvin pointed to the dining room table. It was bare. It took Scott a moment to understand.

"Pinot's skeleton. Oh my god. Someone stole Pinot's skeleton!" Scott said.

"The curator's gonna be pissed," Marvin muttered.

"You had Pinot's skeleton?" Bruin asked. There was a sparkle of curiosity in his eyes.

"Among other things," Curt said. The moment the words left his lips his eyes widened and he looked at Scott. Scott looked at him. They looked at Marvin. Marvin looked at them. In unison the three men rose and rushed to the kitchen. The oven light was on. The twine lay in a clump on the floor.

"I had turned that light off," Marvin said as they approached, "and I had tied the door shut."

Scott quickly knelt down, followed by Curt and the professor. They were staring at the empty plate when Bruin entered the kitchen behind them.

"Marvin, think hard. You didn't get hungry and eat the Kilgotian did you?" Curt asked.

Marvin glared at Curt.

"I can't believe this. Someone stole Pinot's skeleton and the Kilgotian," Scott said.

"I'm going to be sick," Marvin moaned rising to his feet. They followed him into the living room where he went to the couch. Scott noticed the pile of papers on the table had been straightened into neat stacks. There was also a Bible in the middle next to the picture of Marvin and his late wife taken at West Palm Beach in the early eighties. The picture was familiar but Scott couldn't remember if it was one of the professor's normal coffee table items.

"You guys would have been famous," Marvin said with a sigh.

"What are you talking about?" Curt asked.

"Shanis called earlier to tell me Mollur had been in contact regarding some findings at the Trascent Cave site."

Scott and Curt, who had taken seats beside Marvin on the couch and in the recliner, respectively, leaned forward.

Marvin continued, "He found a name. A signature, if you will, toward the base of the tunnel. "Shem" was etched on the wall. Actually, it was not far from the drawing of your fish."

Bruin, who had been standing several feet away from the coffee table, sat down on the carpet. Marvin watched his every movement with wariness. He still didn't know who this man was or why he was in his house.

"You can grab a chair from the living room," Marvin said to Bruin.

Bruin shook his head from side to side.

"Go on, Marvin." Scott said.

"Shem was one of Noah's three sons who traveled aboard the Ark. Mollur found the signature but no others. Shem appears to be claiming credit for the pictorial manifest. This will go a long way in substantiating Mollur's claim that the cave drawings are authentic and directly tied to Noah's Ark. It's quite a find."

The others nodded in agreement including Bruin, who finally seemed to have interest in the conversation.

"But that's only the beginning. There's much more," Marvin said.

Scott broke in, "There's even more than you know. After you're done, Mr. Bruin has a story to tell us as well." The words came out a bit sarcastic but he was not the least bit apologetic. It was now 1:38 a.m. on Wednesday.

Out in the Atlantic Ocean, *Laura Sun*, a U.S. Air Force Reserve hurricane hunter was closing in on Damon's eye. Flying strictly by radar, the location of the eye, or the "fix," had been determined from global positioning satellite vortex data received several hours before. The Lockheed Martin WC-130 and crew were preparing to deploy a package of instruments, called dropsondes, which would send back readings as it parachuted down to the ocean. Onboard, The Omega Dropsonde Wind finding System (ODWS) would receive and process navigation data of temperature, humidity, atmospheric pressure, and wind speed and direction.

At 10,000 feet, the dropsonde was deployed in absolute darkness as the four-engine turbo prop plane passed over the eyewall. The parachute opened perfectly and was tracked on radar as it made its slow descent.

Three minutes later, from the mid-section of the WC-130, Ensign Carlos Rainor watched the real-time data populate across the ODWS screen. He could only stare in disbelief. Typing in some commands, he recalibrated the settings but with the same results. The equipment was in perfect working order and the information was valid. The readings confirmed what he feared.

He opened the intercom and called to the cabin.

"Captain Dupree."

"Yes, Ensign."

Rainor hesitated. "We've got a category *six*."

"Ensign, please repeat. I thought you said six."

"I did. We're officially over the most powerful hurricane ever recorded."

Ambrose C. Ridden (he told his college coach the C stood for cover) woke up on the rough cement pavement to a riveting headache at 2:38 Wednesday morning. Although his watch face was cracked from the impact with the wall, it was still ticking. He had been unconscious for nearly five hours and was not happy about the incident. *If I ever catch his ass I'm going to turn him inside out* he thought, trying to clear his head.

He slowly rose and brushed himself off. In retrospect, he was happy to be alive, but the pain coursing through his head left him with a throbbing skull. He had had a concussion once in high school and it hurt less than the pain that he felt now. Standing erect, he teetered to the side and caught himself on the wall, barely stopping his fall. He reached his right hand to the back of his head fearful he would find blood. He was pleasantly surprised when he didn't.

Ambrose staggered out of the alley and across San Marco Boulevard. He reached the pay phone just outside the entrance to the drug store and dialed 911. Seven minutes later a patrol car pulled into the parking lot as Ambrose sat resting on the hood of his classic 1969 Chevy Camaro Super Sport.

Now he was as vindictive as he was in pain.

After relaying the account of what had happened, and upon the advice of the officer, Ambrose drove to the emergency room at Flagler General Hospital. He was released at 6:15 a.m. after x-rays showed no permanent damage.

As he drove back to his apartment and thought more about his attacker the angrier he got. He wondered if the woman had escaped from the madman.

He also considered how close he had come to dying.

"I'm sure you boys remember the Dead Sea Scrolls discovered in 1947?" Marvin began after retrieving a glass of water and waiting for Curt to return from the open-air bathroom.

"Of course," Scott replied. "The scrolls were a collection of Books from the Old Testament. A shepherd boy trying to find one of his sheep came across the documents in a cave. It was one of the flukiest discoveries of all time. If they were only all that easy."

"But are you aware of the significance?" Marvin asked staring at Scott.

Scott was about to respond but then stopped. He wasn't exactly sure what Marvin was driving at. Curt sat quietly.

"Go on," Scott finally said.

"Until the Dead Sea Scrolls were found, the earliest copy man had of the Old Testament was from around 900 A.D. The original was thought to have been written about 400 B.C. This meant that of all the copies ever made, we were no closer than having a version less than 1,300 years from the original."

"How come the earliest copy is from 900 A.D.? Wasn't it considered significant before then?" Curt asked.

"Its significance was far reaching and its impact profound from the initial edition. The problem was that its value to mankind was considered spiritual, not tangible."

"What do you mean," Scott asked.

"Around the time of Jesus and in the subsequent millennium, old worn out copies of the Old Testament were thought of in such high esteem they were typically buried in the earth in reverence. And you know paper doesn't preserve well in dirt. Fortunately, the Dead Sea Scrolls were stored above ground in special Baratot root shoot casings capped at either end with a hardened gel made from sap. Their preservation was immaculate. With this amazing discovery in the Palestine cave we now have copies of Old Testament books, which were written during the period between two hundred to one hundred years *before* Christ. This means mankind now has copies some 1,000 years earlier than we did previously."

"This is all well and educational but what's this leading to Marvin?" Curt asked.

"What's really astonishing is how the Dead Sea Scrolls agreed with the later ones in existence. It's well documented how much care was taken when copies of the Old Testament were made. Copying was done line by line. Letter and word counts on each page assured the accuracy of the new copy. In some cases it took years to complete. But as is human nature, it was inevitable there would be some differences through the centuries."

"I remember reading that the differences are extremely minor. Wordsmithing," Scott remarked.

"That's what Biblical Scholars would have you believe. Pope John Paul II once remarked, after being briefed by his advisors, how the insignificant changes between the Dead Sea Scrolls and the 900 A.D. version doesn't affect any teachings of the Bible." Marvin added.

"Of course that's what he's going to say. Admitting any inconsistency opens the Bible up to intense scrutiny by skeptics. It allows us to question its accuracy. The contention by mankind all along is that it was written by God's help to insure the truth," Scott said somewhat sarcastically.

"That's a good point, Moses wrote the first five books of the Old Testament but did it from stories passed down through generations. He wasn't alive when most of the events transpired. The church implies that God played a major part in his efforts to document accounts like the creation of the heavens and the earth, the Great Flood and the life of Abraham." Marvin added.

"But the Dead Sea Scrolls did have some differences that were less than subtle from the later copies of the Bible. When Dr. Mollur first returned from Turkey with the photograph of the single fish drawing, he didn't think much about it. As you know the symbol of the fish represents Christianity. This reference didn't seem out of place in a cave that appeared to house such spirituality. It wasn't until he was preparing to embark on his latest expedition that he began to reexamine the evidence and photos collected during the first trip. It was then that the picture of the lone fish caught his attention. Really raised his curiosity. The vicious nature of the drawing admittedly bothered him when compared to the passive image of everything else etched on the cave walls. Before leaving he asked Shanis to do some research on the Dead Sea Scrolls. Specifically, Genesis Chapters 6 through 8. The Noah's Ark account."

Now Marvin had the men's complete attention. Marvin was reverting back to the master lecturer he once was. Back to his days of teaching when his style of orally recounting an event was mesmerizing. He could tell a story laced with historical foundation and philosophical depth like no one Scott had ever known.

For Scott, it was a welcome return to the past.

"And he found something," Bruin said.

Scott and Curt looked at each other. Bruin had been quiet so long they were wondering if he was even listening.

"Yes. Yes, he did," Marvin said looking at Bruin. "When I talked to Mr. Shanis the first time he didn't feel at liberty to release the information. After a brief conversation with Mollur, who was more familiar with me than I knew, and binding me to silence, Shanis faxed me this," he said holding a sheet of paper that the men could see contained several paragraphs.

Marvin picked up his Bible and opened it to the bookmark. "But first, I'm going to read Genesis 6:19. It's one of the verses where God is giving Noah precise instructions."

> *And of every living thing of all flesh,*
> *two of every sort shalt thou bring*
> *into the ark, to keep them alive with*
> *thee; they shall be male and female.*

"Now here's the version of Genesis from the Dead Sea Scrolls. Same verse." Marvin looked down at the fax and began to read.

> *And of every living thing of all flesh,*
> *two of every sort shalt thou bring*
> *into the ark, to keep them alive with*
> *thee **as the waters assist**; they shall*
> *be male and female.*

"Excuse the pun, but on the surface, the words *as the waters assist*, don't appear to be much of a variance from the Bible as we know it. Now I'm going to read Genesis 6:20," Marvin said as he laid down the fax and again picked up the open Bible.

> *Of fowls after their kind, and of cattle*
> *after their kind, of every creeping*

> *thing of the earth after his kind, two of every sort shall come unto thee, to keep them alive.*

"Now this version," Marvin said picking up the fax and laying it upon the open pages of the Bible in his lap.

> *Of fowls after their kind, and of cattle after their kind, of every creeping thing of the earth after his kind, two of every sort shall come unto thee,* **and finned creature** *to keep them alive.*

Scott was astonished. "You mean to tell me the thousands of biblical scholars and historians who have been studying the Dead Sea Scrolls for 50 some-odd years missed this?" he asked. "And now some wet-behind-the-ears graduate student makes the discovery?"

Curt nodded his head in agreement with Scott's comment.

"Initially, I had the same reaction. It wasn't that scholars had missed the word differences. They've been through the Dead Sea Scrolls with a fine-tooth comb ever since they turned up. The pressure from the religious sect was enormous to validate its authenticity and accuracy as we knew the Old Testament. As you mentioned Scott, these folks surely wanted to dispel any difference that would have to make them rethink the guidelines by which the congregations have been instructed to go about their daily lives. So in every instance where a discrepancy was found, it was cataloged and studied. And studied and studied and studied. More importantly, each was justified."

"So how did these little phrase variances slip by?" Curt asked.

"They didn't slip by. Shanis conveyed Mollur's reasoning and it makes perfect since. Think about it boys. Think about the additional words. One week ago would they really have meant anything to you?" Marvin said in a rebutting tone. "Both phrases; *as the waters assist* and *and finned creature* seem to imply God's plan for the passengers of the Ark to have an infinite food source. Fish. Remember, fishing was big back then and while aboard the Ark, there was quite an abundance of water."

Marvin handed the sheet to Curt who gave it a quick look and then passed it to Scott to review. Marvin was right. The words were simple. References to water and fish fill the pages of the Bible. No wonder these phrases were not considered material during examination of the scrolls. And the truth was, the religious majority probably had downplayed any inconsistencies.

But as Scott gazed at the sheet, its meaning was crystal clear to him.

Curt turned toward Scott watching his friend examine the paper but directed his question to Marvin, "Did you verify with what's-his-name..."

"John Shanis."

"With Shanis, did Shanis verify the term *finned creature* wasn't *finned creatures*, as in plural?"

"You know I did, Curt."

"Did you tell Shanis we had the Kilgotian?" Scott asked.

"Negative. Dr. Mollur's going to be famous for his discovery and its magnitude to history. But you boys..."

"Us, Marvin." Scott interrupted.

"Well then, us, I also wanted us to share in some limelight. Of course that's all out the door now."

"Looking for the glory and fame?" Scott said with a smile.

"Not so much the fame but I wouldn't mind some additional income. Living on a professor's retirement isn't all it's cracked up to be," Marvin said.

Scott and Curt laughed bitterly. The professor was right. Based on Mollur's findings, they had an amazing discovery. A discovery tied to Noah's Ark by more than mere coincidence. The evidence was formidable. But now the remains of the fish were gone and they had no idea who would have stolen it, not to mention the human skeleton thought to be Pinot LeFlore.

Marvin sat back as a disconcerted look spread over his face. "What I'd really like to know is exactly what that damn fish is capable of. I wonder if it was ever meant to be found. And if it was on the Ark, how the hell did it wind up in Northeast Florida? We're more than a stone's throw from the Turkey-Soviet border."

"What bothers me is that if the Kilgotian was created for good, how come there's an air of evilness that seems to surround it now," Curt said.

For a moment, no one spoke, each in reflective thought about Curt's comment. All but Bruin.

"God let go of the Kilgotian many years ago. It now belongs to the pond," Bruin said breaking the silence.

Startled, the three looked at Bruin, who slowly dropped his head in deep concentration and closed his eyes. Ten seconds or more passed before he looked up again at the three men seated around him.

"Where to start," he softly said to himself.

"Start at the beginning," Scott said sympathetically as he suddenly sensed whatever information Bruin had to share would not be without anguish. There was a void in the park ranger's eyes that Scott was sure had contained meaningful substance at one time. Now the vacancy reveled in despair.

"The beginning," he said with a disheartened look. "That's going to take us way back." He paused. "Understand what I'm about to tell you

I've never told anyone in my entire existence." The phrase *existence* instantly struck Scott as peculiar.

"The pond or lake, no matter what you call it, at Fort Caroline has been around long before the Timucua walked the land. And for as long as it existed, the Kilgotian has been a vital part. The two coexist. That's why, long ago when the fish was removed, the pond vanished."

"How do you know this?" Marvin asked.

"I'll explain in a minute. The Kilgotian does have biblical powers as you suspected. From what you've just said, I finally understand what I was told as a small child about the fish being a tool that the heavens delivered to the white man. With the fish's ability to resurrect . . ."

"So it really can resurrect," Scott said in awe.

"Yes," Bruin replied.

"How? How does it happen?" Curt said. His hostility toward Bruin had worn off.

"The fish regenerates the original parts. But a sacrifice has to be made, although it's a small sacrifice for a chance to defeat death."

"What sacrifice?" Scott asked.

Bruin had nestled against the coffee table. He raised his left hand. His palm faced toward him and his fingers pointed to the ceiling. The glove was firmly in place. Without saying a word, he used his right hand to tug at the material covering each finger starting with his thumb. One at a time, the material slid off. Slowly, the glove lifted and when his fingers had been sufficiently freed, he grasped the top of the glove and gave it a final pull. As the material exposed his hand, the men stared awkwardly. Like a magnet, their attention was drawn to Bruin's middle finger, or to where it was supposed to have been.

Between the pointer and ring fingers there was a gap. A small rounded nub barely rising from the base was all that was left.

Scott couldn't believe what he was seeing. He asked the next question as if he was in a dream. He hesitated, then spoke. "You were reincarnated? By that fish?"

Bruin nodded.

"When?" Curt asked when he finally got his mouth to work.

"Four hundred thirty-one years ago."

Marvin began choking as if he'd swallowed a peanut and it had lodged in his windpipe. Scott stood up and began smacking him on the back as the professor leaned forward coughing. Several hacks later the professor made one final gag and then sat back wiping the tears out of his eyes.

"Are you all right Marvin?" Curt said after he'd retrieved the professor's glass of water from the coffee table and handed it to him.

"I'll be fine if your new friend doesn't also tell me he's Elvis."

"That's one claim I can't make," Bruin said with a brittle smile. Then his expression turned serious again. "As for the Kilgotian, it takes a small body appendage to induce the resurrection," he said looking at his four fingers as he dropped them back into his lap. "In order to be reincarnated, the body must be placed in salt water."

"The Ocean," Marvin commented.

"The severed appendage, usually a finger for humans, is fed to the Kilgotian who resided in the pond."

"In fresh water," Scott commented slowly.

"Exactly. It's the two forms that make the transformation from the dead to the living."

"All waters are joined," Curt said thinking back to the display at Fort Caroline and the documentation he'd acquired.

"Yes," Bruin said.

"That's why it was on the Ark. It must have been God's way of assuring the survival of Noah, his sons and their wives," Marvin said in a moment of revelation.

"The Timucua believed the Kilgotian could resurrect any creature, human or otherwise. It seems to me the Kilgotian could have also served as a means of assuring all the creatures made it to dry land," Bruin said.

"But the Ark didn't exactly have the pond aboard," Curt said.

"True," Bruin began, "but it wouldn't have to. All the fish needs is fresh water. At least that's what the Timucuas believed. In that case, Noah could have kept the fish in a pail. If any of the passengers died, man or beast, an appendage could be cut off and fed to the Kilgotian after the corpse had been lowered by some device, a pulley maybe, into the sea."

"That makes sense. As much as it can. But back to you. Are you a Timucua?" Scott asked.

"That's right. My Indian name is Tibu."

Marvin had just taken a swig of water when Tibu spoke. Again he choked. For the second time, Scott rose and patted him on the back. Curt sat in the chair with his mouth wide open.

"Holy shit!" Curt said as Marvin barked.

"Is the old man going be okay? Can he handle this," Tibu asked looking at Scott and pointing to Marvin.

Marvin took exception to anyone who called him an *old man* but he was temporarily unable to respond. Breathing correctly was a priority at the moment.

As Scott continued tapping Marvin, he stared at Tibu in astonishment. Before him was a man who claimed to have lived longer than seven consecutive average life spans. Who had been alive at the time Ribault and the French settled Fort Caroline and Menendez and the Spanish had founded St. Augustine. It was simply impossible!

"We read a story about you. You and the LeFlores. You're the Tibu in that story?" Curt asked.

"I'm not sure what story you're talking about but I'm the one who . . ."

"Who told the brothers about the pond," Scott finished his sentence.

"Yes," Tibu said sadly. "And I've been paying for it with horrific dreams of the future ever since. That's why after telling the LeFlores, several years later I took my own life."

"You resurrected yourself?" Marvin asked.

"Yes." Tibu explained how he had cut off his finger and positioned it on the leaves before drowning himself in the ocean. He mentioned how important it was for the events to occur in order; the Kilgotian consuming the appendage only after the body had been submerged in saltwater.

"Oh crap, I think we've done something incredibly bad," Scott said glancing at Curt then Marvin.

"You're referring to the murders?" Tibu asked to their surprise.

"How did you know?" Scott asked.

"I told you. I have dreams. Nightmares."

"And these dreams told you Sherri's alive?" Curt asked.

"Reece LeFlore has her."

Although the words were shocking, the three men had already come to the unimaginable conclusion that Reece might somehow be alive again.

"What's to stop him from killing her?" Scott asked.

"They need her. She's a translator."

"Of course," Marvin said.

Tibu was silent and lowered his eyes to the floor. Then he raised his head gazing at the wall behind the couch.

"But how in the hell did Reece return?" Curt began. "Was it something we did?" he said looking in Scott's direction.

"I don't know, but it was inevitable," Tibu said trying to ease their guilt. "These events occurred because they were predestined. You had no option but to follow this course of action."

"Did you know the Kilogotian was in the Castillo de San Marcos?" Curt asked.

"I took the job at the Fort because I could sense the presence of the fish. I just didn't know exactly where it was. After you two left on Monday, the feeling was gone."

"That's amazing!" Marvin said.

"A Soulful One can sense the Kilgotian. In essence, there's an eternal link."

"I do have a question about the reincarnation. Once you're *a Soulful One*, do you live forever? You've been around four centuries and don't appear to be in bad health," Scott said.

"The legend speaks of a man living an additional 100 to 150 years after the process," Tibu said.

"What's your secret?" Curt asked.

"I don't know. I believe my purpose, my existence, can't conclude until the final resolution"

The room was silent.

"I know you found the Kilgotian under a stone slab in the powder magazine. I went in afterward and saw it had been pried away from the other slabs. Did you find anything else?"

"Yeah. A knife." Scott said.

"That's all? Just a knife?" Tibu asked.

Scott nodded.

"That's odd? Reece must have been resurrected sometime yesterday. That's when the killings started," Tibu said.

"By the way, did you know it was Pinot's remains they found when the powder magazine was opened?" Scott asked looking at Tibu.

"No. But I did sense it was a Soulful One," Tibu replied. "In a way, all Soulful Ones are linked."

"Pinot had been reincarnated?" Marvin asked.

"Apparently, yes," Tibu said.

"Hold on a minute, if Pinot was a Soulful One, then how did he die? Surely sealing him in the powder magazine wouldn't kill him," Curt said.

"Every man needs to eat. Even a Soulful One. For the most part, we're perfectly human," Tibu replied.

"Besides, sealed in that room, his air supply would have run out in less than a day," Scott added.

"Well, that wouldn't have mattered," Tibu said.

"You're kidding?" Curt exclaimed.

"No."

Curt stood up from the chair and walked around behind Tibu. He leaned over and placed his flat hand in the middle of Tibu's back. He left it there for least fifteen seconds before looking up at Scott. "He's not breathing," he said in a mild voice.

Scott rose and walked behind Tibu, repeating Curt's actions. "I guess that clears up any doubt that you're just a whack," Scott said.

Scott could tell Tibu felt uncomfortable having the conversation focused on his condition. Scott equated it to being handicapped.

"So you think that it was Reece who broke in and took his brother's remains?" Marvin asked.

"I'm sure of it now," Tibu responded.

"How did he know Pinot was here? In my house?" Marvin asked.

"Obviously he could sense his location. The brotherly tie might have enhanced their bond," Tibu said.

"Do you think that's why Reece retrieved the remains and the fish? Is he going to resurrect Pinot," Curt asked.

"Probably," the Indian said, "and more."

"And more? And more what?" Marvin asked excitedly.

"I believe he intends to resurrect all the slain French Huguenots. I've had dreams of this occurring," Tibu said softly.

"So that was their plan. That's why they gathered the bodies and were moving them. They must have been transporting them to the ocean somewhere closer to Fort Caroline in order to resurrect the men. They probably severed a finger off each corpse and were planning to feed the Kilgotian. They were caught before they could complete their revenge. It all makes sense now." Scott exclaimed.

"What do you mean plan?" Tibu asked.

Curt told Tibu about the document he had acquired from the LeFlore's descendants. How it had mentioned Tibu and the brothers and referenced their plan of revenge against Menendez and the Spanish occupying St. Augustine so many centuries ago. Tibu was fascinated. He had no idea his story, at least a small portion, had been captured in writing.

"But that was their plan then, do you think they still intend to carry it out? Even after all these years? Hell, Menendez has been dead for quite sometime and the Spanish don't exactly have control of St. Augustine," Scott said.

"But Reece doesn't know that. The time between death and resurrection is instantaneous no matter how many years have passed. To the Soulful One, there is no *time*. I recall walking into the ocean, a brief moment of darkness, and then walking back out. For Reece LeFlore, he's still living in the sixteenth century and he plans to exact revenge on the inhabitants of St. Augustine, no matter who they are," Tibu said.

"I guess it's not like he'd know the difference between Spanish and Americans. Back then, there were no Americans. Only settlers from various European nations and the native Indians," Curt added.

"That's right." Tibu said. "All Reece LeFlore knows is the people around him are not speaking French. He's assuming it's Spanish.

"I wonder how baffled he is by the changes that have occurred over the last few centuries," Curt said. "They didn't exactly have automobiles, two-story stucco homes and paved roadways."

"Even more confusing to him is that this happened in an instant," Tibu added.

"So all Reece LeFlore wants to do right now is kill anyone he runs across who doesn't speak French? Is that what you're telling us?" Scott asked.

"Yes," Tibu responded.

"And that's why Sherri's alive?" Curt asked.

"Yes. Somehow he knows she speaks French and what he assumes to be Spanish," Tibu said. "Her value as a translator can help gain access to enemy strongholds. At least that's what he thinks."

"So what happens next? Are events occurring exactly the way you dreamed they would?" Marvin asked.

"No. Let me explain. When I've dreamed of the final resolution . . ."

"Final resolution?" Scott asked.

"How things will end. When I've had the dream of how things will end, it has varied. You two," Tibu said pointing to Scott and Curt, "I've never seen. But you, I have," he said pointing at Marvin.

"Really?" Marvin was stunned.

"Yes, you help the cause," Tibu responded.

"What happens? What do I do?" Marvin asked.

"The dream is different each time. I've dreamt hundreds, no thousands of endings. Each time there is a different outcome. Sometimes good wins. Sometimes the evil succeeds. Either way, it will be played out soon."

"You're sure because of the murders and the robbery here tonight?" Marvin asked.

"That and certain visions in my dreams that are consistent. One of the consistencies is that a large storm is approaching. Last year, when Donya almost struck I thought the final resolution was about to play out. But the day before the storm was predicted to hit the coast, I knew it was not to be."

"How? How did you know?" Scott asked.

"Across the street from the Old Jail on San Marco Boulevard there is an Eckerd's Drug Store. Last year the windows were taped up crossways with masking tape to support against wind damage."

"You've been in Florida long enough to know that's a common tactic in preparation for strong storms," Curt added.

"In my dreams, its windows are boarded with plywood, not taped, as they are now. I checked this evening."

The four men sat silent for a few minutes gathering in the sum of the conversation. Each processed the discussion and how the previously unknown components fit. But there was one question that Scott doubted Tibu had an answer for.

"Tibu, Bruin, whatever you want to be called, have you ever heard of a man named Tucker Chalet?"

"No."

"He was murdered yesterday near Ponte Vedra. They found his body on the beach. He was decapitated," Scott said.

"I knew of the murder," Tibu said.

"A detective visited Marvin this evening and referenced the notes they found in Tucker's hotel room. Something about him looking for fingers. Based on what we believe to be the LeFlore brothers' plan, I'm beginning to wonder if Tucker was searching for the appendages of the French Huguenots when he ran into Reece," Scott said.

"But why would he be looking for the fingers? How would he know about them?" Tibu asked.

"I have no freakin' idea. It's just too coincidental," Scott said.

"Do you know that Jean Luc LeFlore is buried in the Nuestra Senora de le Leche cemetery?" Curt asked.

"No," Tibu responded. "But then again, I don't know the man. I'm assuming he's a descendent of the brothers."

"Yes," Curt responded. "It's just another odd coincidence."

It was now 3:48 Wednesday morning. The men all seemed to lose energy within a few minutes of each other as the sporadic questions and comments about Tibu, the Kilgotian and the brothers slowed. Finally, Marvin suggested they all get some sleep. Tibu had assured Curt that Sherri was all right and convinced them the final resolution would not occur until the following night. There were indications in his dreams that convinced him of this. Objects, such as certain types of cars and fortification against the storm, were not in place yet. With the hurricane predicted to hit St. Augustine Thursday morning, Wednesday night would hold the pivotal showdown between the past and the present. Between history and the historians.

That night Tibu slept on Marvin's couch while the others each occupied a bedroom. He would dream his last dream. The end played out differently than it ever had.

Tibu woke before dawn at 5:36 a.m. and stared out the living room window, pushing the drapes aside. In the distance he saw a deep blue glow captivate the sky followed by a yellowish tint that lasted only a moment. Then it was gone. Tibu lay back down and fell asleep.

Before light, Pinot was back to join his brother.

CHAPTER-TWENTY-NINE

Sherri walked over to Curt and touched his face lightly with the back of her hand. She sat down on the bed beside him.

"But you're . . ." He began with a look of bewilderment.

"Shhhhh," she said placing her fingers to his lips.

Sherri was wearing very little. A low cut blue lace bra with matching silk underwear. She smelled fresh. Her gaze was seductive. Her full wet lips glistening. Her eyes cascaded an inviting smile as she reached her hand over and touched his thigh.

Curt grinned and she returned his pleasantry with a delicious bite of her bottom lip. Her red hair was lying gracefully about her bare shoulders and along the sides of her cheeks, delicately framing her face.

As far as Curt was concerned she was an angel.

He stared down at her fingers as they traced a gentle trail from his knee to his upper thigh. Her touch was captivating and he could feel his body responding to her simple flirtation.

She looked down. Curt was clad only in his maroon briefs and she could see the effect she was having on him. It pleased her. The smile again spread across her mouth as she raised her head and leaned toward him. Her green eyes radiated desire and they gently kissed. As their lips locked into a firm grip, their tongues sought out for more. Twirling and darting, tasting each other, their hands wandered. Hers running up his chest and back down on his thighs and his, racing to her stomach and moving slowly between her cleavage.

Sherri moaned as she eagerly dragged her fingers across his lap, scraping the material gently with her nails. He encircled his hands around her body and pressed her lips to his in a passionate embrace as they fell upon the bed. Each allowed their hands to seek those strange and provocative places reserved for men and women during intimacy. He massaged her neck and then lowered his fingers to her chest.

In an instant she was free from the constraining material as his lips ventured upon her chest. Seeking out the swollen mounds, his tongue eased along the skin and found the peaks as she moaned with approval.

Sherri was busy rubbing him through the material. She could feel his swelling continue. She slowly slipped her fingers underneath the elastic and found what she desired. Holding it and massaging the taut skin, the pleasure was nearly overwhelming and Curt had to restrain from allowing it all to end too quickly.

Without warning, Sherri flipped Curt onto his back and quickly removed her panties. In one swift motion, she tore off his underwear. The ripping noise was completely decadent. It represented raw, unbridled urges that she no longer wished to contain. The delicious sound almost sent Curt over the edge.

She proceeded to climb on him and settle in a raised position. Her treasure was just beyond his aching reach but he was able to extend his hands upward and firmly clutch her dangling skin. But it was not the end to what he craved. He wanted more. He wanted to feel her wet warmth on him. Her mussed hair, fiery eyes and the glimmer of perspiration beckoning off her soft skin.

She leaned down and sought out his lips with hers. He suddenly became aware of how salty she tasted. A moment later as their tongues probed, she arched her back and pushed her pelvis slowly down on him, taking the length . . .

"Hey, Curt. Wake up,"Scott said nudging his friend. "Come on buddy, rise and shine.

"I know, I know," he said groggily. "Scottis-interruptest. Best birth control on the market," Curt whined as he sat up and wiped the sleep from his eyes.

"The hurricane is still heading this way," Scott said walking out of the room as Curt tried to focus.

Curt slowly slid out of bed. He put on his shirt and jeans. He grabbed his socks and stopped by the doorless bathroom to urinate and rinse out his mouth with Listerine before heading to the living room where the TV was blaring. It was 7:19. The professor and Scott were intently watching the local coverage of an emergency update on Cable Channel 5. Even though they trusted Tibu, curiosity about Damon's position and strength and gotten the better of them.

"Am I the only one who sleeps around here?" Curt asked as he entered the room and saw the others completely dressed as if they'd been awake for hours. Scott and Marvin were drinking coffee. Tibu was sitting on the floor facing away from the TV. To Curt, he appeared to be in a trance.

"Shhhhh," Scott said raising his finger to his lips.

At exactly 7 a.m. the cities of Jacksonville and St. Augustine called for an immediate evacuation. The TV channels and radio stations began airing live broadcast from the Office of Emergency Management from downtown Jacksonville. Damon was officially a monster. The most powerful recorded hurricane of all time. It had sustained winds topping 198 miles per hour and was currently positioned 336 miles southeast of St. Augustine, still on a straight path at 14 miles per hour. It was expected to make landfall in approximately 24 hours. The probability of a direct impact on St. Augustine's shores was 94 percent.

St. Augustine residents were ordered to leave by 3:00 p.m. Jacksonville residents east of the Intercoastal Waterway, including Atlantic Beach, Neptune Beach and Ponte Vedra had until 4 p.m. Because most had fled the previous day, the snarled traffic that occurred last year was expected to be minimal. And based on the experience from Donya, when the limited number of multilaned roads heading away from the coast turned into parking lots, authorities had devised a plan to use traffic reversal signs to keep the flow moving. This combination of foresight and experience would not lessen the terror of the storm but it would ease the frustration of getting away safely.

"Well, that settles that. Lunatic revenge-minded French Huguenots or not, we've got to leave town," Marvin said rising from the recliner and heading toward his bedroom to pack.

"NO!" Tibu screamed. His voice echoed down the hallway. The professor stopped dead in his tracks. Curt was still sitting and Scott had just begun to lift himself from the couch when the Indian spoke. He quickly sat down.

The men looked at Tibu like he had three heads.

"What the hell are you talking about? This damn hurricane is going to smash the coast. We have no choice but to leave. Not even your *Soulful* French buddies can survive if it makes a direct hit. And from what I just heard, it's going to eat Northeast Florida alive." Scott said.

"Scott's right, Tibu," Marvin began. "There is no option. Nothing will survive this close to the coast. Damon's a Category 5. The storm surge alone will kill you. Who knows how high the water's going to rise. San Marco Boulevard goes underwater anytime a northeaster hits. I guarantee my house will be more than just a few feet deep. That is, if its standing at all. Which I strongly doubt."

"NO!" Tibu screamed again. His face became red and puffy. Tibu's head appeared it might burst.

"NO WHAT!" Scott yelled at the Indian. Curt remained quiet for the moment. He knew Scott and Marvin were right. Without question they were right. But he also knew he couldn't leave without Sherri. What was equally frustrating was that she was somewhere within the city. At least that's what Tibu believed.

"You don't understand," Tibu said in a calmer voice. He was attempting to compose himself but his face was still a burnt red tint as if the embers just beneath the dark skin still glowed. "The hurricane is not going to make a direct hit. I've seen it in my dreams. It will skirt the coast. At least the coast of this area."

"Not going to hit the coast? You're willing to go against 94 percent odds? And these damn dreams of yours, are you willing to risk your life on them?" Marvin asked.

"Every day. Year after year. Decade after decade. Century after century," Tibu said softly.

Marvin realized what an inane question that was the moment the words flew from his lips.

"I'm sorry," Marvin said as his eyes fell upon the carpet in front of Tibu.

"No need. But listen to what I have to say. In my dreams, the hurricane has never hit the coast with full force. There are strong winds and all the elements that accompany a storm but never any significant damage. I promise this," Tibu's earnestness was unexpected and it helped to soothe the tension that had flared. Four men existing off limited sleep, trying to digest mind-boggling, science shattering discoveries, seasoned with a healthy dose of violence, kidnapping and a nasty hurricane, had mixed to form quite a volatile environment. They each seemed to instinctively understand this. Now it was a matter of concentration, to keep cool heads and disciplined attitudes. It was the only way they had a chance.

Tibu continued speaking slowly, "We must end this. They cannot be allowed to exist. These are monsters walking the earth. They have no place here and will kill many innocent people."

"But who are they going to kill if the city is evacuated?" Scott said as calmly as he could.

"After the city is empty, except for the few who refuse to go and can avoid the authorities, two things will happen. The brothers, and I'm saying brothers because Pinot has been resurrected by now, will find the appendages of their fellow Huguenots slaughtered at Matanzas. Because their bodies were placed in the Atlantic long ago, all the LeFlores will have to do is revive the Kilgotian and feed him the bones. The second thing that will happen once the hurricane misses the city is that the Soulful Ones will venture out beyond St. Augustine destroying everyone they come across. It will make no difference be it a man, woman or child."

As Tibu spoke, Scott remembered there were more than 300 Huguenots killed at Matanzas. His skin crawled as he thought of his own kids. What a horrifying thought that anyone might lose a child, let alone to a resurrected cold-blooded killer wielding a sword, the likes of which he and Curt believed they were responsible for. In essence, this was all their creation.

"How many lives justify you taking the risk of what I'm saying if true? How many deaths would it take you to stay and try and stop the brothers? Your lives are forever wrapped in the outcome. No matter how hard you try, you're bound as part of this," Tibu said.

"That's the part that bothers me. Of all the things, the events and the things you've dreamed, I wish you could be a little more specific on the outcome," Curt said.

"I'd tell you if I knew. I have noticed over the last several months the dreams have become more consistent. Certain events have been occurring repeatedly. This never happened before. The background had always remained stable but the events themselves had continually shifted. This gives me encouragement," Tibu said. He did not want to alarm them by describing the dream he'd had only hours before. The one that had ended like no other. The one that concerned him.

"God help us," Curt whispered.

The room was silent. Scott and Curt stared at each other and then at Marvin.

"So what happens next, other than me updating my will?" Marvin asked looking at Tibu as the Indian stood up.

"Nothing."

"Nothing" the professor said incredulously.

"Nothing. Everything will occur this evening. And it will begin at the fort. And it will begin with you and him going inside," Tibu pointed at Scott and Curt.

"Gee. Now I feel much better," Curt said with the utmost sarcasm.

"So what do we do in the meantime? Is there anything we need to prepare?" Scott asked.

"You two need to rest and preserve your energy. He and I will load some items in your vehicle," Tibu said pointing a gloved finger at Marvin.

"What items?" Curt asked.

"The items you'll need," Tibu responded with authority.

"Boys, if we're staying in town, which, for the record is utterly insane, we'll need to avoid the cops. This is a mandatory evacuation," Marvin said.

"In that case, we'll need to hide the cars. Marvin, you'll need to place yours and Scott's in the garage," Curt said.

"But what about your Mustang?" Marvin asked.

"I can have Scott follow me to Sherri's. I'll leave it in her garage since it makes more sense to take Scott's Blazer this evening. It's bigger and . . ."

"No. You'll be in the Mustang tonight," Tibu interrupted.

"Did you dream that, too?" Scott asked.

"This morning," he replied.

"OK. Then we'll drop Scott's Blazer off at Sherri's and hide my car in Marvin's garage. We're going to have to be careful and keep the house shades closed starting around noon. I suspect the authorities will go door to door by then to flush folks out," Marvin said.

"I still can't believe we're staying," Scott said reluctantly.

"There is one thing I'd like to do this morning before we have to hide away. I'd like to drive to Ponte Vedra and check on Pierre, see if he's evacuating. I've been unable to get him by phone for days and I'm worried," Marvin said.

"That's fine. We can all go. The traffic should still be relatively light," Scott said. Then he continued, "Tibu, you didn't dream of us all getting killed in a traffic accident did you?"

"No." For a moment Scott thought he saw the faintest of smiles break across Tibu's face but then the Indian turned and headed to the back bedroom.

"I need to call Kay first," Scott said. "I don't know what the hell I'm going to tell her. Anyone got any good lies because she damn sure won't believe the truth."

That reminded Curt he needed to contact Charlene.

At 7:34 Wednesday morning, Jim Beam arrived at the beach for another leisurely day of fishing. Instead of Ponte Vedra, he'd decided to fish on the outskirts of St. Augustine at Vilano Beach. He gathered the gear from the bed of the truck that was sprawled out haphazardly, tackle box and net in one hand and the two Shakespeare rods and a small cooler in the other. As he crossed the roadway and moved toward the dunes and the beach just beyond, he thought about Monday afternoon's excitement. How he'd discovered the body of that poor man and then Officer Dipshit busting his nuts on the corpse's collarbone. The expression on the face of the other cops when he described the sliding, panicking ball-busting crash of Tankersley gave him a story to tell for the rest of his life. And the topper was that he'd made the Channel 12 News. His eyewitness account of finding the body had his phone ringing off the hook all night.

Charlie and Eddie had immediately called from Massy's Pool Hall to say they'd seen him and he looked much younger than 42. Shelly Brock, a waitress at Shoney's that he had dated several months ago, also called. She was obviously awed by his newfound celebrity status because she asked him over Friday night for a few beers. Mr. Johnson, a friend of his father's at O'Brien's Hardware, called to say he might have a job opening soon in the paint-mixing department. Yes, you might say, life had become more enjoyable overnight. Just by finding one lone headless stiff.

But for now, it would be another day of fishing. Another day of collecting unemployment at the expense of the American government. Hell, he had tried to find a job for two weeks straight. Even with the labor market being so robust, his minimal skills shielded him from most opportunities. Besides, something would come up soon and he was not one to pass up an opportunity to get his line wet when the opportunity presented itself. He had been a little fearful, being on the Channel 12 News and all, that he might jeopardize his unemployment status. If someone had seen him they might question his efforts in securing work, so he had spent Tuesday beatin' the streets again. But two days removed from the incident made the decision to grab the tackle and head to the beach an easy one. Hurricane or no hurricane. Plus, it wasn't like he had a wife and kids depending on him. They'd left years ago when he was binge drinking. These days, he kept his consumption under control. At least that's what he told himself as the 12-pack chilled under the layer of ice in the cooler.

As he crested the sand dune and the ocean spread out in front, he looked down to see if this morning held any surprises. Nope. It was a corpseless day. Monday, it was ironic he had not noticed the body when he had arrived around 2:30 p.m. In reflecting back, he realized he must have come damn close to stepping right on it as he approached the beach. The only thing he could figure was that he was so excited about hooking into some whiting and bluefish that he had paid no attention to his surroundings. It wasn't until he was leaving, and the wind had shifted, that he caught the foul smell of the decaying body and spotted the crumpled mass near the base of the sandy incline.

He continued down the backside of the dune and made his way past the soft sand and onto the hard moist beach. Several seagulls broke into a gallop and went airborne as he approached. He stopped several feet before the watermark and laid his equipment down. The sun had cleared the ocean and was making its way upward but the dark lumpy clouds consuming the sky kept the light to a minimum. In the distance, an oil tanker slowly moved north on the horizon, evacuating in anticipation of Damon's approach. "Chicken." Jim thought shaking his head and chuckling. "There's plenty of time to get out of town before this stupid hurricane gets here."

As the salt air filtered through his lungs and the sound of the crashing waves mingled with the squawking birds, he opened the small cooler and pulled out a plastic bag. Unzipping the bag, he reached inside and withdrew a raw shrimp that he de-headed and broke in half. He placed one half back in the bag and the other neatly on the hook of the six and a half-foot rod. Carrying the rod, he moved forward until he was standing in about 14 inches of water and pulled back the bale on the reel. Angling the rod back to the right, he quickly slung the tip forward and released the line letting the shrimp and the two-ounce sinker sail over the waves. It landed about 45 yards past the breakers. Jim immediately backed up and hand-stripped the line until he was again out of the water and on the hard sand. He reached into his tackle box and retrieved a rod spike that he promptly drove into the ground. Once secure, he tightened the line to make sure he had drawn out the slack and placed the base of the rod in the holder. As it stood perfectly horizontal, he clicked the lock to prevent reverse winding. He repeated this process with the second rod, placing it in a holder parallel to the first about 10 yards to his left. Then Jim plopped down on the sand in the middle of the two rods and began the waiting game. He was now content. He was fishing.

For the first 27 minutes the lines were still. Not a nibble. The waves could be very deceiving by tempting the line back and forth but Jim was savy enough to know the difference between the current's motion and a fish bite. The breakers would cause the rods to bow in slow, long, drawn-out bends. On the other hand, a fish would attack with quick, sharp jabs that would cause the rod's tip to jerk rapidly. They were two very distinct motions and Jim wondered why some fishermen were too damn stupid to know the difference.

As he sat on the shore, his blue jeans soaking in seawater from the wet sand, a flock of pelicans skimmed the beach in formation, their long bills counterbalancing the less than sleek bodies, yet wafting their wings with grace and perfection. Jim watched the birds pass and then looked beyond the breakers. Since he had broken his sunglasses the previous weekend when he had jumped in the driver's seat without looking, he was thankful for the cloud cover. If the sun had been out, it would be reflecting off the water and making it almost impossible for Jim to see.

On the 28th minute after flinging the first bait and sinker into the Atlantic, the line to his right suddenly went limp. Jim sprang to his feet and plucked the rod from the spike holder. The lack of tension signaled a fish that was running inward. It also meant a fish he would miss if he didn't quickly reel in the slack and set the hook properly. He began winding in the excess line. After a dozen or so rotations of the handle the line became taut. Jim lifted the rod tip upward and, with a sharp pull, sunk the hook. As he did, his prey heaved violently and ripped off line, sending the rod into an inverted U shape. The drag screamed a whiny, high pitch sound and Jim could feel his muscles straining.

"Damn, oh damn! I got me a biggun!" Jim screamed as the line continued to sing from the reel. He looked up and down the beach to see if anyone was around and was disheartened to find the shore still barren in both directions. There's nothing better to a fisherman than to land a prize catch in front of an audience.

With the waves, it was difficult to tell which direction the fish was running. While holding the rod at chest level, still arched high above his head, he strained to follow the line from the tip outward. From what he could tell, the fish was running in the opposite direction, out to deeper water.

The drag screamed for 30 seconds and then the run suddenly ceased. The fish was still on, practically bending the rod in half, but it had stopped, maintaining its position. Jim's muscles were growing tired quickly and had begun to ache, yet the adrenaline that surged through his veins wouldn't allow him to focus on the discomfort. As the fish remained in this holding pattern, Jim began to wonder if it was still on. The feel of the line was inconsistent. Although heavy and stretched, the lack of movement made him fear the fish had wrapped around either a rock or shell bed and then slipped the TruTurn hook.

As he stood firmly positioned on the beach, Jim maintained his statuesque pose keeping the pressure on. Damn, oh damn, please still be on. I ain't got no witnesses to back this up if he gets off, he thought.

Several minutes later there was still no progress and Jim's patience wore out. Holding the rod in his left hand, he used his right to increase the drag tension . . . 7 . . . 8 . . . 9 . . . 10. There, dammit, 10 should do it. He brought his right hand back to the handle and began winding. At first the fish would not budge and he feared the line would snap as it whistled in the steady cross breeze that had blown up during the battle. But several revolutions later, the rod suddenly arched further as Jim leaned back to put more stress on the beast. The pole was now in the shape of a horseshoe that Jim had hanging on the wall over his bed at home. Once again the fish took line but in a slow, methodical manner. Creeping out inch by inch. The excitement rose again, as Jim knew he still had game. Goddamn, how big is this sonofabitch. It must be a huge freakin' redfish, he thought.

What seemed like hours passed as the fish crept away from the shore, gradually clicking off small increments of line. Jim's arms were aching more and he could feel his muscles knot. The pressure had been relentless for 22 solid minutes. He had chosen not to try and gain any ground on the fish until it stopped its momentum. When it did, he figured it would have expended a considerable amount of energy, giving him a good chance of landing it.

Six more minutes passed with the prey taking line and then it paused. Jim waited to see if the fish would make a further push. Nothing. But the line remained rigid and the rod bowed. The pole was now at a ninety-degree angle as Jim had leaned forward, prompted by the stiffness in his back.

"Okay you sonofabitch, it's my turn now," Jim said out loud as a piece of spit shot from his mouth and he realized how thirsty he'd become. Again he searched the beach looking for company but the only life was the seagulls to his left tiptoeing on the scattered shell fragments just beyond the water's reach. Jim reached for the base of the reel and adjusted the drag level to 11 and then 12. That's it you bastard. That's the maximum. Let's see what you can do now. Then he began winding. The moment he made the first revolution the line soared again stretching the rod outward, almost ripping it from Jim's hands. He desperately held on and jammed the rod skyward in an attempt to gain back some leverage. As he did, he felt a momentary slip as if the hook had been stuck in a seaweed bed and then torn itself free. After gliding freely through the water about 12 inches it again caught on a firm object and, after a fraction of a second, the line went slack. Jim instantly knew the outcome.

"Shit, shit, shit!" he screamed for the benefit of the seagulls who chattered on the sand as they danced between the incoming waves. "Goddammit! Shit, shit, shit!" With each *shit* he stomped his feet on the moist ground which kicked up water in all directions, soaking his pants up to his knees. Looking down, he now realized enough time had lapsed during the fight for the tide to migrate in and place him in several inches of water with each press of the waves. "Dammit, dammit, dammit!" he continued to rant as the frustration of losing the fish to a broken line and splashing water on his pants made him seethe. He turned and walked out of the surf, tossing the rod and reel away from him.

"You sonofabitch!" he screamed as he turned to face the water. The sun had risen higher into the sky and he gazed into the churning waves and soft flat waters that lay beyond. Jim dropped onto the beach sitting with his legs extended in front and his arms behind propping him up as he continued to mutter profanities. "Goddammit, I should have been patient! Shit, ain't no one gonna believe me when I tell 'em"

As he sat dejected, the seagulls that had accompanied him on the beach took to flight and were busily mocking from above. "Git the hell outta here, ya dirty birds!" he barked looking upward.

As Jim Beam mentally replayed the events that led up to the broken line, he became aware of a unique sound that was unrecognizable. It was a tortured, scraping noise that jolted him out of his misery and back to the present. He looked right and only saw the empty rod holder as a reminder of his failure. He glanced left attempting to locate the sound and felt his heart bounce in his chest cavity as he spotted the straining rod. The sand spike of the second rod had been pulled at an angle and now leaned toward the water as it struggled to hold its contents. The rod was curled harshly with the tip reaching out. For whatever reason, Jim had set the drag on this rig at 9 and whatever was hooked at the moment was unable to strip the line off. Or maybe it just hadn't chosen to. Either way, the pole was continuing to bend and stretch and taking the spike, that was giving way in the water covered sand, with it.

Jim rolled to his left and pushed himself to his feet. There was a 25-foot gap between the man and the straining sports gear. Jim broke into a full gallop knowing the spike could completely give way at any instant and the equipment would be traveling out to sea. He took his first step almost running into a seagull that had decided to take a flight path directly in front of him. Shithead, Jim thought as he raced to the rod.

Halfway there, he saw the holder dip further. It was now at a 40-degree angle and he knew the equipment was about to tear loose. As his heart raced, each step dislodged wet sand and water that slung on the back of his pants. Again the rod holder dipped, positioned now at 35-degrees. Goddamn fish is back, trying to screw me again, he thought.

Seven feet away Jim had made up his mind to dive. He was mentally and physically prepared. As it turned out, the decision had been a sound one, probably not born as much out of careful consideration as it was from a surging rush of warm blood to his cerebral cortex. As the spike gave way, it whipped from the sand and began to stream out still snuggly attached to the rod. Jim made a quick burst and then left his feet. As he sailed through the air, he knew he had miscalculated his jump almost immediately. The rod and holder were moving but not at the rate he had anticipated and his speed would surely send him past the objects. But before Jim landed, the prey on the far end of the line pulled with an extreme force that caused the rod's speed to quadruple. Jim hit the shallow surface with his hands extended as far as they could and barely seized the end of the spike. He held onto the slippery plastic with the fortitude of a warrior. Instantly, he felt himself being dragged through the mud at a slow, constant pace as water sloshed into his gaping mouth.

This can't be happening. I must be imagining that I'm moving. But he was. He slid along the mud as the micro shells slipped inside his jeans and ground into his underwear. He traveled eight feet, choking down seawater but determined not to release his hold. If he were to save himself from drowning, he would have to get to his feet and quickly.

The first attempt was unsuccessful as the beast yanked him back into the water as if it knew his plan. But on the second try, he worked to his knees and then to his feet and rose smartly, holding the spike in his hand. A sickening feeling ran through his stomach as he realized that was all he had. The rod was gone! Consumed by the ocean without a trace.

Jim Beam realized his only chance, albeit slim, for finding the rod was to proceed deeper into the water and hope it was lying on the bottom. Maybe it would dig into the mud or the fish would tire.

As he strolled through the surf he thought how odd an episode of fishing this had been. First he hooked a monster that he couldn't turn and eventually broke his line. Now, a creature literally tore the fishing gear from the earth and decided to make off with his tackle.

No one, but no one's, going to buy any of this. I'm not even sure I believe this shit, he thought.

As he moved forward on the last known course the rod had been traveling, he gently shuffled his feet on the bottom hoping to feel the long fiberglass rod or, at minimum, come across the line.

Nothing.

Soon he started a serpentine pattern to cover more ground. By now, the water was up to his mid-thigh and rising quickly. Walking farther out, the water level actually dropped signifying he had come upon a sandbar roughly 20 yards from shore. The shallow water was a relief to Jim as the thought of traversing outward always brought back memories from a certain 1970s movie. Even though this wasn't Amity Island, the Florida coastline was littered with sharks. Not the Great White variety, but carnivores such as Tigers and Hammerheads nonetheless.

When the water became shallow, barely reaching his shins, he felt a twinge against his ankle. He lurched backward, peering into the greenish water for whatever had made contact and barely kept his balance. As the waves pushed over the sand, in between the incoming and outgoing pulls, he spotted the line. It was running perpendicular to the beach, as it was the last time he'd seen it. Without much thought, he reached down and clutched the thin blue monofilament and stood up. The line escaped the water and began sliding out of the swells ahead of him. Then, without warning, the creature on the other end began to run. It had felt the tension from Jim's grip and bucked vigorously at the resistance, bolting toward deeper water.

Jim released the line but not before it neatly cut a fine burn across his right palm. Grabbing the wound with his left hand he turned to his right as the rod, that he had somehow passed on his way to the sandbar, catapulted out of the water behind him. Only by quickly springing his neck back did he narrowly miss having the end of the rod driven through his left eye. The remaining length of the pole whizzed by with the exception of the reel, that jutted out three and a half inches from the fiberglass shaft, that struck his right temple before falling into the water and torpedoing outward.

The contact created a thudding crunch and Jim Beam grasped the side of his brow as he fell to his knees and sank partly into the mud. The ocean began spinning and black and purple colors temporarily covered his sight. For a few moments he wasn't sure which way was up as he tried to rise to his feet and found his head dipping into the water.

"Sonofabitch. I'm gonna get that bastard and chop his balls off!" Jim shouted out loud. His head slowly cleared from the radiant colors streaming past and he focused on the watery horizon until the dizziness faded. A splitting headache parked itself in a square inch of his skull at the point of contact. Then he chuckled at what he had said. He wasn't even sure fish had nuts. He'd never seen a pair of balls dangling off a back dorsal fin.

As the world settled, he rose to his feet looking at the water in the distance. Generally a hooked fish, and one toting around gear, would boil the surface. But the swells were masking any activity.

Jim pulled his hand away from his temple and was mortified to see the bright red fluid dripping the length of his fingers and into the palm, mixing with the blood from the cut sustained from the line.

"Shit, shit, shit!" he said as he wiped his hand in the water and grimaced at the pain from the salt entering the wound. Knowing the action would not be pleasant, he cupped a handful of sea water in his left hand and closed his eyes. He quickly splashed the water onto his temple and the slicing pain felt like it would rip his head apart. As the water dripped down his face and neck and the pain subsided, he lifted his shirt and cleaned the moisture from his eyes. Although the throbbing was constant, he didn't appear to be bleeding significantly. Several pats of his shirt on the wound and he deemed the flow to be at a minimum. To Jim Beam, this meant the battle was still on, concussion or no concussion.

He lifted his right leg and almost lost his balance on the first step.

"Easy there Jimbo, take it slowly. You don't wanna rush things."

The next step went smoothly yet his legs had become extremely heavy. He trudged along, trying to sense the slightest anomaly under the surface. He soon felt the water creeping back up his legs. On the far side of the sandbar, the angle was not as gradual as when he'd approached from the beach. Four steps off the ledge and he was waist deep in the Atlantic.

"To hell with the sharks," he said defiantly as he spit. "I want that goddamn fish." It was more a pep talk to himself than a statement of absolute truth. He was still thinking about sharks and wondering if the time was approaching to cut his losses and make his way back to shore where an ice cold Budweiser was calling his name from the cooler.

Moving slower, now in water somewhere between his potbelly and his chest, he again felt an object graze his foot. For the second time, the contact startled him. But this time he could tell it was not the line. Whatever he had brushed against was solid. He tried to run his foot along the side but the object gave. This was a good sign as it signified that it was not something permanently secured to the bottom. It was also not a fish, or it would have darted away upon contact. Even a shark would have been spooked enough to flee. It must be the rod. All I need to do now is reach down and grab the damn thing.

Hopefully that damn fish is still attached to the other end and I'll have quite the story to tell tonight at Massey's. I'll probably get a free beer on the house for such great fiction. Or is it nonfiction? I always confuse the two, Jim thought.

As he took in a deep breath, he closed his eyes and submerged. Dropping his left hand straight down, he felt his way toward the bottom where his foot had made contact. The object was gone. The injury on his forehead briefly tingled but then stopped as if the water had cauterized the wound. He frantically spread his arm in all directions to try to locate the rod on the sandy bottom but he came up empty. Eyes tightly closed, he moved ahead a half step blindly feeling the emptiness around him as the water gently swayed.

Holding his breath, still submerged, he became frustrated. Then he became scared.

What if the object had not simply floated away? What if it had not been inanimate? What if it was alive! The thought made him yearn for dry land.

It's just a stupid fish, Jim. You'll get 'em next time.

As he argued his way toward this new perspective, his right hand briefly brushed something on the back swing. He was quickly running out of air and had to make a snap decision to grab the object or surface and risk the current moving what he assumed was the rod farther away. He instantly thrust his hand back to the point of contact and wrapped his fingers around a thin coarse object. Immediately he knew it wasn't the rod. But he also knew it was not the fin of a shark. Whatever he held was comprised of two parallel sticks slightly separated.

He suddenly released the object regretting he had ventured out into this godforsaken water. But before he could get clear, something firmly grabbed his wrist. Terror seized Jim Beam's mind. Air burst from his lips escaping to the surface. He frantically tried to pull away but the lock was solid. His heart hammered as if ten thousand gallons of water was upon him.

Shark! A freakin' shark has my arm! He's gonna eat me alive! Jim's mind raced. But somewhere between the dreamlike predicament and the unmistakable reality of the situation he knew it wasn't a shark. The texture of whatever held him was not that of razor sharp teeth. It was something else. Something rugged. It was a grip. A firm human grip. Similar to the way a man shakes another man's hand. He could feel the lean hard fingers tightening on his wrist! My God. What or who in the hell has me!

As he struggled to get loose, Jim brought his free hand around to try and fend off the attacker. He attempted to wedge his fingers under the grip to gain leverage. But it was useless. The claw-like grasp was cutting into his skin. He was powerless in his efforts.

His eyes had been closed as he feared the burning salt water but the time had come to either open them or give in to death's calling. As he pried them apart and focused, the horror of what he saw was paralyzing. The image in front of him could have only been created during the dark mental anxieties of sleep. There was absolutely no way this *thing* actually existed.

In an instant, a second hideous hand reached toward him through the murky water and momentarily placed its rough bony fingers on his neck. When it withdrew, Jim sent the last few air bubbles bounding to the surface. The thing was holding Jim Beam's Adam's apple as the water displayed a floating line of red from his neck to its closed splintered fingers. Jim convulsed and then his world went dark.

On the surface above, the water gently rolled and blended the bright red into a saucy yellow tinted fluid. The ensemble resembled a mini oil spill of unnatural colors that coated the water and then drifted out, riding the undertow to the great ocean beyond.

With the kill, Pinot LeFlore slowly made his way toward shore.

CHAPTER-THIRTY

Curt spoke to Charlene very candidly. He admitted they had had no luck finding Sherri but again he guaranteed to continue his search. She had slipped into the hotel bathroom to talk to Curt while Tina bounced on the stiff mattress watching "Tom & Jerry." Charlene was in tears, unable to control her emotions as she had the previous night. Another nine hours had passed and the notion of Sherri being alive was fading.

There was nothing Curt could say to ease her mind. He informed her that they had contacted the local police who had unofficially begun searching. He also assured her that if Sherri did not turn up by 6 p.m., he would follow the appropriate legal process and report her as missing, to the authorities. If I can find any, he thought to himself.

She thanked him for everything he was doing but, as she spoke, her concerned weeping rattled Curt. In the background he could hear Tina happily chatting at the TV. At that moment, he realized he would not leave St. Augustine without finding Sherri Falco, hurricane or no hurricane.

The call ended with Charlene still sobbing but appreciative to the extent it made him uncomfortable. His assurances to her had all but guaranteed Sherri's safe return.

What the hell am I doing? I don't have the right to lead this poor lady on. I can't control the entire situation. It's beyond me, he thought.

As Charlene hung up he could hear a gleeful Tina laughing in the background.

Curt sat in silence, promising Tina he would do everything he could to assure the safe return of her mommy. Even if it cost him his life.

A second later the dial tone hummed in his ear.

Standing outside in Marvin's front yard, Scott called Kay. She had left the number of the hotel on their home answering machine and Scott had retrieved it after contacting his office and learning the business was officially shut down till Monday.

Kay answered on the third ring. "I'm glad you called. I was getting worried. I heard they evacuated the beaches this morning. Are you on your way here?"

"Not yet," Scott said hesitantly.

"What's the matter?" she asked suspiciously.

"I'm going to be at work a little while longer."

"If you're at work, how come you're calling from your cell phone?"

"I'm at the hardware store," he said thinking quickly. "We're putting plastic tarp over every PC in the building in case of structural leaks."

"Oh," she said. Scott suspected she was skeptical of his answer but at least it sounded plausible.

"Scott, work is not worth risking your life over." Her voice was sincere and he was automatically riddled with guilt for the lie he had just told. He couldn't think of what to say next.

"Scott? Are you still there."

"Yeah, honey, I'm here. How are the kids?"

"They're fine. You know how much they love traveling," she said with a forced laugh.

Again there was silence.

"Scott, what's going on? What are you not telling me? We've been together too long for you to play games with me."

"Kay," he started. His voice was uneven and searching for words. "Curt and I have become involved with something I can't even begin to describe. It's nothing illegal or immoral but it would take me four hours to explain and then you still wouldn't believe me. Hell, I don't even believe it."

"Scott, what are you talking about? I'm your wife. I have your kids with me. When are you coming?" There was desperation and anger in her voice.

Scott could sense the concern flowing amid her words. "Baby I can't," he said softly. It was the hardest thing he'd ever said to his wife.

The buzzing on the line was torturous. He patiently awaited her response.

"I knew something was going on last night when you wouldn't come with us. I knew you were lying then."

"Kay," he said firmly, "understand I love you more than life itself. I love our kids more than they'll ever know. But I have to stay. Curt and I have unfortunately started something we have to contend with. It's something I have to do."

"Scott, you're scaring me. This sounds supernatural. What are you talking about?"

"Kay, I can't explain now. I have to get going. I'll contact you when it's over. Just remember, I love you. Tell the kids I love them."

"Oh Scott," she said openly crying, "what about Damon? It's going to decimate the coast. You have to get out! You can't . . . my God, you can't stay. You'll be killed!"

"Baby, you have to trust what I'm doing. I haven't gone insane and I'm thinking and acting very clearly. The hurricane is going to miss hitting St. Augustine directly and . . ."

"What are you talking about!" she said sobbing.

"It will miss. And when it does, you'll know I was right. I have to go now, honey. I have things to do."

"Scott, please, listen! Oh God, I'm so confused. What . . . what's going on?"

"I have to go. I love you." Scott was nearly in tears.

"I . . . I love you. Please get out! Please . . ." her words trailed off as the tears consumed her.

Scott hit the *off* button on the phone and he looked up into the blue sky. The tears that had pooled around his eyes somberly trailed down his cheeks. He sniffed trying to hold back the moisture but it was too late.

Curt came out the front door with keys in hand.

"You ready?" he asked.

"Yeah," Scott responded reaching into his pocket for keys. He turned toward his Blazer and used the opportunity to casually wipe his face dry with his bare hand out of Curt's view.

The men proceeded to Sherri's in their respective vehicles.

Inside, Tibu created a short list of items to gather and load into Curt's Mustang later that afternoon. It contained items Marvin considered sensible and some that just made him shake his head. Regardless, he was going to follow Tibu's instructions. There was a certain mystical force about the man. Even Marvin could feel it.

After stowing Scott's Blazer in Sherri's garage, the men returned to Marvin's house in Curt's Mustang. There, Marvin and Tibu joined them and the four men headed north along A1A toward Ponte Vedra. It was 9:15 a.m. They made a decision to leave the radio off. Since they were putting their trust in Tibu, there was no need to listen to the weather report. They had no idea that Damon was officially classified as the strongest hurricane on record.

Marvin had attempted to contact Pierre all morning with no luck. Scott could tell the professor was unusually sullen and sensed that whatever occupied his mind was far beyond his concern for Pierre. Marvin continued to be strangely quiet throughout the trip offering no sarcastic comments about Curt's driving. That in itself was odd. Marvin could be cranky and his comments could be very annoying, but it was usually just to get a reaction. Today he held his remarks to himself. Scott wondered what was mulching around in that head of his.

Traffic was heavier than anticipated. The residents of St. Augustine had been proactive in leaving. Visions of the bayside shops in two feet of standing water from Donya's swipe at the coast last year had left a lasting impression. But their neighbors to the north, primarily in the affluent sections of Ponte Vedra, did not heed the early warning and now were scurrying to make up for lost time. What would have normally been a 30-minute trip turned into a two-hour adventure. Traffic was near a standstill as they hit the outskirts of St. Augustine and approached the Usina bridge leading over to Vilano Beach. From there, it was a slow grueling experience. For miles upon miles, Curt's Mustang crept along. At least the beach was visible for most of the ride, which made it far more attractive than the time Scott had spent last year stuck on State Road 16, looking at barren land and mobile home parks.

Occasionally, they hit a stretch with homes, most on stilts, proudly saddled against the beach in defiance of the anger the ocean would extend if Damon came anywhere near.

"I wonder if these homes will be standing this time tomorrow?" Scott said.

"I've always thought I'd love to retire in one of these," Curt said pointing to a two-story house on his right as the car edged ahead at less than 10 miles an hour. Between it and the adjacent house, he could see the ocean churning several hundred feet away. The waves kicked onto the shore as the foam rolled and fluttered down the beach. Seagulls dove and sailed low across the water looking for scraps of food.

The Mustang crawled along the single lane road. The silence in the car was reflective of the mood. Scott began thinking about the Kilgotian and the awesome force he and Curt had witnessed in Marvin's partly decimated bathroom. He wondered why God, if there was such a thing, would cut loose such an entity upon mankind. If it had truly been a useful Ark passenger, why was it now the red-headed stepchild, forgotten and left to its own devices? Had the Devil somehow managed to recruit the Kilgotian to the dark side? As far as Scott was concerned, the fish reeked of evil.

But it was an archeologist's dream. A one-of-a-kind. Not to mention a fish that traveled upon one of the most high profile stories of the Bible and was probably held at some point by Noah himself. Noah, the man who talked to God, for those who believe in such stuff. But even beyond the religious contentions, what a piece of history. It was the discovery of the century. Possibly even more significant than the Dead Sea Scrolls. For the fish was proof of a nonhuman force. Another entity beyond mankind's existence. It would not only shock the historians it would floor the scientific community, the religious sects and philosophers. The Kilgotian's far-reaching impact was immeasurable. But the persistent irritation inside Scott begged to ask the question: But at what cost?

The discovery had resulted in multiple deaths from what they could tell. Obviously, this was not the way Scott wanted to be remembered if his name was ever to be printed in the history books. And, moreover, he felt a certain degree of guilt in considering the fish in any other way than as a killer. They had revived a beast that created those who had killed and would continue to kill if not stopped. His first and foremost thought of the Kilgotian should be how to destroy it. Not to savor its significance. What if that had been Lindsey the police had found mutilated? How would he feel about claiming the Kilgotian as the archeological prize of the century then?

Several miles from Pierre's the traffic cleared somewhat and Curt drove along at a brisk 25 miles an hour. "We're about to break the sound barrier. Everyone strap in," he quipped.

Scott, sitting in the front, facetiously fastened the shoulder harness as a supplement to the lap belt he was wearing. "I'm ready," he said with a smile.

A few minutes later, Curt cut the Mustang right onto Shackle Avenue and came to the stop sign at the intersection of Turner Street. Across the way, on the opposite corner, was Pierre's place. It was one block from the ocean.

Curt crossed the intersection. Cutting across the left-hand lane, he pulled the car onto the grass and parked along the strip of lawn next to the chain link fence. They were on the right side of the house, which faced onto Turner. Toward the back, Marvin saw the chain link gate was wide open.

The four men climbed out of the car and proceeded toward the opening. It was another mild day. The sea breeze swelled and met them head on with a moderate gust.

On the distant ocean surface a cloudbank was building. It occupied the entire horizon blanketing the vast expanse in degrees of darkness from light gray to charcoal black, ominously shrouding the water as a solid wall. Short whitecaps churned past the breakers, seemingly the result of a trembling surface.

All Scott could think about was that if Tibu were wrong about Damon, he would never see his wife and kids again.

As the men approached the open gate, Curt saw a man, woman and young girl walking toward them from the beach. They were heading up Shackle Street, probably toward the parking lots two blocks to the west on A1A. The little girl reminded him of Julie and he suddenly missed her dreadfully. He paused to watch the happy family approach, the girl's blonde hair bouncing from side to side as she held her parent's hands and skipped between them. They were clad not in beach attire, but in everyday clothes as if they were going to see a movie. The threesome had probably been strolling the shore to see the larger than normal waves.

As the family approached Curt, he noticed their lackadaisical attitude. They seemed carefree and unconcerned. Probably on their way out of town, they had taken one last stop to view the beach.

Marvin, Scott and Tibu passed through the gate and Curt refocused his attention and followed. The backyard lawn was in an irreversible state. The warm air combined with the salt spray from the ocean, and apparently not much watering, had left the grounds a virtual dessert. Low cut isolated patches of grass and weeds were all that remained. This was common for beach property not thoroughly attended to.

Marvin led the way up the steps onto the wooden deck. There were two chairs and the small table as he had remembered them. Pierre spent a lot of time outside reading and gawking at the pretty young things heading to the beach. It was his little paradise.

Marvin had known the older man for only a year. Pierre had been referred to him through a colleague at Florida State. The Frenchman had advertised his services simply out of boredom and the two had met when Marvin needed a 19th century diary translated that he had found on an obscure internet site. It turned out to be quite humorous. The diary itself was a fake and the stories were descriptions of explicitly erotic encounters, threesomes, orgies and the like. Although, less than Marvin had hoped for, he still accepted the translation and kept it around for late night reading. He still laughed about it, thinking how Pierre told him he had nearly had a heart attack with each sentence he transcribed.

Although somewhat bitter, and self-confined with his background, the professor acquired respect for Pierre Couperin. After completing Marvin's initial assignment, the two had dinner at First Street Grill at Jacksonville Beach. During the meal, Pierre had insistently refused a glass of wine despite Marvin's repeated offering. (Pierre jokingly asked if the professor was getting a commission on the sale of *Turning Leaf* Merlot.) It was only after Marvin's prodding that Pierre opened up and related his story of Piana Franco. How he had accidentally killed the daughter of a co-worker while driving intoxicated. This left Marvin with an appreciation for the man's demeanor and lifestyle.

As the men approached the house, Scott picked up a pad of paper face down on the deck and placed it on the table. When Marvin reached the screen door he realized the inside door was wide open, which he found peculiar. The air conditioning compressor outside was pumping at full speed yet Pierre had the place wide open. Marvin knocked on the screen door and placed his face flush against the mesh. Cupping his hands around his eyes, he peered in. There was light coming from the kitchen and a solitary lamp upon the buffet in the living room.

"Pierre! You home?" Marvin shouted, banging on the screen door.

No reply.

"Pierre! It's Marvin! Are you here?"

Marvin pulled on the screen door and to his surprise it swung open. He immediately had an unpleasant feeling. The four men entered one at a time and walked into the living room. Marvin was the first to spot the dark red-splotches at their feet. The light colored hardwood floor wore the crimson fluid like a wax covering. The patches were clumped in circular pockets, some large, some small. But all of it was dried in.

Tibu bent down and rubbed a spot. A slight trace stuck to the tip of his finger and he placed it in his mouth.

His nonverbal stare toward Marvin disclosed his finding. *Blood.*

Scott scanned the rest of the room and saw the phone receiver hanging by the cord from the wall unit. Along the cord, were red specks of dried blood.

"Look at this," Scott said walking over to pick up the receiver.

"Don't touch anything!" Curt yelled. We might be contaminating a crime scene. Scott stopped short.

Curt pointed to the suede couch. There were dark blemishes. On the floor along the baseboard was a sword.

"PIERRE!" Marvin yelled as he moved down the hallway, past the empty bathroom and into the first bedroom. The others followed. This was Pierre's bedroom. It was empty and undisturbed.

The second bedroom was closed but light appeared underneath. Marvin retrieved a handkerchief from his pocket and gingerly gripped the door handle.

His pulse quickened as he twisted the knob. After a half turn the door opened inward on its own. A violent, harsh aroma rushed from the room. Marvin released the knob and used the handkerchief as a filter to cover his nose. Curt and Scott used their shirts, raising the collars up to breathe through the material. Tibu never flinched.

The sight before them was atrocious.

Pierre had set up the second bedroom for guest accommodations. It contained a four-post bed, which was positioned in the back right-hand corner and ran against the wall toward them. There was only one other piece of furniture; a dresser underneath the window against the opposite wall. The small lamp on the dresser was hardly enough light to brighten the room, which was oddly dark because of the heavy brown curtains completely drawn in front of them. There was a small multicolored area rug in the middle of the room.

The dim lamp created a mosaic of black, gray and pale white on the macabre setting. Propped upon the bed, nestled in the corner, was the headless body of Pierre Couperin. Pierre's back was positioned against the bedpost as if he were reading a book. His hands lay by his side with the palms down on the blood soaked sheets. The bed was void of a bedspread. The body rested upon what had, at one time, been virgin white sheets. But now almost the entire covering was, in one fashion or another, dark red. There were scant pieces of white visible. Likewise Pierre's pants and shoes were stained with the nauseating color. His shirtless chest bore a grizzled design. Blood had flowed forth from the carving and streamed down, leaving a series of vertical lines. Between his shoulders, there was a divot where his head belonged. From their position, the poor lighting caused a shadow to fill the opening and gave the appearance of a bottomless pit.

On the far-left post against the wall, Pierre's head was speared and prominently displayed, his deformed, wrinkled face withering toward the men. Elongated internal arteries and muscle flopped from the inside base of the neck hanging like a jellyfish. The decapitation had not been clean. The skin on his skull looked leathery and bloated. His eyes were closed but the eyelids appeared translucent as the red pupils glowed through.

His nose had a slight trickle of hard blood forming a perfect line from his nostril to his top lip, which was puffy and remarkably pale.

Scott turned and ran toward the bathroom, heaving as he went. This had a snowball effect on Marvin and then Curt, who in turn, each became sick on the hallway floor.

Unaffected, Tibu pushed past them into the room and walked up to the bed. Without a word, he leaned down closely examining the design whittled into Pierre's chest. He was sure he knew what it was but he had to be certain. The bleeding had made the design somewhat difficult to identify.

Close up it was obvious.

The Huguenot cross. More work of Reece LeFlore.

Scott was still bent over the toilet convulsing. Curt and Marvin had gone into the backyard to expel any remaining undigested food.

Tibu carefully turned and exited the room, closing the door behind him. He wasn't concerned about leaving fingerprints. By this time Scott was coming out of the bathroom holding his aching stomach.

"He has the sign of the Huguenot cross," Tibu said in a slow, deep voice.

"How could you tell?" Scott managed to ask.

"I took a closer look." Tibu responded.

"How did you . . . didn't the smell bother you?" Scott asked.

Tibu pointed to his nose, "It doesn't work."

"Oh yeah," Scott replied. He wiped his lips with his hand. "Let's get the hell out of here."

It was a good thing Tibu couldn't smell. When the four got back in the Mustang, it reeked of vomit. Scott had done an adequate job of missing his clothes but Marvin and Curt had initially thrown up on each other before scrambling into the backyard. Curt blasted the air conditioning and they kept the windows cracked to allow for circulation.

Several miles away, Curt turned on the right blinker and pulled into a Gate convenience store and gas station. He drove across the parking lot, past the gas pumps and stopped in front of two freestanding payphones.

"I'm calling the cops," Curt proclaimed as he began to get out.

"Wait a minute, Curt," Scott said placing a hand on his shoulder.

"What? We just discovered a body. A murdered body at that. I'm going to phone it in anonymously," Curt said.

"No," Tibu replied firmly.

"What the hell are you saying?" Curt said turning in his seat to face Tibu.

"He's right, Curt," Marvin began, "Pierre was my friend and what happened to him is unspeakable, but if you call the police, they're going to be on a heightened degree of alert. It's best to wait until this is over."

Curt drew in a breath of air and exhaled slowly, "I guess you're right. It won't matter. We'll probably all be dead by this time tomorrow anyway," he said gunning the engine and steering the vehicle out to the road.

"Tibu, I sure hope you're right about Damon," Scott said looking to the east. The ominous weather pattern presented distinct rows of dark lines stacked upon one another, not unlike an army assembling to attack, Scott thought.

Tibu was staring out the window and didn't respond. It was 12:20 in the afternoon. As the car made its way south, Curt pulled the notepad out of his pocket he had picked up from Pierre's deck and handed it to Scott.

"What's this?" Scott asked.

"It's the notepad from Pierre's backyard. I grabbed it after losing my stomach a few hundred times. I thought we might want to see if there's anything good on it. I noticed it had something scribbled inside."

Scott lifted the first several pages. They were blank. But on the third page, there were some notes. A few sentences. Scott tried to read but had difficulty with the sloppy writing.

"Messing part?" he read aloud. That doesn't sound right.

"Here, hand it to me." Marvin said. "I have more experience reading Pierre's writing."

Scott gladly passed the pad to Marvin in the backseat.

"*Missing part*. It says *missing* not messing," Marvin said. He continued reading the rest aloud:

> *The power of the pond will only occur after the skeleton has been given to the ocean and when the appendage is consumed by the Kilgotian fish from Noah's vessel. No more than 300 days should pass between the time the two occur. The process should not occur more than one time per soul. If any part of this process is violated, the penalty will be torment for the soulful one and havoc for the living.*

"Sounds like Pierre didn't give you everything he translated," Scott said to Curt when Marvin had finished.

"Well we have our answer about bastardizing the process," Tibu said.

"Yeah, sounds like we're pretty much screwed," Marvin added. "If Reece LeFlore really has returned, it's been a little over 300 days since he died."

"I wonder why the old man kept that passage from me?" Curt commented.

"We'll never know now," Marvin said sadly. Then his voice picked up. "By the way, I just remembered something about Pierre's house. Something that was taken."

"What?" Scott asked.

"One of his antique swords on the living room wall. I knew something was gone but it just came to me. Remember, we saw one on the ground."

"You're right. I remembered seeing the swords Saturday. I guess we know what was used as the murder weapon," Curt said.

"The one that has been used multiple times," Scott added rubbing his forehead.

Just outside of St. Augustine, Curt spotted a rusty brown Ford Ranger parked off to the right. He suddenly slowed the Mustang and pulled in behind the truck.

"What are you doing?" Scott asked.

Curt reached over Scott's legs and opened the glove compartment. He pulled out a screwdriver and handed it to Scott.

"Here. Get the license plate," he said.

"Why?" Scott asked, confused.

"Because if I have to avoid the police in St. Augustine, I don't want them to know who I am in case they get a look at my license plate," he replied.

Scott got out of the car, still unsure he was doing the right thing. He looked around, paranoid of being caught. I'm going to get my ass shot off by some big redneck he thought as he dropped to his knees and quickly unfastened the plate. Although rusty, the screws came off easily. They had not been secured very tightly. After removing the plate he scampered back to the car. "Drive down the road a couple of miles and I'll attach it," he said to Curt.

Curt hit the gas and sent sand flying. The tires caught the pavement with a bark. Just across the Usina Bridge, Scott replaced Curt's plate with the newly acquired one and stored the original in the trunk.

Two minutes later they were back in the historic section of St. Augustine. It was strange to see such a quaint tourist laden town so desolate. The streets were barren of traffic and pedestrians, and most of the buildings and attractions were boarded up tight. Police squad cars were nonexistent. Curt had mentally prepared himself to run a roadblock, but, as it turned out, they had no trouble getting back into the city.

CHAPTER-THIRTY-ONE

At five minutes after noon, Ambrose prepared to leave work after doing a final check of the property. The store had not been opened for business but it was his responsibility to make sure all was secure. He was working on two and a half-hours sleep after his little run-in last night and was ready to get home to gather some things before evacuating town.

He left the store and climbed into his metallic green Camaro and fired up the engine. The motor surged with power as the headers filtered the exhaust in a pounding, steady rumble. The car carried 325 horsepower stock and Ambrose had taken the liberty to tweak the engine even further to gain 50 extra horses. He was not one to be careless or drive 125 miles per hour but he liked the thought of having the power if he ever needed it.

Ambrose was about to pull the vehicle onto San Marco Blvd when he happened to look into the same alley where he had been attacked the night before. To his utter dismay, the man in the ragged clothes was back, standing toward the far end, leaning against the wall and looking at Ambrose. For a moment, Ambrose simply stared back. In the dimly lit alley, the man looked severely pale.

"No way," Ambrose said. He gunned the motor, causing the tires to screech and the headers to flare. The car leaped across the street. He cut the wheel hard to the left and aligned the Camaro in a parking space along the boulevard as he came to a sliding halt.

With the engine still running, he threw the vehicle in park and jumped out. He raced to open the unlocked trunk. Inside was a 34-ounce aluminum bat he kept for extreme situations -- or whenever he happened upon a softball game. He snatched the bat and slammed the trunk lid shut. Ambrose was not one for guns. As a junior at Los Pablos High in Hot Springs, Arkansas, two friends had been killed by gunfire. To this day, he had never owned a firearm.

With the bat in his right hand he sprinted to the opening of the alley. When he arrived, it was empty. He ran to the back, stopping short of the end as he remembered how the man had ambushed him the previous night. He judiciously looked in both directions with the bat on his shoulder, prepared to swing. The end of the alley emptied into a paved lot behind the shops. Beyond that was a six-foot chain link fence, which backed up to other older, run-down buildings.

To his left, Ambrose caught a glimpse of something moving through the trees away from him. The clumped pines disguised the man's departure as Ambrose broke in the direction only to be frustrated by a maze of trunks. He slowly sorted his way between them, careful not to be the victim of another ambush. As he dodged ahead, he caught the aluminum bat on one of the trunks and the impact startled him.

"Crap!" he screamed and then realized it was from his own doing.

Once through the trees, he saw the ragged man running 100 feet ahead of him. He was carrying a long metallic object and angling toward the back of the Prince of Peace Church.

Ambrose took off after him. He hit full stride and immediately began closing ground. But again he lost his prey as the man disappeared from sight behind the church. Ambrose followed. At the back corner, he surveyed the landscape. Across the field was the cemetery and to his right, the massive steel cross. The man had simply disappeared.

Ambrose continued on, trotting in the direction of the nearest graves marked by the dull gray headstones. The cemetery seemed the only logical place the assailant could be. There was an assortment of trees and structures to hide behind. To the left was the clearing. And to the right was the bay. The man surely hadn't climbed the 208-foot cross. So Ambrose picked up his pace and was soon amid the sacred grounds and turning in every direction, looking for any sign of movement.

There was no one in sight but Ambrose was not about to call it quits. He had a knot on the back of his head that needed redemption. Besides, the man had brutally handled that poor woman last night. Who knows what he had done to her? Ambrose was aware of the recent homicides and felt a strong sense of responsibility.

As he strolled along the sidewalks that wove through the cemetery he immediately noticed the small stone building near the center. In the 16 months Ambrose had lived in St. Augustine, the cemetery was the one historical attraction he had missed. This was ironic given the fact he worked so close to Nuestra de la Leche. As such, he was unfamiliar with the layout of the grounds.

He carefully approached the back of the chapel, noticing the heavy folds of ivy covering the outside walls. He circled to the left cautiously anticipating any sudden movement from around the side.

His bat was cocked and ready across his right shoulder. With each step, he kept an attentive watch on the structure and what might be lurking just out of sight. His heart was still chugging from the wind sprint. Now his adrenaline was on full bore as he sensed his attacker was near.

Arriving at the front of the chapel he found the door closed. For a moment he hesitated. Then, with sudden determination, he grabbed the handle and pulled. To his surprise it flew open. Inside, the light cascaded through the stained glass windows. His initial reflex was to back away. If the ragged man was standing against either inside wall, Ambrose would be a sitting duck. So he backed away from the opening.

"I know you're in there you son-of-a-bitch!" Ambrose yelled after a few seconds. "I have a gun and if you don't come out I'm going to use it to ventilate your cranium!" I'm not bullshitting. Get out here!" Ambrose's voice reverberated inside the small chapel and he began to doubt anyone was inside.

Thirty seconds passed. Ambrose was losing his patience.

He stared inside at the 12 rows of wooden bench seats. There was nowhere for the pale man to hide except against the inside walls. Ambrose stepped back and picked up a small stone. He threw it toward the opening and it hit just shy of the doorway. He watched it bounce four feet beyond anticipating what he hoped would be a startled man attacking the thin air.

Nothing.

Either the pale man had nerves of steel or the chapel was empty.

Ambrose boldly approached the open doorway and slowly held out the aluminum bat. He carefully inserted it through the opening at chest level, anticipating a downward blow at any second. Farther and farther he extended his arm until half the bat was through the threshold.

A rustling sound behind him nearly caused his heart to stop. He dropped the bat and the aluminum-coated object fell to the stone walk with a tremendous sound. He spun on his heels and saw a small, furry tailed animal scoot up the side of an oak.

"Shit," he yelled and then turned to make sure no one was charging at him from the chapel. But inside, all was disturbingly quiet.

He picked up the bat, which had rolled several feet to the right onto the grass. Again he held it firmly by the handle and stood in front of the door considering his options.

He carefully surveyed the inside. The chapel was no more than 40 by 20 feet and 12 feet from the floor to the arch of the roof. The stained windows were cut eight feet from the ground on the left and right walls.

If those windows were lower, I'd go on the side and look in at the bastard, Ambrose thought.

Losing the last shred of patience, Ambrose stepped within three feet of the entrance. He gripped the bat by the handle with both hands and silently counted to three as sweat dripped from the left side of his brow.

One.

He could hear the sound of the squirrel frittering in the grass behind him.

Two.

A robin chirped somewhere from above.

Three!

Ambrose lowered his head and charged through the opening holding the bat taut in front of him. He passed through without incident and lunged all the way to the small wooden pulpit near the front before spinning around. In one quick motion, he wheeled and swung the bat with force. If anything or anyone had been within reach, the blow would have been lethal. But all he caught was a load of air.

With no resistance to stop his roundhouse swing and his adrenaline surging, he fell off balance to his left. His sweaty hands lost their grip and the bat sailed into the back right corner smashing into the wall with a resounding metallic crash. Ambrose hit the floor smartly on his right side, facing away from the door. Although he was briefly disoriented by the hard landing, during his out-of-control swing he realized he had not visually verified he was alone inside the chapel. Someone still could have been waiting just inside the entry way. He quickly rolled over and scurried to his feet to make sure the pale man wasn't descending upon him.

But the chapel was mired in solitude. Ambrose noticed the long brass candleholders emanating from the floor and positioned on either side of the door. Atop each were two neatly burning gold candles. But he was alone.

He guessed it was possible the man had escaped as he had charged past the entry, but he doubted it. Ambrose was sure he would have at least seen some motion out of the corner of his eye, enough at least, to know another human was present.

Ambrose stood up and quickly checked his left leg. Although his thigh was sore from the impact with the floor, the knee seemed in perfect working order. "Ten months of rehab and I almost rip my ACL again chasing a lunatic," Ambrose muttered to himself. He reached down and picked up the bat. It had careened off the wall and rolled back to him.

He looked around at the rows of benches on either side. They were free standing but in perfect alignment. Two benches per row, separated by a couple of feet. It was this aisle he had blazed down before turning and falling. He was lucky he hadn't taken a spill over any of the flat pews or he might have done serious damage to his body.

He looked down at the first bench to his right closest to the pulpit. Oddly, the last section of the bench appeared to be covered with a fine white mist, possibly talcum powder, he thought. (If this were New York, LA or Chicago, he would have thought otherwise.) Along the length of the white haze, perfectly centered, was the distinct outline of a long object, which he instantly recognized as the shape of a sword.

"What the hell is this," he said out loud. "I've entered the Twilight Zone."

He bent down to touch the white powder and was amazed to discover it was firmly affixed to the wood.

"This isn't powder," he told himself. "It must have been spray painted. Someone painted their damn sword on this bench." Ambrose had had enough of this place. He'd lost his assailant and the artwork on the pew was unsettling.

He walked outside, again careful to check any ambush points. As he walked back to where he had left his car, Ambrose thought about the metallic object the pale man carried as he had given chase.

He realized it *had* been a sword. He went half a dozen more steps and then stopped. "That mother swung a sword at me last night!" he said out loud. "Christ!"

As the combination of anger tainted with fear boiled inside him, Ambrose made his way back to the sidewalk. He approached the row of parking spaces on San Marco Boulevard across from the drug store.

He stopped abruptly. "Oh no, this shit is not happening to me," he said in disbelief. The parking spot where he had left his Camaro was vacant. There was not a single car in sight.

Then he remembered leaving the car's engine running.

As Curt brought the Mustang down the boulevard on the way back to Marvin's, Scott spotted a familiar face in uniform on the left.

"Curt, pull over. It's our buddy Schultz," he said. "Let's check in."

"You think that's a good idea? He might try and send us out of town," Curt replied.

"C'mon Curt. This is Schultz. Remember, he's concerned about Sherri's safety too," Scott said with a smile.

"Shut up," Curt said as he pulled the vehicle over to the right and parked.

"You two can wait here," Scott said looking at Marvin and Tibu, who were crammed in the back seat like children.

"Yes, Daddy," Marvin said.

Scott and Curt crossed the road and approached Officer Schulz on the sidewalk. He was listening to an excited man and furiously scribbling notes in a pad. The conversation instantly caught their attention.

"Yeah. I'm sure it was that same pale dude who tried to whack me last night. This dude carries a sword man. Bro is pyscho."

"And you think he stole your car?" Schultz asked, never looking up from his notepad.

"No, man. This dude's probably only a murderer. I don't think he's a thief. I think someone else stole my ride," Ambrose said sarcastically.

"Mr. Ridden, I know this is a ridiculous question, but I'm required to ask. Did you possibly leave your keys in the car when you got out to chase the man?"

Ambrose turned to the side and mumbled something.

"I'm sorry. What was that?"

Ambrose noticed Curt and Scott standing near and listening in. Again he turned and, brushing his hand across his lips as he spoke, said something that was mostly incoherent. Only the words *left* and *ignition* were audible.

"Did you say you left your keys in the ignition?" the officer asked loudly as he chuckled. "Why didn't you just leave the car running so the thief didn't have to worry about wearing down the battery?" Schultz asked with a suppressed laugh.

Ambrose just glared at the officer. His expression exposed his stupidity.

"You're kidding me right? You didn't really leave it running did you?" Schultz said with the most solemn expression he could muster. "I'm sorry," he finally said, composing himself. "I've just never heard anything like this. First you chase after a guy carrying a sword who vanishes into thin air and then you return to find your car, which you had left with the keys still in the ignition and running, gone. Sounds like a very bad day, Mr. Ridden."

Scott looked at Curt, then interjected, "I'm sorry to interrupt your fun Officer Schultz, but can we have a quick word with this man."

"Do I know you two?" the officer asked and then nodded slowly. "Oh yeah, you're the guys from last night. Did that redhead from the shop turn up?"

"That's what we wanted to know. She never came home last night. Anything from your guys?" Scott asked.

"Nothing," the officer replied. "But we'll keep a lookout. If I remember right, you said she went missing at six o'clock yesterday, correct? Well, you'll be out of town by that time tonight so you'll have to file a missing person's report in another city or when you get back. Sorry I can't really do any more."

"Thanks," Curt replied discouraged.

"Mr. Ridden, I'll be right back. I need to check in," Schultz said. "I'll get the rest of your statement in a minute." He turned and walked back to his cruiser.

Scott took the opportunity to approach Ambrose.

"Mr. Ridden, I'm Scott and this is Curt."

"Call me Ambrose."

"Ambrose, this is going to be very hard to explain in just a few minutes but we're after a man who's probably carrying around a sword as you described."

"No shit?"

"No shit," Scott replied.

"Hey, your woman. The one missing," Ambrose began looking at Scott, "what'd she look like?"

"She's a tall, attractive redhead," Curt said.

"I think that's who this man had last night," Ambrose said.

Curt arched his eyebrows. "Ambrose, since you're short of transportation at the moment, we'll be glad to give you a lift home when Officer Friendly's done taking your statement. We'd like to hear more about what happened to you. Last night and today."

"Okay. I'd appreciate it. Let me go see if Captain Comic over there is about finished with me."

Ambrose walked to the patrol car and Officer Schultz stood up and retrieved his pen and pad from his front pocket and began writing. Curt and Scott waited as the officer occasionally let out a chuckle when Ambrose stopped talking. Ambrose wasn't the least bit amused by Schultz's lack of professionalism.

When Ambrose returned he was thoroughly agitated. Scott and Curt walked him across the street to the Mustang.

"Tibu, can you let Mr. Ridden in please?" Curt said, hopping in the driver's seat. Tibu opened the door, stood up and allowed Ambrose to slide in. He followed behind and closed the door.

"And who might you be?" Marvin asked.

"This is a man who's seen Sherri," Curt said before Ambrose could respond.

"And our French buddy," Scott added. "This is Ambrose."

"Pleased to meet you Ambrose. You're the only one we know who has met Reece and lived to tell about it," Marvin said with a somber smile. "Where'd you see him?"

"You mean the man who attacked me last night? His name is Reece huh? I ran into him in the alley across from Eckerd's where I work. He was manhandling some nice looking babe. She sounds like the girl they're looking for," he said pointing to the front seat. "I tried to be the Good Samaritan. I should have learned my lesson from *DieHard 3*. That shit doesn't pay. I guess I'm just old-fashioned. Never could stand to see a woman abused. I get into more fights that way."

"By the way, where do you live?" Curt asked throwing the car into drive and pressing the accelerator.

"You know where the Alligator Farm is on Anastasia Blvd? I'm in the apartments just across the road."

Curt nodded his understanding to the man in the rearview mirror.

"So can you tell us what happened to you last night. What'd you see?" Scott asked looking at Ambrose.

Ambrose relayed his story of the encounter with Reece and how he barely avoided the assault.

"Come to think of it, if it hadn't been for your woman taking off, that watery eyed pale bastard would have hacked me to pieces. I think he gave up on me to go after her."

Curt felt his heart sink. No matter how many times Tibu had assured him that Sherri would be unharmed, at least till this evening, he felt agony. The panic and fear she must be going through had to be enormous.

"Watery eyed," Tibu repeated. It was definitely Reece.

"So what happened today?" Marvin asked.

"I saw the bastard again. Down the same alleyway. Pretty arrogant if you ask me. Since I owe the guy at least a blow to the skull, I chased him north past the church and somewhere near that cemetery. That's where I lost him. I thought he was in that tiny chapel-looking-thing, but I was wrong. He must have been there sometime though."

"What makes you say that?" Tibu asked.

"I saw where he colored his weapon. There was a white sprayed paint outline of a sword on the front wooden pew. What I can't understand is when I saw him running with it, the thing looked pretty shiny to me. I remember it catching the sun and sparkling. Must have been cheap spray paint."

Tibu angled his head up and moved his lips without speaking. Marvin watched for a moment. "What are you doing?" he asked the Indian.

"Thinking," Tibu replied.

Marvin shrugged.

"And you say he just disappeared?" Scott asked as the Mustang came down off the east side of the Bridge of Lions. Ambrose's apartment was a mile away on the left.

"When I came around to the back of the church, the dude was gone. And I'm pretty fast so I'm not sure how he did it."

"What I can't figure out is why he ran from you?" Marvin asked. "He doesn't seem like the frightened type."

"I did have an aluminum bat," Ambrose said as he pretended to hold a bat in his right hand and slam it against his left palm.

"You look familiar," Curt said. "Have we met before?"

"I don't think so, but if you're a football fan, you might know me as a Jaguar. I was on the practice squad last year. Someday soon I'll play again. Soon as the knee is back to 100 percent. There's my apartment over there. I'm the second building on the right. Number 4."

Curt pulled the car into a space directly in front of his building. Parking spaces were easy to come by today in St. Augustine.

Tibu let Ambrose out as Scott cranked down his window. "So are you leaving town Ambrose?"

"I was. I still think I can get a ride. My neighbor said he wasn't leaving until 3 o'clock. He's got a Ford Explorer and it's only him and his wife. I'll probably catch a ride with them."

"Good luck."

"Hey!" Ambrose yelled as Curt began to back up. "You never told me why you're after that guy Reeces or whatever his name is. Are you guys FBI or something?"

"Yeah, I'm Molder and he's Scully," Scott said pointing at Curt. "Take care Ambrose and be safe."

"If you find him, kick him in the nuts a few hundred times for me will ya!" Ambrose yelled as the Mustang pulled out onto Anastasia Boulevard.

Ambrose turned and noticed his neighbor's Explorer gone from its normal parking space. "God, I hope they didn't leave early," he said walking up the stairs to the second floor. Three steps from the top he realized his apartment keys were attached to his car keys.

"Ambrose, if there wasn't a hurricane bearing down on this place it would have been a good day to stay in bed," he said going back down the stairs with dim hopes the front office would be open.

The men arrived back at Marvin's house a little after two o'clock. The skies covered the area in a sickly dark haze.

"Cumulus nimbus," Scott said pointing upward as they walked to the front door.

"Right," Curt replied.

The wind was gusting in steady streams and the air had cooled considerably. Damon was not far away.

"Tibu, I hope you're right about Damon," Curt commented as they entered the house.

"I told you, we will not sustain a direct hit," Tibu said calmly.

"A direct hit? You said it wouldn't hit at all," Curt said incredulously.

"I never said that."

"You did," Curt said as they sat down at Marvin's dining room table.

"We will feel the effects but the town will be spared of any major damage. From the hurricane, that is," Tibu said.

"You damn well better be right or we're in deep ca-ca," Scott added.

Marvin had gone over to his desk and booted up his PC. As it initialized, he strummed his fingers impatiently on the mouse pad. He was still in a mild state of shock from their discovery of Pierre's body, although he was attempting to hide it. All the way back from Ponte Vedra he had continued to experience flashbacks to the horrible bedroom scene and the mutilated body of his friend lying on the blood-soaked sheets.

Scott turned on the TV to keep tabs on Damon. His faith in Tibu's prediction had slighly waned.

Once the hourglass had changed to the pointer, Marvin clicked the appropriate icon and immediately saw he had new mail. Monday night, when he'd first read about the Kilgotian, he'd e-mailed an ex-colleague, a history professor at Oregon State, to see if he was familiar with the legend. He had been hoping for a faster reply from Dr. Trace and was anxious to see if he had responded.

Marvin clicked on the new mail icon and a list of e-mails appeared on the screen. Seven in all. Initially, every one looked like SPAM. But upon further examination, one seemed to be from a legitimate source. The title caught his attention because it was from an attorney.

Steven F. Walbash, Esq – Last Instructions

Later he would think about how close he had simply come to deleting it along with the other garbage he had received. Upon opening, he noticed it had been sent at 12:18 that afternoon. Curt and Scott had been copied as well. It read:

Dear Sirs,

Upon the request of my client, the late Tucker Chalet, I am forwarding you this document as instructed after his untimely demise.

Sincerely,

"What is this?" Marvin said out loud. Scott walked up behind him and began reading over his shoulder.

"Curt, come here," Scott said after he had finished.

Curt walked over and read the e-mail.

"Go ahead and open the attached word file," Curt said to Marvin. Marvin clicked on the icon and the word program initialized. They patiently waited for the document to open but it was view protected and prompted them for the password.

"What password?" Marvin asked, looking at Curt and Scott.

Scott and Curt gave the Professor a blank look.

"Well, it wasn't in the e-mail," Scott finally said. "Tucker intended for the three of us to get this. He must have known it would be something we could figure out," Scott paused. "Marvin, try *friends*."

Marvin typed in the word and immediately received a message that the password was incorrect. Marvin clicked on "OK."

"Next," Marvin barked like a counter clerk at McDonalds.

"How about *archeology*," Curt said.

Marvin typed and hit enter. Again the error message popped up.

"Let's try *fingers*," Marvin said as he typed. Again the message appeared.

"Are we gonna get locked out if we try too many times?" Scott said looking at Curt.

"No. But unless we come up with the password, we'll never get into the file," Curt replied.

"I thought you were a PC whiz?" Marvin said to Curt.

"I am, but I never learned to hack," Curt replied.

Marvin tried several other words based on their suggestions. They all failed.

"We're not being very smart, gentlemen. Tucker must have known it was a word or phrase we would know. Something probably exclusive to us," Curt said.

It suddenly occurred to Scott. Of course. The thing they had teased Tucker about the most.

Scott stood up straight. "Marvin, type in *dirty face*."

"Ah," Marvin said as the men watched the screen intently. Tibu sat quietly, displaying his usual disinterest.

Upon typing the phrase, Marvin hit "OK." Again the error message occurred.

"Damn!" Scott said.

"Marvin, did you type it as one word or two?" Curt asked.

"Two."

"Try it as one."

The professor typed again, this time combining into *dirtyface*. Marvin hit "OK" and the document opened. The screen filled with words. Marvin sat back grinning victoriously. They had cracked the safe.

Marvin clicked the print button and a few seconds later his laser printer was humming and kicking out the two-page document.

Scott picked up the paper and sat down at the dining room table. The others congregated around with the exception of Tibu, who was sitting cross-legged on the floor in front of the coffee table.

Scott began reading.

> Dear Friends,
>
> I hope to God you never read this. If you do, it means my anxieties were correct and that I've met with death via some untimely event.

The words were chilling and Scott briefly raised his eyes from the page to look at Curt and Marvin. Each man wore the same solemn expression.

> I'm assuming by the time you get this, you have already heard of my passing and probably wondered why I would be in the Jacksonville area without letting any of you know. There was good reason. I have involved myself in something I believe is dangerous and do not want to put anyone else at risk. Especially good friends such as yourselves.
>
> First, let me be perfectly honest and say I'm petrified of what I'm doing. A deceased man named Jean Luc LeFlore, through provisions of his will, has hired me to find the remains of a legendary one-of-a-kind fish. All I know is that I've had nightmares and horrifying visions for the last week while I've been looking for this thing. But LeFlore's estate is paying me more money than I could ever imagine turning down! (If you read this it'll be a moot point but I was going to take you guys to a 5-Star restaurant if I ever located this damn fish.)
>
> I'm leaving this word file with my attorney with explicit instructions to send to the three of you if anything should happen to me. Since you're reading this, you obviously figured out the password. I'm sure it wasn't that difficult for three brainiacs such as yourselves.

Scott kept his head down but felt an inward smile. Even in the midst of despair, Tucker kept his biting sense of humor.

> The lawyer for LeFlore's estate refused to give me a lot of information about the fish skeleton I'm searching for. He shared some documents, actually a journal of one of LeFlore's ancestors that ties the fish to the Jacksonville/St. Augustine area. The document reads like science fiction and sounds absolutely absurd but the money talks. The fish itself is supposed to have powers beyond mankind's comprehension but all that is just a silly legend, or so I think. The

Lawyer won't tell me why LeFlore wanted (or should I say wants?) the fish's skeleton.

If found, I am to receive further instructions from the attorney on what to do with the fish. If I carry out these instructions, I will receive a tremendous bonus on top of the ridiculous sum of money he's paying me to find the thing in the first place.

You guys know me. I'm firmly rooted in science and don't believe in such fairy tales of mysticism. But recently, my dreams are beginning to make me wonder if I'm going crazy. My gut tells me there's something more to this. It's like I'm not searching for a fish. It's like I'm searching for an entity, or a soul. I can't really explain it. All I know is that I'm confused and scared.

I recently found out LeFlore is buried in the Nuestra de La Leche Cemetery on San Marco Boulevard which is odd because he lived in California most of his life, or so I was told.

Anyway, I get the sense this fish really does exist somewhere but that it's not meant to be discovered. I know how bizarre that sounds but I can't help it. As yet, I've found nothing. And searching for it is like a needle in a haystack. Additional notes left to me by LeFlore suggest it's buried with a box of human metacarpals. Don't ask. I have no idea why.

I do know Jean Luc LeFlore died after contracting AIDS. His death was slow and agonizing. But why would a man pay me millions posthumously to find an artifact based on a legend? Even if I don't find the damn thing, as long as I search for nine months the estate is paying me enough money to retire on.

Of course money's not of much value to me now. I just wanted you three to know the truth and know that I always appreciated our time together.

You were good friends.

One last caution. Please do not pursue the fish if you ever come across any information regarding it.

Sincerely,
Tucker Chalet

P.S. I put your three names on an Internet e-mailing auction site as interested parties for one of the documents in LeFlore's estate sale. I thought you might find it fascinating with its content directly related to St. Augustine. I never had an opportunity to read it as I began looking for the fish but I hope you had the chance to get your hands on it.

Take care friends.

Scott finished reading and placed the paper on the table. "Damn," he whispered as he rubbed his eyes.

"That's why I got that e-mail asking of my interest in Jean Luc's ancestor's document! I thought it was pretty damn coincidental. I thought maybe they got my name from a magazine mailing list," Curt said.

"I don't remember getting an e-mail," Marvin said.

"Me either," Scott added.

"It looked like SPAM. I almost didn't look at it either. It was from some auction house and the title sounded pretty hokey," Curt said.

"Isn't it ironic that if Tucker had read the document he suggested we obtain, he would have known considerably more about what he was looking for. Jean Luc didn't pass Tucker the right information. Tucker would have picked up on the powder magazine connection just as we did and he would have had his fish. Maybe he would still be alive." Scott's voice trailed off.

"Sounds like Jean Luc didn't want Tucker to know about the entire legend -- the fish's ability to reincarnate," Tibu said from the living room floor. "It's obvious Jean Luc wanted the fish for self-serving reasons."

"He wants to be reincarnated?" Curt said.

"It sounds pretty obvious. That's why your friend was limited to the nine months of searching for the Kilgotian. That's about 270 days. The note Pierre left mentioned the 300-day limit. That's also why the man was willing to pay vast amounts of money. The man saw the opportunity for a second life as invaluable," Tibu said.

"Then that explains LeFlore being buried in St. Augustine. He wanted to be near in case Tucker did locate the fish. I'd bet anything the estate's next set of instructions for Tucker was to exhume the body and use the fish to spawn a new Soulful One," Curt said.

"But why would Jean Luc LeFlore wait until he was dead to start looking for the Kilgotian?" Marvin asked.

"Maybe he just discovered the document shortly before his death. Maybe he's been paying people for years to look for it with no luck. We'll never know," Scott said.

"Maybe he's got several hundred archeologists looking for the damn thing," Curt said. "Why put all your eggs in one basket? Tucker could have turned down the offer so I'd bet there are other treasure hunters."

The word *hunter* stuck in Scott's head momentarily. It had a disturbing ring. If there were others, would they be treasure hunters, or more appropriately, would they be "bounty hunters? To what extremes might someone go to reap the reward?"

The room was silent as each man reflected on Tucker's words and Jean Luc LeFlore's audacious plan of reincarnation. Then Marvin broke the silence, "Hey, Curt, you need to put your car in the garage before the cops see it. I'm surprised they're not going door to door yet."

"I forgot." He proceeded outside. Marvin raised the electric garage door from an inside switch and Curt drove the vehicle inside.

CHAPTER-THIRTY-TWO

Per Tibu's insistence, Scott and Curt were to rest. The limited sleep over the last two days had left both men fatigued. Tibu advised them of the need to be able to expend energy this evening, which had both men anxious.

Although they pressed him for answers about what was to occur after dark, Tibu was vague. He remained firm in his instructions that they were to go to the Castillo de San Marcos at sundown. He would join them afterward. A bit frustrated by Tibu's lack of explanation, Scott and Curt each sought a bedroom and attempted to nap.

"I guess we just have to trust a man who doesn't breathe and has been around for four centuries," Curt said to Scott as they made their way down the hall.

Scott nodded in agreement.

While the men rested, Tibu and Marvin went about locating the items Tibu said were needed. Between Marvin's closets and garage they were able to fulfill the list.

At ten minutes after six, Scott came out of his room. Sleep had been sporadic and unfulfilling. Curt was already sitting at the dining room table. Marvin had cooked a light dinner for the men and Scott sat down and prepared a plate of food.

"Last meal," Curt said with a smile.

"You're not that funny. Have I ever told you that?" Scott said with a slight grin.

Marvin came from the kitchen with a couple of cans of Coke and placed one before each man.

"What, no beer?" Scott said.

"Sorry. Fresh out. Plus, according to Tibu, you need to stay sharp," Marvin replied.

Tibu was kneeling on the living room couch peering through the snuggly closed blinds. Marvin had shut every blind and curtain in the house in case the police were sweeping the area looking for stragglers or those who refused to leave Damon's path.

"Aren't you going to eat?" Scott said looking at Tibu.

"Already did," Tibu responded still looking out the blinds through a crack.

After dinner and with little fanfare, Scott and Curt piled into the Mustang. Marvin desperately wanted to go but they wouldn't allow it. Tibu agreed.

"So we'll see you soon?" Curt said.

"Yes," Tibu said.

"Can you tell us this? Exactly what are we supposed to do when we get to the fort?" Scott asked.

Still ambiguous, Tibu replied, "You'll know when you get there."

It was just after seven when they pulled out of Marvin's garage.

By evening, the wind blew in gusts and there was an air of impending struggle weighing heavily in Scott's thoughts. His mind was dancing between the memories of what he'd witnessed, the dreams he had experienced and the improbable knowledge he had acquired over the last four days. Why me? He thought to himself. Why did I have to become involved in this mess?

But then he thought about Tucker and Pierre and the grotesque manner in which they must have experienced death and realized things could always be worse. This had always been his philosophy about life. Actually, he had two philosophical rules he lived by: Things could always be worse and you control your own destiny so don't bitch at anyone for what you have or don't have.

At that very moment he wasn't sure he was in complete control of his destiny and he realized it with a morbid dash of irony. If there is a God, he's just playing a joke on me for the time I shot that sparrow with my Daisy BB gun when I was eleven. I knew sooner or later he'd catch up to me for that one. In an odd way, Scott now felt relieved. It was as if he'd rationalized the actions he was undertaking and understood the role he had to play. But what bothered him was that he was unsure if it was the role that he had chosen to play or one that had been chosen for him.

The car made its way along Anastasia Boulevard as his mind reeled off images of his wife and children. How dearly he missed them at this particular moment. Kay's somewhat cynical grin and the way her decadent smile could still get him aroused even after years of marriage. He also thought about the impish grins of Cody, Katie and Lindsey when they tried to keep a secret. The way they fought, the way brothers and sisters should fight, hating each other's guts one minute and then having more fun than children could possibly have the next. Scott said a silent request asking for the opportunity to see them all again.

Curt's thoughts too were on others. From the moment he had met Sherri, he had been captivated with her. Her mannerisms, the self-confident nature by which she went about things and the cute way in which her red bangs hung across her forehead. He knew it was somewhat ridiculous feeling this way since they had just met. It's just that he had a very comforting assessment from the looks she gave and the body language she displayed. God knows he had misread women before, but he was certain this was different. He just hoped she was still alive.

As Curt steered the Mustang to the foot of the Bridge of Lions, Sherri's face and smile ran through his thoughts compulsively. She was all he could think about and he yearned to spend some time truly getting to know her. His thoughts were averted as they reached the crest of the bridge and he could see the fort standing solemnly on the right.

Curt realized the absurdity in which he and Scott were now caught up. A flesh eating fish skeleton, Soulful Ones, a bizarre manuscript, Tucker and Pierre's deaths, a 400-year-old Timucua Indian and the two of them riding around in his car in a coastal city expected to experience hurricane strength winds in less than 12 hours! What else could possibly happen?

The night was void of the humidity that had covered the landscape for the last week, and the clouds formed heavy bonds locking out the stars that lay beyond. As the gray light of the day vanished, the city became a shell, devoid of life. The residents were well on their way to Orlando, Tampa, Tallahassee, Pensacola or to Georgia and such cities as Valdosta and Macon as they fled the imminent storm. Damon had become a hurricane of such great magnitude it was expected to do billions of dollars worth of property damage to the coastal areas.

For the St. Augustine Beach residents, the prospect was beyond glum. Ocean front homes were expected to be decimated. Areas as far west as the Intracoastal Waterway would experience extensive flooding and, because of the hurricane's size, land 60 miles inland from the coast would be substantially impacted. It would take years to rebuild the area, as it was for Charleston, South Carolina, after Hurricane Hugo struck in 1989.

Of course, if Tibu was right, and they were betting their lives that he was, Damon would sweep by to the north and spare northern Florida from any major damage.

Scott's attention also turned toward the fort as they drove across the bridge. He wondered what impact the storm would have on it. Surely it would suffer substantial damage as well, if not a complete annihilation. Even though the coquina was sturdy, nothing could withstand the force this storm packed.

As they approached the far end of the bridge, before turning right onto San Marco Boulevard, they passed the two stone lions on either side, keeping watch over the span.

"They'll probably both wind up in Daytona by 8 tomorrow morning," Scott said, pointing at the figures. Curt chuckled and Scott joined in. With both men's nerves frail and exposed, the humor was a nice diversion, a tension breaker at a time when it was sorely needed. Like ice cream after a fine meal it had a loosening effect on the rigid atmosphere within the car.

The Fort was now directly ahead of them and within seconds they were parking in the lot located to the south.

"You can't get prime parking like this anytime you know," Curt said as he angled into the first space closest to the walkway.

"I imagine you had to call in advance," Scott said.

"You bet your ass I did," he replied. "They said I was second in line, but the first guy was some Frenchman who didn't have a car."

Scott grinned as they unbuckled their seatbelts and exited the car. The tension had returned full force but neither wanted to admit his fear. The winds coming from the east were brisk and steady but far from what they feared would come.

The two men made their way along the walkway to the guard station, the place where they had met the man called Robert Bruin on Monday morning. Ahead was the sally port, the fort's entrance. Across the moat on the opposite side, was the ravelin, the entry fortification against unwanted visitors. They immediately noticed something they had not accounted for. The drawbridge was not only up, but it was locked. Secured with the biggest locks and chains they had ever seen.

"Do you believe this?" Scott said.

Curt just stood in place. They knew the drawbridge would be up and secured but they also knew the switch for lowering it was in the guard station and they were prepared to break inside to reach it. Tibu had given them the exact location of the controls. What they were not prepared for were the massive locks clinging to the thick metal chains securing the fort's entrance, obviously put in place in preparation for Damon's attack.

"You know that's going to make it somewhat difficult to get inside. Got any ideas?" Scott asked.

"Who says we have to go inside? Tibu told us to come to the fort. Not a word about going inside," Curt exclaimed.

Scott stared at his friend. This whole weird situation had started inside the fort and both men knew that whatever awaited them that evening would be inside.

"Okay, okay. I have an idea, but you're not going to like it," Curt said.

"I don't like any of this."

"Mr. Marvin packed all kind of goodies in my trunk before we left, one of which was a long rope with a grappling hook."

"You're right. I don't like where you're heading with this," Scott responded.

"C'mon. Haven't you ever wanted to be Errol Flynn? The daring Swash Buckler type? Now's your chance."

"So Indiana, what you're proposing is we toss the grappling hook with the rope over the moat and onto the top wall and scale the fortress?"

"In essence, yeah." Curt replied.

"If I die, I'm going to haunt you as long as you live," Scott said.

The two men walked back to the car and found the items Curt described, including a knife in the event that they had to adjust the length of the rope. They made their way to the stone bulkhead across from the drawbridge. Then they set about the task of tying the hook on the end of the rope and then made knots every few feet to help with their grip. Curt lifted the hook and the rope. Positioned with the ravelin at their back and the moat immediately ahead, the men stared up at the raised drawbridge embedded in the far wall.

"So exactly how do we do this?" Scott asked.

"Well, I think it will probably be best if we attempt to throw the hook directly over the wall above the entrance here. That way we'll be able to use those big locks as footing as we're scaling the wall. Plus, there's a ledge a few feet above the water at the base of the drawbridge, which will add some security in case we slip."

"This is insane. You know that, right?" Scott commented. Suddenly a gust of wind pushed both men slightly to their left. The breeze hit them very unexpectedly and then was gone.

"Stand back," Curt motioned to Scott with his left hand as he took the grappling hook in his right. "Hold onto the end of the rope."

Scott did so and moved to Curt's right and slightly behind. Curt began twirling the grappling hook on two feet of rope in a motion perpendicular to the drawbridge. As he increased the speed, Scott backed off a few more steps. That thing could do significant damage if accidentally released in his direction.

"Here it goes," Curt yelled out as he stepped forward and opened his fingers. They watched the hook leap from his hands, flying high into the air and heading backward landing deep inside the Ravelin.

"Nice shot Errol," Scott quipped.

"Okay, so I'm not a pro at this."

The two began gathering in the rope as Scott walked back through the narrow passage leading into the ravelin. Through the darkness, he could barely see the hook lying at the far end. He continued to reel in the rope as he walked toward it. He moved cautiously and slowly through the blackness using the rope as his guide. Halfway in, his left foot bumped into a very hard object that did not give. He stumbled and nearly fell. Because of his slow pace, he was able to catch himself.

He stood upright and looked down at the cause of his surprise. Below, barely visible through the darkness, was a one-foot-square box. He knelt down and touched the top. It was uneven and rough. He placed his other hand around the sides and noticed their smooth surfaces.

Curt yelled, "Hey, you OK in there? I'm ready to give this another shot."

"Come here with the flashlight," Scott called.

A few moments later, Curt was standing at Scott's side. "What's the deal?" he asked.

"Shine the light down," Scott said as he pointed to the ground. As Curt did, the beam raced onto the box. The light was almost blinding as it reflected off the chiseled stone lid. Both men were speechless. The deeply etched Huguenot cross was indisputable."

"This is either very good or exceedingly bad," Scott remarked.

"Care to make a prediction?" Curt asked.

"The only thing I can predict with any certainty is that I'm scared to death of what's inside."

The two men looked at each other and squatted in unison. Another strong gust of wind ran along the fort's entrance. They could hear it whistle by, but the walls of the ravelin and their low position to the ground, protected them from its force. Curt kept the light on the lid as the men each grabbed a side with one hand and gently lifted. Scott could hear his heart pounding in his eardrums as they raised the lid several inches. He had been expecting the same airlock pop they'd experienced when removing the stone slab in the powder magazine and was somewhat pleased with the ease in which it came off. Gently moving it to the side, Curt followed the lid with the flashlight to make certain not to lay it on their toes.

Once on the ground, Curt looked at Scott and then quickly shined the light inside the opening. The light settled on a mass of three and a half-inch objects, neatly aligned in a stack like firewood. Each object had two short portions segregated by joints and a smaller portion at the stem, bearing a combination of colors from pale white to black and brown. Although grotesque, both men could tell the box contained human fingers that had decayed over a long period of time.

As the two men moved to get a closer look, they were overcome by the smell. For the second time that day, Scott rose and fell to the side, convulsing. Curt quickly stood and backed away, holding his nose tightly between his fingers and coughing. The effect had been immediate and overwhelming. What was "stewing" inside had generated a fragrance worse than Limburger cheese.

As Scott knelt to the side, forcing air and spit out of his mouth, Curt composed himself and walked over to his friend.

"Are you okay?"

"I'll be okay in a moment," Scott replied. "It's not nice for you to eat cabbage and not warn me," he said attempting humor as he hacked up some more of nothing.

Curt helped his friend to his feet and then reached down to grab the flashlight lying on the ground. Each pulled his shirt collar over his nose and used a hand to hold it in place to filter the smell as they approached the box again. This time they remained standing as they peered at the array of bones inside.

"This is a very good sign," Curt said.

"Maybe, maybe not," Scott replied.

"What do you mean?" Curt inquired.

"Well, how many Huguenots were slaughtered at Matanzas inlet? Do you remember?"

"Yeah. About 350," Curt said. As the words left his mouth he knew where Scott was going.

The two gazed back into the box and, while holding their collars on the top of their noses, palms pressed against their nostrils, they bent down. Scott counted the bones out loud and discovered there were 22 across the top row. Since neither felt quite comfortable reaching inside and repositioning them, they estimated from the outside there were 12 or 13 rows deep. This meant approximately 286 were in the box. If the 350 figure was accurate, there were 64 unaccounted for.

"You know, there's always the possibility Pinot and Reece didn't retrieve them all and only had 280 to begin with," Curt said optimistically.

"And there's also the possibility they did and have already removed some."

"Either way we need to get rid of these. Reece and Pinot have the Kilgotian and obviously plan on creating an army of Soulful Ones using these," Curt said pointing to the box. Scott nodded in agreement as the two men grabbed the lid with their free hands and placed it back on the box. They slowly lowered their shirts and tested the air for acceptability as they backed away from the spot.

"I think it's okay now," Scott began. "Let's move this thing where our French buddies won't find it."

With that, the two walked over to the box and reached down to one side and tilted it on end in order to get a grasp underneath. Neither was surprised at the weight since it was made of stone and they strained to stand upright.

"I'm open to suggestions on where to put this damn thing," Curt said. "I can tell you now we're not going far with it or I won't have enough strength to scale the wall." Scott nodded in agreement as they proceeded from the ravelin and onto the walkway in front of the raised drawbridge.

"Let's dump it in the moat," Scott said as the two men knelt down and placed the box on the sidewalk.

"Excuse me for being negative," Curt began, "But what if that fish thingy is in there. We'd be playing right into their hands by feeding it a month's worth of rations. Think of the unwanted additional company we might drum up."

"Good point. We can secure the lid with a section of rope."

"I have a better idea", Curt replied. "In the trunk is a rubber strap with metal hooks. The type people use to hold books and things on the backseat of motorcycles. We can use that to secure the lid."

Not waiting on Scott's reply, Curt once again made his way to the car leaving Scott kneeling by the edge of the moat. Once alone, it suddenly occurred to him that he and his friend had been less than quiet these last 20 minutes while outside the fort. If Reece and Pinot were inside the Castillo de San Marcos, had they heard and seen what he and Curt were doing with the stone box?

A cold chill flowed up Scott's spine and didn't stop until it reached the top of his head, setting the hair on his neck at attention as it passed. Awkwardly, he gazed up at the top of the walls, starting at the farthest point to his left and then sweeping to the right. There was no sign of movement, but then again, it was relatively dark. Another gust of wind bore down on him, running along the fort's walls and spilling out onto the surrounding field.

Suddenly, he heard a creaking noise directly in front of him coming from the raised drawbridge. The sound jarred him and he tilted backward from his squatting position, landing solidly on his rear. As he sat motionless, heart racing, he strained to catch the sound again but all was quiet. Half delirious with fright, Scott began nervously chuckling to himself.

He slowly lifted himself and felt his nerves tighten as he stood upright. As something touched his right shoulder from behind, he screamed a brief, but stark, yelp. He wheeled around almost falling as his feet became tangled. He struggled to maintain his balance as he took a step forward to gather his composure. His vision quickly focused on Curt as he swallowed hard.

"Holy cow, Curt! You trying to scare me into a coma?"

Curt laughed. "Come on," he said with a smile. "This is no time for fun and games. Help me slide this strap underneath." Scott slowly inhaled and exhaled to steady his breathing and then bent down. He angled the stone container to one side and Curt quickly slid the rubber strap underneath and locked the two hooks on top.

"That'll hold it shut," Curt said as he and Scott positioned their fingers underneath and raised the heavy box. They moved to the edge of the walkway and stared down into the moat. The surface was 12 feet below. They were unsure how deep the water was since it was not permanently filled. The moat encircling Castillo de San Marcos only held water after periods of extensive rains like the region had experienced lately with the multitude of near hurricanes. At most, the box would only be three or four feet under the surface.

Since they needed to ensure the lid stayed on, they held the stone box level over the edge and, on the count of three, dropped it. It fell and entered the water exactly as they had released it with the bottom smacking the surface and a loud sound emanating upward and echoing through the moat. As the two watched the splash that resulted, the box became lost in the dark water. They felt confident it had settled safely to the bottom intact.

"Let's just hope it stays there," Scott commented. "OK, time to get inside."

Curt turned around and went inside the ravelin. In a moment he returned with the grappling hook and went about recoiling the rope.

"Time to try this again," he said as he began swinging the rig in a circular motion. As he increased the velocity he intently eyed the top of the wall directly above the drawbridge. With a grunt and a couple of steps forward, Curt released the rope and it sailed beautifully out and up toward the top of the wall. Suddenly, Scott realized no one was holding the end of the rope. As the hook continued on its journey, he dove to the ground and grabbed a section just as the hook cleared the wall and was sailing toward the courtyard beyond. The line became taut and stretched Scott's arms to their fullest extent as the hook settled.

"Ouch!" Scott moaned as he stood holding the end and rubbing the scratches on his elbows.

"Yeah, that would have been a bad thing," Curt said. "Thank god for your cat like reflexes and the fact you grabbed the rope at a spot which allowed the hook to clear the wall."

"Austin, my cat would have been proud of me," Scott began. "Some swashbucklers we are. If that hook lands inside the fort taking all the rope with it we'd never get in."

Curt took the rope from Scott and gave it a sharp tug and felt the grappling hook firmly lock in place over the edge. He then moved away from the edge of the moat slowly as he trailed the excess rope through his fingers until he was at the entrance to the ravelin. On one side, there was a tall stone beam. Curt made a lasso and hopped onto the wall and secured the rope over the structure, yanking it abruptly to test its durability. He then lapped the excess rope around it repeatedly until the last bit of slack was gone. They now had a 75-foot tight rope that stretched at a 25-degree angle from the Ravelin to the top of the Castillo de San Marcos wall.

Curt bounced down from the low wall beside Scott and pulled two pairs of gardening gloves out of his back pockets and handed a set to his friend.

"Are we going to be pruning the hedges in the courtyard?" Scott asked.

"Hey, it's better than ripping your hands," Curt replied.

Curt climbed back onto the wall and Scott followed. In a slow methodical manner, Curt grasped the rope and allowed his body to hang free. He carefully placed one hand over the other and proceeded along the rope's path. Scott waited until his friend was five feet away and then followed in like manner. Curt was right about the gloves. With them there was some discomfort. Scott could only imagine how hard it would have been to move upward at such an angle without cushioning their hands.

The two crept along steadily and within a minute were crossing over the edge of the moat. It was a laborious task and each man's arms began to feel the tingle of muscle strain as they continued on and upward. Scott actually caught up to Curt and had to slow down to wait for his friend. As the two dangled 20 feet over the moat, Scott gazed down into the water and gasped at the swirling waters below.

"Look at that!" Scott said in an excited yet quiet voice. Even though what he saw had him on edge, he had enough restraint not to talk too loud. The last thing he wanted was for the brothers to come to the top of the wall and cut their lifeline. The fall might not kill them but it wouldn't be pleasant.

Curt and Scott stared at the murk below. They could see the dim reflection from the surface and the turmoil of water churning and erupting in a five-foot circular pattern. Within seconds, the swirling area sunk downward as the speed of the flowing water picked up and the splashing sound spread in all directions.

"There's a mini-whirlpool," Curt said in a low breathless voice. "It's like someone pulled the plug."

A small charge of electricity shot through Scott's brain. "It's flowing counterclockwise," he said mouthing the words so they were barely audible to Curt.

"What?"

"It's flowing counterclockwise," he said again in a monotone, far-off voice. Scott thought back to Friday night in the upstairs bathroom with Cody in the tub. How father and son watched the maroons caught in the funnel spiraling downward as he toweled Cody off. That's what had eaten at him that night, what had made him lie in bed awake. It was the way the water reacted, carrying the plastic figures on a childlike joyride, spinning them around and around and around.

But not in the manner objects should behave when funneling downward. Water funnels clockwise in the northern hemisphere. The maroons had spun counterclockwise.

But Scott understood the Coriolis effect, as it is known as, is greatly influenced by the size of the body of water and how long it's been at rest. He had done a paper on this very subject in high school. For the bathtub drain to send the water spirally downward counterclockwise was due to the fact the gravitational impact was so limited and the water was still active from the way it had been dispensed from the faucet (not to mention Cody's activity).

But the moat was a different story. If, for some strange reason it was actually draining, it was large enough and calm enough to exhibit the Coriolis effect.

"If that's a natural drain, it should be flowing clockwise," Scott whispered to his friend. What they were witnessing should not be happening. At least not naturally.

"It must be the Kilgotian," Scott stated in a trembling voice.

As Scott cleared his head and looked below, the water continued its counterclockwise gyration and the inverted funnel drove deeper. Scott became aware of the water splashing upward on his pants legs. He immediately thought of doodlebugs and the two-inch, inverted cone-shaped sandpits the insects create in order to trap nourishment. When other insects, such as an ant, falls into the pit, they struggle to climb out. The doodlebug uses the natural incline of the dirt walls, and its ability to embed itself at the bottom and fling sand upward, to prevent the ant from escaping. The pelting sand knocks the ants back into the hole and the prey falls into the bottom of the pit from exhaustion. There, they are grabbed by the claws of the doodlebug and carried into the earth for consumption.

Hanging now above the swirling surface, Scott wondered if he and Curt were the ants.

As the two watched the activity with amazement they each felt a building degree of fear. They were gazing at the circling water barely visible below when suddenly they were blindsided by a gust of wind that sent them horizontal, flapping in the night air like a flag. The surprise force of the air caused Curt to lose the grip in his right hand and he desperately held on with his left.

The wind had crept upon them with an evil presence. It had struck at a most inopportune time with the Kilgotian waiting below. Scott strained to hold on. He couldn't help but think the fish had somehow created the effect for its own self-service.

"Oh God!" Curt yelled as he clung perilously to the rope with his one hand, desperately attempting to reconnect with the other. It was no use. Secured at only one point, his body waved to and from and twisted back and forth in the wind, making it impossible for him to grab the line. Scott could see his friend was in trouble and his adrenaline surged. The persistent gust, was only a few seconds from defeating Curt. The vicious wind would surely send Curt careening onto the hard ground or into the natural earth side of the moat, where he would slide down into the realm of the Kilgotian.

"I can't hold on any longer!" Curt shouted as Scott watched his friend struggle in vain.

"Grab onto my belt to help steady yourself!" Scott screamed as the howling wind kept the men horizontal. With every bit of energy Scott could willfully call upon, he was able to edge over toward Curt and was now within reach. Curt's left hand flailed at Scott's back erratically. He could feel himself close to becoming consumed in panic. He flipped off the glove and let it fall into the waters below. After three attempts, he finally caught the belt on the right side of Scott's pants a split second before the wind caused him to release the rope. As he did, the second glove flew off and his body turned upward as he slid underneath desperately grabbing the belt on Scott's left hip with his right hand.

Suddenly, the air was calm. As quickly as it had struck, the wind was gone. The two men swung back perpendicular as Scott struggled to hold onto the rope and Curt to Scott's belt. It was as if some force had turned on a giant oscillating fan and then, 40 seconds later, the circuit breaker tripped.

Each man fought to catch his breath, panting in the sudden quiet. Below the water was calm. The Kilgotian was nowhere in sight.

"I can't hold on much longer," Scott yelled. Simultaneously, Curt realized Scott's pants were giving way under the strain and he could feel the belt easing down over Scott's hips.

"Scott," Curt yelled back, "I have a plan." He let go of his right hand and quickly reached into his front pants pocket and pulled out a knife still holstered in a sheath. He quickly raised it upward. "Take this!" he shouted to Scott. Scott hesitated for a second but then let go with his left hand long enough to grab the knife.

"Cut the rope behind us!" Curt panted. "And hurry. If your pants give out, I don't think there's anything big enough down here for me to hold onto with two hands."

"Are you crazy? What do you mean cut the rope?" Scott shouted.

"Hurry," Curt screamed. "Cut the rope behind that last knot and hold on like hell. It looks like we have just about the right length to swing down to the ledge of the drawbridge." Scott glanced below at the base of the raised drawbridge. The ledge looked to be about 12 inches wide and ran the length of the opening. If they could safely swing down, they'd be able to roost on the ledge.

But cutting the rope could result in a multitude of trouble. For one, they might swing directly into the drawbridge, bounce off the hard wooden door and plunge into the moat. Another possibility was that a miscalculation of the distance versus the length of the rope might land them below the ledge, smacking violently into the earthen wall. Worse, they might hit the ledge itself. At its best, the plan involved crashing into the door and then maintaining their balance once they came to a stop. But as each man's grip weakened and Scott's belt slipped, cutting the rope was their only option.

"Scott, you've got to do it now," Curt said in his calmest voice under the circumstances. "I won't be here much longer if you don't." Scott knew it was true as he felt his pants slowly sliding over his hips. Scott's hands ached with pain as he positioned them close together on the rope and, while still holding on, he was able to remove the knife from its sheath. Taking a deep breath and closing his eyes, he exhaled slowly.

"Hold on," he shouted to Curt. Then in one swift move he took the knife in his right hand and swiped the rope past the last knot. He quickly returned his hand to the rope as he inadvertently let the knife fall into the water below. The blade cut the surface with a faint splashing sound.

But they were still suspended over the moat.

Scott's slice had not been clean. He had gashed the rope rather than severed it. Scott glared at his work with extreme disappointment.

"Damn it!" he said, "I didn't get it through." Curt considered retrieving his pocketknife from his pants since he'd seen the knife fall into the moat. But before he could, the weight of the two men effectively bore down on the damaged area of twine, and the rope quickly began to fray. In an instant, they tightened their grip and the last tendons of the rope separated. They fell in a direct path toward the drawbridge ledge, each man clinging to his respective lifeline. For Scott, the second and a half journey seemed to last an eternity.

Sailing through the air, he could tell almost instantly they had miscalculated their point of impact and were on a direct course to smash into the protruding ledge itself. They were five feet from contact, and possible death, when a massive gust of wind hit them from the side and pushed them to the left, slowing down their descent. This had the effect of stretching the rope at an angle and causing the men to strike the far-left side of the drawbridge door with a much softer impact. As they made contact with the wall they were both amazed at the lack of pain.

Curt was still hanging onto Scott's belt less than a foot above the ledge when he let go and softly landed on the ledge. Once there, the wind died down and Scott held on as the rope swung slowly toward the middle of the drawbridge door. As it did, the rope extended, easily lowering Scott and allowing him to gain footing on the ledge.

One gust of wind had nearly killed them and the other had most certainly saved them.

"God works in mysterious ways," Curt said, still shaken from the event.

Scott did not respond. He almost wanted to admit that they'd just experienced intervention by some outside force. As malevolent as the first wind had been, the second gust had the makings of a miracle. Almost but not quite.

As the two men stood on the ledge rubbing their aching arms, the rope straightened itself out. The end hung to their left directly down the middle of the drawbridge door. Scott looked up as a brisk breeze, but not nearly as strong as the last two, swept across his face, blowing his hair straight back.

Curt was silent as he slowly eased his way along the ledge to where the rope hung.

CHAPTER-THIRTY-THREE

"You ready?" Curt asked. Scott nodded as he grabbed the rope. Curt motioned his friend to proceed. Scott held the rope firmly and began walking up the wall. Again it was meticulous going as the 22-foot facing loomed above as a towering travesty in the darkness, eerily hiding secrets within the confines of the coquina fort. Through the blackness it was difficult for Scott to gauge how far it was to the top as the structure blended seamlessly into the night sky. After he had climbed a short distance, he looked down and estimated Curt to be 12 feet below on the ledge. His friend had retrieved the flashlight, which had survived the impact, from his pocket and was blinding Scott with it.

"What's the matter?" Curt yelled upward and then cupped his mouth as he realized he probably should not have spoken so loud.

"Nothing," Scott whispered back. "You going to join me or just wait there for that fish to evolve suction feet and come get you?" Curt looked down into the moat uneasily and then back up at Scott. "I'll be right there, dear," he replied.

Scott focused his attention on scaling the wall and soon reached the top. Wrapping his left leg over, he pulled himself onto the edge and paused to rest. Sitting on the wall he looked down at Curt who now appeared to be halfway up.

"Damn, you're pretty fast," Scott whispered down to him.

"Very funny," he said excitedly. "I thought I heard the water churning again."

A minute later Curt was standing on the gundeck beside Scott, panting heavily. "And I remember when they said it couldn't be done. I think you just broke the four-minute wall," Scott said.

The two men turned around and scanned the perimeter. The lighting on top was only slightly better than within the moat. To their right, the bay looked like a vast flatland before plunging into the dark tree line of Anastasia Island.

The two walked forward. Suddenly, Scott grabbed Curt's arm and came to a dead halt.

"What! What's the matter?" Curt whispered in a worried voice.

"What's our plan?" Scott asked.

"What do you mean, *What's our plan?*" Curt responded. "We have to stop the brothers before they turn this place into a blood soaked-Gay Paree. It's actually pretty simple."

"And exactly how do we stop them?"

"I have no idea. I just know we're responsible for unleashing something that should have been left alone. And you know what? Even though I might not attend church regularly, I do very much believe in God and I don't think he will let us fail."

There he goes talking about God. I really wish I had your faith, Scott thought to himself.

After Scott and Curt had left, Tibu had Marvin drop him off at the Nuestra de la Leche cemetery. Tibu knew it was more than coincidence that led to their meeting of Ambrose Ridden that afternoon. It was another sign.

Tibu walked into the cemetery as dusk was settling on the town and the storm clouds approached. Looking beyond to the bay, he noticed that the normal array of sailboats anchored just off shore were gone, stowed away in preparation for the impending storm.

The grounds were beaming with life as birds and squirrels played in the leaves above. Tibu paused for a second to take in the natural beauty of the surrounding as a gentle breeze played through the high trees, swaying the branches back and forth.

In the last hour his thoughts had become unsettled. Nothing was playing out like any one particular dream he'd had. It was a combination of various pieces from different nights. It was as if the events and the outcomes were constantly changing by the actions taken or decisions made. The dream that morning had been very depressing. In it, Reece and Pinot survived to breed hybrid Soulful Ones with the help of the Kilgotian. Many hundreds, maybe thousands, of innocent people died as a result.

On the drive to the cemetery, Tibu had been quiet.

"Tibu," Marvin finally broke the silence, "How did you see me dying?"

"In this car. When it's much darker."

Marvin looked around. "In this car?"

"That's why you're dropping me off and going back home. Don't stop for anyone. No matter what. Understand?"

"Yeah, I understand. I feel like the fifth wheel," Marvin muttered.

Tibu saw no need for the professor to put himself at risk. Although Marvin had been in a few of Tibu's dreams, he had never played a vital role.

Now, as Tibu stood in the cemetery, he used nature to gather himself in. The trees, grass and water. He realigned his thoughts to the tasks at hand. The night was young and there were many battles to be fought. He had to be strong. He had to be determined and use his mind. He had to recognize the various images from multiple visions as they occurred and use all the resources at his disposal in order to have a chance.

Then maybe he could rest.

Tibu strolled toward the chapel making sure he was alone. The door was closed but a firm tug brought it open. There was no light inside and he warily entered, quickly checking both directions once inside. He knew Reece or Pinot had been here recently. He could feel it.

In the insipid light, shadows fell about the floor. He watchfully walked up the middle aisle and arrived at the first set of benches. He pulled a flashlight from his pocket and shined it on the dark bench. Even before the light reflected off the steel he knew the weapon would be there.

It was a sword. A sword owned by Reece. Tibu could tell from the marking on the handle that it was a match to the one in Pierre's house. He leaned forward and picked up the mighty blade.

Now it was time to enter the fight.

The diamond shaped gundeck of the Castille de San Marcos Fort supported four small bastions, one on each corner. There were 14 cannons positioned at various spots on the deck with the majority facing out to the bay on the eastern side.

Curt and Scott walked to the inside edge of the gundeck and peered over the three-foot wall, down into the fort's courtyard. They were met with darkness.

As they nervously looked for signs of life, or resurrected life, Scott thought back to the times he had brought his kids to the fort. Specifically, the times when mock cannon firings were orchestrated by the park rangers.

He remembered the time Cody had cried when the blasts hurt his three and one-half-year old ear drums and had continued to whimper for the next 30 minutes until bribed with a souvenir from the gift shop. But this was unlike those lazy spring Saturday afternoons when the fort was inundated with tourists clumsily meandering through the rooms and strolling up the winding stone steps to the deck. The times when parents allowed their kids to climb on the cannons (contrary to what the signs forbid) as dads created the perfect home movies on their camcorders. Those were casual times, times for relaxation and making childhood memories for your sons and daughters. Times for families from all over the country to explore history and realize how important and how much depth the rich heritage of St. Augustine has to offer.

But on this night, there were no tourists or kids bantering about. No park rangers tending to the crowds. Tonight there was only an ominous atmosphere. An atmosphere of tension and anxiety unlike any Scott had ever come close to experiencing in his thirtysomething years.

For 10 minutes or so, Scott and Curt knelt down and held their position waiting for something to happen. Actually fearful something *would* happen. Neither knew what they would do if they spotted the brothers. They just knew they had to stop them. The wind picked up from the east and a steady breeze blew in.

"What if they're not even here?" Scott whispered to Curt.

"Then we'll be giving Tibu some strong feedback," Curt replied. "But waiting here isn't accomplishing anything. We're going to have to go in search."

"I guess you're . . ."

Before Scott finished his sentence, the silence was abruptly penetrated by a loud noise. The two were so startled they fell into each other from their squatting positions and banged their heads together.

"What was that?" Curt said holding his temple. From their position on the south deck they stared down into the darkness.

"I think it came from over there," Scott said pointing to the northeast bastion. They strained to hear any activity on the other side of the gundeck. But the air was deathly silent again.

"C'mon," Scott said standing up and rubbing his temple. "I must've been wrong. From here, we would have seen them if they were in or near that bastion. It must have come from one of the rooms off the courtyard. And guess which one we're going to check first?"

No response was necessary. Curt knew the answer. It was time to visit the place where it all started. The room that they had so interestingly probed Monday morning.

Sherri sat leaning against the wall of the outer corridor near the entryway to the powder magazine. In the last hour, darkness had settled over the fort quickly. It seemed like an eternity since Reece had placed her left foot in the iron collar and sunk the attached spike with the bulky chain deep into the wall. With less than two feet of links, her movement was severely limited.

Two years ago, during Tina's scare with the severe headaches, Sherri had sat by her daughter's bedside on the first evening in the hospital holding her baby's hand as the intense surges of pain rattled through the little girl's head. Tina cried in agony as she squeezed her mommy's hand. Sherri could still picture in detail the scrounged up face and streaming tears that fell down Tina's cheek as she tossed back and forth moaning. Pain medicine was minimally effective and always wore off too soon. As the rushes continued to pulse every 15 seconds, for the time prior to the Loratab kicking in, Tina would became delusional.

"The real me! I want the real me! I want my real self! Tina would scream. The words had alarmed Sherri. It was as if Tina was trying to disconnect herself from the little girl lying in the hospital bed, the girl suffering from the sharp pains shooting through her brain. She imagined what was going through Tina's thoughts as she struggled. *This can't be me! I don't have pain like this!* In her daughter's irrational state, Tina must have believed that there was really someone else experiencing this torture. Somehow Tina had become joined with this other soul by mistake, bearing its discomfort. A terrible, terrible mistake. Now it was time for the game to end. She'd had enough of this. It was time for Tina to become Tina again and be done with this place where men and women dressed in strange clothes and carried sharp needles, searching the halls for little kids to stab, and liquid pain medicine that tasted so nasty.

This perception by Tina during moments of duress, an outsider thrust in the middle of someone else's shell, had never made sense to Sherri. The separation her daughter had contrived actually frightened her at the time. It seemed to suggest a form of schizophrenia. But being incarcerated, as she now was, incapable of managing her own freedom, she understood Tina's perspective. It was simply a form of mental self-defense. A way of projecting away the reality. Hoping the pain and fear that latched on, could be easily cast aside and inviting the return of normality.

Once the thoughtful awareness of her daughter's words had sunk in, Sherri spent 20 minutes desperately attempting to work the spike loose and screaming for help. Screams not born of panic but of necessity. She was not a woman easily rattled. She prided herself on understanding the value of keeping a level head in situations where most would let their fear and other regressing emotions rule. So even as she sat on the dark, cold stone floor facing the doorway leading to the courtyard, her mind remained focused and calm. And in a short time, she came to the obvious conclusion that she did not possess the physical strength to pull the spike from the wall.

As for screaming, she also realized that from where she was positioned, her voice would barely carry past the courtyard and surely would not be audible enough to extend over the gundeck and into the streets of St. Augustine, which itself now resembled a morgue. Besides, what if her captors became annoyed? After resigning herself to these logical conclusions, she opted to sit down and rest, saving any strength for the appropriate moment, if it ever came. Regardless, she would not give up.

In the increasing darkness, she occasionally heard the wind howl outside. The first big gust startled her as she mistook the sound for Pinot and Reece returning. But subsequent gusts only reminded her of the approaching hurricane and that she would not be in an enviable position within the next few hours.

She tried psychologically to argue to herself that the fort had been here for centuries and that it was indestructible. But her rational side retaliated with a more subjective demeanor and deep inside she knew that a hurricane the size and force of Damon had never directly hit St. Augustine.

These thoughts made her uneasy and she knew that letting fear interrupt her logical mental state was dangerous. She tried to focus on something to occupy her mind. An image of an adorable little blonde girl sitting at the dining room table watching the Cartoon Network while eating a bowl of Fruit Loops appeared. The child sits intently staring at the TV as Daphne and Scooby watch Shaggy and the ghoul go sliding by on a large carpet and careen into the wall as the bookcase comes toppling down upon them and the villain. And, astonishingly, the ghoul really turns out to be Mr. Bickle, the town blacksmith. Turns out Mr. Bickle would have made a fortune by scamming the heirs out of the property value. Except those melding kids in the colorful van had to interfere. Curses!

Sherri could picture the grin on Tina's face as the gang solved the riddle and all was well in Scooby land. As the theme song ended the episode, the cute little adorable blonde would get down from the table and applaud with vigor as if saluting Arthur Fiedler's last performance with the Boston Pops. Yeah, all was right with the world.

Sherri thought of her daughter in other familiar scenes that were forever etched in her mind. Those innocent, humorous, embarrassing, scary memories that every human seems to magically store for a lifetime and can recall as vividly as if just experienced. Some are significant events such as those Christmas mornings or the first day of school but others are far less relevant in the book of life. They just happen to be moments we, for whatever reason, latch onto and remember for the rest of our lives. Ask me what I had for lunch two days ago and I couldn't tell you, Sherri thought to herself. Ask me about the one night Tina crawled into my bed at two in the morning because she was afraid of the lightning and thunder from a distant storm and I can give you every last detail. How she looked, what she was wearing and how her small body felt nestled against mine as she shivered and then slowly faded off into a peaceful sleep. But thoughts of Tina also made Sherri feel sad and she knew the tears would soon be flowing if she kept thinking of her precious daughter.

"Okay lady," she said out loud in a firm voice. "Let's change the subject again." Speaking of what she'd had for lunch two days ago she suddenly remembered it had been awhile since she had eaten.

What she wouldn't give right now for a big, juicy, medium rare T-bone steak cooked on the grill with french fries and an ice cold beer.

She spoke in a louder voice, "Curt, you witty handsome man, you rescue me and I'll buy you lunch. I'll even be your dessert." She smiled as she spoke. She thought about how she had become instantly attracted to the man. His humor and wit. There was just something about him she found extremely appealing. It was hard to put into words.

As a stream of words penetrated the corridor, she fell awkwardly to her side and then scrambled to sit upright. "I'll take you up on that lunch as soon as this is all over," a voice said softly.

Gazing at the shadowy figure in the doorway to the courtyard, Sherri could make out the image of a man. Her heart fluttered.

"I have an idea, why don't we just skip the main course and go right to the dessert tray." Curt said as he moved toward Sherri and turned the flashlight on.

"You have no idea how glad I am to see you!" Sherri tried to catch her breath. "How did you get here? How'd you find me?"

"Find you? Sheer luck," Curt said smiling and wiping the sweat from her brow. "I had no idea you were here until Scott and I got close enough to hear you talking to yourself. I've been searching for you since last night. What happened?"

"A man named Reece grabbed me at the cemetery and he and another man named Pinot brought me here and chained me down." Curt shined the light around her ankles until he spied the restraint.

"Yikes," he said. "Where are the brothers?" he said raising the light and surveying the inner surroundings.

"I haven't seen nor heard them in over an hour. Brothers? You know these men? What's going on? Honestly, I think the only thing that saved me was I spoke to them in French. It seemed to scare them. They couldn't determine if I was friend or foe."

"It's a long story. I don't have time now to explain. You probably wouldn't believe me anyway."

"Curt there's something not right about those men. Why did they kidnap me? Do you have any idea? They kept talking about bones and horrible things. They seem consumed with revenge for something. They also look like they're decaying. They're absolutely grotesque."

"Yeah, I know why they kidnapped you and I know what their plan is. Scott and I have to stop them. They're not exactly good citizens of St. Augustine."

"Where's Tina? Did Charlene get her out of town?"

"Yeah, last night. I insisted. She only left after I promised to find you."

"Thank God. It looks like you kept your promise," she said obviously relieved. A smile broke across her face.

Curt turned and walked back to the entryway. Sherri was about to ask where he was going when he called for Scott to come inside. Scott had remained at the entryway as a lookout.

"Well if it isn't Sherri. Girl don't you have better things to do than hang out in a dark damp fort?"

"Yes, I do. Like go have lunch with your friend here," she replied and then spoke seriously. "Look guys, I appreciate the humor but I'd really like to get out of this ankle bracelet. Think you might be able to lend a hand?"

"Well," Curt began, "remember when I said yikes a minute ago? There was a reason."

"This is not sounding very positive," Sherri said.

"That contraption is going to take a tool to set you free. And at the moment, we're fresh out of tools," Curt said.

"Great. I'm attracted to a guy who doesn't have a tool," she replied. "So what's the plan?"

"Ah, yes, the plan," Scott began. "Go ahead Curt. Tell her the plan."

"We, uh, really don't have one," Curt stuttered.

"You're not very good at this 'hero saving the damsel in distress' stuff are you?" Sherri said.

"I'm working on it," Curt replied.

Scott interrupted, "C'mon, Curt. Let's see if we can get into some of the other rooms. We might be able to find something to help free her."

"By the way," Scott said as he shined the flashlight over the length of her body, "how'd you get so wet?"

"I went for a swim before we got here. I couldn't tell you how we came inside because I was blindfolded, but it involved going through water. Next thing I knew, I was here," she said.

"The moat," Curt said and Scott nodded.

"Guys, you're not going to leave me here alone are you?" Sherri asked in a distressed voice.

"We'll be right back," Scott said.

Sherri forced a smile as Curt handed her his flashlight. "Here, take this."

She watched the two men depart into the darkness. For now, she would keep the flashlight turned off behind her back just in case her captors returned. She didn't want to give them any indication of Curt and Scott's presence and she might be able to use it as a weapon.

"Hurry back now," she quietly called out as they turned right and out of sight.

Scott and Curt walked along the stone sidewalk and checked two storage rooms but found them securely locked. They continued around the courtyard past the fort's chapel, the British Room and nine more storage rooms and eventually arrived at the staircase along the south wall.

As they paused at the foot of the stairs they noticed a distinct drop in the temperature as a fierce gust of wind scoured the gundeck above. The skies had darkened as the moon became hidden by the solid layers of clouds hovering over the coast of northeast Florida. Suddenly, they heard a strange sound emanating from somewhere on the deck above, a noise muffled by the wind and barely audible.

Then it stopped.

Scott and Curt looked at each other as if to question the reality of what they'd heard. They waited for a repeat but heard only the savage wind.

"What do you think?" Curt turned to his friend.

"I think we go upstairs very carefully," Scott replied as he ascended the steps with Curt close behind. They followed the steps up the south wall until the open stairway veered 90-degrees and continued up the north wall. When they tentatively reached the gundeck, Scott switched off his flashlight and the two crept slowly forward searching for any signs of movement. Again they heard what sounded like muffled voices but the deck was devoid of life. But now they could tell the sound was coming from the northeast corner, known as the San Carlos Bastion.

Curt and Scott quickly ran over to a nearby cannon and hid behind it.

"Where are they?" Curt whispered, convinced that what they heard were voices.

"Can't tell," Scott replied.

As they remained behind the cannon, the voices fluttered in the night air again, but still gave no indication of their exact origin.

"Let's move closer," Scott mouthed to Curt.

Curt nodded his approval and the two moved clumsily through the darkness. Curt led the way and they ran to the next cannon, using it as cover and briefly stopping to survey the bastion again.

Proceeding very slowly, their eyes straining through the nonexistent light, they came to the first of three cannons positioned on the San Carlos Bastion. They were less than 60 feet from the corner tower. The northeast tower was the fort's tallest, standing some 15 feet high and, like the others, had been used as a sentinel post.

Wrapped within the constant breeze chasing past them, it was now apparent the voices were not coming from within the fort. They were coming from beyond the walls.

"It's coming from down there," Curt whispered to Scott, pointing out and then downward as they peaked over the cannon, still fearful about exposing their position.

"C'mon," Scott whispered and he slowly rose and made his way over to the last of the three cannons before the tower. Curt was on his heels. So much so, that Scott made an abrupt halt and Curt collided into him.

Scott turned to look back at his friend when he saw a figure approaching, coming up quickly behind Curt, hands grasping a long object. In an instant, it had rushed their position and Scott had no time to warn Curt. In the dim light, Curt was unable to detect the surprise on Scott's face.

The figure coiled the long object in its hands toward the right and Scott only had a moment to react. By turning quickly and planting his right leg alongside Curt's right knee and grabbing his friend's left shoulder, Scott pushed hard and toppled Curt to the deck. Curt's expression made it clear that he had absolutely no idea what was happening.

As Curt fell, the figure unloaded from the right and swung the long object horizontally. Slicing through the air chest high, the object ripped the air and missed Curt's scalp by no more than an inch and a half. Unfortunately, Scott realized his momentum, in stepping forward to save his friend, may have cost him his own life. He was now directly in the attacker's wheelhouse swing. With no time to move, Scott desperately sunk his chest in, involuntarily exhaling, and pulling his arms back. In the split second the object drew across, a flash of lightning in the distance broke the darkness and Scott could make out the long thick blade of the sword stretching toward him and the crazed look in his attacker's eyes. A look of frustration and exploding anger, face pinched, and lips parted with only a few teeth still intact. The look of a madman. As the tip of the blade reached Scott's chest and scraped along his shirt, gashing a section of the material, it tore into his skin with ease. But for Scott's expulsion of air, the blade would have sliced deeper, terminally deeper.

As it was, the gash traced a path just below his nipples. The crazed man had expected to make solid contact which would have stopped, or at least slowed the momentum of the swing. But the nearly clean swipe was unexpected and the sword's weight and momentum were too great and it continued its arc. The attacker's entire body spun 180 degrees and he fell backward landing flush on the deck, face down, still holding the sword in one hand.

Curt, still on the ground, turned to see who or what had attacked while Scott was working to keep his balance by shifting his feet to compensate for his displaced weight. As he attempted to step backward, he found himself caught up in Curt's legs and fell across his friend. He barely had a chance to extend his palms to brace himself before he smacked the stone flooring. His hands hit the deck with a thud. The pain of the fall on his palms was excruciating. Scott lay there stunned. Then he felt another unwelcome sensation, a warm pulsating pain emanating from his chest.

"Scott are you okay?" Curt shouted. "Where in the hell did he come from?!"

"I don't know," Scott responded to both questions. The shock of the fall and the surprise by which they were attacked had left him feeling like he was in a dream. It had happened so fast. All he wanted to do now was to wake up, go to the bathroom and get his morning cup of coffee without losing his footing down the stairs as Austin wove in and out of each step.

But the sound of the attacker stirring brought him back to reality. He lifted his head to see the madman slowly raising up, still clutching the sword.

"Scott, you've got to get up!" Curt shouted. "He's coming back for more."

Forgetting the pain, Scott quickly lifted himself as Curt tried to do the same but he was still hindered by Scott's position. When Scott finally rose to his feet holding his throbbing chest, Curt bounced up. By this time, the madman had risen and was glaring at the two men, the sword firmly clutched in his left hand. The lightning in the distance was becoming more frequent.

The madman stood 10 feet away from Scott and Curt and the lightning flickered again, partially illuminating the deck and providing a horrid view of a figure standing 5'6" tall with a very thin build. Its face was sunken in and gave the appearance of an anorexic about to give in to death. Its tattered clothes hung loosely and its hair was thin and matted. Except for the fact it wielded a 42-inch sword, the thing itself was not that ominous, save for one exception -- the nearly indescribable, exceedingly white eyes. Eyes that practically glowed in the darkness, glistening as if full of water. The pupils bobbing within the eye sockets, angrily swaying from side to side, combined with a facial expression of disdain and utter hatred.

It stood motionless before them. Curt whispered to Scott turning his head slightly but keeping an eye on the thing, "Is that what I think it is?"

"I don't know what in the hell it is," Scott responded softly and slowly. Still holding his chest, he looked at his friend and Curt returned the stare.

"On the count of two, run," Scott whispered. Not waiting on Curt's approval he began to count, "One, two!" Curt and Scott turned and ran toward the northeast corner. They had taken only a couple of strides when a second watery-eyed man met them head-on in the darkness, just beyond the second cannon on the bastion. The shock caused both men to fall back against the cannon's barrel. Armed with a sword, the second attacker made a vertical swing. The blade descended quickly and with substantial force. Scott and Curt barely had time to separate before the weapon struck a spot of iron inches between, sending sparks flying into the darkness. The lightning frantically flickered in the distance as Scott and Curt remained against the barrel, paralyzed in fear. As the thing raised the sword high above its head again, Scott saw it was aimed at him and felt his mouth go dry as he came to terms with the reality of the situation. "Oh no," was all he could muster in a quivering defeated voice.

Suddenly the sky lit up. But this time, the flash was accompanied by a tremendous burst of air, which hit the attacker full force. Scott and Curt's flush positions against the cannon kept them shielded from the wind's effect and they watched their attacker get knocked to their left across the gundeck as the sword flew out of its hands. The madman slid along the ground, sailing toward the ledge overlooking the courtyard some 25 feet away. The sword struck the wall with the handle slightly embedded in the coquina and the blade extending five inches perpendicular above the deck. As the thing slammed headfirst into the wall, he landed to the right of the sword, his skull crushing on impact and his lifeless body curling against the ledge.

Scott and Curt had watched as the thing was catapulted by the wind and sent sprawling into the wall as they leaned backward against the cannon's barrel, breathing heavily. When suddenly it occurred to Curt they better be concerned with the first attacker that they now had their backs to! Spinning around, he strained to see through the darkness, aided by a constant flurry of lightning that cascaded upon the deck. Scott turned as well, understanding Curt's concern. Searching intently, the two were surprised to find they were once again alone.

"Where'd he go," Scott asked.

"I don't know. Are you okay?"

"Yeah, he just nicked my chest. It's like a very bad paper cut. It just stings like hell," Scott replied.

Curt looked at Scott somberly. "Scott, I don't even know how to begin to . . ."

"Please, don't get sappy," Scott cut in with a slight grin, breathing in big gulps of air. "I believe I owed you."

As the men scanned the deck in search of movement, they walked over to the still, crumbled body against the wall.

"Hey, how about that wind," Curt said. "I think someone up there likes us," he said pointing to the cloud covered sky.

Scott did not reply.

They approached the body cautiously to make sure there were no signs of life. Scott removed the flashlight from his pocket and hit the "on" switch. But it was not working, obviously damaged when he fell. But drawing close, they could tell the body was not breathing, which was not unusual for a Soulful One. The lightning again flickered in the darkness and they could see a milky substance excreting from the skull, which was mashed against the wall.

"I don't think he's alive but you better check," Scott said to Curt as he turned and looked down at the shadowy figure.

Curt gave his friend a scowling look but because of Scott's heroics, felt compelled to do anything asked at the moment. He slowly knelt as Scott kept a lookout. As Curt neared the body, a familiar smell arose and slammed him in the face. The same stench as the hundreds of French Huguenot metacarpals lying in the stone box.

Holding his breath, Curt examined the body. The thing's right arm was awkwardly twisted behind its back, surely broken in several places. With the next flash of lightning, Curt got a glimpse of the thing's hand on the ground with the palm up and fingers slightly curled. At least the four fingers it still had. Curt motioned for Scott to see. This confirmed their suspicion.

"Do you think this one and the other one that attacked us are the brothers?" Scott asked.

"There's no way of telling. If so, we're half way home." Curt replied.

Looking at the lifeless mass, Scott felt a chill run up his spine. Curt placed his hand on the thing's back to feel for movement. The skin through the material was rubbery, almost like silly putty, and the bone of the spinal column was coarse and exposed, as if uncovered by the epidermal. He quickly retracted his hand, which made Scott leap backward.

"What's the matter?" Scott asked excitedly.

Curt turned to look back at Scott, "Well his skin feels like jelly and I think his spinal cord took a vacation without him. Other than that, and the yellow shit oozing out of his cranium, I think he'll be back to playing the piano in no time."

"Seriously," Scott said.

"Seriously?" Curt replied. "This thing bought the farm, it kicked the bucket, whatever you want to call it, he's dead."

"Glad to hear it," Scott said with an obvious amount of relief.

As Curt placed his left hand on the deck and pushed himself up, the dormant corpse rolled on its back and gazed into his eyes with the pupils floating and the white brilliance screaming. Curt struggled to catch his balance but fell backward in panic. The thing raised sharply to a sitting position with its right arm dangling ineffectively by its side. More reacting than thinking, Scott raised his right foot and kicked the thing square between the eyes, sending the front half of his shoe deep into the skull and it stuck there. The thing raised its left arm, grabbed Scott's foot, ripped it out and pushed him to the ground not far from Curt.

As Curt and Scott lay dazed on the cold stone, the thing rose to its feet, milky fluid pouring from its head. Because of Scott's kick, only one eye was operable and it was attempting to focus. Nonetheless, the thing quickly approached their position.

From out of the darkness, a swoosh cut the air. A steel blade caught the thing directly in the neck. Its detached head lazily flew over the edge of the wall and into the courtyard below, landing with a disturbingly dull thud. The body collapsed and fell beside Scott, who immediately rolled away and scurried to his feet. "Jesus Christ!" he muttered.

"Home run," Tibu said in a matter-of-fact manner, holding the sword with two hands in front of him.

"If I get another scare like that my heart is going to drop into my scrotum," Curt said, panting as he wiped the sweat from his brow.

Scott stood up and brushed himself off, grabbing his chest which began throbbing again after the contact with the ground.

Tibu sat down on the ledge as Scott and Curt composed themselves. Curt explained to Tibu how they had heard the voices, which were now gone, and their run-in with the soulful Huguenots.

"Tibu, is this one of the brothers?" Scott asked hopefully.

"No," Tibu replied but offering no explanation.

"How can you be so damn sure? This one's face is pretty nasty. It could be Scott and I wouldn't know it," Curt said.

"Thanks," Scott added.

"It's just not," Tibu responded firmly. "It would not have been that easy."

The man was so confident in his answer, Curt didn't pursue further. Besides, Tibu had known these two when they were mortal.

"And just so you know," Tibu began, "my sword will only kill Pinot."

"What do you mean?" Scott snapped.

"A Soulful One can only be destroyed by his resurrector's weapon. Obviously, Reece brought Pinot back and this is Reece's sword," Tibu replied.

Curt gave him a disgusted look as Scott spoke, "When in the hell were you going to share this little secret with us? We spent the last 24 hours trying to figure out a way to stop these guys and you knew the answer the whole time?"

"I had another dream."

"You and your dreams," Curt barked. "You have more dreams than Dr. Martin Luther King. Why don't you dream we're on a tropic island with Bahamas Blues in our hands?" he said sarcastically.

"And how did you come about acquiring Reece's sword?" Scott asked.

"Actually, it belonged to your friend Pierre but once Reece killed with it, it was his. If this had been Reece," he said pointing to the headless body "it would have been ineffective."

"And you're sure this isn't Pinot you laid to waste?" Scott asked.

"Positive," Tibu responded.

Scott and Curt were silent as they looked out over the sullen deck.

"I guess it's safe to assume we're too late to stop the brothers from amassing the slain Huguenots," Tibu commented.

"Not exactly," Curt began. "It's obvious that the brothers have some of the fingers but Scott and I have assured they won't be bringing back the whole force."

They described how they had accidentally found the stone box and had restricted the contents and then dumped it in the moat. They told him how Sherri was chained up in the room adjacent to the powder magazine.

"Well, at least we're not up against 300 or more. How many bones did you estimate they retrieved?" Tibu asked.

"Sixty to sixty-five," Scott responded.

"Which is not good news if we've only got one sword to try and kill 65 of these things," Curt chimed in.

"You never answered my question. Where'd you get Reece's sword?"

"From the chapel at the cemetery. Reece left it there," Tibu replied.

"But how did you know . . ." Scott cut his own words off. "That's what Ambrose saw. The outline on the bench."

Tibu nodded. "Unfortunately, as I said, it won't help us against Reece. We still don't know who resurrected him. It may have been your friend Tucker. It may have been someone else. Unless we find out who that is, we'll have no way of permanently stopping Reece LeFlore."

The men were quiet.

Finally, Tibu spoke. "We can use this," he said pointing to the sword with its handle stuck in the wall.

"Well, you two stay here and pry it out," Curt said. "I'm going back down to check on Sherri. There's at least one of those monsters still roaming around in here."

"Then I'm going with you," Scott said and started to move when Tibu grabbed his shoulder.

"I need your help," Tibu said forcefully.

"Scott, stay here with Tibu. I'll be right back," Curt said as he turned toward the stairway.

"Curt, be careful," Scott said to his friend as he vanished in the darkness.

CHAPTER-THIRTY-FOUR

Curt made his way from the bastion along the length of the east wall, which paralleled the bay, and down the stairway. He was exceedingly cautious and ready to bolt at the first hint of trouble. He reached the bottom and walked on the rock pathway that bordered the courtyard. Before he reached Sherri's holding room, he stumbled upon an object that he inadvertently kicked onto the grass. He was surprised the object gave so easily.

Then he realized it was the head of the Huguenot Tibu had decapitated. A cold shiver ran over his body. He continued on as morose questions ran through his mind. Exactly what did I kick? Not what, what part, what feature? The image of the decaying face on the deck appeared and it gave him the shivers. Then images of Pierre flashed in his mind. How the veins, arteries and other innards, that he didn't know the name for, had hung haphazardly from his head affixed on the bedpost. The way it had seeped blood onto the mattress until it had dried into a crimson pool. The carving in his chest.

Seconds later he welcomed his arrival to the room. Forcefully, he flung the thoughts of head entrails, ruptured pupils and all other morbid considerations out of his mind. But the expected satisfaction of seeing Sherri waned and he became troubled when he saw the doorway to the corridor was bathed in black. He had expected to see glints of light. It was possible Sherri had heard someone approaching and didn't want to let on she had a flashlight. It would make for a nice weapon. She was probably inside scared to death, assuming he was one of the brothers approaching. He suddenly felt very sympathetic to her predicament and wanted more than anything else in the world to set her free and get her out of this god-forsaken place.

But outside the entrance he knew something was wrong.

He tried peering through the opening, anxious to proceed inside.

"Sherri," he called. His pulse quickened when there was no immediate response.

"Sherri, are you here?" he asked softly. Still no answer.

"Sherri, please answer." Nothing.

He began imagining her fate. Maybe one of those *things* he and Scott had encountered had killed her. Maybe she'd fallen asleep or passed out from exhaustion. Those were two plausible explanations as to why she might not be responding. I wish I had a flashlight, he thought.

But if she were still alive, he'd be damned if he were going to leave her here to perish. He moved through the entryway and made contact with the left wall with his outstretched palms. Continuing, his hands glided along the stone as his heartbeat bounced off his eardrums in the dead quiet of the enclosure.

Several steps in he called for her again.

No reply.

Sweat congregated on his brow. Each step became smaller and more deliberate. The last thing he wanted to do was step on the woman or possibly fall on her, injuring both of them.

Lightly touching the stone, he gradually came upon the area where he expected her to be, based on the distance from the doorway as he remembered it. He thought about how she had smiled at him and told him to hurry back. This image now tortured him.

Using his right foot as a probe, he stretched out and felt the ground and wall ahead and came up empty. Taking another step to the right he repeated the search, extending his leg as far as it would go and using it to seek her position.

"God please don't let her be dead," he said out loud. His fear began to multiply when he took another step to his right and still nothing. He had a horrible feeling the next step would have him happening upon her deceased body.

"Sherri. Please, please don't be here," he now said realizing that it was better if the brothers had taken her from this place. But his heart sank and his body went almost limp as his foot tapped something hard on the stone floor that gently gave way. The way a limp head might fall to the side if easily kicked.

For a few seconds he stood motionless making countless pleas into the darkness. His thoughts strained and his muscles tightened as he slowly eased his foot and placed his toe against the object and pushed again. This time the object moved aside with a sound Curt clearly recognized before hitting the wall. It was the sound of an object rolling. The crinkling sounds of plastic rotation. He quickly knelt down and felt along the wall until his hand came to rest on the cylindrical shape. Gathering it in, he found the "on" switch. The beam of light shined on the embedded spike and attached chain, minus its captive.

He scanned the room with the flashlight but it was barren. For the moment he felt relieved. He still had no idea where Sherri was and felt badly about the situation he had left her in. He had departed, providing her only with a flashlight and a promise that he would soon return to free her. A flashlight she no longer had and a promise Curt could no longer keep.

After several hardy tugs, with Tibu and Scott sitting on the deck and bracing their feet against the wall, the sword came free.

"What good is this thing going to do us?" Scott said standing up. "You said in order to kill these things it had to be the weapon of the person responsible for bringing them back to life."

"That is true," Tibu began. "Although this sword will not destroy Pinot or Reece or any of the other Soulful Ones for that matter, it can help slow them down."

"I'm not sure I follow you but I'm not going to argue."

"Where did you say you heard the . . ." Tibu began before Scott interrupted him.

"Shhhhh," Scott whispered holding his finger, to his lips. In the distance, from the direction of the San Carlos Bastion tower, the voices had resumed and this time it was obvious they were coming from the other side of the wall outside the fort.

Without saying a word, Tibu's facial expression hardened and he began walking. Scott followed closely behind, struggling to keep pace with the Indian without breaking into a trot. As they approached the small tower in the northeast corner, the voices intensified and Scott could make out the sound of splashing water, as if someone was dropping golf balls into the moat one by one every few seconds.

When Tibu reached the tower, he strained to look out the center of three windowed openings. Scott came up fast behind him. The opening was too narrow for both men to look through at the same time so he stood behind Tibu frustrated.

"What's going on down there?" Scott whispered excitedly as he heard the voices in a language that he assumed was French.

Tibu was silent. He raised up on his tiptoes to see more of whatever was occurring below.

"Who is it? Is it the brothers? What's going on?" Scott asked in a tone one degree above a whisper.

"You white men have no patience. Been that way for 400 years. I kept thinking you'd evolve," Tibu muttered as he backed away from the window and Scott wasted no time moving into place. "Yes, it's Pinot and Reece."

In the scant light below, Scott could easily make out the figures of two men. One wore a white shirt and the other a dark blue or black shirt. They stood facing the fort on the thin stone ledge bordering the side of the moat. As they conversed back and forth in French, every so often, the man on the right would lift his arm and toss an object into the water below. At the conclusion of each throw the water would thrash and churn violently for a few moments and then go still. A sick sensation settled in the pit of Scott's gut. He knew exactly what the brothers were doing. He pulled himself out of the window and looked at Tibu.

"These guys are chumming with fingers. We have got to do something to stop them," Scott said quietly and slowly trying to hide his fear. Tibu again said nothing but nodded his head in agreement.

Tibu stuck his head through the opening again but this time he was not so discreet. "Hey you," he screamed. "Come and get us!" Then he drew away from the window and faced Scott again.

"Well, I stopped them," he said as Scott stared at him with an expression of blankness.

"What have you done!" Scott blurted out.

"I did what you wanted. I stopped them from resurrecting more soldiers. Of course now they're on their way up here to kill us."

Scott leaped to the window and scoured the area below. Pinot and Reece were gone.

"That's some plan you had there, Tibu!" Scott yelled sarcastically as he ran from the tower onto the gundeck with the Indian following. "Bet you put considerable thought into that one. You're a regular General Patton you are," he shouted as he hit the stairwell at full speed. The two descended the stairs skipping steps at a time the best they could in the darkness. They were fortunate neither rolled to the bottom. Scott stopped short of the last step causing Tibu to almost run him over.

"Wait a minute, wait a minute," Scott said panting. "How in the hell are they going to get in here?" Then he suddenly remembered Sherri. They had already been inside the fort once.

Tibu broke ahead of Scott and streaked across the courtyard. When Scott caught up to him, Tibu replied as he ran, "The same way I got in probably. There's an opening on the west wall just under the moat's surface that leads to the middle storage room. The corridor angles up slightly, which brings it above the water line. Inside, it's covered by a slab of stone in the floor that can be removed and snuggly nestled back into place. It's been there since the fort was built in 1675. A secret tunnel you might say."

That explains Sherri getting wet, Scott thought as they reached the walkway on the west side of the courtyard.

"So did you replace the opening when you came in?" Scott asked through labored breathing.

Without answering, Tibu struck the door of the middle storage room with his shoulder at a full gallop and crashed inside landing on the floor and rolling on his side twice before coming to a stop. Scott followed Tibu inside the room. Tibu quickly got up and felt his way along the right wall until he found a switch. A quick flip and a dim light came on. It reminded Scott of Cody's nightlight, except that it covered a much more expansive area than his son's bedroom.

The room was barren save for a small wooden stand with a cement head capped by an angled metal plaque with an inscription against the left wall. It contained some historical information about the origin of the room and how the Spanish used it to store wheat and barley. The back wall had a solid five-foot wide ledge that jutted out to form a three-foot high stair step. Tibu moved to the right corner at the base of the stair step and stood in place looking around.

"Where's the opening to the tunnel?" Scott asked.

Tibu looked down. "Below me," he said staring at the slab beneath his feet. Just then voices could be heard coming from the ground followed by a scraping sound against stone. Pinot and Reece had arrived and were trying to gain entry back inside. Tibu sat down on the single slab. If not for the fact that the sand had been knocked out of the bordering cracks, the piece would have fit seamlessly within the puzzled flooring. As it was, it was still a perfect cover. In all these years, no one had ever discovered that below the stone was a passageway between the storage room and the outside.

As Tibu waited patiently the voices and myriad of underlying sounds increased. Apparently, the brothers were becoming annoyed that the doorway had gained weight. Tibu remained still, with his arms folded across his chest.

"You need me on top as well?" Scott asked feeling useless.

"No. Go and get your friend and then return," he said very nonchalantly.

"Why?" Scott asked with a confused look.

"Just do it. I can hold them out," the Indian replied.

Knowing it would be a waste of time to question Tibu's reasoning, Scott turned and headed through the door and back onto the walkway in the courtyard. Outside, the sky had turned an eerie orange shade and visibility had increased ten-fold. He could see the clouds rapidly passing by and could only imagine how strong the winds must be to force that type of motion. Scott glanced at his watch. 10:38. How can it be this light in the middle of the night? Is it possible I lost complete track of time and it's 10:38 Thursday morning? It can't be. That's a twelve hour difference!

Scott continued toward the powder magazine, completely confused. It was like awakening from a sound sleep and having everything and everyone around you going full speed without waiting for you to comprehend.

He made his way to the corridor and through the entrance leading to the powder magazine where he expected to hear Curt chatting with Sherri. As he drew close, the unexpected silence was awkward. He turned on the flashlight and aimed the beam at the wall.

Sherri was gone and Curt was nowhere in sight. Scott speculated that his friend might have found a way to free Sherri and the two had left, possibly going back to the gundeck. Then again, they might have been captured -- or worse. Scott entered the room using the light to survey every inch of the enclosure. Thankfully, there were no bodies lying about and no blood stains that he could see. But there was also no trace of Curt or Sherri. Moving farther into the room as quietly as he could, he stopped in the middle and turned to collect his thoughts.

Remain calm, he reminded himself. If you lose your head you're defeated. Scott did something he had not done in a long time, he said a silent prayer. He prayed to God that his friend was somewhere else in the fort looking for him at that very moment. His doubts about God were still solid but for the benefit of his friend he wasn't going to close out any aid which might generate his safe return.

"C'mon Curt," he whispered barely audible, hopeful his friend would somehow reply. After waiting several seconds, he discouragingly turned to exit the room when he heard a slight knock coming from behind. He wheeled around aiming his flashlight at the nondescript back stone wall. He carefully surveyed the flat surface and waited for the sound to repeat itself. It suddenly occurred to him that the noise might have come from the opening to the powder magazine just below the lighted area. He slowly moved toward it. Were my ears deceiving me? No, he felt confident he had heard *something*. Maybe it was the stone settling . . . like the fort hadn't had 400 plus years to settle already. Then again, maybe it was the other Soulful One. The first one that had attacked them on the gundeck.

As he gathered his nerve to proceed under the ledge and enter the powder magazine he paused to kneel down and shined the light in. From his vantage point, the enclosure was empty. But he also couldn't see the entire room. The walls adjacent to either side of the opening were not in view and wouldn't be until he entered. It would be a dangerous move to enter if someone was lying in wait. He would be an easy target as he crouched down to get through.

He stood up and retreated backward a few steps, listening for any further sounds emanating from inside. When he heard none, he considered his options. One, get the hell out of there. A nice safe play that would assure he would live to fight again. But what if Curt and Sherri were chained and gagged inside against the wall? Two, proceed through the opening and, once inside, defend himself as best as he could. This would leave him severely susceptible to an ambush and the thought made his stomach swell and turn as if a bad case of diarrhea had invaded his intestines. Or Three, charge in.

Three was the craziest and it came to him out of the blue. It would require some precision, a great deal of skill and a certain amount of insanity. It would also require something he didn't have but knew where to find. He backed out of the room and turned into the courtyard, moving quickly. He ascended the stairwell and cautiously made his way onto the gundeck. He continued along the east deck past the Huguenot's headless corpse, but not before inadvertently stepping in the pool of yellow fluid resonating from the body and flowing toward the third cannon. He looked away but it was too late. He gagged, fighting back the stomach juices that had risen in his throat and landed at the back of his tongue. Although it initially felt like the warm bile would fill his mouth, it regressed to leave a lingering putrid taste.

With the image of the grotesque body glued in his mind, he kept shuffling his feet rapidly on the stone flooring in an attempt to wipe the fluid from his soles. He continued on and reached the tower on the San Carlos Bastion where he'd left the sword propped inside when he and Tibu had left in a hurry. Given the oddities of the evening, he was surprised to see it was still there. He grabbed the weapon and walked back to the gun-deck, carefully taking a path that kept him well clear of the body and the fluid. Then he descended the stairway to the courtyard.

When he reached the stone walkway, he looked across the courtyard in the direction of the storage rooms on the west side and wondered how Tibu was doing. The doors to all the rooms were closed and Scott desperately tried to think back to whether he had closed it upon leaving. He could not recall. Nor was he sure which room Tibu was in. They had rushed in so fast and he had left not paying much attention. But since there was no sign of Pinot and Reece, he felt sure Tibu was still preventing their entrance or at least he hoped he was.

Scott made his way carefully through the entryway into the corridor leading to the powder magazine. The room was still painfully quiet. Not wanting to give his presence away, Scott moved stealthily. He turned the flashlight on and shined it just to the left of the opening to the powder magazine, careful not to allow any light to get inside. Scott gently placed the flashlight on the ground keeping the light's destination on the wall constant.

Now for the hard part, he thought. He moved silently back to the entryway. Moving into the courtyard, he retrieved the sword he had left on the walk and stood 20 feet in front of the opening. Scott took several more steps backward as his mind calculated the distance. He reached into his pocket and pulled out his key chain with the Walt Disney World pen light that Katie had bought for him during their trip last April to the Magic Kingdom. He held the sword firmly in front at a slight upward angle and took several deep breaths.

Waiting wasn't doing him any good and his blood pressure was rising. It's now or never, he thought. He started forward quickly, focusing on the beam of light against the back wall. Remember, the opening is to the right and I need to go lower than three feet to clear, he reminded himself. If I do that, I'll be fine, he thought, as he increased his speed and entered the corridor. He approached the wall at a full gallop with the sword extended as doubt clouded his thoughts as to whether there was really an opening to the right of the beam in the absolute darkness. But there was no time for second-guessing. In essence, he ran forward with blind faith.

When he was 10 feet away, he dove forward, flipping the small penlight on but not attempting to guide the light. He felt relief as the sword continued through the opening instead of jamming back into his face. Clearing underneath, he slid on the smooth rock. But before he stopped, the sword hit the far wall. He had forgotten to take into account how small the room was and that he might cross completely to the other side.

Fortunately, his momentum had slowed so that the contact was abrupt but not too forceful. Unfortunately, the sword flew out of his hands upon impact and careened away from his body leaving him defenseless.

As he lay on the cold stone clearing his head, a light pointed directly in his face blinding him. Scott tried to shield his eyes with one hand while frantically searching for the sword with the small flashlight in the other. He had a horrid feeling, waiting for some violent act to be committed against him. He lost all bodily functions as he urinated on himself.

"What are you doing? I nearly took a whack at you!" a familiar voice asked excitedly, trying to keep the volume down. With trembling fingers and through sweat that had fallen into his eyes, Scott focused on Curt's face. He still couldn't speak.

Scott rolled onto his back and glared up at his friend. "What are you doing in here?" he asked exasperated.

"I was hiding," Curt replied. "After I came into the room and found Sherri missing I heard people coming down the stairs in a hurry and didn't want to take any chances."

"Between you and Tibu, with his ingenious plan of getting the LeFlores attention, you two could teach a military tactics course," Scott said as he rose to his feet with the help of Curt. His shoulder ached from where he had smashed into the stone and the pain from the gash on his chest flamed up again. "What happened to Sherri?"

"They must have taken her," Curt replied. "Hey, what smells?"

"Don't ask," Scott said with a serious voice.

"You didn't," Curt said.

"Shut up," Scott replied firmly.

"It's only normal for a human to lose control in a terrifying situation," Curt said. "Good thing you haven't eaten solid food in a while."

Even Scott smiled at that comment as he felt the warmth congregate in his crotch and partially down the legs of his blue jeans. "If I have a choice between pissing on myself or dying I'll take the self inflicted golden shower anytime," he said.

As they left the room and returned to the outer area, Scott explained what had happened with him and Tibu and how the Indian was holding the brothers at bay. Curt commented about the bizarre sky as they hurriedly walked across the courtyard, constantly watching against attack. They approached the door of the storage room where Scott was reasonably certain he had left Tibu and gently pushed it open to find the man sitting silently on the stone with his arms folded.

The sound of the brothers conversing and occasionally scraping the earth below continued to rise from the ground.

"What took you so long?" Tibu asked looking at the stain on Scott's pants.

"Scott had a little bit of an accident," Curt quickly spoke up.

"Sounds like they don't give up easily," Scott said referring to the Frenchmen and ignoring Curt's comment.

"They have no choice," Tibu replied.

"What do you mean?" Curt asked.

"They're stuck. Before they left the northeast corner of the fort they must have somehow distracted the Kilgotian. Maybe they threw him a few extra fingers. I don't know. But whatever they did, it kept him at that corner long enough for them to make their way to the west side of the fort, jump into the moat and climb up the tunnel," Tibu said. "If they go back into the moat now the fish might be waiting for them. They're not willing to risk that fate."

"And exactly what would *that fate* be?" Scott asked.

"You still don't understand do you? The Kilgotian fish is the key. Not only will it give life but it will also destroy it."

"You're right. I don't understand," Curt said.

"Well Pinot and Reece do," Tibu began. "If they go back into the water and the fish sees them, they'll be destroyed. It'll rip them apart."

"I thought the fish had one favorite food. Fingers," Scott said.

"That fish was born of good but now dwells in evil. If you give him any flesh to consume, living or dead, he will do so without remorse or feeling. And will devour it with amazing tenacity."

Tibu continued, "When I was a young boy, I was playing alone near the pond at Fort Caroline late one afternoon. As the sun began to set, a man and a woman from the fort were strolling along the woods and happened upon the pond as they were playing lover's games and hiding amongst the thick trees. The woman happened to wedge herself between several oaks and found herself on the bank of the water. She called out to the man to join her and they would bathe in the quiet surroundings in their own secluded pond. He eagerly joined her and together they undressed each other. As they disrobed, they placed their clothes neatly on a bush at the water's edge. Being a boy of 11, I watched anticipating their actions. As they stepped into the water near the bank, they went waist deep standing on the algae coated bottom. When they turned to kiss, their screams filled the air at a feverish pitch as the water churned all around them. I watched from behind a tree. I screamed out and began crying. But the suffering and agony didn't last long. A few seconds later they were gone as their bodies crumbled below the surface and the lake turned a burnt shade of red. Then, the area was as silent as it had been before their arrival. Even the birds chose to remain quiet as the evening settled on the land. I never went near the place again nor did I tell anyone about it. I was afraid of the punishment I might suffer for being there. As you know, it wasn't until some years later I found out about the pond's true secret and realized the power of the fish.

"From what you've shared with me," Tibu continued, "it was created by your God for a purpose. Now it needs to leave this world. You two need to get the Kilgotian from the moat. I'm going to stay here and guard this entrance," Tibu said.

Scott and Curt looked at each other with blank expressions and then turned back to the Indian. The stone slab he sat on slowly lifted at the front an inch and a half and Tibu leaned forward shifting his weight causing it to fall back into place. The voices underneath became more and more agitated.

"Hurry," Tibu said. "I will not be able to hold them out for much longer."

Still wanting to ask Tibu how they were supposed to get the Kilgotian out of the moat if it had the appetite of a platoon of piranha, a more important question took priority.

"How are we supposed to get out of the fort?" Scott asked.

"Lower the drawbridge," Tibu replied looking down, watching the slab for any movement. "The switch is to the left of the door".

"Okay, and how do we get the Kilgotian?" Curt asked.

"Anyway you can," Tibu responded. There was a trace of discouragement in his tone.

"Great," Scott commented and turned pulling Curt with him.

The two men exited the room and turned right. The sky was still a brilliant orange and Scott glanced down at his watch. If Tibu's forecast was wrong, Damon would hit with full force in less than eight hours.

Scott and Curt stood on the moat's ledge peering into the water below. Exiting the fort had been considerably easier than entering, as the switch to lower the drawbridge had been exactly where Tibu had told them it would be. The massive locks that had appeared so ominous to the men as they had crossed the moat were more to keep the door itself intact than to secure the bridge. A simple flip of a lever and the mechanical ramp slowly fell into place and the two walked around the rope still hanging from the top of the gundeck. They were anxious as to what they might find outside but all was clear.

Now, standing at the northeast corner of the moat in the same spot the LeFlores had been feeding the Kilgotian, Scott and Curt looked down at the fish hovering near the surface. It continuously boiled the water with its tail as if to say, "Feed me or leave me alone. But if you stay and get careless, there will be a deadly price to pay."

They were awed by the amount of natural light coming from the sky. It was as bright as full morning and, if not for the extensive cloud cover that preceded the impending storm, it would have been time to don sunglasses. The only possible explanation was that the hurricane had triggered some bizarre atmospheric condition.

Scott looked to the left out across the water and to the far side at Anastasia Island. The wind had died and the water was serene. For one of the few times he could remember, the bay resembled glass. It was as if a huge sheet of saran wrap had been gently placed on top to keep any ripples or disruptions in check and preserve the pristine setting. The disparity between the calmness of the bay and the frantic rush of the clouds above seemed to epitomize the week for Scott and Curt.

"You know what's really bothering me? Besides the fact Pinot and Reece are still around and they've got Sherri?" Curt asked.

"The bright orange sky at midnight?" Scott replied.

"Besides that. What's really bothering me is you said you saw them feed this creature right?"

"Pretty sure. It was dark but they were feeding him something. It stands to reason it was the missing fingers," Scott said.

"So when do we get to meet the new Soulful Ones, as Tibu calls them?" Curt asked.

"I'm sure it will be sooner than we want. What we better do now is get this thing out of the moat," Scott said pointing down at the disruption in the water.

"I can tell you right now, we're not going in there after him," Curt said shaking his head back and forth.

"You got that right," Scott said and turned. "C'mon, I have an idea."

Curt did not reply. He had nothing so whatever Scott had would be their strategy.

As they walked, Scott told Curt his plan. Although somewhat ludicrous, it made considerably more sense than the alternatives. They made their way back to the parking lot where they opened the trunk and grabbed the necessary gear. Rod & reel, scoop net, and a tackle box full of an assortment of hooks, line, sinkers and lures. Everything an angler could ask for. Scott remembered seeing the items on Tibu's list at the house and had a feeling why they were included.

The men returned to the northeast corner of the fort with the equipment. They continually surveyed the landscape for activity but saw no signs of life. For the time being, it appeared the only Soulful Ones around were being held captive by Tibu.

Scott's plan was simple. The natural aggressiveness of the Kilgotian fish would play right into their hands. Scott figured he could rig a topwater lure, make a single cast, pop the line a few times and hook the fish.

Tying on a Floatin' Beetle, Scott clipped off the excess line and tested the strength of the knot with one long tug. The knot held secure.

Curt gazed into the dingy green water below and could see the swirling fish just beneath the surface, moving rapidly then slowing as if someone was turning a blender from puree to beat and then back to puree. A single gust of wind blew and Scott waited for it to subside. When it did he reared back and let loose. The lure floated lazily through the air and, with sufficient force, smacked into the side of the fort's wall, disintegrating into multiple pieces. Scott had considerably overshot the mark.

"Oops!" Scott said.

"Yeah, oops buddy," Curt mocked.

Retrieving the partial lure, Scott tied on a replacement.

Curt watched Scott prepare the rig and then turned to look down at the fish. The water was still. The Kilgotian had been circling eight feet out, directly in front of the bulkhead and had either gone deeper into the stained water or had moved away from the area.

"Great. I can't see him," Curt said.

"Neither can I."

The two waited patiently for several minutes. But the ripples and other telltale signs of the fish were gone and the moat appeared lifeless. Curt turned to the right and scanned the entire north side. For as far as he could see, the water was calm. Maybe the Kilgotian had swum around to the other side of the fort?

Scott considered roving the edges in search. It should be easy to spot. The creature always seemed to swim a few inches below the water, never breaching its environment, but revealing its position by the commotion it created.

"I'm open for suggestions," Curt finally said.

"Let's walk the moat. There are three more sides he may have gone to," Scott replied. He started to walk and then abruptly stopped.

"What is it?" Curt asked.

"It's just odd. Hold on, I'm going to make one more cast in the last location we saw it." With that, Scott flipped the bale open and drew the rod over his head slowly. In an instant, he brought it forward, releasing the line with his finger and the lure glided gracefully through the air. It landed just before the wall with a splash. Floating on the surface, Scott imparted no human intervention, rather, letting the lure lay motionless.

The tiny circular waves flowed away from the lure and quickly disbanded. The surface again became peaceful, reflecting the orange tint from above. The silver three-inch lure remained stationary and undisturbed. Scott intently watched for any sign of the fish as both men focused their attention on the floating deception. After a minute Scott decided to create some artificial movement. He tightened the line and made a short, abrupt tug. The Floatin' Beetle twitched, dove under then quickly rose to the surface. In distance, it had traveled three inches. The lure's motion, combined with the smart pop, presented a stark contrast to the stillness and Scott felt his muscles tighten in preparation for a strike.

Again the lure lay still as the ripples diminished and the fort's gray wall reflected off the water's glassy covering. The men stood frozen on the ledge in anticipation. Another short, quick pop and the lure temporarily submerged then reappeared. Scott took a deep breath and twitched the lure again, relaxing the rod tip to a 45-degree angle. It was obvious the Kilgotian had moved on.

Scott glanced up at the top of the wall, scanning the gundeck for any sign of movement. Content, he turned his head to the right and looked out at San Marco Boulevard, one hundred yards to the west. It was completely barren. Scott perceived the city as a shell of its former self. San Marco Boulevard was usually lined with tourists visiting the Oldest City and locals making a living by carting patrons through the streets in horse drawn carriages and on historic trolley car tours. Scott's mind wandered as he could picture the out-of-towners canvassing the streets with their baggy shorts and tee shirts wearing cameras around their necks and, in some cases, a bright orange round sticker on their chest that represented participation with an organized tour group.

Suddenly, Scott felt the rod being yanked forward. He nearly lost his grasp as his arms extended.

"He took it under!" Curt said excitedly.

Scott turned his eyes back to where the lure had been floating. The serene water had been replaced with churning bubbles. The area appeared to have been flushed and was now boiling back to the surface. Scott quickly rebounded from the initial shock and raised the tip of the rod into the air and held firm. The rod bowed and the drag screamed as he hooked into the beast. For a 12-inch fish, it began putting up a tremendous battle.

"That damn thing is strong!" Curt added as the two watched the fish head west down the moat taking line. The streaking creature made a path away from the men cutting a wake in the tranquil water. The rod strained as the powerful fish swam furiously. Unlike a large mouth bass, which Scott was accustomed to fishing, this thing never broke the surface in an attempt to throw the hook. Instead, it chose a strategy of hiding beneath the surface and twisting and fighting with tremendous agility and force.

The line continued to strip off as the fish ran. Scott glanced down at the spool of 12-pound test racing from the reel. The reel was fat and it appeared he still had plenty of line to give. His strategy was to just let the fish go, let it expend large amounts of energy fighting against the drag. Eventually, maybe 10 or 15 minutes later, it should tire and Scott would be able to turn its direction. Then again, this thing had been resting for centuries. It might never tire, he thought worriedly.

Thirty seconds into the fight the line went limp and Scott had the same disheartened feeling he experienced anytime he lost a fish. Hoping the Kilgotian had simply changed direction and was heading toward them, he began to wind furiously attempting to catch up. If the fish had turned, it would be much easier for the beast to dislodge the hook with the line slack. But as Scott kept winding it was soon painfully obvious that the Kilgotian had gotten off. Fifteen yards out, the lure rose unattended to the surface.

"Damn!" was the only way Scott knew how to respond. Retrieving the lure the men were amazed at what they saw. The lower third of the Floatin' Beetle was missing -- snapped off just above the last treble hook.

"Ever had a bass do that?" Curt asked.

"I've never had any fish do that," Scott replied. Ironically, this exchange of words reminded Scott of a scene from *Jaws*.

"That's a comforting thought," Curt remarked. "Look! He's back!" he said pointing out where the water was swirling and churning, more tumultuous than before. "Scottman, I think you upset the little guy!"

Without another word, Scott quickly tied on a new lure. He reared back and cast again with precision into the middle of the fray. The lure landed with a subtle splash. After several quick pops he reeled in and repeated the process with another masterfully accurate cast. After allowing the lure to settle, he tapped several times but to no avail. The Kilgotian had either lost interest or had a much higher level of intelligence than the average fish.

"He's ignoring you better than my ex-wife when I wanted sex," Curt said after the third fruitless cast and retrieve. "What do we do now?"

"We try again but with different bait," Scott said.

Curt looked bewildered as Scott reached into his pocket. "We're going to use this," he said raising his hand to Curt's face. Stunned, Curt pulled his head back with a distasteful expression.

"Don't do that!" Curt said as he stared at the object and held his nose trying to avoid the stench.

Scott bent down and placed the object on the ground and then reached into the tackle box to get a number five hook.

"Do you always walk around with fingers in your pocket?" Curt asked.

"Only when I'm trying to catch the Kilgotian," Scott replied as he clipped off the Floatin' Beetle and tied on a single hook. He tested the knot for durability and then picked up the metacarpal still baring the stench of time. Standing up, Scott drove the hook in the middle joint of the bone. It went in with a crackling sound both men could have done without hearing.

"I think I'm going to be sick," Curt commented.

About an inch and a half of finger hung on one side of the hook and another inch on the other. It reminded Scott of a large, very thick earthworm but smelled considerably worse.

"A fish that eats fingers," Scott said more to himself than for Curt's benefit. "What kind of messed up situation is this? This is like some asinine headline you'd see on the cover of a grocery store tabloid or maybe the lead story on one of those stupid TV shows. Are we really here doing this?"

"I'm afraid so, buddy," Curt replied. "What's even worse we still don't know what good it is to catch this thing," he said pointing to the disturbed water.

Scott shook his head in agreement and cast the hook with the foul smelling bait into the swirling water. Hand feeding several additional feet of line, he waited patiently for the rod to bow and the action to begin. But after a minute of waiting his impatience took over and he retrieved the bait. More accurately, he retrieved an empty hook. It had been picked clean. No bone, no bone marrow, even the smell was gone.

"My God," was all Curt could say.

"I never felt him." Scott reached into his pocket and retrieved another finger as Curt looked at him with surprise. "Was there a sale on those things at the bait shop?" Curt quipped.

Scott did not answer. He had transitioned into the serious fisherman as he was known to do when he felt he had been outsmarted by the prey. He baited the second finger in the same manner as the first and flung the rig directly into the center of the churning activity. This time he did not supply any additional line, but kept the monofilament as taut as possible. A minute passed and he raised the hook to find the thief had struck again.

"Do you believe this?" he muttered raising the line and grabbing the hook in his left hand while holding the rod in the crux of his right arm. "I'm down to the last one," he said.

"Good," Curt responded, trying to loosen Scott up. "I was beginning to think you started a collection. Tell me though, genius that I am, I know where you got these disgusting things but how did you know we would need them?"

"I just had a feeling." Scott looked at Curt and forced a slight smile and then returned to the business of removing the last finger and securing it to the hook.

"Of course you realize you've just increased the Soulful population by two?"

"Yeah. Yeah I know," Scott said with a sigh. "But do we have any choice?"

"Nope. Now let's catch this bastard."

Scott opened the bale and secured the line in his finger. Raising the rod over his head, he gently whipped it forward and the rig landed two feet beyond the area of water where the Kilgotian swam in an amazingly furious circle. Disappointed by his inaccuracy, he started to retrieve in order to recast. But as he did, the Kilgotian slammed the bait with full force, straining the rod tip and almost knocking Scott off balance.

"Got ya!" Scott yelled as the beast followed the same strategy as before, swimming horizontally away from the men and heading west to the far end of the moat.

"I'm not losing you this time!" Scott growled as Curt watched in amazement.

Again, the fish was amazingly strong. The drag, which Scott had set on 6, alternated between a high pitched squeal and a low pitched whine depending on the creature's speed.

Thirty seconds passed and Scott tightened the drag to 8 and watched for the effect. The torturous strain on the drag was merciless and the line continued screaming out. He glanced down and now felt uncomfortable with the amount of line remaining.

"More drag!" Curt said excitedly.

Scott increased the drag tension to 10, not chancing the maximum of 12. Surely this would slow him down. But the sound remained constant as the line spooled off. In his estimation, Scott believed the fish had to be near the northwest corner by now. If it made the 90-degree left turn toward the south, it would stand a good chance of cutting the line on the Fort's corner.

"We've got to move," Scott said with amazing calmness.

Scott walked along the moat's edge, rapidly attempting to gather in any excess line with each step. At this pace the fish was still winning. Scott began a slow trot, winding furiously. Moments later he was into a full run followed closely by Curt. Scott could tell the fish had turned the northwest corner and was moving south along the wall. The line briefly hugged the corner but Scott's speed brought him around to the west side. Several more seconds of friction against the coquina would have shredded the line. Once Scott cleared the fort's corner and the line was free, he stopped to resume the fight.

"I don't know if this is possible," Scott said panting. "He's too strong."

Curt watched his friend look down at the reel and hesitate. He was struggling with the decision. Scott's mind flashed to his backyard pond and the fish he had lost Friday night by overcompensating the drag.

"Do it man. You have no choice!" Curt shouted.

Scott reached behind the base of the unit and gently turned the knob displaying 11 and then 12 as the line whined and went silent. Scott held his breath as he looked at the rod and the monofilament stretching into the water.

Both men stared into the water and then at each other.

Scott slowly began winding. It was dead weight. It was as if he had hooked the bottom and was bringing in a 75-pound rock. He began to fear that either the line or the bowed rod itself would break. There was no fight or movement on the other end. Just a slow, steady, monstrous weight.

It was Scott's will against whatever was hooked on the other end.

"I don't know," Scott said in a worried voice. "There's no action. The line is lifeless. I'll be surprised if he's still there. I feel like I'm bringing in a cannon."

"Just keep winding," Curt encouraged his friend auspiciously.

A short distance from the ledge, the fish rose beneath the surface and stared at the men. Was he baiting them? He slowly flapped his fins but put up no resistance. Its eyes were bright yellow, possibly capturing the reflection of the tinted sky. The pupils rolled fluidly first from side to side and then up and down. The creature appeared completely diabolical. It was a frightening sight. But the ancient fish also had a distinct intelligence. Scott was sure of it. He could sense its thoughts, sense its manipulation. It was beyond evil. It was something menacing, completely lacking compassion.

"Am I catching this thing or is he hunting us?" Scott asked.

"Don't say that," Curt replied nervously as his skin crawled. "I had a dream about this thing dragging me under the water. It looked just like it does now."

"I don't like this at all," Scott said and stopped winding. The fish was dormant in the water, still eyeing the two of them, gently moving its fins and pushing water through its gills, its body glowing below the grainy surface.

"Nevertheless, let's get him on land. I feel better about my chances with him up here," Curt said bending down to grab the line in order to hoist the fish up to the ledge. But before he could, the fish dove and turned, leaving a bubbling trail. The drag sang out at a blistering pace. Curt had barely gotten a grip on the line and paid the price. It cut a four-inch rip in the palm of his hand and nearly pulled him into the moat. The rod bent in half as the fish ran.

But then, after the short burst, it paused. Was it resting or was it just teasing them?

Again the Kilgotian made a short run and Scott prayed the line would hold. He had lost his share of large fish by trying to horse them in before they were exhausted. He was determined to remain patient and allow the fish to wear itself out, if that was possible.

"Are you okay?" He turned briefly to check on Curt.

"Yeah, I'll be fine," Curt responded, clamping his left hand over his right palm to stop the bleeding. "Now I'm pissed. As soon as you land that thing I'm going to fillet it."

The fish was 75 feet out and still heading south from the northwest corner of the moat. But it seemed to be losing momentum and energy as it took the drag more sporadically.

"He's running out of juice," Scott said.

"Good. You got a sharp knife? Oh, forget that, I've got the trusty sword I'll use to slice him open. I can't believe I had the bastard in my shirt against my skin Monday morning! I'll be right back," Curt said as he turned and ran back to the northeast corner, picked up the weapon and returned.

Curt approached the stone edge of the moat next to Scott. Getting down on his hands and knees, still clutching the sword, Curt begin to sing, "Here fishy, fishy, fishy," in a monotone voice. His hand dripped blood into the water.

The Kilgotian had stopped again and Scott suspected he had the creature turned. As he began to reel the withered fish in, a piercing scream shattered the silence. Holding the rod upright, Scott spun around as a man dressed in tattered clothes charged with a sword extended outward like a bull aiming for a matador. The chilling grimace on his face was nearly as terrifying as the watery eyes floating in their sockets. Just before the weapon reached Scott's chest, Curt rose up on his knees, turned and hurled his sword forcefully with both hands. The point drove into the attacker's chest, striking the rib cage with a crunching sound. To Curt's astonishment, the sword not only went in, it disappeared into the torso and then magically came out the other side, landing five yards behind. The thing momentarily wobbled in placed with its eyes rolling back and forth, then fell backward and convulsed violently on the ground. Curt stood up and quickly ran over to get the sword. It was covered in the same yellowish substance Scott had stepped in on the gundeck from their headless friend. Scott, who had nearly slipped into the moat, tried to compose himself. He checked the line for tension and was relieved to find the fish was still on.

As Scott leaned over to catch his breath he looked at the body still convulsing on the grass beside Curt. Curt had taken a handkerchief out of his pocket and was wiping the yellow substance off the blade.

"You know he's not dead, right," Scott said.

"He's got to be close. The sword went through him."

"But remember what Tibu said. It would have to be the weapon of the one who made him soulful," Scott said.

Curt stood up and walked toward Scott as the body on the ground ceased shaking and now was silent. "That sonofabitch over there is dead," he said pointing to the still body. "He isn't going anywhere. Besides, if Tibu is right, maybe he's one of the ones we accidentally brought back feeding that damn fish. In that case, this is the sword of the one who brought him back."

"I don't think so, buddy," Scott said easing back against the ledge.

"I'm sorry Scott. I just don't believe everything Tibu says."

"Well, turn around and tell me what you believe," Scott whispered slowly as his gaze was fixed beyond Curt. Curt slowly turned with the cleaned sword in his right hand. The thing was again wobbling, standing fully erect and slowly speaking French in a low-pitched, possessed, demonic voice. The thing was hideous with discolored skin, floating eyes and yellow fluid rapidly gushing from the wound in its chest.

Curt raised his sword and the thing attacked, screaming as if its feet were on fire. The shrill sound made their eardrums ache as he came at them head on. Curt drew back the sword and swung hard from left to right deflecting the thing's blade to the side as the two weapons collided.

Unfortunately, Curt had not accounted for Scott who was standing close behind and was forced to lean back to avoid having his gut sliced open by the back swing. Scott lost his balance and teetered momentarily on the ledge before plunging into the murky waters of the moat with a harsh smack.

He was now in the domain of the Kilgotian.

CHAPTER-THIRTY-FIVE

Scott stood up clinging to the rod, relieved he could touch bottom and still have more than a third of his body out of the water. He grimaced as he felt the sliced skin on his chest burn from the impact. God, how it stung. Then the reality of where he was sank in with a cruel harshness. Oh my God, I'm in with this thing, he thought, trying to remain calm. He was standing four feet from the side and quickly moved over to try and scale the wall but it was useless. It was six feet over his head and much too smooth to get a handhold. Think, the voice inside kept screaming.

Above in the distance, he could hear the clanking of steel. He knew Curt was in a battle for his life and at the moment, so was he. He tried to visually locate the fish. Maybe it has no idea I'm in the water. Just don't move Scott, he thought. Just freeze and don't move a muscle and he'll never know.

The surface of the water was calm. The fish was somewhere out of view. Scott could feel his pulse quicken. He looked at his right hand, which still held the rod. It took a few seconds to register in his paralyzed mind that he was *only* holding the rod. The handle of the reel was free. If the fish was still on, even remotely trying to run, the handle would be back-winding. But it wasn't. The demonic fish was no longer moving away.

The cold water caused Scott to shiver uncontrollably. He moved the rod into his left hand and started winding furiously with his right, trying to minimize any bodily movement. "God please let me catch up with him, please, please," he whispered out loud as the clanging continued above. As Scott cranked the handle, the free line loaded onto the reel and a sick feeling pervaded his stomach. The Kilgotian must be right on me! Winding as fast as humanly possible, Scott was sure he had already wound in more line than the fish had taken. Where in the hell is he? Is he a foot away from my ribs preparing to attack?

Suddenly the line became taut. He held the rod high over his head and, from the angle, was able to estimate there was approximately 20 more feet of line extended. Feeling slightly encouraged, he continued to wind vigorously. It was obvious the fish was heading straight for him. His only chance was to draw in the slack and use the rod itself to keep the fish from tearing him apart.

On the grass above, Curt was awkwardly fending off the slimy attacker and had slowly disarmed his opponent, literally. Curt had severed its left arm and its right leg at the knee, but still it came. Curt stared at the thing in bewilderment.

"Why don't you just die," he said to the Soulful One. "It would be a lot less painful."

But the thing bounced forward as Curt took a position a few feet from the edge of the moat. He was trying to see Scott. "Scott, you OK," he shouted.

"No!" Scott yelled back still winding. "This thing's about on top of me!"

As the Soulful One neared, Curt hacked off its right arm and watched it fall to the ground still holding the weapon.

"I'm tired of playing with you," Curt said and drove the blade through its neck, almost decapitating the dismembered creature. It fell to the ground, convulsing a second time. But this time Curt quickly moved to the thing's side and, using his sword, stabbed it in the chest. With the sword firmly embedded, Curt began to drag the quivering corpse.

Down below, the fish had stopped some 15 feet away from Scott, at least by his best estimation, and remained at bay, keeping the line taut. Wherever it was, it was staying deep enough to remain out of sight. Scott was shaking badly and his teeth chattered. What the hell is it doing? Should I try and pull it to me? Scott wondered. At least if I can draw it up to the end of the rod I can keep it that far away from my body. That is, if the line doesn't break. The thought made him even more nervous but, nonetheless, he began winding again, his hand shaking with each slow revolution. He peered into the water looking for any motion; any flaws in the surface.

Suddenly, a large object entered the water between the Kilgotian and Scott. The sprawling mass showered Scott, as he jumped back. He wiped the liquid out of his burning eyes with his sleeves while trying to maintain a steady hold on the rod and handle. As the object settled in the water he could tell it was a body, face down. For a second he feared it was Curt. But the thing lifted its head slightly and he knew otherwise. The Soulful One raised itself up and attempted to gain footing on the bottom, but before it had a chance, the water started churning and swirling. Scott held a tighter grip on the rod as it vibrated, nearly jumping out of his hands, pulling left and then right and then up and down. The water stirred violently and the Soulful One screamed a ravenous cry. It went under as if it had been sucked down in a large whirlpool, and the water turned a gooey yellow. The waters continued to churn where the body disappeared, its shrieks echoing horribly in Scott's mind.

Reacting more than thinking, Scott yelled up to Curt, "Get ready!" Then lowering the rod tip within inches of the surface, he began winding as fast as he could. The resistance was still constant. The fish couldn't have been more than eight or ten feet away. Scott kept the tip low as he wound, concentrating on the surface just past the end of the rod. Less than three feet away, the fish came into view gliding toward him barely under the surface. Scott estimated he had six revolutions of the reel before he'd have to react. He counted down as he saw the horrid yellow tint in the Kilgotian's eyes as it approached. 6! . . . 5! . . . 4! . . . 3! . . . 2! . . . 1! and lift!

With every bit of energy he could muster, and with the help of pure adrenaline, he flung the rod tip high into the air, lifting the fish out of the water. The rod pointed up, initially bowing under the weight but then straightened. The Kilgotian launched upward and Scott flipped the bale open to release the line. As the spool unwound, the creature sailed out of the sanctity of the moat and onto the grass near where Curt stood. It had been a desperate plan that had worked with amazing precision.

As the fish lay flapping on the ground Curt looked down at it with vengeance. He raised his sword to slaughter the creature but stopped to watch in awe. The skin and meat of the fish literally fell away from the bones and disintegrated before he could blink twice. An instant later, the evil yellow eyes hardened, cracked and then broke into dust. The only thing that remained was the skeletal structure as Curt had first found it in the powder magazine. A slight breeze caught Curt in the face as he gazed down at the lifeless remains. He was speechless.

"Hey, how about helping me out of here!" Scott yelled up, interrupting Curt's trance. "Did you get the fish? I don't want him floppin' back in here. Curt! You okay? Did you get the fish?" he yelled again.

"I'm fine," Curt called while standing on the ledge. "And *you* got the fish."

Curt rescued Scott from the moat by using his belt. Leaning over the edge and extending his arm, it was just long enough for Scott to grab. Scott ascended to the ledge with the rod stuck in his pants. Once on top, he walked over to the skeleton of the Kilgotian and shook his head in amazement.

"He dissolved a few seconds after he landed," Curt explained. "Now he looks just like he did when we found him. But I bet if you put him back in the water he'd come to life just like a sea monkey."

"Well, I have a nifty idea. Don't get him near any water," Scott said enunciating each word slowly and deliberately.

"So what do we do with him. I vote we crush his little skeleton into pieces so fine you could mistake him for cocaine," Curt said with a grin.

"That would not help us," Tibu suddenly spoke up, startling the men. He had come up from behind and now handed Scott the sword from the Huguenot consumed by the fish.

"I wish you'd stop doing that," Scott said startled, as he turned to face Tibu.

"Don't you ever make noise when you walk?" Curt asked.

"I'm an Indian," Tibu said with a serious voice.

Curt cocked his head to the side looking at Tibu. "If you're here, then who's keeping the brothers out of the fort?" he said barely beating Scott to the question.

"It doesn't matter," Tibu replied. "We need to leave."

"Good point," Scott said raising his eyebrows. "They can have the fort. We have the fish. So what's our next move?"

"We move away from the fort and out of sight quickly," Tibu said. He reached down and grabbed the skeleton and began jogging away from the north wall. Scott and Curt followed. They angled toward Matanzas Bay and reached the bulkhead stretching along the water. Running on the embankment, they continued north and reached a series of trees. Three hundred yards from the Castillo de San Marcos they stopped for Scott and Curt to catch their breath.

"Bruin, I mean Tibu, why did we just leave the car back at the fort?" Scott asked.

"Because there were six Soulful Ones in the parking lot. I was able to get by without being seen."

"So there are more. But why are we running?" Scott said.

Tibu did not immediately answer. He looked back at the fort to make sure the trees were blocking the view of their position.

"While I was on the slab, I put my ear to the stone and heard the LeFlores talking very low. They were about to go back through the moat and risk meeting the Kilgotian," Tibu said. "I decided to quietly get up and leave the room and walk through the drawbridge opening. I flipped the 'up' switch and raced over the bridge and leaped onto the sidewalk. Fortunately, the drawbridge lifts very slowly and I didn't have far to jump."

"Weren't you afraid of landing in the moat?" Curt asked.

Tibu looked into his eyes and stared a few seconds before responding in a chilling tone. "If you hadn't caught the fish by then, we were doomed anyway."

"What next?" Scott asked, hoping to bring some optimism back into the conversation.

"We go to the cemetery," Tibu replied almost whispering.

"Why," Curt asked.

"Because there's something there we need to do," he responded, straining to look out into the bay.

"What? Please tell me that's where Sherri is," Curt said.

"It is," the Indian responded.

"Tibu, how long will it take for all the new Soulful Ones to arise, assuming there's more than the six you saw in the parking lot and the ones we ran into?" Scott asked concerned.

"They might already be here. It depends where they were laid to rest in the salt water."

What they didn't know was how many Soulful Ones the brothers had reincarnated. When the men had stumbled upon the stone box full of Huguenot metacarpals they estimated about 60 to 70 bones had already been removed. This was confirmed when Scott saw Pinot and Reece feeding the Kilgotian. But since they interrupted the brothers, they had no way of knowing for sure. Plus, whatever the number was, Curt and Scott had added two or three more to the count by their unique baiting technique. Either way, the odds were not going to be in their favor. Even more unsettling was Sherri's fate. Curt remembered the worried look on her face as he'd left her chained in the room and how she tried to conceal her fear with witty remarks. I should have never left her alone, he thought and wondered if her ability to speak French would keep her alive much longer.

The three continued along the bulkhead. For about the 15th time that evening, Curt said a silent prayer for Sherri's safety. If he ever found her again he would never let her out of his sight. And from what Tibu said he was inspired to push on to the cemetery.

The sky above the bay had darkened into a burnt orange. The lightning show that had accompanied Scott and Curt on the gundeck earlier had moved on. Clouds still hung over the landscape trapping the night and the events below.

The men made their way from the shoreline to San Marco Boulevard. The pavement was brightly cast in light from the street lamps hovering high above merging with the orange glow, presenting a strange shade of yellow.

Not far ahead on their right was the Prince of Peace Church and just beyond was the cemetery where Tibu said Sherri was. But even Tibu was unsure if she was dead or alive, although he did not admit it. Curt took the lead as they left the street and trotted through the grassy field toward the rear of the church.

Scott looked up and saw the massive stainless steel Beacon of Faith Cross towering into the sky. Standing resilient against the orange colored background it appeared taller than its advertised 208 feet. It reached upward with determination and grandeur. In some ways it seemed almost alive. Scott felt placated in its presence, a certain comfort that he would never have admitted to Curt.

The three men made their way behind the chapel. Carrying the swords was tiring and they paused to catch their breath, except for Tibu who was beaming with energy. Scott wondered how his blood carried oxygen to his heart without breathing. Then again, maybe his heart was nonfunctional as well.

They looked across the field at the grounds of the cemetery. The night had darkened, the sky turning from an orange shade to brown. The clumped trees that resided amongst and over the area gave the surroundings a clouded manifestation. The nearer tombstones were visible but beyond that, their shapes were obscured.

"We've got to be very careful here," Tibu said. "I sense there are many."

It suddenly occurred to Curt. "They can sense you too, can't they?"

Tibu nodded.

"That's why you didn't come to the fort with us initially. You were afraid of tipping them off," Scott said.

"Yes," the Indian replied. "And I needed to retrieve the sword."

"So they know we're here?" Curt asked excitedly.

"At the fort, Reece and Pinot knew there were no others close. They could probably sense I was in the city but it would have been a weak signal. Because there are more Soulful Ones, my presence is now masked. They'll believe me to be one of the other Huguenots they've resurrected."

"Makes perfect sense," Scott said.

Curt shook his head in agreement. "I have to give it to you Tibu. You have this all thought out."

"I've had a long time to prepare. I can't make a single mistake." His voice trailed off and he appeared introspective.

"So what's next," Curt asked.

"I believe the woman to be in the chapel. Our best approach is to head back to the street and come across the small bridge that spans the saltwater pond in front of the cemetery. Their attention will be focused away from us, toward the bay, waiting for others to return," Tibu said. "We have to move quickly. Soon, they'll be too many and only my sword is capable of permanently stopping them. And don't forget, we have no weapon against Reece. The sword I have will allow me to defeat Pinot but your weapons will only slow them down."

"Tibu, are we going to survive this ordeal?" Scott asked hesitantly. He wasn't sure if he wanted a truthful answer and held his breath waiting on the response. Curt gazed at Tibu.

The Indian hesitated in his response and dropped his eyes to the ground, "Not all of us," he said quietly with despair.

Curt and Scott looked at each other allowing the reality to slip in. Tibu sprinted toward the road and the men followed as quietly as they could, their swords becoming heavier as they went. Tibu tracked the pavement to the parking lot of the Nuestra de la Leche cemetery and angled in. He moved to the foot of the 45-foot walkway bridge, waiting for Curt and Scott to catch up.

Tibu led the way, cautiously watching the far side for movement. The darkness lingered underneath the trees, blocking the view and causing a black walk to appear on the other side. They made their away across the bridge and settled on the grass off the path, squatting to reduce the chance of being seen. Ahead, the stone walkway broke into two directions. To the right, it led to the cross. To the left, into the cemetery toward the chapel. They rose and slowly made their way, as their eyes became accustomed to the dark.

"The tombstones are gone," Curt whispered to Scott who was behind him.

Scott looked around and saw his friend was right. The additional headstones that had appeared the night before were nonexistent. The cemetery, at least what they could see, was back to normal.

The walkway meandered left and then right. As they neared the chapel, there was a dim light shining through the stained glass windows high along the side but still no indication of Reece, Pinot or any other Soulful Ones. The only visible signs of life were from the chorus of crickets and frogs bellowing loudly in whimsical bursts.

Tibu silently pointed out the light but Scott and Curt had already noticed. They paced carefully around the front of the chapel and made sure the entrance was unguarded. The door was closed.

Inside, they could hear a human voice. Curt was sure it was Sherri's. She was pleading something in French out of desperation as she wept.

"Bastard," Curt whispered loudly as he rushed the door.

Tibu stopped him. "Knock on the door and move out of the way," he whispered.

Scott stood back and Tibu moved to the left. Curt stepped in front and rapped on the wood briskly. Sherri's voice ceased and Curt moved away. The door swung out toward Tibu's. A haggard man with glowing white, milky eyes saw Curt and took two steps before Tibu kicked the door closed behind him. As the thing turned toward Tibu, the Indian was already in mid swing. The sword caught the Soulful One high and gashed into his skull, sending a yellowish substance splattering across the door and entryway. Its head broke off just above the nose as the bone fragments and skin splintered against the wall. The body dropped in its place and Tibu quickly kicked it aside.

"What's with that yellow shit?" Scott asked excitedly.

"These men should never have been brought back. Remember the warning. After 300 days it's too long." Tibu pointed to the clump of bones and flesh on the ground. "This is what happens."

Curt had not waited for Tibu response to Scott's question. He reached for the door handle careful to avoid any contact with the substance that was dripping along the wall. He swung the door open and felt agony at what he saw.

Sherri was tied up with her hands above her head on the wall behind the small pulpit. Her head drooped to the side and her hair was matted in her face. Her dirty blouse was torn and hung loosely. One shoe was lying on the ground to her right. She did not appear to be breathing.

Curt rushed to her. He grabbed her face in his hands pushing the hair out of the way. With her eyes still closed she snatched her head from his grasp and moaned.

"Thank God! It's OK, Sherri. It's Curt. I'm so sorry I left you," he panted. Her eyes opened slowly and focused in the dull light.

"He hurt me," she said weakly and with a slight slur. Curt could see the abrasion on her left cheek under her eye. The pink skin had already risen slightly and was quickly discoloring. "He hurt me," she repeated and began sobbing. Curt placed his cheek against hers for comfort.

Scott and Tibu entered the room and began working on the knots that bound Sherri's hands. Soon she was free and Curt sat her on the first bench. Frightened and tired, she needed a moment to recuperate before moving on. Tibu kept watch through the slightly cracked door. Scott looked down at the bench and searched for the white outline of the sword Ambrose had mentioned. It was nowhere to be found.

"I was so scared," Sherri said trembling in Curt's arms. He held her firmly and stroked her hair. It was moist from perspiration. "How did you know I was here?"

"Just luck," he said looking at Tibu who had turned to face them. He didn't want to explain now. "Did he . . . Did it rape you?"

"No. Thank God. But I think it was about to," she said as she pulled away and wiped the tears from her eyes. "What was that thing? Was it even human?"

"Sherri," Scott began as he sat down beside Curt, still holding his sword, "these things, these men who captured you, are reincarnate souls. They're four-century-old French Huguenots."

Sherri looked past Curt at Scott, then back to Curt. "What is he talking about?" She had turned fear and pain into agitation.

"He's telling the truth. As wild as it sounds, it's real. But we now have the one thing they need. Tibu, show her."

Tibu reached into his shirt and pulled out the skeleton of the Kilgotian.

"You've got a dead fish. What are you trying to tell me?" she asked. "What is going on?"

"There's too much to explain. We've got to get out of here before they return. We have no way to defeat one of the brothers," Scott said.

Sherri stood and looked at Curt in amazement.

"Don't ask," he said.

"I won't now but somebody will be answering my questions later," she replied with a faint smile. Even battered, her beauty came through.

The four warily walked outside into the night. There was no sign of movement. They followed the walkway around the chapel.

As they reached the back of the church they were attacked.

Five screaming Huguenots wielding swords came at them, their watery eyes glowing with cries that ripped the night. Curt shoved Sherri to the opposite side of the sidewalk and raised his sword just in time to glance a blow. The impacted steel sparked the darkness.

Scott was so caught off guard he never had a chance to raise his sword. Instead he jumped backward, losing his grip. The steel clanged on the pavement as it fell. Tibu, unfazed by the ambush, stood his ground like a battle hardened warrior. He spun and caught one attacker with a swipe through the midsection cleanly separating the Huguenot in two. The crumpled remains heaped on the ground in a pool of ooze.

Scott was avoiding the swinging blade of another when Tibu turned and drove his sword backward through the attacker's rib cage, spilling yellow fluid everywhere. Without confrontation, Scott retrieved his sword and caught a third Huguenot at the kneecaps. As the thing fell backward, legs severed, Tibu quickly moved over and plunged the sword into the left eye socket until the tip of the blade made contact with the stone below. Then the thing went still.

Three down, two to go. The last two had chosen to go after Curt. He awkwardly fended off their blows but knew he could not hold out long. As yet, they had not coordinated blows, instead following a pattern of duplicating high or low attacks. Sooner or later they would assault at different angles and, unable to defend two places at once, Curt would be bludgeoned. But one of the Soulful Ones broke off and moved toward Sherri, who had taken the opportunity to slowly back up on the grass as the fighting had continued.

Scott ran up behind Curt's foe and brought his sword down. The steel crushed the skull. Fragments of brain matter mixed with the yellow substance dripped down its body before tumbling to the earth. Incredibly, the thing rose only to be smashed by a violent blow of Tibu's sword decapitating what was left of its head. This time it fell and remained down.

The fifth Huguenot had cornered Sherri against the back of the chapel. Curt positioned himself behind and, with two hands, sunk the point of his blade down through its neck at an angle. He forced the weapon up to the hilt with the point protruding out from the chest. He turned the thing and flung it to the ground as it screamed in pain. Sherri covered her ears and cringed. Curt's sword easily pulled out as it fell. Tibu walked up and sedately slashed the neck with a searing swing, separating the head and body.

Scott sat on the ground and rested as Curt went over to Sherri and hugged her. Tibu watchfully gazed around, prepared for another attack.

"Five down. Sixty or 70 to go," Scott said breathing deeply. "Were any of these Pinot?"

Tibu shook his head side to side.

"Damn," Scott said.

"We have to get out of here. We need to destroy this fish," Tibu said.

"Exactly how are we going to do that anyway?" Curt asked lifting his sword to his shoulder.

"I don't know," Tibu admitted.

"Why don't we just rip it apart," Scott asked.

"It can't be done," Tibu said.

"Bullshit," Curt said. "Bring that thing out."

Tibu reluctantly pulled the fish from his shirt. He laid it on the paved walkway and looked around for any signs of danger.

Curt lifted his sword high over his head and dropped it directly on the Kilgotian's skeleton. With a quick downward blow he struck the fish sending sparks flying off the stone. But the skeleton remained intact.

"My turn," Scott said moving the fish into the grass. He took an overhead swat that simply deflected off causing the skeleton to bounce up. He bent down to examine the fish and realized that neither of the two blows had left a mark. "Unbelievable," Scott said, "Not even a scrape."

"Are you satisfied I'm telling the truth?" Tibu asked.

The men nodded.

"Now let's get out of here," Tibu said taking the fish from Scott's hand and placing it back in his shirt. The three men and Sherri walked to the bridge and crossed over. The parking lot ahead was clear and they discussed returning to the fort to get Curt's car. If it were still guarded they'd have to come up with a plan to divert the attention of the Huguenots. It was mindboggling to think the Soulful Ones knew to watch the vehicle. Reece must have done enough observation to understand this new form of transportation.

Tibu heard a faint sound behind them. It was the patter of feet upon wood. He turned to see three Huguenots, clothes dangling loosely, armed with swords and knives coming over the small bridge.

"Run!" he yelled to the others as they turned to see what had caught his attention.

The foursome began to sprint toward the road when four more soldiers came at them head-on carrying similar weapons and yelping, their eyes glowing in the faint light. The three men and woman froze in their tracks as the two groups quickly converged upon them.

Tibu turned toward the three coming from behind. "Defend the front!" he yelled to Scott and Curt. Tibu made a sweeping motion with his sword once the soldiers were close enough and caught two across the chest. But the third deflected the blow with his sword and fell to the side. Scott and Curt were able to successfully fend off the other four long enough for Tibu to turn and help. Sherri did her best to keep between the men without getting in the way.

Tibu quickly disposed of two. One, by driving his sword through its chest and the second by decapitation. He was prepared to assist Scott when the third Huguenot caught Tibu with a glancing blow on his left shoulder. Tibu grimaced as he turned and embedded his sword in the attacker's mouth driving the end through the back of its skull as the yellow substance poured out. Tibu momentarily grabbed his shoulder in pain as blood soaked his shirt. Scott and Curt were locked in battle when Sherri moved toward Tibu and tried to grab his sword.

"No!" Tibu shouted at her.

"Give me the damn thing!" she barked back.

Sherri took it from Tibu's hand as he winced. He didn't want to give up his weapon but at the moment she was more capable of using it.

Sherri lifted the heavy blade and rested it on her right shoulder. Scott had turned his opponent so that its back was to the woman. With all the strength she could gather she swung the sword at a three-quarter angle striking the thing in the side of the neck. The blade carved deep into the collar and the head limped to the left, hanging gingerly as its carcass collapsed to the ground.

She raised the sword to her shoulder again, positioned to the side of Curt's attacker. But before she could strike, Tibu stepped in front and took the sword away.

"Thanks, but I'll handle this." His voice was stable and calm.

She obliged and stepped aside. Tibu took his place alongside Curt and Scott who were busy clinking swords with the Huguenot. This particular one seemed more skilled in technique and Tibu knew his inexperienced allies were no match. The Indian had been practicing his swordsmanship for more than five decades in preparation for this night. It was time to put his training to use.

"He's mine. Move aside," the Indian said calmly yet with determination. Scott and Curt didn't question the order.

The battle was fierce but Tibu's superior experience was evident. Even with a bad shoulder he fought like a machine. With precision and speed he soon knocked the Huguenot to the pavement and sent a crushing blow across its thorax sending the yellow substance spurting into the air.

Tibu rested his sword tip on the ground as the pain in his shoulder reminded him of his wound. He was angry with himself for allowing the soldier to sneak up behind and advance such a strike. He had gotten careless and it had cost him.

The other three came over, "Are you all right? How bad is it?" Scott asked.

"I'll be fine. It's not too deep," Tibu responded, pulling his collar aside and examining the area.

"Tibu, something occurred to me while you were fighting. You are a Soulful One. You can't be killed can you?" Curt said.

"Yes, I can."

"But you said . . ." Scott started to say.

"Not in my case," Tibu interrupted. "A Soulful One should only exist an additional 100 to 150 years. I've far outlived that, probably with the sole purpose of fighting this battle tonight. Once the 150 years had passed, in the early 1800s, I noticed I was susceptible to diseases and other human afflictions. I had to use your medicines to remain alive and avoid disease. I was fortunate not to contract yellow fever when it spread through St. Augustine in the mid-1800s. I personally knew a lot of the folks buried in the cemetery across from the fort who died from it. Until that time, I never even had a runny nose. I am quite capable of dying."

Sherri looked at Tibu in amazement.

"Don't worry, Sherri. As you can see, he's on our side," Curt said.

The four were still tense and on edge from the last attack and the next minute would not get any better. From the left, coming at them from the church, were eight more screaming soldiers running at a full gallop.

"Christ!" Sherri said. "These guys are everywhere!"

Scott and Curt looked at Tibu for direction. He was slow to speak. His energy was obviously draining. Curt turned back toward the bridge where four more were crossing. Their eyes bulging white, sliding back and forth.

"Not good," Curt said. "Coming up from behind again!" he screamed. The men held their ground despite an overwhelming urge to run.

"God! There's more!" Sherri screamed as three more approached from the right. The Huguenots had triangulated their position and were moving in quickly. The three men formed a circle around Sherri with their backs toward her.

"We're gonna die," Curt said.

Scott swallowed hard.

As the first group of eight approached to within 10 yards, a dark automobile screeched its tires and jackknifed into the parking lot. The engine roared, as the car diverted to its right and skidded into the pack of soldiers spreading them in all directions. When the vehicle stopped, Marvin rolled down the window of the Buick Regal.

"Get in! Your ride's here!"

With the four attackers coming from the bridge now upon them, Scott and Tibu fought to hold them off while Curt and Sherri jumped in the car. Marvin punched the gas and circled around to intercept the three approaching from the far side. Without hesitation, he steered into them. The car pummeled over the soldiers and bounced up and down like it was traversing a series of speed bumps.

"Scott, Tibu! Get in!" Marvin screamed. But at the moment there was no opportunity. Tibu had quickly dispensed with one of the soldiers but there were still three left that he and Scott were fending off. Curt climbed back out of the car to assist. He raced over and engaged one of the two Tibu was battling.

A moment later Scott knocked his man to the ground and the Huguenot fell against Tibu, knocking the Indian off balance and careening to the pavement. The Kilgotian spilled out of his shirt and slid several feet away. Tibu scurried to try and get it but his opponent was on him. In defense, he stood up swinging viciously. The tip of his sword passed through the thing's cheeks deep enough to be fatal. The body fell limp. Tibu turned and stabbed the soldier on the ground that Scott had toppled. For the moment, Tibu left the Kilgotian on the ground.

Curt was struggling with his opponent as Tibu crept up behind and thrust his sword through the thing's chest cavity and out the front. The Huguenot's watery eyes burst and the pupils fell lifeless as its arms dangled at its side and its weapon hit the hard ground before it collapsed.

Sherri was hanging her head out of the backseat of the Buick when she screamed at the sight of the monster. An enormous man, if that's what he was, had come up behind Scott, Curt and Tibu. He bent down to pick up the Kilgotian. He was nearly seven feet tall with a massive frame. His body was coated in a slippery brown, blotchy substance that resembled off-colored mud. He moved fluidly as if his joints were completely flexible in any direction. His actions defied the laws of nature, as his knees bent inward and out when he straightened.

"Oh my God!" Marvin said slowly in amazement. "Now what!"

The three men turned.

The sight even caught Tibu off guard. Never had a giant monster played a role in his dreams and he had no idea if he was facing friend or foe. For the first time that day, with everything they had experienced, fear nearly overwhelmed him.

Once upright, the men could see the thing had used a handkerchief to lift the fish and now wrapped it tightly around the Kilgotian.

Scott looked carefully at the beast. Even through the dirty covering he recognized who it was. "Holy shit," his words escaped through clenched teeth as he attempted to keep his voice low. "It's the park ranger formerly known as Tatterhorn."

Curt's mouth fell open.

CHAPTER-THIRTY-SIX

Pinot and Reece gazed into the water and saw the stone box just beneath the surface. They had been intent on locating the missing box since discovering its disappearance. Reece lowered Pinot into the water with the rope they found secured to the Ravelin's small tower. It was the perfect length to extend into the moat.

Pinot climbed down and dropped into the moat to the left of the box. The water was slightly above his knees. Because of the terrain, it was not nearly as deep on this side as where they had fed the Kilgotian. Pinot trudged through the water, leaned down to grab the box and realized it was propped on its side. Feeling around the moat's bottom, he found the lid lying flat and lifted it up. There was some form of rope underneath. Having no use for it, he pushed it aside.

He reached into the box and then felt around the outside.

It was empty.

Tatterhorn stared at the men. Lightning flickered in the background. He held the Kilgotian tightly as his massive hand dwarfed the fish in the dirty handkerchief. The ooze dripped from its body and speckled the ground.

The others watched in amazement. They felt a combination of bewilderment and fright. Scott finally spoke up, attempting a manly voice that projected timidness.

"Wh-What do you want, Tatterhorn?"

There was a moment of silence and then the large structure spoke in a deep, guttural tone. Curt almost regretted teasing Scott about his little liquid accident earlier as his own kidneys refluxed and he barely held on.

"MINE!" the man-beast growled as he held the Kilgotian to his chest.

The men stared with eyes wide open.

"I think he's got a little problem with being over possessive," Curt whispered back to Scott and Tibu.

"You have no idea how right you are," Tibu replied, never taking his eyes off Tatterhorn who remained frozen as the mud packs globbed to the pavement. The lightning again flickered in the distance. For an instant, the stray light beamed on the giant's face, revealing an undercoating of facial skin that was tight and dry. It was cracking as if it had been very poorly embalmed.

The sight caused Sherri to scream a muffled cry as she threw her hands over her lips.

"Give us the fish," Tibu said calmly. "We will return it to the pond."

Scott and Curt looked at the Indian confused. Then each seemed to understand his strategy.

"MINE!" the thing yelled again. His voice was deep and more gravelly than before. Scott wondered if the brown mucus was draining down his esophagus. Maybe, with any luck, the thing would just choke to death. Another burst of lightning lit up the air. For the first time, the rumble could be heard in the distance several seconds later. The storm was drawing closer.

Curt looked at Tibu as if to say, "Are you sure Damon's not going to decimate this town?"

Tibu never removed his eyes from Tatterhorn.

On the next flash of white, Tatterhorn turned around as if on cue.

"FREEZE!" Marvin screamed. He had come out of the car and stood to the right of the men. He raised a 12-gauge doublebarrel shotgun he had dug out of his closet to his shoulder and aimed. Tatterhorn kept moving away with his knees bowing in and out.

"LAST CHANCE! STOP!" Marvin yelled taking half a dozen steps forward. For an instant, he looked back at Tibu. "Is he human?"

"Not anymore," the Indian replied.

With that, Marvin turned and aimed. Catching the broad back of the beast in his sights, he gently squeezed both triggers.

The sound of the dual chambers unloading ripped the night. Sherri threw her hands to her ears a split second too late as the ringing enflamed her head. The spray impacted the thing's glossy back, entering with a muffled thud as if shot into water. Buckshot passed through the porous body and dug into a small church parking sign 20 feet beyond, shredding the upper half of the metal away. Large chunks of brown globs accompanied the fragments and pelted the remaining piece of the sign. The impact tore the Kilgotian out of Tatterhorn's hands and it flew across the parking lot.

Tatterhorn never wavered. The shot had absolutely no effect. Marvin, on the other hand, was sent backward six feet and landed sprawling on the hard pavement. The shotgun ended up farther behind. Scott and Curt helped Marvin to his feet as they watched the beast slowly move over to the Kilgotian's skeleton and again lift it carefully, keeping it wrapped in the folds of the cloth.

"Marvin, you okay?" Scott asked.

"Yeah. Did I get him?"

"Not even close." Curt replied.

The beast turned to gaze at the men and then slowly began walking toward them.

"I think you did succeed in pissing him off," Tibu said. "I suggest we get going." His words were rational but his eyes showed a degree of excitement none of them had seen to this point. The men didn't need to hear the recommendation a second time.

Tatterhorn approached at a steady pace, knees bowing in and out. The men moved quickly to the car. The giant wore a ferocious scowl and was not to be challenged.

"GET IN! GET IN!" Sherri yelled. "IT'S COMING!" Scott raced to the driver's side and was about to get behind the wheel when Marvin commanded him to move over.

"It's my car and I'm driving!" he screamed. This was no time to argue so Scott obeyed. Tibu and Curt climbed in the back through Sherri's open door, careful not to injure each other with their swords. Tatterhorn was within five feet as the doors slammed and Marvin cranked the engine. The Regal fired up as Tatterhorn lifted his massive right hand into the air and brought it down like a sledgehammer through the right rear window. Glass shards spilled onto Tibu's lap as Curt and Sherri cringed against the far side, giving the Indian as much room as possible to escape from the thing's grasp. Tibu lifted his blade and sunk the steel into the thing's arm with a thrust firm enough to have severed the appendage just above the elbow. But the blade passed through like butter.

Tatterhorn retracted his arm and the blade withdrew with a slosh. There was no response from the beast, which apparently felt no pain. Marvin gunned the motor and dropped the car into drive. The tires lit up as he cut the wheel hard to the left. Tatterhorn momentarily stood in place, watching the vehicle circle in the parking lot.

Marvin was intent on running this bastardly thing down. He spun the car around and caught Tatterhorn in his sights. But before he kicked the accelerator, Tatterhorn was on the move. Not at the slow, awkward motion they had witnessed, he was gracefully gliding out of the parking lot at a steady clip.

"What in the hell!" Scott said.

"Go after him!" Tibu shouted. "We cannot let him get that fish to the pond!"

Marvin squealed the car through the parking lot and banged harshly onto San Marco Boulevard, screeching tread. He turned left bouncing everyone in the car as the shocks fought to steady the car. Another flash lit the sky as the beast headed south on the boulevard in the direction of the fort, running with long, hideous strides. His legs appeared to grow longer with each step and his knees bent in malformed directions.

"Look at that thing run!" Marvin said excitedly.

"This is the man you said attacked you at Fort Caroline?" Tibu asked.

"Yes," Scott and Curt replied simultaneously.

"And he fell into the water?"

"He fell where he said the pond had been," Scott replied. "He fell into the sand. What in the Hell happened to him? You said he's not human?"

"After sending that blast clean through, I'd have a hard time arguing he is!" Marvin said, mashing the accelerator to try to catch up with Tatterhorn as he streaked past the fort. The road made a slight bend left and then straightened out along the bay.

"No, he's not human. The pond owns his soul. When he fell in, it consumed him."

"But the fish wasn't there . . . and he didn't fall into the pond. It was freakin sand!" Curt said.

"It was still the pond and it consumed him. Now the pond wants the fish back. It's using Tatterhorn's body to that end."

"So now we're also battling a disciple of the pond?" Marvin said incredulously.

"The Kilgotian and the pond formed a symbiotic relationship. Unlike the fish that could exist anywhere, the pond needs the fish," Tibu responded as the creature stretched out its long legs and turned left onto the Bridge of Lions. Marvin squealed the radials as he made a hard turn sending the Buick onto two wheels.

"I have no idea what you guys are talking about," Sherri said, shaking her head back and forth.

"Don't worry. When I get about four days, I'll explain it to you. Just trust us. We need to get that fish back or a lot of bad things are going to happen to a lot of innocent people," Curt replied.

"I have no choice but to trust you," she said giving Curt a small smile.

"So where is he going with the fish?" Scott said looking back at Tibu. "Fort Caroline is north and he's moving farther south."

"I have no idea. This thing has never been a part of my dreams."

"That's not good," Scott commented as the car came across the Bridge and onto Anastasia Boulevard. The night was becoming more and more alive with picturesque bursts of light creeping in from the coast several miles ahead. The wind had intensified as gusts met the Buick's grill but Tatterhorn never slowed. Marvin watched the speedometer eclipse 74.

They passed the foot of the bridge and went by several small businesses. Curt caught something out of the corner of his eye. He wheeled around and looked through the back window.

"What is it?" Sherri asked.

"We've got company."

Tibu turned and saw the group of sword-carrying Huguenots trotting slowly in their direction. They faded away as the car sailed on.

Scott turned to look when Marvin screamed out, "He's stopping!"

The beast, which had been gliding along at warp speed, suddenly stopped and turned into the St. Augustine Alligator Farm parking lot.

"Is there a body of freshwater inside?" Tibu asked hastily.

Marvin whipped the car into the parking lot as the thing easily scaled the high wooden fence and was gone.

"You mean you've lived around here for 400 years and you've never been to the Alligator Farm?" Marvin asked in an almost comical manner.

"IS THERE A BODY OF FRESHWATER INSIDE?" Tibu screamed. Sherri cringed in the backseat. Scott and Curt gazed at the Indian whose head bore a pulsating vein glaring out from his temple.

"Yeah, yeah! There's a wooden walkway across a swampy area in the back right corner of the park. It's full of gators," Marvin responded out of fright.

Tibu dashed from the car. Marvin had stopped near the spot where the creature had climbed the 10-foot fence.

"C'mon!" Scott said turning to Curt. The two men exited the car with swords in hand.

"Marvin, stay with Sherri!" Scott yelled back. "Get the car out of sight in case those soldiers make it here."

By the time Scott and Curt got to the side gate, Tibu had destroyed the lock with one solid blow of his sword and had pushed his way through.

"Not much security," Curt said.

"Who the hell but us wants to break into an alligator farm?" Scott said running inside. He picked up the silhouette of Tibu racing down the walkway. Scott and Curt dashed after. The frequent lightning brightened the area as they pursued the Indian who was hot on the heels of Tatterhorn.

The cement path led to a small wooden walkway that carried over a pit of large alligators. As the men crossed, there was little motion below but they could easily make out the defined shapes of the carnivorous reptiles lying in wait.

Once across, they caught up with Tibu. He seemed almost unaware of their support. He ran down the sidewalk to the right, past a small gift shop and the open-air theatre where daily shows of the reptiles were conducted. Scott had brought his kids here on many occasions so the layout was quite familiar to him as it was to Curt.

Continuing at a trot down the walkway, they came upon the former home of Gomek. Gomek had been a prized exhibit at the farm for many years. A 17-foot alligator worthy of his own holding area and pond in which to live out his days in captivity. Gomek had died in 1997 and the park had yet to do anything creative with the containing area. As they passed, the men could hear the clogging footsteps ahead and saw the wet residue on the ground as the lightning again struck off shore. Incredibly, they seemed to be gaining on the creature. Either it was losing energy or it had slowed to navigate the narrow path.

The sounds of thunder sent shivers down Scott's spine.

"Tibu," Scott asked panting as they ran, "where's it going? Why did you ask about the body of water?"

"If it gets into a natural body of water it will be able to travel the aquifer back to the pond. Probably the same way it got here," Tibu replied, completely unwound, which was easy when you didn't need to breathe.

"That would be bad?" Curt panted.

"That would be the end," Tibu said firmly.

The men reached the start of the wooden walkway that spanned the swamp. Scott knew it ran about 75 yards over the marshy water, bending in a semicircle to the left and returning back to land where the *Alligator's from Around the World Exhibit* had been permanently established.

Tibu abruptly stopped and lifted his hand to motion for Scott and Curt to do the same. They scurried off the pavement and hid behind some shrubbery. From its actions, the creature had not seen nor heard their approach. It had stopped a short distance onto the walkway and was busy bending down, intently doing something with the Kilgotian.

"Is he going to put that damn fish in the water? I don't want to have to go through what we did to get it out again," Scott whispered.

"Besides, you're not using any of my fingers," Curt said.

"He has no intention of reviving the fish until its back in the pond. He's probably preparing it," Tibu said.

Scott looked at Curt. He wasn't sure what that meant but also didn't want to risk talking too much for fear of being overheard.

Tibu suddenly stood from their hiding spot and charged the beast with his sword lifted above his head. It saw the Indian coming and wobbled to its fully upright extension, appearing even larger than before. It glared a look of complete disdain as a bolt shot across the sky, flaming against the darkness. It took one step forward to meet Tibu, leaving the empty cloth lying on the wooden deck. Tibu could see a rubber coated sash draped across its neck.

Scott and Curt stood up to watch.

Marvin pulled the car around to the side of the attraction underneath a huge oak that had been protected when the parking lot was paved. He backed the Regal up against the wooden fence that enclosed the entire complex. As he and Sherri anxiously waited in the car, Marvin gave Sherri details of what they'd uncovered and what had happened over the last few days that had led to these events. He also admitted, although reluctantly, their belief in Tibu's prediction that Damon would skirt Northeast Florida. His words lost their self-assurance as the crisp lightning flashed and the roar of thunder embellished the clouds above.

They talked, keeping a watchful eye out for the Huguenots. Marvin noticed a large scrape across Sherri's arm and reached over to the glove compartment box for the first aid kit when the backdoor on the driver's side popped open and a man jumped into the seat.

Sherri screamed as Marvin jumped forward and slammed his face on the dash just above the radio as he tried to right himself.

"Mr. Sellon," a voice sprang from the back, "how's it going?"

Marvin whirled around to see Detective Sean Cowens closing the back door and looking at him. There was a gash above Marvin's left eye that began to ache.

"Jesus Christ, Cowens, you scared the crap out of us!" Marvin said. Sherri stared at the younger man with a void expression as thunder roared above.

"Mr. Sellon you lied to me," the detective said, leaning forward against the back of Marvin's seat. "You pretended like you knew nothing about the Kilgotian when all along you had it. You had it in your house when I was there, didn't you! You little bastard, you had it all along!"

"Now look here detective! I didn't see what the relationship to . . ."

Marvin gasped before his voice trailed off and his body stiffened. Sherri saw his horrid expression of surprise then his face contorted into grimacing pain and Marvin rolled lifelessly against the side of the door. Sherri saw the ghastly blade retract into the blood stained seat, its exit accompanied by the macabre sound of tearing cloth. The man in the backseat held the weapon up by the handle and wiped it clean with a dark piece of cloth that he casually threw on the seat beside him. Sherri looked at Cowens in disbelief. She could feel herself sliding into shock.

"Now my dear, what's your name?" he said with a decadent grin.

"Sherri jammed her hand into the side and found the handle. She flung open the door and had begun to stand when Cowens grabbed a handful of hair. "Wait a minute, deary! You're a witness!" he shouted pulling her head back violently against the headrest. The pain was excruciating. It felt like her scalp had been ripped from her head. The force of landing in the seat caused Marvin's limp right hand to flop onto her left leg. It was warm and gooshy. A second later it slid off.

"You seem like a sweet young thing. Let's talk for a few minutes," Cowens said in a hauntingly sedate tone. He held a firm grip on her hair pinning her against the seat.

"Sorry to muss such beautiful red hair but I'm sure you understand. Business is business. Millions of dollars speaks volumes!" he laughed. "Don't you think?"

Sherri was looking at the dashboard. Seeking out anything she could use as a weapon. Still holding her down, Cowens leaned forward and reached across Marvin's body and triggered the automatic door locks. He sat back pulling her head tighter against the headrest as he switched his grip from his right to his left hand. "Just to make sure you don't go anywhere missy."

Sherri was near panic but commanded herself to remain composed. She continued scanning everything in sight for a possible weapon.

Anything, God please, give me something to use.

"This is just a goddamn shame," Cowens mumbled.

The words sent waves of fear through her mind. Her head became so blood filled she almost passed out. For a few moments, the pain of the man's grip was nonexistent. She believed her scalp had gone numb as colors circled in her vision. She felt herself beginning to black out..

As the next brilliant spark of bony fingers shot across the sky, Sherri saw the keys glimmering in the ignition. They were her one chance for survival. Her only chance.

"You, you like my hair?" she asked in a quivering voice.

"Yeah and that's too damn bad."

"It's red all over," she said nervously as the man positioned his face on the right side of her neck, nuzzling the tip of his tongue onto her skin. She had to fight from jerking her head away. For now, playing along was her best defense. From the position he was in, she knew he was shielded from seeing her left hand. She reached for the ignition.

She was able to grab the keys without him noticing as he continued to snuggle his lips against her neck, licking the salt from her skin. Moving slowly at first, she realized her best chance was to yank the keys out instead of attempting to remove them slowly. Any jingling sound might cause alarm, but at least she'd have the keys in her hands by the time he understood the noise. But her initial tug proved fruitless. There was some sort of release lock or the angle was bad as the keys were frozen in place. Fortunately, Cowens had not noticed the brief clinking sound. Now she could feel the man's hot breath as he brought the knife around in his right hand to her chest, never moving away from her neck. His tongue flicked around her earlobe.

He held the knife casually in front of her. The blade caught each glint of lightning as the skies erupted. She had a brief notion of attempting to dislodge the blade from his hand but the price of failure was too high. He seemed psychotic enough to jam the blade in her neck without a second thought.

Again she tried to pull the keys from the ignition. Gradually, quietly. As she did, her fingers accidentally rubbed two keys together creating an abrupt click.

Her heart nearly stopped. Surely that sound was loud enough for this lunatic to hear! No it wasn't, it barely made a noise. Remain calm, Sherri. Calm.

"You like this?" Casanova Cowens said as he heard her sporadic inhaling.

This idiot thinks putting his tongue in my ear is some kind of turn on, Sherri thought as her fear began to evolve to anger. She gently leaned her neck to the right, into Cowen's lips and then slowly leaned away as his mouth followed. He dropped the knife slightly to the right and away. As he did, she reached her right hand to the ignition and ripped the keys out. At the same time, she pinned the hand holding the knife against the door with her knee. She caught him completely off guard and he was unable to react before she drove her right hand back over her shoulder and plunged the long car key into Cowen's right eye. Blood and fluid shot onto the windshield as the wounded man dropped the knife and screamed a sickening yell. Cowens flew back in his seat grabbing his face. Sherri dropped the keys on the floorboard at her feet.

"You bitch! God dammit!"

Sherri felt her stomach flop as the man's fluid streamed down her cheek and she leaned forward almost throwing up. The watery substance dripped on the dash and splotched the glass. She had to get out within seconds or he would kill her as he'd done Marvin Sellon.

She leaned over Marvin's limp body and flipped the door locks open as Cowens writhed in the back seat screaming obscenities. The man began to flail his left hand forward attempting to grab anything in his reach and choke it. Preferably, the bitch's pretty little neck.

Sherri quickly found the handle. She flipped open the door and saw blood streaming from a cut across her right knee. Pinning Cowen's hand with the knife had caught some of the blade. She lifted herself from the car and could barely stand. Fear had wound her muscles into knots and she nearly fell to the pavement.

She turned and slammed the door behind her and, through sheer will, forced herself to run toward the opening in the fence where Scott and Curt had followed Tibu into the Alligator Farm.

Tibu met the beast with a perfectly aligned downward swing. The blade cut into Tatterhorn with a thud, having no effect as it passed through the skull and out through the crotch. Tatterhorn swung his left arm and sent Tibu crashing into the wooden rail several feet away. The Indian was slow to rise and suffered another blow from the monster's massive arm, which sent Tibu staggering into the far rail. His back struck the framework hard, nearly splintering the wood.

"We've got to do something!" Curt shouted as he began moving toward the fight.

"Leave your sword here!" Scott commanded.

"What!"

"Trust me," he said laying his sword on the deck.

Curt looked at Scott and dropped his sword. He wanted to argue but understood Scott must have had a reason. At this rate, if they didn't intervene quickly, Tibu would be dead in a matter of seconds.

The two ran toward the beast.

Tatterhorn bent over and lifted Tibu into the air when the two men body-slammed the sopping monster square in the back. Curt wasn't sure what to expect and imagined sliding through the body and landing among the alligators. But the blow was startlingly sound and forced the creature off its feet and headlong into the deck. Tibu fell across the rail and desperately clung to the outside with his feet dangling dangerously close to the alligator infested water. He could hear the surface stirring below as he looked to see Scott, Curt and Tatterhorn slowly rising in unison. The creature spotted Tibu as the Indian struggled. With a grotesque expression, Tatterhorn moved toward the battered Indian.

Scott raced toward the monster and clipped him at the knees with his entire weight. For a moment, the creature buckled back and forth and then Curt, sensing the unbalance, blasted him from the side, grabbing the sash and ripping it from its body. The blow sent the torso of the beast against the rail with its upper body and head leaning over, facing the water below.

Tatterhorn let out a grueling howl but the men were persistent and managed to continue to push the beast over the edge while its arms swung helplessly in the air. In a final effort, it tried to hook its withered soggy toes on the wood but Scott was able to pry them off. The creature fell with a splash into the bog. The water became alive in every direction as the reptiles approached to investigate in their typically inquisitive nature.

Curt and Scott ran to help Tibu while the water where Tatterhorn submerged became a carnival of activity. The frantic slashing on the surface gave way to an animalistic scream that carried seven or eight unique voices with altering pitch. Vicious slaps of water signaled the feeding frenzy. Eventually the cries ceased and the water became calm.

Scott and Curt stood panting on the deck as the clouds lit up and the mountainous noise rumbled closer and closer. Tibu would not admit it, but he'd broken several ribs. The Indian had difficulty standing erect after bending down to grab the sash and withdrawing the Kilgotian. Scott picked up Tibu's sword.

"Scott," Curt began as they started to walk back, "how did you know our bodies would be more effective than the swords."

They arrived on the land where Scott and Curt had left their weapons.

"I wasn't positive but when Marvin's buckshot and Tibu's sword seemed useless, it was just a hunch."

"The thing was made of water. Our bodies are mostly water. Smart observation," Tibu said laboring.

"Are you going to be all right?" Curt asked.

"I'm fine. I'm better than fine," Tibu said looking down at the Kilgotian.

Sherri had nearly made it to the opening in the fence when she stopped. To her disbelief there were nine raggedy men clutching swords by their sides, approaching from the west on Anastasia Boulevard. They were less than 40 yards away.

God, this can't be happening, she thought.

She ran back in the direction of the vehicle and jumped behind one of the two pillars in front of the main entrance to the Alligator Farm. From there she could still hear Cowens in the closed car screaming in pain and anger.

Shut up you bastard! You're going to draw them over here, she thought.

Sure enough, as the soldiers approached with their floating eyes glowing in the darkness, they heard the man's cries and rushed toward the parking lot. Sherri was petrified and stood motionless behind the pillar. They passed in front of her and one of the leaders greeted Cowens as he emerged from the vehicle with a decapitating blow. Cowens' head launched from his vertebrae and rolled lazily onto the ground. His right hand holding his eye socket was also detached in the swing and plopped against the wooden fence and slid to the base. His body wavered momentarily and then dropped forward.

God, please don't let them see me. Please! Sherri could feel the tears straining to come out but she fought them back. Out of nowhere she felt a cold object touching the nape of her neck. She nearly screamed but a hand capped her mouth.

If it's going to end, then kill me quick, she thought.

The soldier ordered her to turn around in a muttering voice. She braced, then felt the object move away from her skin. She spun around in time to see an African American man crush a fist deep into the skull of her captor from behind.

"Damn, this mother's head just caved in!" Ambrose said louder than he meant to. He suddenly lunged behind the pillar with Sherri. The other Huguenots glared toward the entrance but saw no one. They turned to examine the car with Marvin's body inside.

"My God, thank you!" Sherri whispered.

"What in the hell is going on? Who are these guys with swords?"

"Just know this. Those men are lunatics and will kill anyone they see. There are three men inside the Alligator Farm that can help us. We have to get in and find them," Sherri whispered. "Where did you come from?" she said looking at the soldiers still by the Buick.

"I live in the apartments across the street. I saw some commotion and came over to see what was going on. Nothing personal lady, but I wish I'd have stayed inside."

"Well, I'm glad you didn't," Sherri said.

"So why did his head cave in? What's up with that?"

"Apparently, these men have already been dead once. Let's get inside that farm before this one gets back up," Sherri said pointing to the soldier on the ground.

Ambrose looked at her in complete disbelief. They watched the group surrounding the Buick and quietly moved away from the pillar when they were sure no one was looking. They had neared the opening when five more Huguenots approached quickly from the opposite direction and surprised them.

Sherri and Ambrose turned and ran. They had no choice. The bloodthirsty soldiers raised their swords and were hollering in hot pursuit. The others by Marvin's car were alerted and approached quickly. The two forces pinned their quarry in the entranceway. Sherri and Ambrose slowly back in, watching their maniacal attackers creep forward, pupils floating back and forth with unnatural ease. A foul smelling wind blew as the skies continued to burn and the sounds crackled overhead. The soldiers stepped forward then stopped, donning their swords. Several uttered some gibberish back and forth, their pupils swilling in the sockets and rage blending in their brows.

Oh my God, it's Pinot and Reece, Sherri thought as she overheard them. Standing behind Ambrose she did not see which two had spoken but she'd clearly heard the names. In unison on command, the soldiers raised their swords and moved toward Sherri and Ambrose.

From out of the darkness behind the congregation of soldiers, Scott, Curt and Tibu came up and attacked the semicircle surrounding Sherri and Ambrose. The first swings by Scott and Curt resulted in decapitations. But even with broken ribs, Tibu was more effective. His first three swipes decimated an equal number of Soulful Ones. Then he quickly moved over to plunge his sword into the chest of the two on the ground which Scott and Curt had defeated. As the remaining soldiers turned and faced the attackers, Ambrose jumped on the back of one and wrenched its head off, rupturing the skull cleanly from the vertebrae with a torrid snap.

"Shit!" he yelled as the headless body fell to the ground pulling him down.

Ambrose retreated, grabbed Sherri's hand and pulled her through the ensuing melee. But before they could get clear, one of the brothers ran at them and sunk his sword deep into Ambrose's back. The vengeful Huguenot twisted the blade inside as it passed through the man's chest. He thrust the entire length of the steel into Ambrose's body, rotating it until the handle was flush with the skin and blood was gushing outward. The thing smiled at Sherri as he placed his foot on Ambrose's back and ripped the sword from the sunken body, extracting a pool of blood and pieces of lung. Ambrose fell in an unresponsive heap. Blood instantly accentuated the pavement in all directions.

Sherri screamed as the rogue turned to engage Tibu. The element of surprise had given Scott, Curt and Tibu a decided advantage but fatigue was becoming a problem. Any soldiers that Scott and Curt were able to defeat would spring back up several seconds after hitting the ground if Tibu was not quick in finishing the job. And now, the Indian was locked in battle with a fierce warrior.

The fight continued for several minutes until only Scott, Curt, Tibu and two Soulful Ones were left. Sherri had moved to the side, away from the action, and had slumped against the fence out of sight, fighting back the tears. Tibu's opponent was proving exceptionally challenging. The two traded blow after blow until the Huguenot caught Tibu's right elbow with a deep gash. Tibu dropped his sword and fell to his knees. The Soulful One moved in for the kill when Scott temporarily broke off contact, leaving Curt to fight the remaining soldier, and ran his sword through the Huguenot's back as he was about to lance Tibu. The Huguenot let out a scream that caused the other Huguenot to swivel and Curt used the opportunity to bury his blade through its neck. The thing fell to the earth with a sputtering yelp. With this sudden break in the action, Scott and Curt raced over to Tibu and helped the Indian to his feet.

There was a series of clicks coming from the left. The men turned to see two dozen more soldiers running wildly toward them, swinging their swords overhead.

"We've got to get out of here. Can't let them get the Kilgotian," Tibu said as they helped him to his feet. The man was bleeding from his shoulder wound in addition to the slash on his elbow.

"Can you run?" Scott asked as they began moving away.

"I have no choice," Tibu replied as they started to run in the direction of Sherri.

"Sherri, come on!" Curt yelled. As they passed she rose and joined them.

They ran east on Anastasia Boulevard as the skies glowed sporadically, giving the impression that God was trying to turn on the sun but there was a short in the fuse. The tremendous thunder continued to blast overhead as the air pulsated.

The four were exhausted as they made their way down the barren street. Behind, in the distance, they could hear the ranting Huguenots. They didn't have to turn around to know that they were being chased relentlessly by the sword-welding soldiers who wanted the Kilgotian. The fish everyone seemed to want. The thing Tucker had wanted, the thing the pond wanted back and had taken over Tatterhorn to get, and the thing the phony detective Cowens, or whatever his name really was, was willing to kill for. The thing that had traveled on Noah's ark, the thing that was now so unholy that it reeked of evil, of death, of the devil himself.

As the foursome trudged on, Scott looked at Sherri who agonizingly tried to keep up with the men. She wondered how they could move so fast carrying the swords.

"Where's Marvin?" Scott said between breaths.

At first Sherri did not respond. She turned to Curt and back to Scott. "I'm sorry. He's, he's dead," she said softly.

Scott turned and looked straight ahead.

Curt looked at Scott.

Scott bit down hard on his lip as he ran. "Which one was it? Do you know?" he said fighting back his emotion.

"It wasn't one of those things, it was . . ." she said, pausing in mid-sentence to recall the name, "some detective named Cowens."

"What?" Curt said.

Scott looked at Curt. "He was no detective, he was one of Jean Luc LeFlore's treasure hunters. Another like Tucker, after the money." He took in another deep breath as they ran. "Bastard! As we thought, Jean Luc had others looking for this goddamn thing. If we get out of this I should resurrect that asshole myself just to kill him."

Away from the Alligator Farm, Anastasia Boulevard broke to the right, paralleling the beach several streets over. Between their current position and the coast, thick woods and vegetation created an impassable wall. Above the trees, the lighthouse loomed nearby.

"We can't go on like this for long. And they're still coming!" Curt shouted.

Scott suddenly had an idea and it involved getting to the ocean. Ahead, beyond a tiny strip mall on the left, was Red Cox road. Red Cox cut back at an acute angle eventually bordering the beach. Not far away, where the lighthouse sat on the left and a restaurant on the right, would be the nearest access to the sea.

When they approached Red Cox road, with the screams and shouts growing closer, Scott motioned for the group to turn left.

"Where are we going?" Tibu asked holding his ribs.

"I have an idea," Scott said and continued running without explanation. Sherri looked at Curt who had his arm around her to help keep pace. A brisk wind blew into their face from the east. A short distance away, they could hear the sound of the tumultuous waves crashing against the shore.

As they fled down Red Cox road they had no idea how many soldiers were in chase but knew if they were overtaken it would mean death. The foursome was too exhausted and too outnumbered to put up a healthy fight.

"Where are we going!" Curt yelled, helping Sherri to push on.

"To the ocean!" Scott screamed.

The skies were sporadically lit from the lightning streaks cascading above. When they reached the dirt road leading to the lighthouse parking lot, Scott pointed right. They cut toward the volatile sea slapping the beach a short distance away.

Then they abruptly stopped.

Ahead in the churning and sloshing white caps of the ocean, there were bodies coming ashore. Some were already trudging on the sandy beach. Others were knee-deep in the surf, or up to their waist, or with the tops of their heads barely breaking the rolling surface. Plodding inland and yielding weapons, heading toward Scott, Curt, Sherri and the wounded Tibu.

"God, look how many there are!" Curt said.

"Where are those things coming from!" Sherri said in a fearful whisper.

Tibu withered from the sight of the number of soldiers climbing out of the ocean to greet them. He rotated his head to the left and then right. "There must be 70 or 80," the Indian said disparagingly.

"Oh my God!" Sherri said feeling faint.

"I don't think the rubber strap held," Scott said watching the onslaught of dripping bodies rise from the sea. The things shuffled slowly as if trying to shake off atrophy. Some had swords, some long knives and others had barbaric axes.

"I don't think the beach is a good option, Scott. Any more ideas?" Curt said.

Scott turned and saw the pack of Huguenots in pursuit approaching from the right. He quickly turned around. With the next gleam of white from the sky, the St. Augustine Lighthouse jumped out of the darkness.

The lighthouse was originally known as the "Anastasia Light." It had been built in 1874 of brick and iron at a cost of $100,000 to replace an earlier wooden structure. It stood 165 feet high and was one of the very few lighthouses with the original black and white spiral design. The beacon was fire engine red. Lighthouses are classified by Orders and this one on Anastasia was classified as a "First Order" with 20,000 candlepower light. But on this night its beacon was inactive. The city had opted to cut the electrical source to the top of the structure in hopes of minimizing the chance of a fire in the probable event that Damon brought the lighthouse down.

Inside at the base was a short narrow hallway with two rooms on either side. To the left was the fuel room where oil had been stored to energize the beacon before being replaced by modern day electricity. To the right was an office. The end of the hallway emptied into the cylindrical structure. Inside the hollow tower, beginning on the left and running against the curved wall, was the first of eight spiral staircases reaching upward. Each staircase had 28 iron steps and was separated from the next staircase by a landing, also made of steel. In all, there were 219 steps. The top led to a walkway that wrapped around the outside of the beacon. In the daytime, visitors who had the cardiovascular stamina to chance the journey, were awed by the breathtaking panoramic view of the Atlantic Ocean to the east and Matanzas Bay and downtown St. Augustine to the west.

The two-story structure in front, at one time the lighthouse keeper's home, now doubled as a gift shop and Maritime Museum for the thousands of visitors each year.

"Come on!" Scott yelled as the screaming soldiers grew near. He led the group across Red Cox and through the dirt parking lot. The Huguenots followed yelling tirelessly, lifting their swords in hungry anticipation of a massacre. The lighthouse keeper's two-story house-turned-museum appeared as Scott ran to the left side of the building and toward the back. Cutting through an open stone gate, the group sprinted to the door at the base of the lighthouse. Scott arrived first. To his disappointment, the door was secured with a state of the art internal locking system. There were no external Masterlocks they could whack away to gain entrance. Scott stood back and gave the barrier several firm blows but the staunch door did not give. The others arrived and immediately realized Scott's concern.

"It's useless," Scott said in a defeated tone.

Tibu stepped forward and pulled a 22-caliber revolver from his pants. The group instinctively backed off as he dropped the sword to the ground and lifted his heavy arms. He cupped a hand under the butt and squeezed off all six rounds into the door handle. The sound cracked the air and sparks flew in all directions.

Initially, Scott wasn't sure the bullets had done enough damage. But Tibu stepped forward and smashed the door with a stern blast from his right foot. It broke open exposing the darkness inside.

The screams behind were again drawing close. Until the sound of the gunfire, the soldiers had lost track of their prey. Now they charged the back of the house, toward the spiraling black and white structure leaping into the sky.

Scott entered first followed by Sherri, Curt and Tibu. He walked with outstretched hands until he found the left wall. Curt located the right wall while Sherri chose to stand within the dim light of the doorway.

"Scott, does this thing have electric lights?" Curt said in a panic. In the next second, there was a click and the room was viewable.

Tibu quickly pulled Sherri inside and closed the door as the Huguenots rounded the corner and entered through the stone gate.

"We've got to secure the door," Tibu said quietly. The men raced into a room on the left, Sherri into the one on the right while Tibu remained against the door. Scott and Curt found nothing of substance. Upon Sherri's loud whisper, they scurried into the other room, which turned out to be an office, and found a large oak antique desk. It would make a perfect block. The men positioned themselves on either side and slowly slid the table into the hallway in short scoots. Fortunately it slid easily. Too easily.

"It's on wheels," Scott said.

"That's okay," Curt replied.

Tibu leaned his back against the door. The soldiers were close outside but obviously had not seen them go inside the lighthouse and were tentative about entering an ambush situation.

But as Tibu listened, the voices increased. More were arriving.

CHAPTER-THIRTY-SEVEN

"Hurry!" Tibu whispered to the men as he adjusted the Kilgotian's skeleton inside his shirt. Scott and Curt, with Sherri's help, pushed the desk toward Tibu and into place against the door. Curt ripped a piece of his torn shirt off and split it, handing one section to Scott. The men wadded the material and jammed the cloth behind the back wheels and then tested for durability. The desk held firm.

"By the way, Tibu" Curt began, "Why were you hiding the gun?"

"I wasn't. I knew it had a specific purpose. It's ineffective against the soldiers."

"Did you dream about this? Coming in here?" Curt asked.

"A couple of times."

"Do you want to tell us how those dreams ended?" Curt asked.

"No."

"Great," Curt said walking away from the door and retrieving the sword he had propped against the wall.

"What now?" Sherri asked.

Scott looked around. His mind was racing with a certain clarity he had not experienced this evening. He attributed it to the adrenaline lapping through his body as the voices outside came near and the handle of the door shook.

"Let' go up," Scott said looking at Tibu. The Indian nodded.

They moved through the hallway as the doorknob again rattled violently. If nothing else, the Huguenots could probably see the light escaping from the doorframe. There was no way of knowing how long the desk would hold and climbing the stairs was the only option.

As tired as they were, the four trudged upward on the winding steel staircase, their fatigue multiplying with each step. The swords began to take on the weight of anvils as they made their way to the first, second and then third landing before stopping to rest. Below, down through the hollow cylinder, they could hear the occasional banging against the outer door. So far the desk was holding.

The lightning flashes inside the stairwell were virtually nonexistent and the only light was a soft glow coming from the bottom floor.

After a brief pause, the four continued up to the fourth, fifth and sixth landings before again stopping to rest and listen to the activity below. While scaling the iron steps it was impossible to hear much more than the clinking of their own footsteps. But once they stopped, the structure would echo anything occurring below. As they paused, the bottom had gone strangely quiet. The soldiers' attempts to make their way inside had either been abandoned or were being rethought.

The utter silence led to fear. Curt took a deep breath and put his arm around Sherri, drawing her near.

"Isn't this romantic?" he said, trying to calm her. "Our own private lighthouse."

She smiled unable to say anything positive.

"We have to keep going," Scott said and took the first few steps toward the seventh landing.

"Why?" Tibu asked. His expression showed his fear for the first time. The hardened Indian seemed to be dissolving. His eyes bore concern and he grimaced from his burning wounds.

Scott hesitated then turned and continued up without answering. In an ironic way, he was now giving Tibu a piece of his own medicine. Answering questions only when he felt like it, only when completely necessary.

Curt and Sherri followed, as did Tibu. They made their way onto the seventh landing in the total darkness. As the four moved slowly along the grate, sliding their feet to make sure nothing was on the steel floor to trip upon, lightning flashed harshly overhead and beamed through the small window on the opposite side.

Standing to Scott's left was a large man. He had been so patiently waiting in the blackness, they nearly walked right into him. Now he was only several feet away braced against the wall. Out of terror, Scott raised his sword to the right and curled it around toward the man's neck. The blade swished through the air and made contact severing the head from the body.

Sherri screamed as the succession of lightning outside kept the mutilated figure in view.

There was a tortured tearing sound as the blade sliced through, nearly hitting Curt on the recoil. The cardboard face of the victim stuck onto the tip of the steel and released on the back swing, gently falling down the hollow stairwell and floating to the floor far below.

"Holy crap!" Scott said panting, "Who in their right mind puts up a full life cut-out of a man on the seventh landing of a lighthouse!"

Curt and Sherri grinned at Scott's embarrassment. Tibu walked over to the wall and sat down. Curt strolled over to the torn figure and read the inscription on the wooden plaque in the scant light, helped by the sporadic bursts of energy from the clouds.

Henry "Hank" R. Mears
Lighthouse Keeper 1889 – 1968

"Hmmm," Curt said. "Same occupation as my ex-wife. Light housekeeper."

Sherri smiled.

"Very funny," Scott said almost grinning. "Let's go."

"You lead," Tibu said in a firm voice to Scott. "In case we run into any more cardboard figures."

On the eighth landing the lighting significantly improved.

"OK," Curt grabbed Scott's shoulder. "Now what are we going to do?"

"We're going on the deck outside."

"Why?" Curt asked.

"To get rid of this fish."

Tibu looked at him and cocked his head. "Explain."

"I have a theory. Hear me out. Everything we've read and heard about the legend describes a specific process of reincarnation. Put the fish in a pond or lake and put the corpse in the ocean. More specifically, put the Kilgotian in fresh water and put the body in the salt. See what I'm getting at?"

Tibu nodded slightly as if he understood the intention but wasn't quite sure of the probability.

"Back up the bus, Scott. Replay that for me because I missed it," Curt said.

"Remember the note we found in Pierre's backyard? The four sentences he translated but didn't give you? The last sentences mentioned that 'the process must not be violated.' We assumed it referenced the sentence directly before it about the 300 day time limit. But what I believe it was referring to as well is the fresh water versus saltwater sequence."

Curt raised his head, "So you're thinking we should dunk this damn fish in the sea?"

"It makes sense," Tibu remarked.

"Oh my God!" Sherri said suddenly. "The papers Marvin had me translate. It made some reference to a fish. Is that what you're talking about? How it should only be placed in pure water! I think Scott's right!"

"What about that 'all waters are joined, crap?' " Curt asked.

"Think about it. Are they? Are they really joined? No, not at all. There's a distinct separation between salt water and fresh water. Saltwater fish can't survive in freshwater and vice versa." Scott said.

Again Tibu nodded and Curt seemed to accept the rationale.

"Well, that's all good and fine but we're at the top of this lighthouse. My best guess is we're about 100 yards from the beach with a street in between. How do you intend to get it there?"

"God willing, if the wind is right, it's going to fly the friendly skies," Scott said.

Curt looked at Scott, not because of the idea, although it did border somewhat on the lunatic fringe, but because it was the first time during this entire escapade that Scott had made reference to God.

"The thing is light. If the wind is blowing favorably, it might make the ocean." Tibu said as he withdrew the Kilgotian from his shirt and unlocked the door leading to the outside deck.

"Wait. I have an idea that might help. Curt, come with me," Sherri said. She grabbed his hand and led him back to the seventh landing where the headless figure of Hank Mears stood. They returned in a few minutes carrying a chunk of cardboard.

"Maybe we can fasten wings," she said.

Tibu took the cardboard and gently wove it between the ribs of the skeleton, wedging it tightly. "Now, if only the wind will cooperate," he said.

"Let's add this," Tibu said as he reached into his pants pocket grimacing from the pain. He withdrew a pen light and a small one-quarter inch roll of duct tape."

"What are you? McGyver?" Scott said facetiously.

Tibu placed the pen light against the skeletal head and wrapped several layers of tape around it. The flashlight would serve two purposes; it would help the men see the Kilgotian and also give it a heavier nose with which to fly, similar to the way a child's balsa airplane has a metal tip attached to the point.

Tibu pushed open the door and was accosted by a deluge of lightning stirring from every direction. The top of the lighthouse was nowhere near the clouds but the proximity to the storm seemed to have increased by tenfold. As he moved onto the deck, grabbing the handrails, he smiled. The wind was gusting directly toward the Atlantic. This renewed Tibu's energy and gave him a feeling of contentment. It's almost over, he thought. The air around him crackled and the hair on the base of his neck rose. But all was right.

Scott and Curt walked out onto the deck. They had seen the wind pushing Tibu's hair toward the ocean indicating their good fortune. From this height, with the strong tailwind, the Kilgotian would easily reach the sea.

Suddenly Sherri's voice burst through the air. "They're coming!" she yelled. Curt looked back to see her leaning over the rail inside, squinting down toward the base of the lighthouse. He moved through the doorway and heard the distinctive sound of footsteps clomping on iron. The noise echoed up the chamber and filled the lighthouse with dread. Their escape path was not only sealed, but they had allowed themselves to be cornered.

Suddenly, Curt concluded that none of them would make it out of this alive. He swallowed hard and returned outside to warn the others.

"She's right. They're coming up!" Curt yelled over the brisk wind.

Tibu had a look of acceptance as the night lit up and the thunder roared. He looked at Scott and back at Curt handing him the Kilgotian. "Let this beast fly."

Then Tibu ran inside, grabbed his sword and bolted down the stairwell. His steps rang out harshly. Curt and Scott were so dumbfounded they never got a word out.

"What is he doing?" Sherri asked, running outside.

"What he has to," Curt said solemnly.

"Scott, let's get this thing in the Atlantic and hope you're right," Curt said as he held the aerodynamic fish high over his head and let it go with the stiff breeze. The thing sailed off beautifully.

Tibu settled on the seventh landing, nestled in the dark next to what was left of cardboard Hank. He could hear the Huguenots rapidly approaching from below. He remained still, not making a sound. The shadows would allow him ample advantage, at least against the first few soldiers that reached the landing. Beyond two or three he could not hold out. His only goal was to buy his comrades enough time and hope they understood what had to be done.

As he crouched patiently, the pain in his shoulder and elbow was immense. He tried to turn his thoughts away by concentrating on the sounds.

He continued to monitor the distance of the approaching men by the sound of their steps. Slowly, and without intention, his mind glazed back in time, to centuries gone by. He flashed to the morning he had awakened after disclosing the pond's secret. The sick, hungover feeling of how the whiteman's alcohol had left him so puny. How the days and years had passed. Then the fateful morning he stopped breathing and became a Soulful One at the mercy of the Atlantic Ocean. The same body of water he now sought as an end to the ordeal.

He thought of his own existence. He was a Soulful One, whether the rules applied or not. He wasn't a man but a thing in a human shell. He had lived a long time, too long. Life is meant to have a beginning and an end. He had seen more things than the mind should have to endure.

And the dreams, those persistent dreams of this one night, never consistent, never ending the same way. Constantly changed by the intervention of circumstances. Some he controlled. Some controlled by another.

He snapped out of his thoughts as the soldiers reached the landing directly below. Tibu's body tensed. He held the sword in his right hand with the tip touching the ground near the wall to his right. He would wait for the Huguenots to reach his landing and move halfway to the next set of stairs before he would venture an attack. His preference would be to catch them from behind after they passed by.

As the seconds crept by, the floor below went silent.

Dead silent.

Then he heard clanking on iron that seemed to be strangely losing volume. He listened keenly to the sound, thinking his senses were deceiving him.

But there was no mistake.

The noise was growing faint.

The soldiers had abandoned their efforts and were heading back down! Tibu started to feel revived and began to rise when the intrusion of steps slapping against metal found his eardrums. The sound grew louder. There were multiple sets of footsteps ascending the stairs quickly. Tibu's optimism sank.

He knelt back down in position, sword angled by his side. Through the darkness, he saw two figures arise from the spiral staircase to his right. They slowed as they reached the landing, realizing the darkness held a perfect opportunity for an ambush.

Tibu was motionless. In his mind, he desperately begged the frequent flashes from outside to hold off for just a few more seconds. The small window across would foil his chances if light found its way through.

Just give me long enough for these two to make their way across the landing.

In the cloak of darkness, Tibu would have every advantage, save the fact it was one against two and he was wounded. More injured than he had let on. Nevertheless, against two, he stood a reasonable chance of surviving the encounter. If the rest had come, he would have been doomed.

The two soldiers cautiously moved through the darkness. One ran his sword against the wall as if checking for foes that might be hiding in wait. The sword scraped the mortar three feet off the floor, head high to the squatting Tibu, creating an irritating whine.

Tibu tensed, gripping his sword tightly in his right hand.

Six feet away from Tibu. Five feet . . . four feet . . .

Tibu slowly raised his sword to prepare for contact.

Three feet . . . two feet . . .

Tibu angled his sword outward. He was about to thrust the blade into the chest of the passing soldier when the scraping ceased. The Huguenot lifted his weapon placing it on his shoulder. The second one following closely as the two picked up speed and looked to the next set of stairs.

In the instant the second Huguenot passed, Tibu jumped to his feet and swiveled his sword from right to left, clipping the soldier's head into the wall. The body fell limp as the first soldier turned screaming a bloody yell. The Huguenot barely had time to react before Tibu was on him hacking away. Amazingly, Tibu had more strength left than he would ever have imagined. But the first soldier was resilient, taking several blows about the shoulders and ribs before joining his companion on the deck.

With the two bodies slain, Tibu doubled over to rest. Fatigue jumped on him, but his mind was clear and his fortitude was firm.

This was the night he had waited for. He would give it everything humanly and inhumanly possible. There were no second chances.

He waited for his body to respond positively. For his tired, wounded muscles to revitalize. But before he was ready, the steps warned again of an opposing force. This time it appeared to be a single man approaching. Running up the stairs at the pace of a marathoner. Tibu backed to the left of the cardboard cutout and crouched against the wall. The pain again declared its presence. Outside, thunder roared and the wind howled as it whipped around the lighthouse.

Whatever was ascending the stairs was approaching fast and with purpose. Tibu closed his eyes and swallowed hard.

The Kilgotian gently moved upon the wind, gliding effortlessly. The skies had again, and miraculously, lightened, this time to a dirty gray. Following the path of the fish was surprisingly easy. And it was going just as they had hoped. Staying aloft and traveling quickly to the cresting waves.

"It's there! It's there!" Sherri yelled jumping up and down.

Curt smiled, "It's getting there but it's not there yet."

The three watched the Kilgotian travel outward. By its height, it was difficult to judge exactly where it was in relation to the ground but even Scott began to smile. It has to be over the sea by now, Scott thought as it continued its flight.

It was uncanny how it had departed and shot straight for the ocean. But that's where the wind was blowing. As it glided farther and farther, Scott thought how odd it was for the wind to be blowing out. With a hurricane approaching from the east, any meteorologist would probably tell you this was impossible. Just our luck, he thought as he smiled.

"It must be 250 yards over the surface by now," Curt said. "It's about time the thing landed. You realize it hasn't lost any altitude? It might make its way over to Africa and miss the salt water altogether."

The words had barely left Curt's mouth when Scott had a gut wrenching feeling. Scott turned to look at Curt. He was going to tell his friend not to say anything negative again. But Sherri's voice interrupted him.

"Oh my God, I don't believe this," she cried.

Scott was looking at Curt and didn't have to turn around to know what had happened. He could see it in his friend's eyes.

The fish was coming back.

CHAPTER-THIRTY-EIGHT

Scott turned to look. At first his eyes would not allow the truth to exist. The small fish with the cardboard wings and weighted nose looked as it had. Gently sliding off the coast into oblivion. But a few seconds of steady concentration revealed the bitter truth.

It was growing larger. And it was doing so quickly. Then the three suddenly felt the wind go slack and change direction 180 degrees. The bursts of air to their faces were brisk and full of volume. It was a steady, relentless flow.

"I absolutely don't believe this!" Curt said.

"I don't know what I believe," Scott said watching the airborne Kilgotian navigate the wind stream.

Sherri lurched forward clinging to the rail as an unexpected sound surprised her. It was a shriek coming from inside. Somewhere down the stairwell.

Scott looked at Curt with concern.

"Look!" Sherri said pointing to the beach now visible through the gray cloud cover. Along the coast, Soulful Ones were coming ashore in mass. The initial wave was congregated on the sand. They seemed to be waiting for their brethren to arrive as several hundred soldiers trekked through the treacherous breakers heading inland, each armed and intent on revenge.

"Oh my God," Curt said.

After briefly glancing at the multitude, Scott focused on the Kilgotian. It was still sailing inland, riding the steady breeze but it had lost substantial altitude. At one time lifting higher than their position, it was now a mere 100 feet off the surface of the ocean and losing height quickly.

"It's landing," Scott said pointing.

From the railway, the three could see the soldiers below. The fish was angling perfectly to the foot of the lighthouse where six Huguenots awaited its arrival. One of the Soulful Ones was laughing, as he eyed the incoming prize.

"There's one of the brothers," Scott said.

"How do you know," Curt asked.

"Because when Tibu and I saw them at the fort, they each had tee shirts on. One was blue, the other white. See the Huguenot with the blue shirt?"

"Yeah, I see him," Curt replied. "Now I remember them at the Alligator Farm. Where'd they get tee shirts?"

"Who cares. At least we can identify them," Scott said.

"Yeah, but we can only kill Pinot with the sword Tibu has. We have no way of destroying Reece. We still don't know who brought him back."

"This is all good and fine that you can identify the enemy but what do we do now?" Sherri asked as the wind blew her red hair across her face.

Scott and Curt looked down where the Kilgotian had landed gently on the ground near the solders. The blue-shirted Frenchman bent down and picked up the fish. He ripped away the light and cardboard, then looked up and choked out a maniacal laugh. His eyes glowed as he lifted the fish high over his head and held it in triumph.

"We're screwed," Curt said dejectedly.

Tibu opened his eyes as the aggressor reached the seventh landing and abruptly stopped where the steps emptied onto the steel flooring. He stood motionless. Unlike the two before him, he was allowing his eyes to focus and Tibu might have to attack before he was ready. The pain in his shoulder and arm was causing them to go numb. He wasn't sure he could even lift the sword. At the moment, time was Tibu's enemy. The faster the man approached the better chance the Indian would have.

But the soldier took small steps, inching his way along. Tibu saw the dirty white tee shirt and knew it to be one of the brothers. The one who violently killed the black man at the Alligator Farm by mercilessly driving the sword through the man's back and churning it through his chest. The heartless thing that at one time had been a man Tibu had come to know and respect as a young Indian. One of the brothers who had tricked him that fateful night and made his life an eternal prisoner of humanity.

It was a soul he had come to hate.

Tibu's rage was nearly uncontrollable. Yet he waited. Waited patiently in the darkness. As he had waited for 400 years. But he did not know which brother this was. If this was Reece, Tibu could not win. If it was Pinot, with Reece's sword, the weapon of the one who had made Pinot a Soulful One, he could destroy the Huguenot.

The Huguenot moved quietly, making his way within several feet of Tibu. Suddenly, lightening streaked the sky and the far window glowed creating light upon the wall where Tibu was cradled close to the landing floor firmly holding his sword. The Huguenot immediately spied the Indian and turned to raise his sword. Tibu was surprised by the sudden illumination and leaned to his left off balance, sliding against the wall as he fell. The Frenchman dropped his weapon toward Tibu's head. The blade narrowly missed, landing on Tibu's sword dragging along the floor. There was a dazzling clink as the two pieces of steel collided and an ominous spark danced free.

The area went dark as the lightning temporarily subsided but the madman's eyes adjusted to see Tibu scurrying to the right. The Indian struggled to rise as he watched the hellish white pupils bob back and forth following his motion. Again the thing slammed the sword down toward Tibu. But this time, climbing to his feet, the Indian was able to raise his sword and cleanly block the blow. The sound echoed inside the lighthouse walls. Thunder struck with an angry scowl and lightning burned outside.

Tibu, now fully erect, went on the attack. He coiled his sword to his right and made a roundhouse swipe slicing into the thing's side with a narrow cut. It was not a firm hit and left Tibu off balance stumbling to his left against the metal guard overlooking the hollow center of the tower and the seven-story drop to the bottom. He caught himself as his stomach crunched into the rail and his chest hovered over the edge. He barely clung to his sword as it hung over pointing at the distant floor below. The collision into the rail left him dazed. With his back toward the Huguenot, he could sense the thing approaching for the kill.

Tibu's body was deteriorating quickly and his muscles were saturated with pain. His strength had nearly evaporated. He knew he'd never be able to spin and fend off the next blow as the sword in his hand was completely out of position to make a rapid defense. His only option was to slide either left or right along the rail and hope the thing didn't anticipate the move. Without thinking, Tibu moved to his left.

The next sensation was a searing warmth streak down his right shoulder blade to the small of his back. Then an agonizing jolt seized his body. Tibu turned and tried to lift his right arm but found it unresponsive. He switched his sword to his left in time to ward off another strike. Tibu was now backpedaling toward the ascending stairs. The burning in his back was almost paralyzing. The crazed Huguenot seemed to feed off Tibu's injury and attacked feverishly, blow after blow.

Tibu was barely able to block the swings. His energy now came from some unknown source. On the next swing, Tibu caught the tip of his opponent's blade across his right forearm and he grimaced in pain.

The thing hesitated and stared at the Indian. The two men had fought to the foot of the stairs leading to the beacon. The flickering lightning from above now shown on them and the Huguenot examined his opponent's eyes.

"Tibua!" it yelled with a fiendish smile. It rested the sword on its right shoulder. It could tell the Indian was a beaten adversary and no longer a threat.

Tibu strained to keep his head up and eyes focused. His right side was useless and in complete turmoil compounded by the earlier injury to his shoulder. He held the sword in his left hand with the tip of the steel blade on the floor. He was exhausted, barely able to stand. He wasn't sure he could raise the blade again to defend himself.

"Tibua!" The Soulful One screamed again holding its side where yellow ooze trailed out. This time the voice was fiery, full of anger. How dare this Indian try to stop me? Attempt to defeat me with a French weapon? Who does he think he is? Soon it will be over for this savage bastard.

Through clouded vision, Tibu focused on the right hand grasping the sword on the thing's shoulder. It looked malformed. He expected one finger to be absent, but there was more. Why would he be missing more than one finger?

Then it clicked and made perfect sense. This is Pinot, Tibu realized!

During the battle, there had been the consistent doubt of who he was up against. Now he knew. And with Reece's sword, he had a weapon that would be effective.

The excitement he felt suddenly energized his left arm. Tibu looked at Pinot and smiled. It was an arrogant expression and the thing's eyes boiled. Tibu quickly raised his sword and before Pinot could stop him, lunged forward, lancing the Huguenot through the chest.

Pinot simultaneously swung his weapon down across Tibu's right shoulder, hacking deep into the Indian. The two fell into a heap, the Huguenot with Tibu's sword securely affixed in its body as yellow fluid pooled around the two. Tibu was on his back, lying across Pinots legs, nauseated as he watched colors and images from his lifetime dance in front of his eyes. Moments later, or was it minutes, he felt a cold, mesmerizing shudder lapse through his legs and rise to his upper body sending the pain slowly away. He briefly closed his eyes and opened them to see several shadowy faces closing in.

Scott led the way down to the seventh landing with caution. They had heard screams and clashing swords but all had gone quiet.

Curt was close on his heels and both had their swords prepared, in case of attack. Sweat was pouring down their faces. Sherri followed two steps behind.

They made their way to the landing and paused to give their eyes an opportunity to adjust to the dim light.

"Look," Scott said pointing to a clump. He moved cautiously closer trying to understand what he was looking at. Curt pulled along side.

"It's Tibu," Curt said sadly.

"What about the other one?" Scott asked. A burst of lightning flickered three times in succession causing the area to reveal its secret. It was obvious the second body was mortally wounded. The sword sunk into its chest and jutted out its back. Behind them, against the wall, two more Huguenots lay slain.

Scott bent down close enough to see Tibu's facial features. Sherri and Curt knelt on either side.

Tibu opened his eyes.

Curt noticed the wounds and traced the blood that had spilled onto his shirt and to the floor. Then he spied the yellow substance leaking from the Huguenot's corpse. "Don't get near that. That stuff burns like hell."

"Tibu, can you hear us?" Sherri asked as the Indian's eyes wandered across the three faces, never stopping to focus on one.

"I . . . I . . . I got . . ." he closed his eyes and swallowed hard. Blood continued bubbling from his right shoulder and flowing to the floor.

"Pin . . . ot. One . . . more."

The last syllable escaped his mouth even as death silenced him. His head rolled to the side and his eyes briefly glowed in the darkness. The light faded as Tibu's body went limp.

Curt reached forward and drew the man's eyes closed.

Scott dropped his head. "A man's life should never last this long he told us. Now he can rest without the dreams."

Sherri wiped her eyes with her hands. She barely knew the man but felt his finality translated to a certain sense of freedom for his soul.

"How did he know this one was Pinot?" Scott wondered aloud.

But Scott did not respond. Instead, he rose, clutching his sword. His anger exploded and he turned and walked to the guardrail where he slammed the blade across the top. The sound vibrated through the landing. He turned to stare as Curt rose holding Sherri's hand.

"What now, Scott?" They've got the Kilgotian. We can't beat them all." Curt said.

Scott was silent as he turned and gazed down into the darkness of the lighthouse.

Before he responded, a shrill screeching sound emanated from the base of the lighthouse. It was an annoying squeal that caused Sherri to place her hands at the sides of her head.

"What the hell is that?" Curt asked.

"That's a sound we've heard before!" Scott screamed as the noise grew louder. He reached into his pocket and pulled out the wax he'd had since reincarnating the Kilgotian Tuesday morning at Marvin's. Twice since then he'd considered throwing the wax balls away. He quickly inserted a piece in each ear. Curt, seeing what Scott was doing, checked his pockets and then remembered he'd tossed his wax pellets into the bathroom wastebasket at the professor's house. Scott looked at Curt who shrugged his shoulders.

Curt grabbed his ears.

"Come on!" Scott screamed running up to the top floor and through the door onto the walkway. Staring down, he could see the soldiers on the ground writhing, holding their heads. There was a light mist falling.

"The rain! It's freshwater!" Curt yelled as he scrunched his face in discomfort.

"Curt, stay here with Sherri!" Scott screamed as the sound continued.

"But . . ."

"No buts. The sound's too loud! With any luck, those soldiers will stay disabled and I can get that goddamn fish into the ocean!"

Scott didn't wait for Curt's approval. He turned and raced through the door.

"Be careful!" Sherri screamed as Curt watched his friend disappear through the dark opening.

Scott made his way swiftly to the seventh landing, sidestepping Tibu, Pinot and the yellow gunk that mired the floor. Once past he continued downward. To the sixth, fifth, fourth . . . the tortured sound consistently growing louder . . . third, second . . . the boisterous noise gaining strength, finally reaching the base. Leaping the last three steps he saw the entrance was open. The oak desk had been pushed away from the door and backed into the office. Two soldiers were in view, writhing on the ground outside the door, clutching their ears. Scott did not hesitate. He ran toward the door, pushing the wax deeper into his ears.

Once outside, he was astonished by what he saw. The rain had ceased and the wind was zinging quick, sharp bursts. Eight or nine Soulful Ones rolled on the ground, screaming harrowing sounds, their weapons scattered about. The LeFlore in the dirty blue tee shirt, which Scott now knew was Reece, was flat on his back. His shirt had a gaping hole and the Kilgotian, head down and tail in the air, was viciously chewing into the Huguenot's ribcage. Wailing, Reece fruitlessly tried to defend himself from the attack. Yellow ooze was vaulting upward several feet with each grinding clamp of the Kilgotian's jaw.

But with the short-lived precipitation, the stern wind was quickly evaporating the water from the skin of the beast. The Kilgotian was transforming back to its skeletal state of hibernation. Scott could see its aggressiveness waning and knew he had to act quickly.

He dashed toward Reece and drove his sword through the mass of the Kilgotian's body, burying the tip into the Huguenot's chest. Reece's screams were nearly as deafening as the fish itself. With the fish nearly dormant, Scott lifted the whining skeleton, barely covered by flesh, and held the point of the blade upward.

The Kilgotian stuck on the end of the sword like a shishkabob. A millisecond later it was a harmless semblance of sturdy bones and the horrifying noise ceased.

"Oh no!" Scott said to himself as the soldiers began to rise. He turned to stare at Reece. The injured Huguenot was coming to his feet as well. The Kilgotian had done damage but not enough. Scott's only chance was to try and make it to the beach. He bolted to the dirt parking area. Reece rose and, grasping his chest, ordered three soldiers back into the lighthouse. He commanded the rest to follow him in pursuit of Scott and the Kilgotian.

Curt and Sherri watched the activity from above. As they saw the soldiers enter the lighthouse they backed away from the rail and looked at each other.

"What are we going to do?" Sherri asked nervously.

"We're going to do whatever we have to do to survive," Curt said. "I just hope Scott gets to the ocean before they can catch him."

"But what good's it going to do? They've already brought back so many."

"If we can destroy the fish I believe it will destroy the army. At least we better hope so. It's our only chance," Curt responded.

Curt grabbed Sherri's hand and they made their way around the outside deck of the beacon to the doorway. Curt studied the knob but, since it opened inward, there was no way to secure it from their side.

Sherri looked at Curt's waist. "Give me your belt" Sherri demanded.

"What?"

"Give it to me."

Curt didn't argue. There wasn't time.

He ripped it from his pants and handed it to her. There were two small poles on either side of the doorway. She looped the belt through the buckle and slid it down the pole on the right-hand side, then stretched the remainder of the belt across the doorway five inches off the ground and guided the end through the two-inch gap between the left pole and the wall. She sat down firmly holding the end. It was stretched taut across the base of the closed door. She used her feet against the pole as leverage, squeezing her body against the wall to stay out of immediate view.

Curt looked at the woman and smiled. She was brilliant. Sherri shot back an encouraging grin.

Curt positioned himself on the far side of the door. He raised his sword as the lightning beckoned nearby, startling the darkness. On the horizon, the night was beginning to give way to the dawn. Clouds bundled together in the sky as the wind hummed a constant strain. The light would soon arrive unless Damon decided to cancel the day.

Scott raced out of the parking lot and headed across Red Cox Road. The screams filled his ears. He pulled the sword down and grabbed the fish from the end. He thought about throwing the sword away to lighten his load but then reconsidered. He might need it. Scott had no idea what he would face when he got near the water. The last time he'd looked, an unholy army was assembling on the beach.

Halfway across Red Cox he saw the assortment of bodies visible on the shore. Simultaneously, they spotted him. A group of newly created Soulful Ones began yelling and charging toward him. He angled left onto Red Cox. Scott had never been past the lighthouse and had no idea how far the street went or if it connected to other roads. He had always assumed it was a dead end and now he saw that the streetlights did indeed end somewhere up ahead. He suddenly had the discomforting feeling that he was boxing himself in. First the lighthouse and now the dead end road. But his only chance was to find a cutover to the beach somewhere up ahead rather than try and make it to the ocean through the pack of waiting soldiers.

For several hundred feet the screams continued. At one point he turned and saw no less than 50 or 60 watery-eyed Huguenots in pursuit. Sweat was pouring from his body as fear kept his exhausted legs pumping. Scott frantically searched for an opening to the ocean, but to no avail. To his right, dense foliage and trees lined the road and although the pavement was well lighted, he didn't want to chance getting caught in the dark wall of underbrush where the light ceased. He had to go on and hope there was a more visible path to the shore before the streetlights ended.

As he ran, the sword became incredibly heavy and the awkwardness of carrying the weapon in one hand and the fish in the other hindered a smooth running motion. He became more and more anxious from the constant shouts and was sure the angry mob was gaining ground. Without further contemplation, as pain and cramps embellished his body, he flung the sword to the side. It clanked along the pavement, coming to a stop along the edge of the grass. How ironic it would be if one of the Huguenots retrieved it and used it for his own demise.

The wind circled in blustery gusts, sometimes helping his momentum, sometimes hampering. All the while the screams drew closer and closer as the end of the streetlights approached. There were only two lamps remaining and then darkness ruled beyond. Dawn was coming but the sun was shielded by the ominous storm clouds.

Suddenly, to Scott's right, was a clearing. It was almost hidden in the shadows without a hint of how deep it reached. For all Scott knew, he still might have to travel a considerable distance in the underbrush before reaching the water's edge. Regardless, he had to chance it. He was running out of road, strength and time. For an instant, he wondered about Curt and Sherri, if they were still alive. Then he pushed the thought out of his mind to contend with his own situation.

He cut into the clearing and glanced back at the pack coming toward him. Reece, with his torn shirt, ravaged chest and murderous expression was leading the way. His eyes reflected the white streetlights and his stare was ghastly. The Huguenot was so enraged, he churned the sword above his head as he ran.

Scott dashed into the clearing. Forty feet in, he ran into a dense thicket. He frantically searched for an opening but to no avail. If he attempted to get through the tangled brush, the Huguenots, with their weapons to hack a path, would catch up and massacre him in a matter of minutes.

Now he was trapped with no options. The screaming soldiers were quickly approaching with their horrid white eyes dancing in the night, anxious to bury their deadly weapons in enemy flesh.

Sherri kept the belt taut as Curt flattened himself against the opposite side of the closed door. Even from the outside with the staunch breeze sending their hair dancing, the drumming sound of the footsteps chiming through the tall hollow structure was audible. It seemed to take an incredibly long time for the sound to stop.

When the inside went silent, Curt clutched the sword in both hands high over his head. He gave Sherri a wink and she smiled tentatively. He could tell she was absolutely terrified. He had made a decision that if he had to, he would give up his life to save hers. For an instant, as lightening spilled across the sky, he saw Julie's beaming face.

Seconds passed and the silence continued. Then the door slowly pulled inward. This was not what they had planned and Curt's confidence plummeted. The best scenario was for the Huguenots to burst onto the deck with wild abandonment. The cautious tact was not conducive to their trap and would leave Curt and Sherri at a huge disadvantage. Sherri bit her lip as a frightened tear streamed down her cheek.

But suddenly, with a menacing scream, the three Soulful Ones charged out single file, so tightly packed together it was as if they were one creature. Sherri leaned back using all her weight to stiffen the belt at the moment the first Huguenot's ankle made impact. The noise and sudden burst through the doorway caused Curt to hesitate as the first Huguenot caught on the belt and lost his balance. The other two could not stop and the three fell against the railing in a clustered heap. The lead soldier lost his weapon over the edge. A second weapon fell to the deck after striking the guardrail and bouncing back near Sherri.

Curt, regaining his composure, offered a swift strike, severing the head of the lead Soulful One who was hanging over the edge watching his weapon fall to the earth below. The limp body dropped to its knees, hovered briefly, then fell on the cement walkway as the detached head fell to the distant ground below.

It was at that moment, Curt thought about the sword he was using. He was still armed with the one acquired from the Soulful One on the gundeck. Just, one floor below, in the slain body of Pinot, was Reece's sword. If he had it, this headless thing before him wouldn't live. As it was, the body would be up again in a few seconds. Of course, unlike the others he and Scott had decapitated during the course of the night, this one would have to go a long way to get his head back.

Sherri grabbed the sword that had ricocheted and jumped to her feet. Raising the steel blade, she caught one of the Huguenots, still crouched against the rail, in the back with a firm swipe. Its body smashed into the steel rail and buckled. The third attacker was not a threat as it had fallen to the ground and Curt now saw why. After being tripped going through the doorway, one of the swords had impaled the Huguenot. The thing was groaning in a puddle of yellow sauce with the blade tip showing through the small of its back.

Curt lopped the head off the Huguenot Sherri had wounded. Now, two headless bodies and a third, with a disemboweling sword, lay quivering at their feet. The yellow fluid was pumping from their bodies and saturating the deck. Curt glanced over the edge. Visibility was becoming better with each minute but the dark clouds would preclude the amount of early morning light normally cast upon the coastline. Looking down, there was no one in sight. Somewhere in the distance, a motor roared between the crisp crackle of lightning strikes and Sherri hugged Curt with tears of joy.

The chilling moans of the injured Huguenots grew louder and louder. When the first headless thing began to rise, Curt grabbed Sherri and pulled her through the doorway. She nearly tripped on the belt still sprawled loosely across the opening. Curt guided her down the steps.

"I thought about throwing the bodies over but I thought it would be more fun for them to navigate the steps the way they are," he said trying to lighten her mood. But as high-pitched screams wafted in from the north, Curt's thoughts turned back to Scott.

The two made their way down the stairs and Curt retrieved Tibu's sword from Pinot's corpse, using the Huguenot's shirt to clean off the yellow ooze. Descending, they carefully checked each landing for unwanted guests.

CHAPTER-THIRTY-NINE

Scott ran back to the lighted roadway in hopes of finding a way out. To his right, he could clearly see the road came to a dead end half a block ahead and the entire area was consumed with the same thick underbrush. To the left were the soldiers led by the crazed Reece, now barely 20 yards away. With no other choice, Scott turned and raced in the direction of the dead end as the cries behind him intensified. Sweat drenched his body as the utter fear of his doom crested. The Soulful Ones knew they had him trapped. They would soon slaughter the man who had tried to take the Kilgotian away from them.

When Scott reached the end of the asphalt, he stopped and turned. He raised the Kilgotian with a trembling arm. Out of desperation, he was prepared to throw the cursed fish as far into the woods as he could. Reece, leading the pack with his sword swinging and white oculars dancing in their sockets, never slowed. Out of terror, Scott turned and rushed toward the solid underbrush when he heard an escalating hum from behind. Suddenly, slivers of light were cast on the underbrush and Scott whirled around. The Huguenots stopped and looked back as the disruption became louder.

Something swift and large approached and the soldiers scattered. A blaring sound disoriented Reece and his tyrants. Scott's view was obscured as he tried to make out whatever was approaching. Then solid beams of light began filtering through the mass of soldiers. The speeding car never veered, careening into the crowd sending bodies flying in all directions as its brakes locked and it screeched across the pavement. Some managed to elude the first run, but the Buick Regal expertly backed up and pummeled through those previously unscathed. Then Scott saw the gray hair of Marvin Sellon behind the wheel.

The car continued to weave through the maze of mangled bodies. Somehow, Reece was able to evade the vehicle. Twice he caught the front windshield with his blade, shattering fragments of glass. After five passes, Marvin finally spotted Scott and brought the car to an abrupt stop. The strewn soldiers picked themselves up and began to regroup.

"Get in!" he yelled.

Scott climbed in as Marvin mashed the accelerator and spun the car about, aiming for the most populated cluster of Huguenots. The Buick bore through effortlessly as some bodies fell under the wheels while others shot into the air, flailing helplessly after impact with the two-ton moving force. Reece again avoided the onslaught and began screaming, "MATANZAS, MATANZAS!"

The words sent a chill down Scott's spine as they drove away. He recalled the translation. "Slaughter, slaughter."

"I thought you were dead," Scott said looking at Marvin's blood soaked shirt.

"So did I," Marvin replied looking nervously in the rear view mirror as the car sped along. "I'm not exactly in prime shape," the professor said, contorting his face as he held his wound.

"Stop!" Scott yelled.

Marvin slammed on the brakes. They had returned to within a stone's throw of the lighthouse. "Why?" Marvin asked.

"Because I've got this," he said removing the Kilgotian from inside his shirt. "And the last time I looked, farther ahead, the beach was seething with raving soldiers. I'll have a better chance if I get out here and go to the left of the restaurant."

"Where are you going?" Marvin said holding his side and breathing irregularly. His talking heightened the pain.

"We believe the saltwater will destroy this thing."

"Where's Curt and the woman?"

"Last time I saw them, they were at the lighthouse."

"Scott, are you sure saltwater will kill it?" Marvin asked.

"No. And if I'm wrong, tell Kay and the kids that I love them with all my heart." Scott quickly got out and slammed the door before Marvin could say a word.

Marvin glanced in his rear view mirror and saw a shadowy figure flash behind the car. In the dim night the reflection was hazy. Marvin spun around and saw a Huguenot wearing a blue shirt darting in Scott's direction. The bastard must have caught a ride, Marvin thought. Marvin laid on the horn and Scott turned. He saw Reece charging at full speed. Scott ran to the side of the restaurant.

Ahead, were the tossing waves of the Atlantic Ocean. Scott was within half a city block of getting the Kilgotian where it *had* to go and, if the assumption was wrong, where he would soon die.

After watching Scott and the Huguenot disappear around the corner of the building, Marvin glanced in the rear view mirror again. To his horror, there were three dozen or so screaming soldiers coming up fast. Most had body parts flopping or missing altogether. He cut the wheel and gunned the motor. The Buick peeled against the asphalt, spinning the car around. Time for more Soulful driving, he thought with a bitter smile. Marvin pulled the shotgun from his left side where he had stored it earlier and laid it on the passenger seat in case the front windshield gave way. At this point, all he wanted to do was buy Scott some time.

Curt and Sherri saw Scott emerge from the Buick and race toward the shore. They were amazed, particularly Sherri, that Marvin was alive. She assumed the knife wound had been fatal. Seconds later they spotted Reece giving chase. As much as they wanted to warn Scott of Reece's presence, they couldn't chance making a sound for fear of tipping Scott's position to the army assembled at this end of the beach. They were relieved and mortified when Marvin had blown the horn.

Curt and Sherri crept through the dirt parking lot toward the road. When Marvin raced the engine and went against the crowd of soldiers, Curt was baffled by the disinterest of the Soulful Ones gathered on shore. Something else had drawn their attention and Curt and Sherri used the opportunity to cross Red Cox unsuspected. They made their way north to the front of the restaurant and then scurried around to the left side. There was no sign of Scott.

Then Curt spotted his friend. His heart sank.

On the beach, several yards from the water line, Scott had been captured. Two soldiers had his arms fully extended. He knelt with his head forward facing the sea. His shirt was completely torn off, lying in the wet sand beside him. Reece LeFlore bent over behind him as Scott screamed in agony. Reece was repeating the fate administered to Pierre Couperin and Tucker Chalet.

Curt turned toward Sherri. For a moment their eyes locked in silence. Sherri could see the desperation in Curt's face.

"I have no choice," Curt said.

Scott bellowed another tortured scream. Curt and Sherri turned to see the vengeful Huguenot carving Scott's shoulder blade with a knife. With the sight of the blade's bloody path, Curt charged.

Approaching the beach, Curt suddenly saw the army of soldiers, previously obscured from view by the restaurant, which had come to witness the tattooing and subsequent mutilation. He knew it was suicide but he continued toward Reece with his sword raised, thinking only of Julie and how he hoped his daughter would remember Daddy.

A quarter mile away, Marvin was bulling his way over and through the soldiers. In the last few minutes his energy had diminished. His wound had looked much worse than it was but he had still lost a considerable amount of blood. Steering through the soldiers, gashing his bumpers into the bodies, he started to become light-headed. The adrenaline rush that had carried him this far was fading. He felt as if he was going to pass out. If Scott hadn't reached the ocean by now he never would, he thought, so he turned the car around and floored it. In Marvin's delirium, he had become disoriented and was now driving in the direction of the dead end. Before he realized his mistake, he blacked out. His foot slipped off the gas pedal and the car rolled leisurely into the thicket, coming to rest peacefully as the underbrush acted as a buffer. To the rear, the vile Huguenots began to gather their weapons and rush the motionless machine.

Curt reached the sand and stopped dead in his tracks. This time, a force beyond his control held him back. Out in the distance, a wave had formed. It was larger than any wave Curt had seen this side of *A Perfect Storm*. It could only be a massive storm surge, he thought.

But it was more than that, huge and churning, rolling with a purpose, gathering momentum with each coil. What made it so amazing was its uniqueness. The storm had given the ocean sizeable swells and blistering whitecaps but this was a monster. It stood out and it stood tall, well over twenty feet. A single wave dwarfing its peers.

As Scott cried out again, Reece withdrew his knife and stood up. Noticing the crowd of admirers, he arrogantly pulled the fish from his pants and raised it into the air. There was chattering and maddening yelps. Curt stood watching the wave, anticipating its arrival. But it was unnoticed by the army, which focused its morose attention on Scott's back.

Curt retreated from the beach and hid behind a palm tree. Sherri stayed hidden to the side of the restaurant. The surging water was almost upon them when the first Huguenot saw the tremendous wall. He howled and the others turned to look. Reece glanced toward the sea and then quickly bolted away, leaving his shell-shocked comrades staring in disbelief. The wave broke with a thunderous collapse, pounding the beach and carrying soldiers inland. The spraying water created a temporary screen as the Huguenots cowered in the vicious surf, their bodies scattered everywhere. Curt saw fleshy parts meshing in the water and washing toward shore as if they were in some kind of a grotesque soup. There was no sign of Scott. Somehow, Reece outran the surf and scampered off the beach, holding the Kilgotian in his hand.

As Reece approached, Curt sprang from behind the tree and drove Pinot's sword through Reece's midsection. Surprised, the Huguenot held onto the Kilgotian. Reece looked down at his wound then sneered a thoughtful, knowing smile at his attacker. Curt withdrew the sword and saw the yellow substance drip from the end.

Reece held himself erect in temporary pain and waited for it to subside. This idiot's blade is ineffective against me, he thought. Curt watched the thing with the floating white pupils curl its lips in a decadent grin. Then he laughed at Curt. A cocky laugh. In the background, scattered soldiers along the beach were slowly rising to their feet and searching for their weapons. The water had receded as fast as it had approached.

Curt stared back at Reece. "I wouldn't be so happy if I were you, Frenchy. I figured out something that might be of interest to you."

Reece had no idea what the Spaniard was saying and continued to laugh.

"In this whole messed up ordeal, the one thing that kept gnawing at me was the finger bone that I lost in my shirt on Monday. The finger that we assumed was Pinot's since Marvin discovered a finger missing from its skeleton when it arrived from the museum. Our theory was that, for whatever reason, while sealed in the powder magazine, Pinot had severed his own finger and hidden the Kilgotian, the knife and his appendage underneath the slab. We assumed it was a desperate attempt to somehow reincarnate himself. In a twisted way, it seemed to make sense.

"Then Tibu told us that Pinot had *already* been a Soulful One. He had sensed Pinot's presence in the fort even before the powder magazine was discovered. This would mean that the missing appendage from Pinot's hand had been severed from his corpse and used, probably by Reece, in the 1500's to bring his brother back. Of course that explains why Pinot had lived to be more than 135 years old and why the Spanish were so afraid they had sealed him alive in the powder magazine."

Reece grinned sarcastically at Curt.

"So you see, the finger I found under the slab couldn't have been Pinot's. His first severed finger was used 400 years ago and he didn't lose his second finger until you removed it to bring him back yesterday. Tibu realized all this when he killed your brother but he died before he could tell me.

"But that still didn't explain whose finger I had found and then subsequently lost. Then I began thinking back to Monday morning and I remembered that before I tried to use the bathroom at the fort and was so rudely pulled away by Bruin, I took a quick drink from the water fountain. I guess some of it dribbled down my chest and onto that damn fish inside my shirt. The drops of water brought the Kilgotian to life just long enough for it to *absorb* the finger I later thought I had lost."

He paused as Reece chuckled softly. Then Curt continued, "All this time we couldn't figure out how *you* came back."

Reece stopped laughing and appeared to be trying to understand what Curt had said. His brother's name repeatedly caught his attention but he had chosen to ignore the Spanish enemy. Then Reece remembered that he had not seen Pinot in a while and didn't know what had become of him.

"Now it's crystal clear. It's the *only* way you could have come back since we had the fish." Curt clenched his teeth and continued in anger. "It was *your* finger that Pinot buried under the slab in the powder magazine with the knife and the Kilgotian. He was probably attempting to reincarnate you when the Spanish captured him. And it was your finger the Kilgotian consumed inside my shirt. I brought you back when I let water drip on that cursed fish and your body was already submerged in the ocean."

Reece's smile disappeared. He sensed the arrogance in Curt's words.

"And since I made you a Soulful One, my weapon is the only thing that can destroy you."

Curt threw his sword behind him and reached into his pocket. He withdrew his pocketknife. The same one he'd had since ninth grade. The same knife Curt had used on Monday to pry open the stone slab in the powder magazine. Then, to Curt's surprise, he saw Scott slowly creep up behind Reece. He was dripping saltwater and looked half-dead.

But Scott wouldn't miss this moment for the world.

He had heard what Curt had said. He grabbed Reece's arms and pinned them behind his back. Curt ran forward and plunged the knife deep into the thing's neck. Yellow juices streamed out as Scott let go and Reece shrieked falling on the sand convulsing. The Kilgotian fell at Scott's feet. The thing's body quivered for thirty seconds before it stopped. His floating white eyes wide open and his body seeping the yellow substance.

Reece LeFlore was dead. Again. Curt's knife, the weapon of the man who had made him a Soulful One, had destroyed the Huguenot. Scott gave Curt a somber smile. But their success was short lived. Two soldiers, still recovering from the wave, heard Reece's screams and charged.

"Go! Go!" Curt yelled at Scott as he pointed to the fish.

Scott bent down, grabbed the Kilgotian and headed toward the surf. Curt grabbed his sword behind him in time to fend off one's swing and then the other's.

"Hurry Scott!" Sherri yelled coming up behind Curt. Six soldiers raced toward Scott as he entered the surf. He would only get one chance and he wanted to make sure this thing didn't fly back onto shore again. As the ranting soldiers drew within a dozen feet, Scott pulled his arm back like a quarterback and hurled the Kilgotian into the air. Because of its lightweight, it began to glide upward.

Please not again, he thought.

Scott continued running into the surf to avoid the soldiers while Curt valiantly fended off the two on the beach. Several more approached as he saw the fish floating above the ocean out of the corner of his eye.

As before and to Scott's chagrin, the wind pushed the Kilgotian back over land to where Curt was engaged in battle, suspended like a seagull riding an updraft. As additional soldiers moved in, Curt broke off and grabbed Sherri's hand. They ran toward the road and circled the restaurant attempting to lose their pursuers. The fish floated lazily over the restaurant as if watching the activity. Curt and Sherri fled past the right side of the building and headed toward the ocean with the madmen in pursuit.

Marvin was still groggy as his eyes flickered opened, then closed. The constant bashing was giving him a headache.

"Knock it off!" he screamed wiping his eyelids rising from a deep sleep. Then the crashing reality occurred to him and he opened his eyes in horror. Four soldiers were on various sides of his car smashing their way through the windows. He reached over and grabbed the shotgun. He had two shots. Two shots and no more. It was only a matter of seconds before they'd break through and slice him to pieces.

.

Suddenly the wind changed. A rigid gale whipped up from the west and caught the Kilgotian, sending it tumbling through the air back over the sea. The flying fish was thrown a hundred yards in a matter of seconds yet remained suspended over the water's surface.

There was a battle going on. Two forces in opposition. One bearing down and one driving up.

The windshield shattered inward as Marvin covered his eyes with his arm. He quickly fired the first set of buck at a soldier attempting to strike. The blast sent the Huguenot sailing, as its right arm detached and was thrown deep into the underbrush.

One more shot.

Another Soulful One came through the passenger side window. Marvin raised the shotgun and gave it a face full of pellets. The yellow substance splattered across the dash and inside door. Two small specks landed on Marvin's thigh and immediately burned through his pants and into his leg. The agony was immense but no more than having a knife driven into his back. The other Huguenots positioned behind the car cautiously moved forward on both sides with their blades raised and their eyes glowing. They sensed the man's despair and thrived on it. Tibu had warned Marvin that he would die in his car. The Indian had dreamt it Wednesday morning. Marvin had elected to disregard the warning and help his friends. Now the premonition seemed guaranteed.

The professor was close to blacking out again from the combination of pain and fear. He knew he would never wake up if he did.

Scott was in waist deep water and began to swim to his right once he saw Sherri and Curt enter the water in an effort to escape. His back burned as the salt entered the raw wound. For some reason, the Huguenots seemed tentative about entering the surf, possibly unable to swim. But their initial hesitation was superseded by their desire to kill the interlopers and gain back the Kilgotian. At least 150 soldiers stepped into the rumbling surf and began wading. Scott joined Curt and Sherri as the Huguenots heaved knives, axes and swords. The weapons cut into the water around them.

"Look!" Sherri shouted.

Curt and Scott looked up at the Kilgotian hovering above the water in the distance as the assorted weapons splashed dangerously close. The fish was motionless, poised in midair as if held by a thin wire.

"That thing has got to drop!" Scott said. "It's defying gravity!"

"And that surprises you?" Curt said treading water. Then his tone changed, "Scott."

"Yeah"

"What do you believe now?" Curt asked paddling.

Before speaking Scott gritted his teeth. The saltwater was seeping into the cuts on his back. "What do you mean?"

Curt, treading water, didn't respond. An axe landed two feet in front and splashed water into his face.

"You mean God?"

"Yes," Curt replied as they continued moving outward to evade the sharp objects landing perilously nearby.

For a moment, Scott was silent, leading the group out to deeper water. Then he paused. "Curt, I believe we've experienced things . . ." he paused accidentally taking a gulp of water and then spitting it out. A sword landed less then a foot away. ". . . things no one should ever experience. I believe we've been facing an incredible evil from the start. Ever since we found that damn fish."

Curt nodded trying to keep his mouth above the rolling waves. Sherri was shaking from fright and exhaustion.

Scott thought back to the images in the cloud Friday morning, the etching in the sand that led Curt to his rescue when Tatterhorn had him trapped at the pond, Ambrose's intervention, including the discovery of Reece's sword, the strange bursts of wind that saved them: once as they swung toward the drawbridge and a second time when the Huguenot on the gundeck had them pinned against the cannon. "I also believe we've had help. Unsolicited, amazing, miraculous help. I wouldn't consider it luck. It was guidance. We would have never made it this far without it."

Curt nodded and smiled.

"If you're asking me if I believe in God," Scott continued, "The answer is yes." As the words left his mouth, a voice inside his head said, "Suspended until belief," and for an instant Scott was reading the words from a hymnal while sitting on a wooden pew in a beautiful church. He recognized the image was from a dream.

"It's coming down!" Sherri yelled staring at the Kilgotian's skeleton against the dark gray clouds hanging low overhead.

The Kilgotian fell from the sky as if its lifeline had been severed. It hit the surface with a bold splash sending water in all directions. For something so light, it had a voluminous impact. It entered the water less than 50 feet away.

The Huguenots froze in their pursuit. And then the multitude of bodies frantically turned and attempted to move inland, ranting as if running out of a burning building, falling over each other enroute to shore. The water where the Kilgotian entered began to bubble creating a spectacular froth as a downward funnel formed.

Sherri, Curt and Scott began to swim ashore as soon as they saw the Huguenots run. The idea of being sucked under and drowned was no more appealing than being hacked to death. At least with the army in disarray they might stand a chance on shore. They could already feel the pull from the churning and were anxious for land.

The funnel started slowly, capturing the nearby water in its downward spiral. It gained velocity as the swirling area enlarged to a circumference of 50 feet. The wind began gusting fiercely. The lightning toyed through the clouds and thunder bellowed from above. All of the elements seemed to grow angry at once.

The soldiers retreated to the beach but became drawn into the phenomenon. They struggled to progress but some flew backward, spinning and tumbling. Scott, Curt and Sherri strained to make the beach, fighting the draw of the whirl as Huguenots sailed by, sucked outward. Countless bodies shot past, some skimming just over their heads while others glided the surface, somersaulting as they passed among the threesome. Their bloody cries were drowned out by the torrential wind, the thunderous booming of the water and the heavens above.

Scott was the first to come clear of the surf. Curt and Sherri soon followed. The wind was rigorous but they were able to manage against it. The vengeful Huguenots were not fairing nearly as well. They continued to fly past the breakers into the open sea, arms and legs fighting the invisible force, drawing them away from the sanctity of dry land and toward the swirling whirlpool. Scott dropped to his knees and turned to witness the extraordinary commotion. Sherri fell onto Curt and the two watched in awe. The wind whistled as it stole a hearty haste. Soldiers continued to stream outward.

The ocean was alive. Swells surrounded the funnel and walled off the outside. The screaming souls, flipping in the water uselessly, shimmied across the surface. One by one they crested the outer waves and bound over, sinking into the vertical pit of saltwater. Ten, twenty, thirty, forty, a hundred bodies went in. Cries of agony flooded the air as the wind yawned and blistered the morning. The sky above the Atlantic's new mouth whipped the clouds in a blend of white whiffs and yellow fluid rising from the epicenter below.

The three watched from the beach as the last few souls scattered through the shallow water and slithered toward the vortex. Desperately fighting the unseen influence, the soldiers wiggled and jerked until the last one soared over the watery hills into the turbulent maze below. Suddenly, a boundless number of dorsal fins cut the settled surrounding water, circling the funnel, drawing inward as the water pooled the yellow substances. The sharks, with their razor-like jaws, feasted upon the mass of flesh and bones until the screams faded into the depths.

Then the sea was still. Full of its capture and content to resolve any further discrepancies another day, another millennium. Whenever the need might arise. But now the process was complete.

The fish had been returned. All those affected were placed where they should have stayed, hidden within the ocean's belly. It had ended as it had begun.

A warm gentle mist fell on the beach as the dark clouds gave way to the morning sun cresting on the horizon. The thunder and lightning had dissipated. It was as if the slate was being wiped clean.

It was a new day.

Marvin had sealed his eyes with his arm. Assuming defeat, he just wanted it to end. A disturbance to the east had arisen but he was oblivious to the event. God, just make it over quickly, he prayed. But God hadn't been listening. He was preoccupied. As the surroundings went silent, Marvin unveiled his eyes to the quiet Buick. To the quiet trees, and thicket and empty road behind the vehicle. To the playful breeze caressing his face through the shattered glass of the windshield. He was dumbfounded but relieved.

Scott, Curt and Sherri scanned the horizon as the sun continued to shine through a gentle opening in the clouds. The beach was isolated, as it should have been at 6:56 on a Thursday morning. The ocean was flaccid. Slow rolling swells bounced inward. Seagulls appeared out of nowhere bickering upon the soft breeze skirting the coast. Hard clouds still drifted overhead but their threatening demeanor was gone. Instead of scowling black, the puffs floating above were playfully gray, resembling the advanced look of cumulus nimbus before a refreshing shower in the spring.

The three gazed in all directions and silently began to question what was real. The scene had shifted in an instant.

After minutes of wonderment, Scott walked off the beach without a word. He felt renewed. Curt and Sherri followed with their arms secure around each other's waist. Curt was hobbling badly from a gash on his right thigh. He had no idea how the injury had occurred but it left his leg simmering in anguish.

"Curt, did I ever tell you I'm kinda rich?" Sherri asked with a straight face.

"Why no you didn't ma'am," he said limping along. "But your sister did mention something about the lottery. Does that mean you'll pay my medical bill?"

"Only if you buy me dinner," she said with a coy smile.

They made their way toward the dead end and found Marvin dazed and resting on the trunk of his car.

"Did we win?" The professor wheezed, holding his side. The crimson stain covered half his shirt. There were two holes in the material covering his right thigh.

"We did," Scott smiled through his exhaustion. His back ached from the incisions and his muscles cramped in more ways than he knew were possible.

"Good," Marvin said weakly.

For a moment they were silent.

"You realize we're the only ones that are ever going to know we had the Kilgotian? An animal capable of being reincarnated, of reincarnating others? A creature created specifically by God for Noah? An entity that traveled *on* the Ark?" Curt asked.

Again there was silence.

"Good riddance," Scott spoke up.

They all laughed and the professor promptly fainted. Scott and Curt caught him before he hit the ground.

EPILOGUE

Seven weeks later, on the second Saturday in November, Scott drove Curt, Sherri and Marvin to Fort Caroline. It was almost dusk when they arrived. The park would be closing within the hour.

The tropical storm that had evolved into Hurricane Damon in late September had graciously missed the North Florida coast. At the last minute, it was diverted by a front sweeping across from the Gulf of Mexico and pushed back out to sea. At least that's how the meteorologist had explained it. Damon never did any damage to the mainland as it followed the coastline and eventually withered away, 500 miles east of Nova Scotia.

Scott led the group out of the parking lot along the dirt trail. They headed toward the fort on the banks of the St. Johns River. Upon reaching the earthen structure with the arched entrance, Scott veered the party down the nature path to the left. It was the same route he and Tatterhorn had taken on that Tuesday in September.

"Exactly what are you going to show us?" Curt asked. "Did you find a hidden bar that sells 20 ounce beers for a dime?" He smiled at the woman whose hand he held on his left. She gleamed back.

"I'm a mature man still recovering from a severe wound and you're leading me on a marathon. Can we at least get a hint?" Marvin complained.

"Nope. All I can say is you'll find this very interesting," Scott replied.

"If you found another fish, I'd prefer not to know," Sherri joked.

"I didn't find the first one," Scott said.

"Don't start with me," Curt said smiling at his friend as they pushed on the trail.

"Poor Tibu," Sherri said thinking back to the ordeal. When they had returned to the lighthouse, Tibu's body, along with Pinot's, was gone. It pained them that they were unable to give the Indian a proper burial.

"I promise you, Sherri, Tibu is much happier where he is," Marvin replied.

"I know, I know. Curt keeps reminding me. I just feel for him, for all the years he spent on earth with those terrible nightmares," she said.

"Yeah, but did he tell you the number of times he had sex? How many different women?" Scott said turning around briefly.

Sherri stared at Scott suspiciously.

"No, he didn't," she replied.

"Shucks, I was hoping he had. Scott and I were kind of curious," Curt said laughing. Sherri popped him in the stomach and he let out a pretend exhale.

The four laughed and continued on. From what Curt could remember, they passed by the point where he, Scott and Tatterhorn had left the trail on that day and angled toward the clump of trees, a feature of the landscape which had inexplicably disappeared afterwards. Scott and Curt had spent considerable time searching for it in the aftermath only to come up empty. It was as if it never existed.

Twenty yards farther, as the path ventured to the left, Scott broke off and stepped over some small underbrush. His three curious companions followed. The grass was sporadic for the first dozen or so steps. Beyond, they carefully navigated thick bushes and dense ivy covering the ground. Farther down the makeshift trail, Scott stopped. He turned right, spied his objective and stepped in front of the huge oak tree.

Scott turned to face his friends. "I was here at the fort recently with Cody, and for probably the 30th time, was searching for the patch of trees I had entered with Tatterhorn when I came upon this old oak."

The tree behind Scott was massive, obviously hundreds of years old. Oak trees have been found in excess of 800 years old in some parts of the world. While not that aged, the huge trunk and sprawling giant arms shot in all directions indicating its longevity, which was not uncommon along protected areas of the St. Johns River.

"Cody and I saw this one late in the afternoon as the sun was setting," Scott said, turning and walking up one of its protruding roots. He leaned against the trunk with his left hand as his right dug into his pocket. When he withdrew, he was holding a small flashlight.

"The sunlight was coming through the trees that afternoon and hit this barkless flat area at an angle." Scott pointed to a barren area of the trunk about 12 inches above his head. It was square and charcoal gray.

"Don't tell me," Marvin began, "Keebler elves live in there."

They all laughed, including Scott.

"No, professor. No one lives in there. But someone once lived around here," Scott said.

Night was approaching quickly and the area was rapidly growing dark. Scott reached up and flipped the flashlight on, holding it at an angle against the bark so that the beam skipped across the area. The other three moved closer to see what now appeared. A series of symbols was visible. Carved into the trunk and unseen before, it now stood out.

"What is that?" Curt asked moving alongside his friend.

Scott stepped off the root and back to the ground. "I had to have it translated because I would never have known." Scott removed a piece of paper from his pocket and read aloud:

I am the one. And I will undo what has been done – Tibu

They were silent as the darkness continued to settle quickly. No one knew what to say.

"And you did," Curt finally said quietly. Sherri wiped her eyes.

"I just hope he knows it," Marvin said.

"I'm sure he does," Scott said with a smile. He turned and led the way back to the path. Curt, Sherri and Marvin followed. Their thoughts driven back to the events of that week in September. When they had come in contact with a runaway from God and a dynasty of evil. When survival had come in the form of a miracle and the waters had been joined for the Kilgotian, ending its stay on earth.

As the sun settled on the horizon, the waves broke in small, harmless heaps along the deserted beach on Anastasia Island. The sea birds had made their way to their nighttime hideouts and left the shore mired in solitude. Small crustaceans burrowed in the wet sand as an ultrasonic hum flowed with the incoming tide.

Author's Note

As with most works of fiction, I will lean against the "creative license" defense if questioned by historical or theological purists for misrepresentation of information in this story. For the most part, the descriptions of St. Augustine and Fort Caroline and the history depicted relative to the French and Spanish occupations of the area are technically accurate. The characters of Pinot and Reece LeFlore are creations from my imagination and interjected into the setting for effect.

Likewise, the gun powder magazine at the Castillo de San Marcos does exist inside the northeast corner of the fort. The amazing discovery of the sealed room with remains scattered about the floor occurred in the 1800's (not recently as I had depicted) when a cannon fell through from the gundeck above. Why it was sealed and whose bones were found inside is a mystery to this day.

Also, no offense is meant toward Native American Indians, the French or Spanish people. The characters are fictional and are not intended as a representation of their culture or ancestry.

Lastly, the song, "You Choose," by "Big Al & the Kaholics," (quoted in the preface) is from the CD entitled, "HYPE." You can learn more about the band, including where to buy their debut CD, by going to www.kaholics.com.

Printed in the United States
22045LVS00002B/43-48